Reinforced by another wave of shock troops, the Minotaurs drove deeper into the earthworks. Front ranks fanned out in a widening arc. Sword and axe rose and fell with killing blows. The ground ran slick with blood and offal. Several warriors slipped, their brethren leapt or climbed over to continue the attack. Suddenly the Minotaur army was in danger of being impossibly entangled. Snarls brought the front line grinding to a halt. Panting heavily, the bulls cut down the remaining Goblins and established a foothold for follow-on forces.

Having been brutalized, the Goblin ranks cracked and broke. Survivors fled back into the ruins to secondary defensive positions. The trench quickly became untenable as more Minotaurs swarmed into it. Soon the large warriors were forced to snatch bodies and toss them across the killing field just to continue unimpeded. Shock units surged through the gaps in the line, taking a new fight to the retreating Goblins. Scores fell, hacked down from behind as they fled for their lives.

Krek was at the center of it all. His dark bear hide draped across his shoulders flapped in the early morning wind. Sweat covered him in a thick sheen. His breath fumed from his nostrils. Naked from the waist down save for boiled-leather armor, the Minotaur king was drenched in blood. He paused at the inner lip of the trench and surveyed the battlefield. Most of the first trench was occupied by his army and the erected battlements were being systematically ripped apart. Reluctant as he was to admit it, the honor-less weapons of the Dwarves were highly effective. Krek brandished his war bar high above his head and roared.

EVEN GODS MUST FALL

Book VI of the Northern Crusade

Christian Warren Freed

Excerpt from *Dreams of Winter* 2021 Christian Warren Freed
Cover design by Melissa Andres
Cover copyright 2021 by Warfighter Books
Author Photograph by Anicie Freed

Warfighter Books
Holly Springs, North Carolina 27540
https://www.christianfreed

Second Edition: January 2021

Library of Congress Cataloging-in-Publication Data
Name: Freed, Christian Warren, 1973- author.
Title: Even Gods Must Fall/ Christian Warren Freed
Description: Second Edition | Holly Springs, NC: Warfighter Books, 2021.
Identifiers: LCCN 20219313434 | ISBN 9781736804469 (trade paperback)
Subjects: Epic fantasy | Military fantasy

Printed in the United States of America

10 9 8 7 6 5 4 3 2 1

ACCLAIM FOR CHRISTIAN WARREN FREED

Hammers in the Wind

‘Freed is without a doubt an amazing storyteller. His execution of writing descriptive and full on battle scenes is second to none, the writers ability in that area is unquestionable. He also drags you into the world he has created with ease and panache. I couldn't put it down.’

‘Gripping! Hammers in the Wind is an excellent start to a new fantasy series. Christian Warren Freed has created an exciting storyline with credible characters, and an effectively created fantasy world that just draws you in.’

Dreams of Winter
Fractured Universe #1

‘Dreams of Winter is a strong introduction to a new fantasy series that follows slightly in the footsteps of George R.R. Martin in scope.’ Entrada Publishing

"Steven Erickson meets George R.R. Martin!"

"THIS IS IT. if you like fantasy and sci-fi, you must read this series."

Law of the Heretic
Immortality Shattered Book I

'If you're looking for a fun and exciting fantasy adventure, spend a few hours in the Free Lands with the Law of the Heretic.'

Where Have All the Elves Gone?

'Sometimes funny and other times a little dark, Where Have The Elves Gone? brings something fresh and new to fantasy mysteries. Whether you want to curl up with a mystery or read more about elves this book has something for everyone. Spend a few hours solving a mystery with a human and a couple of dwarves - you'll be glad you did.'

Other Books by Christian Warren Freed

The Northern Crusade
Hammers in the Wind
Tides of Blood and Steel
A Whisper After Midnight
Empire of Bones
The Madness of Gods and Kings
Even Gods Must Fall

The Histories of Malweir
Armies of the Silver Mage
The Dragon Hunters
Beyond the Edge of Dawn

Fractured Universe
Dreams of Winter
The Madman on the Rocks
Anguish Once Possessed
Through Darkness Besieged
Under Tattered Banners*

Where Have All the Elves Gone?
Tomorrow's Demise: The Extinction Campaign
Tomorrow's Demise: Salvation
Coward's Truth*
The Lazarus Men
Repercussions: A Lazarus Men Agenda*

A Long Way From Home+

Immortality Shattered

Law of the Heretic

The Bitter War of Always

Land of Wicked Shadows

Storm Upon the Dawn

War Priests of Andrak Saga

The Children of Never

SO, You Want to Write a Book? +

SO, You Wrote a Book. Now What? +

*Forthcoming + Nonfiction

ACKNOWLEDGEMENTS

This book is dedicated to my mom and dad. The first movie I ever went to see was Star Wars in an old drive in western New York. Thanks for giving me the ability to dream.

EVEN GODS MUST FALL

The 6th and final volume of

THE NORTHERN CRUSADE

PROLOGUE

Dawn. The sun broke the horizon, crisp and bright against the eastern sky for the first time in days. A late winter storm had blown through, covering the lands, yet again, in a perpetual blanket of austere white. While residents huddled in front of sputtering hearths, a sense of prevailing turmoil settled over the world. Rumors of struggles, whispers of titanic battles to the east, reached the villagers of the almost forgotten town. War was sweeping across the northern kingdoms. Yet it was a war that left them largely unaffected. A few favored sons had answered the muster and marched off to join the ranks. The old grieved while the young dreamed. War did funny things to all.

Eldric and Bjorn, eldest of six sons, slipped into their heavy winter clothing and collected their bows on the way out the door long before their mother awoke. They'd ached to enlist when the Wolfsreik recruiter visited back at the beginning of winter. A great, unstoppable crusade was underway that held the implications of liberating the entire north of Malweir under Delrananian flags. Who wouldn't want to become part of such grandeur? Glory was not for the boys, however. With their father long in the ground from an unfortunate plowing accident, their mother insisted on keeping all her boys close. Wars were no place for youth. Not if they expected to mature into decent men.

Abandoning the confines of their home, the boys hurried off down snow-covered trails in search of a stag or brace of rabbits. Winter had been a successive string of miserable storms confining them to the relative security of the house. Eldric grew inspired by the dawn and led the way. All thoughts of war and, given the circumstances, abject misery associated with too many feet of snow, dissipated the deeper into the woods they stalked.

A lone rider had come through the village a few weeks past with devastating news. Eldric and Bjorn learned for the first time of the insurrection against the throne and the destructive civil war raging across Delranan. The sheer incredulousness of it left both boys in doubt. Any aspect of war would surely have trickled down into the minor villages peppering the Delrananian countryside. The rider, claiming to be a messenger from the rebellion, rode off in disgust. Not a single villager answered the call and Eldric and Bjorn watched as their ancestral home quietly returned to the way life had always been.

Still, there was an urgency in the rider's words that inspired a fire within Eldric's heart. Questions of legitimacy sprang forth. He suddenly wanted to know more of what the rest of the kingdom was like. What it was undergoing. Bjorn chastised his older brother for being brash. The impudence of youth was often misunderstood. Why should Eldric's desires be any different? Eventually he calmed down. The rider was long gone, presumably off to other villages in search of able-bodied fighters to join the cause. Eldric forgot his dreams, brief as they were. His life was here, with his family.

"Look," Eldric announced in a hushed voice.

Bjorn knelt to gingerly touch the cloven-hoof print. A light splattering of snow had settled in deeply. Bjorn grinned. "Fresh. These can't be more than an hour old."

"Come on, looks like we're in for fresh meat tonight, brother."

The boys loped off on the hunt. Eldric's eyes scanned the woods as they followed the deer tracks deeper. Both boys stalked with arrows strung. Their stomachs growled hungrily. A long winter of too many old potatoes and slightly rotted vegetables left them salivating over the prospect of fresh meat. This past winter was among the worst in recent history, leaving many old and young naught but frozen corpses stored behind homes until the ground thawed enough to dig their graves. Worsening matters was the intense stir-crazy feeling gnawing away at every villager. It was time for the sun to shine again.

Trees began to thin. They were drawing to the edge of the forest. If either boy was thinking clearly they might have given pause. Deer preferred the security of camouflage, seldom venturing far into the open air. Eldric reached the tree line first and jerked to a stop. Bjorn, more worried over losing the trail, slammed into his brother's back.

"Hey, what did you stop fo…,"

"Shhh," Eldric hissed. "Look!"

Bjorn lowered his bow to peek around his brother's solid frame. What he witnessed stole the warmth from his soul. The plain stretching out before them had turned black under the steady wave of Goblins pouring into Delranan. Thousands, perhaps tens of thousands of the vile creatures choked the fields. Harsh, guttural orders were issued as Goblins slowly broke away into companies. Sword and axe, spear and tulwar gleamed in the morning sunlight.

"Where did they come from?" Bjorn whispered.

Eldric could only shake his head. A flicker of unnatural light caught his eye, drawing his attention to the magic-infused atmosphere on a small hilltop. The very air was warped with sickening shades of rot. Larger than a house, the rent continued to belch forth the Goblin army. Unending waves of infantry flooded Delranan.

"How?" was all Eldric managed to ask.

Frightened yet not understanding what he was seeing, Bjorn nervously clutched his brother's arm. "We need to leave, before they see us."

Eldric continued to stare as the Goblin army grew. He briefly considered killing one, if for no other reason than to brag to his friends, but quickly discarded the notion. Any unwanted attention would draw the entire horde down around him and there'd be no hope of escape. Not against so many. Reluctantly, he withdrew his gaze from the Goblins, creatures he'd only heard of. To see so many in Delranan this close to his home was impossible.

Bjorn, sensing his brother's hesitation, tugged harder. "Eldric, come on. We must warn the village."

Shaken free from the horrible scene continuing to unfold around them, Eldric nodded and began to duck back into the trees. Three squat, barrel-bodied Goblins emerged from the right and attacked. Bjorn cried out, dropping his bow as his small hands scrambled to draw his hunting knife strapped to his belt. Eldric was not so careless. He quickly drew and fired into the nearest Goblin, more reflex than anything else. The Goblin grunted and fell dead. Eldric's arrowhead punched out the back of the dead warrior, killing him instantly at point-blank range. The other two fell on the young villager with curses and sharp steel. Bjorn screamed as he watched a Goblin short sword plunge into Eldric's stomach.

"Run," he mouthed and fell dead.

Bjorn ran for his life without looking back.

The impossible army continued to swell.

Thunder echoed down from the mountaintops yet no lightning slashed the sky. No storm darkened the world. This was the thunder of two hundred booted feet. Locked in step, the heavy crunch-thump reverberated down through the jagged rock passes, knocking boulder and stone loose in massive cascades. Avalanches filled long-forgotten defiles and ravines. Dust clouds rose to choke the air. Red and heavily mineralized, the dust was the life blood of the very mountains.

Song soon accompanied the baritone of the march. Deep and ominous, the words were lost upon the rocks. Their meaning, however, wasn't. The song returned a forgotten people to old glories they'd abandoned for personal reasons. It whispered of past triumphs and the promise of new glory. There was unparalleled pride drifting on the winds. At last, after centuries of seclusion and the continuing downward spiral into obscurity, the Giants of Venheim were reborn.

Called into action by the Dae'shan and the gods of light, the Giants couldn't abandon the rest of the world to the depredations of the evil threatening. At long last the time for Giants had returned. Coerced to march down from the mountaintop fortresses, the Giants headed into Delranan to claim their rightful place in the future history of the world.

Joden, eldest and most revered of the Giant smiths, paused at the rear of the column to give a last, longing glance at the home he'd known for over one hundred years. He knew, deep within the warmth of his soul, that this would be his final look at fabled Venheim. Old and fragile--for a Giant--he'd lived a long, full life. The world was changing, irrevocably moving towards a finale very few even realized approached.

The elder Giant had come to accept that his purpose in life had been to train, mold, and sculpt young Groge into the bearer of the Blud Hamr, the weapon capable of ending the dark gods' quest to reclaim Malweir for good. The war would be fought by blood and steel, the destiny of a dozen races, but the battle for the soul of the world rested in the hands of a young, inexperienced Giant and his small band of companions. That task completed, or at least en route to completion, Joden took his rightful place in the one hundred marching to join the allied army.

Artiss Gran, last of the true Dae'shan, mentioned the momentous occasion rapidly approaching. The world had not seen the likes of such an alliance since the days of the Mage Wars: Giant, Dwarf, Elf, Minotaur, and Man fighting an unimagined army of Goblins. Such prospects robbed the very strong of will and crumbled city walls in anticipation. The Dae'shan offered no promises, no delusions of victory or promise. This war threatened to exceed the reach of all mortals involved.

Unhindered by emotions, Joden accepted his fate. Lord Death rode his chariot straight for the combining armies, ready to reap his terrible reward. The Giant forge master would be among the casualties, carelessly slain for reasons only he valued. Joden grinned as he took in the smooth, stone walls and well-worn paths of Venheim. Content with his inner peace, the Giant turned and joined his troop. The Giants were finally returning to war.

ONE

Grim Dawn

"This is madness." Orlek angrily crossed his arms over his chest as he paced through the ankle-deep snow. His eyes were stern, narrowed from the fierce glare of sunlight burning brightly.

Ingrid finished pulling her long, blond locks into a braid. She repressed her sigh, knowing his protests stemmed from the awkward combination of affection for her and the strain of leading a rebellion he deemed bound to fail. Frustrations abounded throughout the beleaguered rebel camps. They'd fought, and died, in the name of antiquated ideals. Yet abandoning the principles with which he was raised was like poison in his blood. Orlek's love of kingdom was mired in hopelessness.

Delranan would never return to its former glory. Harnin One Eye had seen to that. Most of the major cities were gutted ruins. Plague had decimated a disproportionate amount of the population. Worse, there was darkness at play in the kingdom. Disappearances continued to rise at a disturbing pace. Children stolen from cribs. Fathers not returning at dusk. Whispers of depraved acts in the east forced an exodus as far west as possible. Delranan had become a kingdom of bones.

Despite the downward spiral they seemed trapped in, Ingrid took hope. The brother of the king's return offered new light through the gloom. Bahr wanted no part in ruling the kingdom, but he'd vowed to do everything within his power to help purify the hatred occupying the northern kingdom. Ingrid's hope was that the dispossessed son would reclaim the title from Harnin and restore at least a small measure of Delranan's normalcy.

Ingrid remained resolute. Feet planted shoulder-width apart, she calmly folded her arms across her chest and narrowed her eyes. "Madness or not we have a civic obligation to uphold. The people of this kingdom have suffered enough."

"What obligation other than removing Harnin from power do you think we have, Ingrid?" he fumed. "We've been pushed across half of the kingdom and kept on the run since the plague struck. This rebellion isn't as strong as you seem to believe. We're…fragile…if nothing else."

"It's your job to change that, Orlek. Each of us knows the cost and risk associated with our actions. This isn't the time to blanch in the face of all we've accomplished."

Orlek's eyes widened with shock. "Just what have we accomplished aside from filling too many holes with corpses?"

Ingrid's mouth opened and closed quickly. Her viperous retort died on the tip of her tongue as she began to recall faces and names, all brave fighters who'd given their lives in the pursuit of a cause they weren't wholly sure of. Did Ingrid truly wield such vast power as to command the life and death of her followers on mere whim? She shuddered to think so. A widow of a former Wolfsreik officer, Ingrid was led to believe that all life was precious and no one person deserved to command that of another. Not when it came to Lord Death claiming your soul.

Ingrid paused, oddly recalling a previous conversation where they'd been on opposite sides of the argument. She'd felt used up. A well long bereft of water. The war had dragged on much longer than their earliest expectations. She'd lost friends and enemies, all the while losing part of herself along the way. Fundamental changes continued to have residual effects. Ingrid held greater understanding of what had happened but lacked foresight to change the future. Where self-induced misery once occupied her mind she was now occupied with orchestrating that singular pivotal moment that would shift the balance of power and drive what remained of Harnin's forces out of power for good.

Tiny laughter escaped her lips.

Orlek narrowed his eyes. "What's so funny?"

"I was just thinking how we had this very same argument not long ago. Only I was the one consumed with grief over losses." She paused, choosing her next words carefully. "Orlek, our raid on the western fortress can't be construed as failure. We ruined Harnin's plans for the west. Think of how much manpower and funding went in to building that hideous fort in the middle of nowhere?"

"Perhaps you're forgetting how many fighters we lost in that engagement?"

She shook her head. "Absolutely not. Every face, every name haunts my sleep. I'll never be alone again, Orlek. None of them died without purpose. Harnin sought to establish a firm base of operations in the west, thus depriving us of our hiding places. Yes, we lost, but Harnin lost a captain, a base, and numerous soldiers. We hold the advantage. All we need to do is reach out and seize it."

"What advantage, Ingrid?" Orlek threw his hands wide in a futile gesture. "We're borderline ineffective. It won't take much to break what remains. You risk losing everything by taking to the field so soon."

"We've all risked much since leaving Chadra. Harnin is weak. Bahr's return gives us a new hope."

"How? He clearly wants nothing to do with the throne or the kingdom."

"So he says," she conceded. "What if he's not being entirely truthful?"

Orlek clicked his tongue on the roof of his mouth. "I'm listening."

Ingrid began to pace around the campfire. "Bahr and his collection of friends are in a hurry to move east. Clearly there is a confrontation brewing that will decide the future of Delranan. Bahr knows what his brother and the One Eye have done here. He's seen the suffering firsthand. There's no way he can willingly walk away from this. Not if he expects to be able to live with his decisions."

"I don't know, Ingrid. Sounds like a lot of speculation. What is your reasoning?"

She paused. A warm grin spread across her face. "The princess."

"Maleela? What about her? No one has heard from her since the Wolfsreik left for the invasion of Rogscroft."

"Precisely. My gut tells me she is an integral player in all this. Could Bahr be heading west to find her?" Ingrid's eyes shone with fresh ideas. The princess of Delranan might well be the answer to all their problems.

"More likely off to confront his brother," Orlek concluded. "Badron's never cared for his daughter. I think you overstate her importance."

"Possibly, but we have to keep that option open. Orlek, I think we need to start driving east. Catch up to Bahr if we can."

His eyes widened in shock. "To what end? You've seen his group. A Giant, Dwarf, wizard, and Gaimosian? That's no meeting I want any part of. If Lord Death is stalking Delranan that group is heading straight for him."

"Harnin will assume the same and move to stop Bahr. There's no love lost between those two. We can use that distraction to slip back into Chadra, seal off the Keep, and bring the One Eye to his knees."

Orlek wasn't convinced. "You're forgetting those five thousand soldiers roaming the kingdom. What about them?"

"We've already bloodied their noses in the west. Harnin's lost significant supplies, weapons, and manpower. Orlek, this is the only chance we're going to have."

"We abandoned Chadra to change the war," he said.

Ingrid nodded. "Now it's time to change it again. We need to move into the end phase of the rebellion. Delranan can't sustain the kind of warfare it's been subsumed with. How many more sons and daughters are there to throw into the flames? This is our chance, Orlek. We can break Harnin. Argis is gone. Jarrik killed himself. The others haven't been seen or heard from since Badron left. Only Skaning remains and his focus is moving east. We have to presume he's chasing Bahr and forgetting about us."

The decision to return to what little remained of Delranan's capital wasn't easy to make. Ghosts haunted the streets, worsened by the plague. Still, Orlek was forced to admit Ingrid's plans bore at least a little measure of merit. Bahr's return was no secret and Harnin would be frothing at the mouth to get his claws on the king's brother. Orlek's only issue was the rebellion lacked up-to-date intelligence on what was happening in the east.

Speculation of Badron's return continued to circle the campfires nightly but without confirmation Ingrid couldn't react accordingly. Orlek knew the rebellion teetered on a constant edge. All it would take to push it too far beyond the recoverable line was one fell move. They *needed* to get back in the fight before idle minds bled them all dry. Reluctantly he began to follow Ingrid's thinking.

"If we succeed, if, we could bring the war to an end before summer," Orlek spoke slowly.

"We can," she affirmed.

He forced a grin. "If, we're going to have to push scouts forward immediately. We can't march on Chadra without knowing what we're getting into."

She resisted the urge to rush forward and hug him. Her personal feelings continued to strengthen towards the normally stoic warrior. Love was forming, but she couldn't allow any more than a passing thought until the rebellion reached its destined conclusion. She'd already lost one husband, the pain of going through it all over again frightened her more than any other aspect of this war.

"Summon Harlan. We need to begin drawing up plans. Our forces need to find a convergence point a day's walk from the city," she ordered.

Orlek agreed. "I'll push out scouts in the morning. Moving against Harnin blindly turns my stomach."

Lord Skaning peered intently through his spy glass. He closed it just as fast, disgust twisting his features. What he had in enthusiasm failed to translate into results. The decision to abandon his persecution of the rebellion hadn't reached Chadra yet. Otherwise Harnin One Eye would have already sent assassin squads. He didn't relish the thought of undergoing the same ordeal his fellow lord, Jarrik, did. The former lord committed suicide during the rebel attack on the western fort a week ago.

Skaning maintained reservations toward hunting down one of his friends. Skaning wanted power, making it easy to cast aside bonds of fellowship and follow orders. Harnin was adamant about Jarrik's removal. Not only did Skaning fail to execute his former friend, he had lost the ex-rebellion leader, Inaella. Her continued existence was proving to be a bane to Harnin's rule despite abandoning the rebellion in favor of the crown. Skaning had never placed trust in the pock-marked woman.

She should have died a dozen times over. The plague ravaged her body while the betrayal of lower-ranked rebels twisted her mind. Inaella was a broken woman. Her worth to Harnin's efforts diminished daily despite delusions of self importance. Skaning saw through her. The woman was trouble. More than she was worth. Harnin's alliance with her would hurt the crown.

Thoughts wandering down paths he didn't care about, Skaning refocused his attentions on the barren fields of snow stretching lazily out before him. Seven hundred soldiers waited impatiently behind him. The hunt was more intensive than anticipated. Thoughts of desertion spread. Being reservists, none of the soldiers wanted to be away from home longer than necessary. Skaning was leading them on a fruitless chase as far as they were concerned.

"Explain to me how a group that large can disappear in the middle of all this openness?" he asked sharply. "No tracks. Not even a pile of horse dung. I'm losing faith in your abilities."

"My lord, we've found nothing," the scout said and shifted nervously, fully expecting the executioner's blade against his neck.

Skaning snarled. "Double your efforts. A group that large can't just disappear. I don't care if we are in the middle of the wilderness. Bahr must be found and destroyed before he reaches his goal in the east."

"We've got more than a hundred soldiers scouring the countryside, my lord. Bahr may be cunning but there is a lot of land to cover."

Skaning swung to the mercenary captain. “Perhaps I no longer need your services, captain?”

The veteran shrugged nonchalantly. “Doesn’t matter to me. Give us our back pay and we’ll be off to warmer climes.”

“Careful, mercenary. I still have enough soldiers to handle your company,” Skaning threatened.

The captain stiffened. “Can you afford to lose them? I don’t need you, Skaning. You need us. We’re the best fighting element you have, and you know it. Like I said. Makes no difference if you keep us or cut us loose. It comes with the job.”

Trapped by his own anger, Skaning had no option but to swallow his pride and push forward. He knew there was no way his reservists were capable of hunting down Bahr and his motley assortment, not with a wizard and Gaimosian with him. The Vengeance Knight alone would be too much for most of his soldiers to handle. Worse, time was running out. Harnin’s rage would be unparalleled once he discovered Skaning’s disobedience. Skaning had to make his move, quickly, if he hoped to retain his place in Delranan’s current court.

“Double your search efforts, captain. The Sea Wolf needs to be found before he reaches his destination,” Skaning said, finally succumbing.

The mercenary grinned savagely. *More like before that one-eyed bastard learns of your traitorous actions. No one likes a man with secret agendas*. “Very well. We’ll find this forgotten son and bring your army down right on top of him.”

Skaning cursed his ill fortune. All bridges behind him were burned. His only option was to continue ahead, no matter the outcome.

TWO

Bitter Homecoming

Cold, almost bitter winds kissed Piper Joach's face. Raw from prolonged exposure to the elements, his flesh was constantly pink with several areas peeling away. His lips blanched. His nose burned. His body ached from continual long days in the saddle. Yet he wouldn't change any of it for the reward stretched out before him. A long winter's campaign robbed him of what might have been. He'd seen friends die and killed enemies who were now considered friends. All for what? He didn't know. The war in Rogscroft was unlike any he'd envisioned all those years ago when he decided to join the Wolfsreik. He was tired--exhausted, more accurately--and he was finally home.

Piper stared down on his kingdom. Delranan, at least this part, was an untouched wilderness. Snow clung to pine branches, covering bushes. The air was crisp, kissed by clear skies as far as the eye could see. He should have been content. The long winter war was over. He was home. Home, however, wasn't what it had been when he'd deployed. Delranan had become a wicked land. Brother murdered brother out of fear. Trust died. Harnin One Eye had turned this one standard for justice into a pit of the foulest quality.

"Seems peaceful enough," Vajna commented. He stifled a short yawn. "It certainly doesn't look like there's much war going on in this sector."

Piper cast a sidelong glance at the Rogscroft general turned friend. They'd ridden together since King Aurec and General Rolnir forged the alliance between Wolfsreik and Rogscroft. Battle honed their friendship and understanding of one another, enough that both old soldiers were comfortable working with the other. More importantly, they had no issues with allowing their soldiers to take orders from the other.

"Perhaps Harnin just hasn't made it this far east," Piper countered cautiously. He'd had the misfortune of working with the One Eye on more than one campaign. Harnin always seemed to struggle with containing an inner rage.

Vajna yawned again. Long days in the saddle left him tired and sore. He, like the rest of the combined army, was more than ready for the war to end. "We should push ahead and secure the immediate area before he realizes we've arrived."

"You realize it might be a trap?"

Vajna snorted. "I didn't get my rank by looking pretty."

Piper laughed. Grey and slightly overweight, Vajna was anything but handsome. Time, battles, and more worries than a sane person should be expected to shoulder brought wrinkles, lines, and liver spots aplenty to the middle-aged general.

"I'm surprised you got married looking like that," Piper quipped. "I'll send out scouts to secure the perimeter. Go back and have the light infantry begin deploying to valley floor."

Vajna wheeled his horse about, back towards the haunting mountain pass. "You don't really suppose he's waiting for us?"

"I wouldn't put anything past that bastard," he replied after a moment. "We'd best be on our guard. The fun part of our travels is over."

"Fun? I'm ready to retire."

Vajna clicked softly and rode back to the first of the main army units. Rolnir's premier infantry were massed by the thousands, filling the slender mountain pass. Rogscroft regulars, militia, and a few small units of Pell Darga fighters composed the rest of the five-thousand-strong vanguard. Cavalry and engineers forced their way through the Murdes Mountains. The air stank of horse flesh and sweat. Heavy weapons, catapults, and trebuchets disassembled for easy moving clogged the pass in anticipation of establishing firing positions. They were a force capable of stopping any army. Getting them deployed in fighting positions before they were overrun was the difficult part.

Each soldier harbored individual demons. More than one held doubts about his ability to attack his own people. Civil wars were vicious acts of desperation from all angles. Fears of returning home only to find relatives or loved ones opposing them threatened to bring the army to a halt. More than one soldier considered desertion, but pride and discipline kept them in place. They were the very best of Delranan's sons. Each languished under the combined weight of tradition and family.

Piper looked back on his soldiers. They were his source of pride, having conducted themselves professionally from the moment the Wolfsreik invaded Rogscroft to their exodus from King Badron's service. While consecutive campaigns were successful, the second in command of the north's most powerful army couldn't help but wonder how many of his soldiers weren't going to live to go home again. It was a sobering feeling.

"Sergeant at Arms! Deploy the scouts. Double screen. Just because we can't see the enemy doesn't mean he isn't there," Piper ordered.

The veteran scout saluted crisply. Flakes of snow peppered his beard. Flint-like eyes took in his commander with a measure of approval, as if saying it was about time. Harnin One Eye went disliked by nearly all the army. Piper hoped it would make his job easier.

It was near dusk by the time the scouts returned with curious news. Harnin had no forces deployed along this stretch of the Murdes Mountains, having little to no knowledge of the Pell Darga's secret passes. Several teams of scouts rode as far west as the line of freshly constructed fortresses running from north to south.

Piper took the news with casual interest. Static defenses always held the same inherent weakness: they could be ridden around and totally avoided while the invading army continued towards the exposed capital. The risk of leaving active combat forces behind the advancing elements was practically negligent considering most of the soldiers garrisoning the forts were ill-equipped infantry. They'd be ridden down and wiped out without causing much hassle to the invaders. That sickening feeling in the pit of his stomach returned at the thought of invading his own kingdom.

Delaying served no purpose. Piper regretted what needed doing but saw little point in avoiding the inevitable. The time for action was once again upon him. He listened as the scouts went into detail, drawing maps with sticks in the fresh snow. Piper recognized many of the prominent land features. Wheels began turning. He knew Rolnir trusted him implicitly, so the slender man started forming plans for attack. The maneuver was risky but might prove beneficial if his forces were able to claim the first fortress before Harnin caught wind of their presence.

"How large is the garrison?" he asked, suddenly impatient.

The scout cocked his head and gently stabbed the bowed stick into the snow repeatedly. "Can't be more than a hundred, sir. Shouldn't be an issue if we hit them in the middle of the night."

"A night raid on unfamiliar ground? The end result may not be what we're looking for," Piper countered. He didn't want to dismiss his scout's suggestion, knowing that in doing so he would effectively severe the free-flowing line of communication through the ranks. "What about pickets? Roving guards? What kind of defenses do they have emplaced to halt our progress?"

"Didn't see any pickets or anything," a second scout said quietly. "We ran into a bunch of trenches and pits, though. Ought to prove troublesome for cavalry and such."

"We can't risk an open charge anyway. The thunder of hooves will alert the defenders well enough in advance for them to reach their positions and open fire with whatever they have. Arrows and scorpions I'm assuming." Piper paused. His mind reeled through various options available to him. A spark ignited. He turned to the lead scout. "Sergeant, bring me the engineer captain. I've got a job opportunity for him."

Nodding at his subordinate, the sergeant folded his arms across his chest and continued studying the crude map. "Got something devious in mind, commander?"

"Perhaps. That all depends on if our wonderful engineers can bridge the defenses and blow a hole in the outer wall," Piper said.

"Light skirmishers or heavy infantry for the assault?"

Piper thought for a moment. Both had advantages and disadvantages. Skirmishers weren't designed for lengthy battles in confined spaces. Their lack of armor and limited selection of weapons reduced nearly fifty pounds from their fighting weight, however, giving them a distinct advantage over more cumbersome infantry. Casualties threatened to be high if Piper decided on them. Without knowing the depth and capacity of Harnin's army, Piper was loath to trade lives for ground.

Heavy infantry offered a different scenario. Slow and unwieldy, they were armed enough to render every living soul within the fort dead without much trouble. Strength in numbers often relied on interlocking shield walls on the open plain. That specialized defense was immediately rendered useless the moment they breached the walls. Conversely, their armor and weapons were enough to literally crush any opponent.

"I want archers to slip down within range as soon as it gets darks. They're to begin firing to cover the infantry attack."

The scout nodded again. "What about them engineers? Oden won't be too pleased with getting shot at while his boys are busy filling in holes."

"He'll get over it. The engineers need to employ without cover. We can't risk giving away our attack plan while they prepare the way," Piper said and grinned.

"I'm sure he'll come looking for you," the scout said and shrugged. The move was well rehearsed, too well for Piper's comfort.

"Good. I need to see him immediately. Time is slipping away from our advantage. Get the archers emplaced."

The sergeant saluted crisply and wheeled about.

"Sergeant, has there been any word of General Vajna's return?" Piper asked, already knowing the answer.

The scout shook his head and kept walking.

"Well, my friend, this appears to be the end of our time."

Venten stood erect, gazing up at his former pupil and friend-turned king. He'd done all he could for young Aurec but it didn't feel enough. The kingdom was slowly rebuilding, but from the raw chaos Badron and his Goblin horde visited it would be decades before Rogscroft returned to any semblance of normalcy. The purifying mission into Delranan would not only remove a tyrant from the throne, but secure Rogscroft's western borders for at least another generation provided Aurec and Rolnir found a suitable candidate for the throne.

The former general–now advisor--struggled with his emotions. He'd been around Aurec since the boy was born. Guiding, leading, scolding when necessary, Venten was the epitome of what a mentor should be. His love for the freshly crowned king of Rogscroft went beyond vocalization. The boy was like a son to old Venten.

"This is not how I would part company, Aurec," Venten said before his voice betrayed him.

"It is what's best for the kingdom. I need to accompany General Rolnir and the army. Rogscroft needs you to come out of retirement, Venten. I can't imagine a snake like Paneolus worming his way back into politics with all us away." Aurec winced at the memory of dismissing the self-serving politician only weeks before. He started thinking more severe actions should have been taken.

Venten frowned. "Paneolus doesn't have the backing to make a bid for the throne. He's more vulture than opportunist. A lesser man can defend Rogscroft while the army is deployed. I won't ask again. Allow me to accompany you on this campaign."

Though it hurt him to do so, Aurec couldn't allow Venten to tag along. "I can't, Venten. Rogscroft needs your experience. You did well while we reclaimed the kingdom and

I need you here. There's no telling how long it's going to take to subdue Harnin and find Badron. The kingdom can't be left without strength. I do not ask this of you lightly. You've been my conscience whispering in my ears for many years. I am going to miss you."

Satisfied yet disappointed, Venten stretched out and took Aurec's hand. "You've grown into a fine man, Aurec. Your father would be proud. I'll do my best to keep reconstruction on pace. Hopefully we'll at least have the rubble cleared away by the time you return."

Hundreds of villagers and refugees were already streaming back to the capital city. The thousand-strong detachment of Rogscroft soldiers left behind were immediately responsible for not only housing the incoming personnel but finding appropriate work for each. If Rogscroft was to be rebuilt it was going to be through the combined efforts of every single citizen capable.

"I've never had any doubts as to your qualities, Venten. Neither did my father. You're the best qualified to…to rule in the event I don't return."

Aurec's voice trailed off. After all they'd been through, from stealing Maleela away from Chadra Keep in the middle of the night to routing the Goblin army out of Rogscroft, Aurec seldom bothered thinking on death. If Lord Death chose to claim him there was nothing the fledgling king could do to prevent it. Standing on the very border of his kingdom, about to depart all he knew and loved, Aurec suddenly felt icy fingers clawing down his spine.

Venten refused to comment. Idle thoughts of death plagued every soldier and king. Aurec should be no different. There were times when it was good to be reminded of the consequence of failure. Venten didn't fear for Aurec's life nearly as much as the king did. Brash at times, Aurec was highly capable. Whether he lived or died was out of either of their hands.

"Go with the blessings of all Rogscroft, sire," the old advisor finally said. "I look forward to hearing of your exploits upon your return."

Aurec grinned warmly and turned his horse towards the mountains. It wouldn't do to allow Venten to see the tears building in his eyes. The king rode off, heading towards a war he didn't fully understand and a fate only the gods might know. Unlike his previous campaigns, Aurec lacked the urgency required for what was to come. He'd never intended on invading Delranan, despite the urgings of his council. He'd already accomplished all his goals save one. Maleela, princess of Delranan and love of his life, was missing and possibly dead.

The young king had already gone through desperation, fear, regret, and the faintest glimmer of hope since having Maleela ripped away from the sanctity of his castle. Vengeance was all that remained. Vengeance and the prospect of avenging all wrongs committed. His shoulders slumped ever so slightly as he entered the shadows of the pass. Delranan awaited, and with it a new phase in this seemingly unending war.

Venten stood and watched until Aurec entered the cold shadows of the pass. The Murdes Mountains were nightmarish on the best days, but this deep into winter they were near impassable. Cuul Ol and the other Pell Darga tribal leaders reluctantly offered up their secret ways to facilitate the army moving rapidly back into Delranan. Trust remained an issue between both factions, but Aurec was confident enough not to let it interfere with the movement of nearly twenty thousand combat soldiers.

"I'll watch over him. Don't worry."

Venten turned to look at Command Sergeant Major Thorsson. The greying veteran was filled with scars, oddly contrasting the freshly sewn-on insignia denoting his recent, and unexpected, promotion. "He needs to stay here in Rogscroft and let one of us act as his proxy."

Thorsson shrugged. "He's king. If you couldn't stop him who can?"

"He's headstrong and young. Two elements necessary for a quick demise," Venten countered. He failed to keep the bitterness in his heart from bleeding into his tone.

"Venten, Aurec is all grown up and you're responsible for the person he's become. Take it as a compliment. I'm comfortable with him leading the army. You should be as well." Thorsson turned his head and spit a wad of brown phlegm before wiping his mouth with the back of his sleeve. "We can win this war. Hopefully the mountains will be clear by the time we come home. I'm tired of winter."

"Winter? Thorsson, there are more inherent dangers in what you're about to attempt than the prospect of another storm."

The lifelong soldier grinned savagely. "I wouldn't have it any other way. Take care, Venten. The war may be finished here but Rogscroft is not a safe place."

"Stay lucky, my friend."

They shook and Venten finally headed back to his company. They'd set out for the capital in the morning, giving Aurec and most of the main body time to begin their short journey back into combat.

THREE

New Allies

The Dwarf army from Drimmen Delf, nearly four thousand strong, continued the long march towards Delranan. King Thord strode at the head of the winding column. It had been many years since the Dwarves last went to war with any other race than their own. Thord harbored no personal feelings on the matter, insofar as he was concerned he was simply repaying a debt.

The dark Dwarf rebellion cost Drimmen Delf dearly but the toll would have been much higher if not for the intervention of Anienam Keiss and Bahr of Delranan. Their combined efforts helped drive Thord's enemies from the field and secured a lasting friendship between the Dwarf Lord and Bahr, the Sea Wolf. Thord agreed to send an emissary along with Bahr on his quest to recover the Blud Hamr. When the Elf Lord Faeldrin informed him of the dire need to march west to the wars of man, Thord was honor bound to accept.

Cool winds blew across the Dwarf's face, at least the parts not covered by the thick moustache and beard. Marching across frozen plains was not in the Dwarf's best interests. He was infinitely more comfortable spending his days in the warmth and familiarity of his halls. Life above ground was meant for others. Still, Thord almost relished the freedom of having an entire world open and exposed before him. The sounds of his army marching behind him comforted him in ways only a soldier would understand. The jostle of armor. The accidental clank of steel on steel. The grumbling, cursing, and joking of soldiers as they marched. All were sounds so ingrained in the Dwarf Lord that he managed to take comfort in uncomfortable situations.

Wagons laden with spare weapons, feed and grain for the animals, and supplies for the army trundled along behind agonizingly slow. The cannons came next. Each was pulled by four oxen and followed by three additional wagons carrying the newly invented ammunition and gunpowder. Armorers roamed the camps at night, repairing the black-powder pistols and axes as necessary while the infantry recovered strength. The road to Delranan was long and Thord planned on having his army arrive, in fighting condition, by the end of ten days. Five had already passed.

Elf scouts of the Aeldruin ranged the fields and forests for sign of the enemy. Reports of the initial battle along the banks of the Fern River reverberated throughout the army. One hundred Dwarves gave their lives against an army estimated at more than fifty thousand. The Dwarves made the Goblins pay but not even Thord's main body was strong enough to repulse an army that strong.

Dwarves and Elves shared no love lost yet were far from being considered enemies. Most of the Elves on Malweir were too aloof, self-absorbed in their own ways, to bother caring what the other races did or didn't do. Thord was taken off guard when Faeldrin and his mercenaries arrived in Drimmen Delf offering to assist the Dwarves in their civil war. Very few individuals in the modern world offered aid without expecting something back in return. True to their word, the Elves performed scouting and light raiding duties without asking for more than food and shelter. Dwarf and Elf bonded almost immediately.

Dusk found the army breaking down into camps. The wagons were pushed into the center of four separate defensive squares. Fires were lit, for Dwarves held no fear of any living creature. They brazenly invited enemies to come closer. Guards were set. The army settled in for the night. Soon the smells of roasting meat invited grumbling stomachs and salivating mouths. Thord and his generals made their rounds among the rank and file. Nothing boosted morale for the lower ranks than seeing their leaders struggle alongside.

Exhausted but unwilling to admit it, Thord finally trudged back to his tent and readied to collapse shortly before midnight. He'd done all he could to get a gauge on the state of the army, stopping to fill his belly along the way. He'd checked the guard lines and the strength of the defenses in what was becoming a nightly ritual. No sign of the enemy had been spotted as of yet but he knew it was only a matter of time. An army the size of the Goblins was unheard of and moved much slower than his meager one. It would take time for the two to clash.

The Dwarf Lord tugged his boots off and leaned back on his cot. His rest was immediately interrupted by the gentle rap of knuckles on the wooden door pole. Grumbling under his breath, Thord reluctantly sat back up. "Enter."

He frowned upon seeing Faeldrin sidle in. "King Thord."

"Don't Elves ever sleep?" he growled.

The Elf Lord cocked his head. "A curious notion. We are told from an early age that there will be enough time for sleep when we are finally put in the ground. Life offers so much it is a shame to miss a single moment."

"Would that I shared your sentiment," Thord said.

"We are each different."

Thord wasn't sure if he appreciated the irony of the statement. "What brings you here tonight?"

Faeldrin gestured towards the empty stool uncomfortably close to the ground. "May I?"

Thord gestured with his head.

"My scouts have returned with their nightly briefings. Normally I don't bother you or the other commanders with their tales of finding nothing of consequence," he said and paused. "Matters discovered this night have changed that. We've run across large tracks converging on our course. We should meet sometime around midday tomorrow."

"What sort of tracks?" Thord sat straighter, suddenly more interested.

Faeldrin held up a staying hand. "Not Goblins. My apologies. It appears our Minotaur allies have finally arrived in force."

The Dwarf scratched his beard, running his stubby fingers through the tangled weave of thick hair. He'd heard of the giant bull warriors but, like most of the world, had never seen one. They were a race belonging to historical records and myths. When Faeldrin first brought word that the Minotaurs were willing to join the war Thord took it with a grain of disbelief.

"I guess hooves move faster than boots," Thord grumbled.

"It would be unwise to taunt them so. I have worked with their king, Krek, before. He is a humorless creature. The two of you should get along nicely."

Thord pointed a finger. "Dwarves have plenty of humor. It's just you surface dwellers don't get it, is all."

"That may be, but Minotaurs have notoriously quick tempers," the Elf countered. He enjoyed their mild sparring. It was a product of the campaign trail.

"I'll remember that when I'm staring up at them," Thord said. "What can you tell me of this Krek?"

"Krek was a young bull when we accompanied Dakeb the Mage on his quest in Thrae. His aid was immeasurable, though we ultimately failed in our quest. The Minotaurs have no love for the Goblins."

Thord's eyebrow peaked. "Did they bring enough to beat fifty thousand?"

Faeldrin paused before answering. "Perhaps not that many but their numbers will be sorely diminished once the battle ends."

"I don't relish the idea of being killed for no reason."

"We all must die, Thord."

He closed his eyes. "In due time. I'd like to see this war through first. That cold throne needs my ass on it for a few more decades."

Life or death were both real possibilities for the meager army. Faeldrin had lived for centuries, narrowly avoiding Lord Death a hundred times. He'd never bothered concerning himself with such thoughts, until now. *The war for the soul of Malweir. Long prophesied and now it finally approaches. If Thord knew a fraction of what I've been shown would he still march glibly towards the inevitable conclusion? What fool would? Were I a lesser Elf I'd have fled back to Elvanara to await the end.*

Thord saw the Elf's consternation. "You're troubled."

"We all should be. This is no easy task we have set ourselves to. I fear many a friend will not be among us when the last sword falls. Perhaps we should have all remained neutral."

"What talk is this? I've never heard an Elf sound so depressed in all my days," Thord chastised. "Go and hide in your trees or me in my caverns? I don't think the gods, dark or light, care for what we wish. If what you believe is true, this is the hour in which our combined might will either win the day or see us all enslaved for eternity. Running from the problem won't help a damned thing, Faeldrin. No. We march to war even if it means none of us return."

Rebuked, the Elf Lord could do no more than smile. "You've had me fooled for a long while, Dwarf. I didn't think your taciturn nature had such an expansive vocabulary. Very well. We shall continue on. I can only hope the kingdoms of Men in our path are just as willing to accept what's to come. This will be a war unlike any ever fought."

Thord leaned closer. Bits of chewed meat were visible between his teeth when he grinned. "What better place for a Dwarf to be?"

"They are moving faster than yesterday," Faeldrin remarked.

Euorn folded his hands over the saddle horn and continued to watch the approaching army go from a dark stain on the distant snow to distinguishable figures. "Big beasts. Bigger than I recalled."

"They are formidable to say the least. They are most welcome to this fight," Faeldrin added.

"I wasn't suggesting otherwise, Faeldrin."

The Elf Lord sighed. "Don't worry about it. Perhaps the Dwarf was right. A little rest might do us all good."

"Ha! I've been with you for more than two hundred years. I don't seem to recall you ever slowing down. Should I go out and meet them?"

Faeldrin stared for a moment longer. "No. There's little point in moving in the wrong direction. Krek and his legion will be along shortly. Head back to the main body and alert them of our impending arrivals."

"I only hope the Minotaurs have brought their own supplies. There's no way we can feed that many extra mouths," Euorn said and rode off.

Faeldrin's wait proved far shorter than anticipated. The Minotaur army moved fast, as if they were in a rush to reach the final battle. The Elf closed his eyes and recalled the last time one of their armies took to the field. Outside the walls of the Mage citadel of Ipn Shal, the Minotaur army was charged with defending the gates. Goblins and wicked men made charge after charge only to die by the hundreds on Minotaur tulwars and stone axes. The great bulls reaped terrible vengeance upon their foes while losing great numbers of their own. Ipn Shal held, if barely, and what remained of the Mages honored the bulls in Paedwyn. That honor echoed down through the years, transposing onto the current generation of warriors.

Fond memories often warmed the Elf. His own Aeldruin rode the flanks for the Minotaurs, preventing the enemy from rolling up on the sides and overwhelming the steadily outnumbered force. Those were days of glory and sorrow. Too many friends and familiar faces were buried in the aftermath of the battle. The war continued for another five years, reaping thousands of souls. Lord Death strode Malweir at will. What remained of the old ways spread out. Alliances disintegrated as war-weary soldiers returned to their ancestral homes. Magic was rooted out. Any bearing the signs were hunted down and murdered in blind rage. Faeldrin took his few surviving Elves and returned to the forest haven of Elvanara where they remained for an entire generation.

The Elf Lord knew that no other kingdom had reached out to the Minotaurs in all the years since. The quest to kill Ramulus the dragon brought the inevitable collision of races. Unexpected as it was, Faeldrin knew Krek, then a young bull who had yet to earn his first kill, was highly praised for his efforts by Anienam Keiss's father, Dakeb. He hoped the ferocity of a single Minotaur was a hint of what an entire legion held.

He watched as the legion ground to a halt. Steam poured from their nostrils. Cold sunlight reflected from freshly polished horns. The Minotaurs were breathing heavily. Plain, boiled leather armor clung to each bull. Weapons were sheathed or slung. There were no natural predators in the northern kingdoms for the vast legion to fear. Faeldrin admired their arrogance.

"Hail Krek, Lord of Malg!" he called out.

Krek, tallest of the bulls, strode towards the Elf. His great cloven feet were the size of small boulders. His horns thick, powerful. Muscles corded every inch of his nine-foot frame. Scars from individual combats ran diagonally down his face. Much of his mane had turned grey. He was old, almost at the point where a successor would be named. The old never lasted long in warrior societies.

"Elf Lord. It has been long," Krek replied. "Malg comes."

Faeldrin gazed out upon the army, judging their numbers to be close to two thousand. "You are well represented. I pity the Goblins that come upon us."

Krek coughed and spit. "No pity for grey skins. All must die."

The Elf feigned a smile. He held no personal desire to kill, not even a Goblin, but knew when necessity demanded otherwise. A reckoning was upon them. Only those with martial prowess could possibly survive. Little known to Faeldrin, the war had already claimed thousands of lives and was continuing to grind more souls towards Lord Death daily. His brief meeting with Anienam Keiss failed to present an adequate sense of urgency in the Dwarves. They were solely concerned with confronting and defeating the massive Goblin army.

"Allow me to lead you to King Thord. The army of Drimmen Delf awaits you not far from here," he said.

Krek nodded and bellowed orders in his brusque language. The Minotaur legions slowly took up the march again.

"What do you mean gone?" Thord demanded.

Anger filled his tone. He clenched his massive fist so tightly the knuckles bled white. The others assembled fell silent, knowing all too well their king's wrath when angered. The Dwarf Lord ground his teeth while looking to each of his generals and advisors.

"Well?"

"Sire, the Elf scouts report there is no sign of the Goblin army. They have…vanished." The younger Dwarf cleared his throat, shuffling uncomfortably from foot to foot.

Thord leaned menacingly closer. "An army that size cannot just disappear without any trace. The scouts must be wrong."

Aleor, tall and slender as most Elves, stood passively with hands folded in front of him. He regarded the smaller Dwarves as curious, yet capable of great violence. For an entire clan to fall to darkness didn't take much imagination. Any race willing to exercise violence must hold natural instincts towards fouler paths.

"King Thord, may I offer a suggestion?" he asked.

Tension left Thord's face, at least some of it, and he waved the Elf to continue.

"My scouts have scoured all the lands east from here to the Kergland Spine. While it is unlikely the Goblins have vanished there is the very real possibility they have altered their route of march. I suggest doubling the scouts and focus on the northern approaches. Fifty thousand enemy soldiers will have left a mass of debris in their wake. We will find them."

"For all we know we could be marching right towards them," Thord replied.

"Possible, but unlikely," the Elf countered. His tone was dry, as if analyzing every aspect of the conversation before commenting. Elves were notoriously deliberate in their actions, often taking years to reach conclusions most races couldn't afford to delay on.

"How do you mean? We can't continue the march to Delranan without knowing where our enemy is, Elf."

"We won't. The Goblin army is massive, larger than any other in recorded history. We would know if they were ahead of us. The signs would be unmistakable. Faeldrin and the Minotaurs should rendezvous with us by nightfall. I'm going to take a team of scouts back to the enemy's last known position and try to determine which way they went. We should return before the dawn. Given your leave, naturally."

Thord lacked options. He couldn't plan accordingly without knowing his opponent's disposition. He relented. "Very well. Find the Goblins, Aleor. Find them fast."

The Elf nodded and exited the command tent, leaving the Dwarf steaming over his sudden handicap.

FOUR

No Rest for the Wicked

The wagon groaned to a stop in the copse of thin firs shortly before nightfall. Another long day's march pushed Bahr's party to their limits. The running engagement with Harnin's forces had drained their energy, supplies, and forced them off schedule. Each suffered from multiple cuts and scrapes. They lost hours of sleep. The trek across Delranan had proved arduous on enough levels to inspire doubt in the hardiest.

Bahr climbed down from the wagon, pausing to stretch the pain of sitting on the hard, wooden planks all day away. He was pushing fifty, an age when most people retired and found a life of fishing on a quiet river. Being the brother of the king didn't allow for that sort of life. Loss and hardship seemed his place in life. His holdings and estate were burned to the ground. All he owned in Delranan was confiscated by Harnin One Eye. His true love, the *Dragon's Bane*, was resting in charred pieces in Chadra's harbor, the crew either dead or pressed into military service. Even his niece, Maleela, was missing.

Through it all, Bahr continued driving towards the final battle. He'd taken his band of reluctant heroes east and then south to Trennaron in search of a weapon few believed in. Along the way he stumbled into a greater conspiracy threatening the future of the entire world. Bahr considered himself a person of honor. He'd given his word to the wizard Anienam Keiss. One way or another he would lead his group to the ruins of Arlevon Gale. He was committed to the course, no matter how foul the potential end promised to be.

"We can't keep on like this, Bahr," Boen, the big Gaimosian said after he finished brushing his horse down.

"What choice do we have?" Bahr echoed Boen's sentiments but couldn't find a way clear of their dilemma. "Arlevon Gale is still a few days away."

“We’re not going to last a few days, not with Harnin’s soldiers hounding us every step of the way. Something needs to change.”

Bahr threw up his hands. “What? We’ve done all we can to elude Skaning yet they’re still on our trail. It’s not as if we can hide easily. Not with Groge. His tracks alone are larger than the rest of ours combined.”

Boen grinned at the thought of the Giant youth stumbling along in the wagon’s wake. He’d initially thought the Giant would be enough of a deterrence to keep Harnin’s soldiers at bay. Such wasn’t the case. Enemy soldiers continually threw themselves at the Giant once they’d overcome the initial shock of facing a twelve-foot-tall warrior. They died just as easily.

“What I don’t understand is Skaning’s willingness to throw away lives,” Bahr added. “Harnin can’t have that many disposable troops to dedicate to running us down.”

“The rebellion’s drawn attention to this part of the kingdom. Ingrid and her people have stirred up a hornet’s nest,” Boen said. “There’s no feasible way to reach the ruins without detection.”

“I don’t think we can make it if that’s the case.”

Bahr’s reluctance to fight was contrary to all they’d been through since initially being hired to rescue Maleela from Rogscroft. Battles followed in a never-ending stream as they crossed half of Malweir. He was tired. His mind wasn’t as sharp as it had been. Age and hardship combined to lower his stamina and esteem. Thoughts of sailing away to another land entertained him on those rare moments when he was alone. It was past time to move on. Delranan wasn’t what it once was, even for a man who turned his back on the throne when he was barely out of his teens.

His easygoing life was in fragments, broken and scattered beyond repair. What remained accompanied him on this quest. A pair of could-have-been sell swords. An enigmatic wizard who spoke of days long past, now blinded by the powers of the gods. A strange woman from the Jungles of Brodein with an affectation towards Dorl Theed. Skuld, the stowaway struggling to find his place in life. A surly Dwarf warrior who enjoyed killing a little too much for Bahr's liking. A Giant with the emotional development of a human child and Boen, the Vengeance Knight who knew nothing but battle. Not the worst of friends but not what he expected after such a long life.

"It's time to change tactics," Boen suggested.

Bahr cocked his head. "How do you mean?"

He knew they couldn't take Skaning's forces head-on. His small band of heroes was no match for a sizeable force--a force neither Boen nor Bahr knew how large. Running accomplished nothing. It was only a matter of time before a stray arrow took one of them out, or worse. They were trapped between the rocks with no plausible escape route.

The Gaimosian continued. "What do you know of this Skaning?"

Bahr took a moment to think. "He's not the best or brightest in Badron's court. Young, brash, that makes him prone to mistakes. What he lacks in experience he more than makes up for with ferocity. He's a killer, Boen, just not one with honor."

"That would explain why none of the soldiers we've killed wore uniforms." Boen grunted. "I doubt they're more than mercenaries."

"Meaning they can do whatever it takes to ensure our deaths," Bahr concluded.

The Gaimosian nodded. "And we can do what needs to be done as well. Mercenaries don't garner the same treatment as uniformed soldiers."

Bahr disagreed. Combatants should be treated accordingly regardless of their affiliation. Executing someone simply because they were mercenaries was akin to murder in his eyes. He purposefully avoided the discussion, knowing Gaimosians were viewed in similar light.

"We can't afford taking prisoners, Bahr," Boen pressed, mistaking silence for acquiescence. "Sooner or later they're going to get the better of us. There is only so much Ironfoot and I can do to prevent it. Our weapons are blunted.

Armor needs to be repaired." He lowered his voice so only Bahr heard. "We're at the breaking point. These people have been through every imaginable scenario you or I can think of. There's only so much left to give."

"What would you have me do, Boen? This quest is committed to stopping the Dae'shan from releasing the dark gods. We've gone well beyond the point of turning back."

Disturbed, Boen folded his burly arms across his chest and began pacing. "We won't make it to Arlevon Gale. Not like this."

"I don't see any other option," Bahr said after a few minutes passed.

Boen glared, briefly, at his friend. "So be it. I'm going out to scout the area. Save me some of that deer."

The Sea Wolf watched him ride off. Once the Gaimosian became angered, there were no words capable of calming him. He hoped a quick ride around the camp would enable him to blow off his rising bitterness. Bahr wished he had such an outlet instead of feeling trapped in a tightening snare.

Tripwires were already set out, roughly one hundred meters from the camp. Knee high, the wires were suggested by the Dwarf captain, Ironfoot, as an early warning system. As of yet they hadn't been discovered, though Bahr debated whether it was by sheer luck or deliberate. Anienam supposedly ensorcelled the camp with a protection spell, preventing the enemy from noticing the fire or the smells of roasting meat. The wizard wasn't the most liked among the group but his acceptance was growing the closer they got to the ruins. Perhaps his unexpected blinding played a large part or, as Bahr suspected, it was due to the approaching battle against the ultimate evil.

Bahr reentered the camp locked in thought. For all his experience and quality, he couldn't find an escape from their current situation. The enemy seemed to be multiplying, as if the entire western campaign had abandoned the rebellion to hunt him down. Logically it made sense. Badron was deposed and his only surviving child was missing. That left Bahr as the only blood relative to the current monarchy. His presence in Delranan remained a threat to Harnin's plans for as long as he lived.

Briefly, so quick a thought he was ashamed to have it, Bahr considered abandoning the others in the hopes Skaning wanted him alone. Anienam and the sole true Dae'shan, Artiss Gran, both insisted that the only way for the group to succeed was by having all members arrive at the final nexus together. *Everyone has a part to play. The only chance Malweir has to survive rests in your combined hands*. Memories of that conversation atop the walls of Trennaron plagued his peace of mind.

He knew he should consider their progress fortunate. Thus far they'd only suffered two losses. Ionascu, the broken former spy, was clearly murdered by Maleela in the jungle. Bahr wasn't surprised. Ionascu was greatly hated. His loss was hardly felt and did wonders for the group chemistry. Bahr never fully understood Anienam's reasoning from bringing Ionascu out of Harnin's dungeons after they'd been captured and tortured. He offered nothing to the group but animosity. The overall dynamic improved in his absence.

Maleela, on the other hand, was the reason they had all come together. Hired by Harnin One Eye after the daring midnight raid on Chadra Keep, they'd ranged into Rogscroft and stole her away. The wizard believed Maleela's future held great portent yet failed to suggest finding her. Bahr feared his niece was already dead. They'd never been close. In fact, Bahr often did his utmost to forget all blood bonds with his brother's side of the family. Their relationship grew the longer the quest prolonged. Now she was gone he could do no more than weep at her loss.

"You need to abandon your regrets, Bahr. They will only make our enemy's job easier."

Bahr exhaled sharply. He hadn't wanted to get into a conversation with the wizard this evening. "Anienam. Can you sense any soldiers nearby?"

"You know my powers don't work like that." The blind wizard cocked his head as if listening to the wind. "This is an amazing world, don't you think? Here we are, a tiny group of the most mismatched races you could conceive and we are all that stands between life or eternal darkness."

Bahr snorted. "Aye. The gods have a sick sense of humor."

"I don't think humor has much to do with it. We were destined to carry out this task. Our wants and needs are nothing to the gods. After all, why should they be? The gods created this world and all life on it. We are nothing if not the playthings of the gods."

"I don't fancy being a plaything for anyone or anything," Bahr said and frowned. "This has gone on long enough. Maybe it's time for the gods to be gone altogether."

"What are you saying? That we'd be better off without their influences?" Anienam asked. His mood visibly darkened at the possibilities intoned in Bahr's train of thought.

Bahr paused, suddenly conscious of where his thoughts were leading. "Perhaps. We've been ignorant tools for far too long. What good have the gods done for us? The good ones abandoned Malweir long before any of us here were thought of. The dark ones only want to destroy everything. We don't need either sect, wizard. Perhaps the time has finally come for the world to govern itself. Malweir continues daily without divine interference. Most of the old races have abandoned their belief in the gods altogether. Look at Groge. His people worship a singular deity. What do your books have to say about that?"

Though blind, Anienam looked down upon Bahr with newfound approval. The Sea Wolf was finally shedding his outer skin and revealing his true nature. Granted, it had taken longer than he anticipated, but Anienam was sure Bahr now had the practical understanding necessary to complete the difficult task appointed to him. *A good sign, but is it already too late?*

"What you propose is tricky. Each race is imbued with the ability to self-govern. We all enjoy certain freedoms that a lifetime of slavish devotion to the old gods disempowers. The gods can be seen as lethargic. The gods of light left this plane long ago, vowing to allow us the right to self-rule."

"They don't seem overly interested in returning to deal with their problems, though, do they?" Bahr added. "They could have come back to stop the dark gods at any point."

"Perhaps they wanted to test us," Anienam said.

"So this is all some grand experiment? For what purpose?"

"An answer I fear we will discover all too soon."

Bahr let the conversation drop. Something he failed to identify in the wizard's tone bothered him for reasons he wasn't sure. All he wanted was to sit down, enjoy his share of roasted venison, and fall asleep. The rest of the world could wait.

He practically collapsed onto a folding stool procured from the fine vaults of Trennaron and listened to the conversation between Dorl and Nothol. Bahr could always count on the travel banter of his favorite sell swords to brighten the mood.

"I'm not saying that, you thick-brained fool," Dorl fumed. His face reddened from frustration. "All I'm saying is that the meat is starting to taste old."

"Of course it's old, dummy. Boen killed it near on a week ago!" Nothol replied, feigning his own frustration. Most of his comments were always meant to incite the infantile feeling of aggression Dorl kept pent up.

Dorl blinked twice as the realization struck. "No. You're not going to get away with this again. This is my point of view. I'm not giving it over to you just because."

Nothol sat back and held up his hands in surrender. "Fine, be that way. I wasn't looking for a fight anyway. It's still too cold for that."

Satisfied with the victory, Dorl said, "Good. That's settled."

"The meat is getting a little rank."

"Damn it, Nothol! I'm going on guard duty."

Laughter spread through the camp as the shorter sell sword hastily snatched his weapons and trudged off to rove the perimeter.

"Why do you do that?" Rekka Jel asked once the merriment died down. Since joining the quest in Chadra, she and Dorl had grown to become lovers. Her newfound emotions failed to translate into understanding for the northerners or their rigid ways. Rekka never bothered thinking of her relationship lasting beyond the approaching battle. There was a good chance many, if not all, of their ragged group would be dead before the end. A life in the north with Dorl hadn't become a possibility until she'd been banished from her village of Teng through a series of unfortunate events.

Nothol smiled warmly. "It keeps him on his toes. Don't tell him I ever said this, and I'll deny it if you do, but I need Dorl around. He's watched my back for years and that's an irreplaceable feeling."

"He cares deeply for you," she said.

"Let's not get mushy. Emotional types don't last long in this profession." *Of course, we're not likely to last much longer anyway. What have we gotten ourselves into, I wonder?* "Just know that I will do everything I can to keep his scruffy hide alive. No matter the cost."

The sudden commotion on the far side of camp broke her thoughts. Her head snapped up. Hands reached for her sword. She squinted in the dying light, relaxing only slightly upon spying Boen's massive frame rumbling back into camp. He was out of breath and exuded danger. The Gaimosian brought dire news. She sensed his adrenhilin and knew he ached for the sweet release only battle offered.

"We're in trouble," he said between ragged breaths.

Bahr looked to his friend. "How close?"

"Not far." Boen shook his head. "I don't know how they're tracking us, either. Every time we stop they seem to make a straight line towards our position."

Heads turned towards the wizard. Sensing their consternation, Anienam lacked the answers they desperately wanted. The truth was he was just as confused. Each night he cast a web of spells intended on confusing their stalkers. It was old magic, from the high days of Ipn Shal and the Mages. The powers able to counter it were few. Anienam reluctantly came to accept that their enemy was imbued with the taint of the Dae'shan. It was the only possibility that made sense. But how to explain that to the others when it was merely a stray thought without evidence?

"I don't understand either," he said reluctantly. "My magic is stronger than any other in this part of the world. We should be safe, practically invisible to any prying eyes."

"But we're not, wizard," Bahr said. "And if they can unerringly follow us across the wilderness how secure are we at night? What stops Skaning from bursting into the perimeter and slaying us in our sleep?"

"Bahr, the situation is more convoluted than you make it appear," Anienam replied. "There are many forms of magic in play. I recognize its taint on the air. Our enemies can't produce such talent on their own. We must assume they are being aided by the very worst the dark gods have to offer."

"You didn't answer the question," Boen growled.

"How would you have me answer when all I have is speculation?"

The Gaimosian pointed an accusatory finger. "With a straight answer for once. No more damned riddles. We're too far along on this quest for child's play. I don't mind dying but I need to know all the facts before I willingly sacrifice my life. You owe us that much."

Anienam hesitated. The last in a long line of magic wielders, he alone was the heir to the wealth of knowledge from Ipn Shal. Many secrets were nestled deep within his mind. Secrets that no other living being should know lest the world was plunged into war again. He'd tried to follow his father's advice. Tried to live up to the majesty of what the Mages had once represented. Anienam wasn't convinced whether he'd succeed.

Malweir grew increasingly dangerous with each new generation. Petty wars sprung up between kingdoms. He often suspected the Dae'shan were pulling strings behind the curtain but never had the numbers to investigate in force. He paused to consider how he'd come to learn of this latest plot threatening them all. Idle in the crumbling libraries at the old Mage citadel, he was visited by a terrible premonition. Darkness approached. Darkness so deep all life on Malweir would be consumed, devoured by eternal rage.

He'd lost years trying to decipher what the vision meant. Anienam didn't believe in premonition. Fate pulled or pushed each individual according to a whim. The directness in the message he'd received left him immobile. How could any one person walk the face of the world knowing that the hour of the dark gods' return was finally at hand? His resulting crisis of faith took him down roads best left unmentioned. He nearly fell along the way, lost to all who truly needed him. The Mages were gone and with them the only capable force with the knowledge to combat the dark gods and the Dae'shan. He was alone. The solitary survivor of a way of life the rest of the world deemed too dangerous. A relic.

Anienam finally rediscovered his passion on a lone mountaintop high above the world. Dragons had once claimed the peak for their roost, but those days had fallen into dust as well. He hurried back to Ipn Shal to discover all he could of his impending doom. At last, after centuries of aimless wanderings trying to decipher his purpose in life, the last wizard knew what he must do. He attached himself to a merchant caravan and headed north to Delranan to find the forgotten son of kings.

"Very well. The Dae'shan lend speed to our enemies. It is not that they can unerringly find us, but more they're being shown which direction we travel. Pointed, if you will, towards us through unflinching desire. Part of me takes heart in this. The Dae'shan have been trying to kill us, especially you, Bahr, from the beginning. I suspect they were already at work on your brother long before we were hired to rescue Maleela from Rogscroft. Those foul creatures manipulated the kingdom and brought war to the north."

"To what end? What value do I hold in their plans?" Bahr asked. Cold fingers of dread danced over his flesh, as if Lord Death stalked right behind.

Anienam turned his head. The rag covering his eyes was frayed and ragged. "You are the key to all this. Your blood holds the power to stop the dark gods, or release them."

"I don't understand. I'm just a man, Anienam. There's nothing special about me. What could I possibly do to affect these immortal beings?" Bahr protested but deep inside he recognized the truth in those words. He'd felt haunted his entire life. Always running from what might have been, never taking the time to fully embrace what he should have been.

"But you're not. You are so much more. I've studied the ancient histories. Each of the three nexuses is centered around powerful bloodlines. Yours is the last. The Dae'shan know this. Through your blood they intend to release the power of the Olagath Stone. Thousands of captured souls will tear the fabric between time and space. Their screams will open the gates to our realm of existence and release the dark gods."

Skuld, sitting open-mouthed in shock, found the courage to speak. "Why is he headed towards the danger? He should be halfway across the world by now."

Anienam smiled softly, quietly approving the youth's growing sense of understanding. He'd grown much since sneaking aboard the *Bane* all those months ago. Anienam envisioned a grand future for Skuld. All he needed to do was reach out and claim it.

"He travels with us because he must. Bahr's blood is important, yet it also flows within his brother's veins, and within his niece. Any of the three can be used to doom or save Malweir. Bahr needs to go to Arlevon Gale." *There he will confront his deepest fears. I only pray his strength of conviction is enough. Otherwise….*

"So I am to confront my brother after all," Bahr concluded. He'd avoided Badron for decades, always staying beyond the scope of vision, yet ever a step ahead of his brother's plotting and schemes. It seemed all his careful planning was crashing to the ground.

"If he still lives," Anienam said. "Who can say what has happened since we've been gone? All we know is that Harnin One Eye has usurped the throne and seeks to transform Delranan into a kingdom of pure chaos. I believe this to be a diversion intended on keeping us distracted enough so that we fail to keep sight of the true goal."

"The ruins," Boen added. "Anienam, that's all well and fine but we're not going to make it to the ruins with Skaning's soldiers hounding us like this."

"He's right," Nothol added. "We need to change the plan."

"There's a village not far from here," Bahr suggested. "We might be able to blend in if we can reach it far enough ahead of Skaning."

"With a Dwarf and Giant in tow?" Ironfoot scoffed. "I think you overestimate the simplicity of your people, Bahr."

"The Dwarf has a point, but it's a chance we should take," Boen said.

Bahr scratched the stubble growing on his upper lip. He didn't like the idea of heading back into another town, especially considering how poorly they'd fared in every village and town on their trek. One calamity after another befell them, from Chadra to Teng. He dreaded learning what new twist the Dae'shan had in store for them in the upcoming village but it was a risk he felt they needed to take. Only a few days remained before the day when the Dae'shan would attempt their ritual. Only a few days to decide the fate of the world.

"We make for the village. I want camp packed up and ready to move an hour before dawn," he ordered. "The faster we get there the less chance of Skaning being able to counter our plans. Not even he is foolish enough to risk a battle in the middle of a village deep in rebel territory. We might just find a few allies along the way."

FIVE

Difficult Decisions

True to his plans, Bahr had the group up and moving well before the first wave of sunlight cracked the curtain of darkness. They pushed their already weary animals harder, hoping each beast had the strength to carry them to the destination. Bahr's route since departing Ingrid and the rebellion was a parallel course due south of Chadra Keep. He wanted nothing to do with Delranan or the rebellion and especially had no desire to run in to the One Eye again. Their last confrontation ended with each of them being tortured mercilessly in Harnin's dungeons. Bahr figured there'd be time enough to deal with Harnin once the quest was complete.

Groge trotted alongside the wagon. The Giant lad barely started sweating and his almost childish grin entertained the others to no end. None of them but Skuld fathomed how anyone could manage to find amusement under such dire circumstances. Groge, still foreign to the ways of lowlanders, struggled to accept his place within the group. That the Blud Hamr could only be wielded by a Giant forced him to become integral in the quest but his lack of social interaction before joining Bahr left him at odds. The Giants of Venheim were vastly unlike any of the other races. More stoic and taciturn, Giants seldom engaged in frivolous small talk. They dedicated every waking hour of their day to the perfection of steel and iron. His interaction with others was limited to the workings of a forge.

The others managed to work well enough considering the variety of backgrounds and races. Groge half expected to find kinship with Ironfoot, but the Dwarf often kept to himself Their conversations were limited. Ironfoot often chastised Groge for his inability to accept his natural strength and power and to use them in battle. At first Groge felt disappointed, knowing their kinship through old blood, but then he came to understand the Dwarf's need for battle. He didn't necessarily agree with it, but strong people seldom changed their ways without proper cause.

He'd been walking for most of the day lost deep in thought when he finally decided to confront Bahr with his problems. The Sea Wolf, to his credit, accepted the Giant's sudden crisis of conviction.

"Captain, might I have a word?" Groge asked.

"Of course, my friend. What's on your mind?"

Groge paused, taken off guard by Bahr's pleasant demeanor. "I have much on my mind. This quest is changing me, and not in ways I appreciate. I'm a simple blacksmith. Not a king or great warrior."

"We don't always get to choose how we live our lives," Bahr told him. "This is not the life I would choose either but it is the one I was given."

"I understand that. I do, but I can't help but question what is the point. Should we prevail and the dark gods are defeated, what comfort is there? We'll have sacrificed so much of ourselves that we won't be the same ever again. I liked who I was. Who I am. The elders tell us change is a necessary evil if we are to continue to evolve as a race, but this is not the change that I need." Groge shook his massive head. "What point is there in continuing when I will never be who I am again?"

Bahr glanced to Anienam, hoping the wizard had some random bit of sage advice, but the wizard remained uncharacteristically silent. Bahr briefly considered pushing him from the wagon on principle. "Groge, you ask questions I don't have the answers for. Each one of us has personal demons to overcome. We've gone through so much with no promise of survival. Would you believe I was not always this way?"

"You?" Groge asked. It had never occurred to him that Bahr, famed sea captain and dispossessed brother of the king of Delranan, might have lived a vastly different life before this quest.

Bahr nodded. "I am the eldest son, meaning I should have been king, but it was a hassle I never wished. I turned my back on the crown and my father to pursue a selfish lifestyle. My decisions are at least partly to blame for all the problems inflicting Delranan now. I lie awake each night wondering if matters would be different if I had accepted my rightful place. Would there still be a war? Would the future be in doubt? I can't answer those questions and I don't feel as if I should. This," he said and gestured to the rest of the group, "is my world now. I am responsible for their lives, and yours, if only for a moment. Nothing else matters to me, Groge. Nothing. Once we destroy this Olagath Stone and send the dark gods back to whatever hells they come from, I will finally be able to look back on my life and decide whether or not I was a good person."

Finding the answers to his potentially life-changing course of action mildly acceptable, Groge shifted the weight of the Blud Hamr on his back. It was no easy thing discovering he must reach his own conclusions while trying to struggle through day-to-day battles. He decided to change his method of approach. "What can I expect in this new village? I don't relish the thought of having to hide in the forests again."

Bahr grinned. "There will be no hiding for you this time, I'm afraid. We can't afford to let the Blud Hamr out of our sight, meaning you will be coming with us the entire way. Don't mistake my simplistic attitudes for lack of apathy. You've become an important part of our little dysfunctional group and I personally enjoy your company."

"I understand. The Hamr is what's important," Groge said, displaying impressive clarity for one so inexperienced. "How then do you plan on concealing my…size?"

"Ha!" Anienam cackled.

Bahr cast a sidelong glance. "Now you comment? Groge, we're going to find a nice warm barn for all us. My precious sell swords might object to having to rough a night in the straw and stench rather than a soft bed but they'll get over it."

Satisfied with the answer, Groge plodded on. He'd learned much and was given more to consider before that fateful moment when he would be forced to use the Blud Hamr and alter the course of future days. Bahr continued glaring at the blind wizard, wondering why he chose that moment to open his mouth.

The village was as far out of the way as possible, an extraordinary feat considering the size and scope of Delranan. Less than twenty houses mixed with a tavern, millhouse, chandlery, and trading post composed the village. Bahr didn't know the name, nor did he have any reason to learn it. His plan called for limited interaction with the locals, despite the possibility that many, if not all, of the villagers might be sympathetic to the rebellion. They could just as likely be loyalists for all Bahr knew.

Holding the group up less than a league outside of the village, Bahr sent Dorl and Nothol in to scout the area. The latent fear that Skaning might have forces stationed close by or garrisoning the village kept him from immediately striking towards the town. Time was steadily slipping through his fingers but he knew they were less than three days from the ruins of Arlevon Gale. A few small delays wouldn't hamper the quest. Or so Bahr hoped.

"How is it we're always the fools getting sent into harm's way first?" Dorl complained. Chimney smoke, thin tendrils of blue-grey, rose into the fading day sky.

Nothol shared his best friend's ire but knew better than to waste time griping about it. They each had a task to perform. This just happened to suit their skillset.

"You're looking at it all wrong, Dorl."

"How should I see it? That we'll get killed before the others and not have to see how badly this all goes at the end?" Dorl snorted in reply.

"Or that Bahr had full confidence in our ability to complete the task. Besides, we get first dibs on where we sleep."

"You don't take things serious enough. What if the village is loyal to Harnin?"

Nothol shrugged. "We fight our way out and keep heading east. One meager village isn't going to do more harm than the hundreds of mercenaries on our tail. I don't think Rekka is doing a good job taking care of you."

"Watch it," Dorl threatened.

"I mean it. If she were, you'd be a lot happier."

Dorl opened and closed his mouth before finally letting a sympathetic laugh escape. Nothol followed suit as they rode closer to the thatch-covered houses.

"We need a drink, Nothol," Dorl said after wiping his eyes from what turned out to be almost uncontrollable laughter.

"More than one."

"A shame Bahr won't let us get drunk. I'd like to forget what we're about for just one day."

Nothol agreed. "It will all be over soon enough. Three more days and we either live or die. There's not much more to it than that."

Dorl's mood darkened again. "At least we've got the right allies with us. That Giant may not be much of a fighter but he doesn't need to be. All it takes is one roar and misplaced boot to give someone a really bad day."

"Groge? He's harmless. Now, Ironfoot. That one worries me. Dwarves like to fight almost as much Boen. Between the two of them we should, theoretically, be able to sit back and watch the show."

Dorl reined his horse in. "You don't expect that, do you?"

"Expect what?"

"Those two brutes to do all the fighting," he replied.

Nothol really hadn't bothered thinking on it either way. "Seems they've been doing most of it so far. Sure, we get a few licks in here and there but it's nothing compared to what Boen and Ironfoot seem to enjoy."

"That's just it. Leaving all the fighting to them weakens the rest of us."

"How so?" Nothol asked.

"We expect them to take the brunt and wind up paying more attention to them than our own business," Dorl said. "I don't fancy taking a blade in my back."

Neither spoke for the rest of the ride into the village. Unwanted thoughts, those stray bits of gloom both purposefully shoved to the forgotten corners of their minds, burst to life, forming new demons in the seclusion of solitude. Lord Death was a powerful motivator. He forced their hands to greater extremes the longer the quest extended. Now that it was all grinding to a rapid halt there seemed little chance of escaping certain, violent demise.

Banks of dark clouds rolled in as the sun sank beneath the horizon. Shades of night crawled across the land, an ominous warning to any foolish enough to be caught outside. Chickens clucked under the eaves of a series of farmhouses running the length of the only road leading into the village. The sell swords would much rather sneak in on a lesser-traveled path but neither were familiar with this part of the kingdom. Deciding there was some measure of merit in being bold, Nothol headed straight for the nearest farmhouse and hoped for the best. A quick barter later and they were granted a relatively comfortable night in the farmer's barn, all for a nominal expense.

Bahr and the wagon rolled in a short time later, after darkness fell. No one noticed the Dwarf or Giant sneaking into the barn before the doors groaned shut. Food was prepared, the horses brushed down. Normally they wouldn't have been allowed a fire but the farmer suffered the effects of the long, severe winter with the same frame of mind. A pit had already been dug out in the center of the floor, low enough to prevent the flames from spreading to the dried timbers of the structure. He reluctantly granted the sell swords permission to do the same, on the condition they didn't burn his barn down or kill his livestock in the process.

Groge found the space cramped but comfortable. His twelve-foot frame snuggled into a stack of hay bales for the night. The young Giant let his mind wander as he stared longingly into the flickering fire. It was moments like this that reminded him of his time in the forges of Venheim. Satisfied and full, the Giant slowly fell asleep.

"That didn't take long," Boen murmured and gestured towards the sleeping Groge.

Bahr glanced up quickly and went back to the fire. "He's fortunate. I haven't gotten a good night's sleep since we left Trennaron."

"The past has a way of haunting us," Boen concurred. "Don't waste your time worrying over it, Bahr. Whatever happens is meant to. Nothing you or I do will change that."

"You Gaimosians are walking contradictions. One moment you are determined to set the course of action for the world and the next willing to let it all ride. I wish I had that sense of confidence."

Boen chuckled softly, knowing it was all for show. He felt Bahr's gradual change the closer they got to their destination. Anyone would undergo the same, as far as he was concerned. Recognizing you were the agent of Fate was no easy task to swallow. Boen often wondered what his life might have been like if he'd been born anything but Gaimosian. The image never materialized. He was a warrior, nothing more. His own demons struggled for dominance in the recesses of his mind. Idle thoughts of retiring to a quiet village to enjoy his final years were overpowered by the growing sense of foreboding that he was going to die soon. He shrugged his personal concern off. Death would happen in its own good time. All he needed to do was ensure Bahr and the others were given every opportunity to accomplish their tasks.

"What are we going to do about Skaning? We can't keep trying to dodge him and expect to reach the ruins in time," Boen asked. He idly poked a large stick into the fire. White-hot coals collapsed in the center of the flames.

Bahr continued to stare into the dancing flames. The over complications that were developing added unnecessary stress to an already stressful situation. As much as he wanted to stand and fight, to force Skaning into a final confrontation, he knew he couldn't afford the delay. Time had grown perilously short without them noticing. His back was against the rocks.

"What can we do?" he said. "I'm sure he's already sent riders ahead to coordinate a blocking force, cutting us off from our destination."

"How would he know where we're going?" Boen asked. "Skaning seems like a minor player in all this. It's that bastard One Eye I'm concerned with. What I would give to plunge my sword down his gullet."

"We can't risk getting stopped by Harnin or Skaning." Bahr frowned. His options continued to restrict.

Boen offered, "I could go out into the village. See who's sympathetic to the rebellion and stir up enough trouble to swamp Skaning's soldiers here long enough for us to get a day's ride on them. I'm sure the people would be more than willing to exercise their anger after the long winter."

"I don't want any unnecessary deaths heaped upon our cause, Boen," Bahr said, rejecting the idea.

"What cause? The way I see it I'm only here to watch your back. You and the others while you destroy this gateway between worlds. This isn't my crusade, Bahr, and I damned sure don't have a problem with a little spilled blood."

Bahr felt deflated. None of his ideas offered a sliver of hope and he was steadily sinking down into feelings of emptiness. "What do you propose, Boen? We incite a riot and let those mercenaries slaughter the countryside?"

The malevolent gleam in Boen's eyes lasted a brief second too long. "No, but it's past time for a blooding. Let me stay behind. I'll lead them off our trail and double back to you before you reach Arlevon Gale. I might be fortunate to take out enough of them to make this Skaning change his mind on pursuing us. Let him go back to Ingrid and fight it out."

The idea wasn't without merit. Boen could single-handedly wipe out most if not all the pack of mercenaries hounding them. All he needed was the proper vehicle to administer Gaimosian justice. Tempting as it sounded, Bahr couldn't afford for his greatest, strongest asset to disappear.

"Anienam and Artiss Gran both said we are all needed at the end," he countered. "We need you here, with us."

Boen waved off his concern with mild disgust. "Bah! I'm tired of these mystics and self-proclaimed wizards trying to dictate our lives. Are we not free men? How much longer are we expected to languish under the control of beings lacking the concepts of free will?"

"I'm not arguing that, Boen, but we've been shown what's to come. I need you by my side, if for nothing else but the strength you possess. The others are capable in their own fields, but you, you are the truest version of a warrior we have. I figure there are less than two hundred on our trail. Who knows how many await ahead?"

"Ahead or behind makes no difference. We've got to confront the nearest threat and neutralize it before it can be allowed to grow. Bahr, you know I'm right. Let me deal with these mercenaries my way."

Bahr hung his head in defeat. His latent fear of losing the Gaimosian was preventing him from making the logical decision. They'd been hounded since leaving Ingrid and the rebellion, causing exhaustion in a matter of days. Boen's unexpected assault would give them time to recover and properly prepare for the coming battle. Still, Anienam's warning hovered in the back of his mind. All were necessary to succeed. The Sea Wolf used both hands to wipe his face, cleansing the doubt and self-castigation in the process. He'd been a slave to inaction for too long. It was time to take the fight back to their enemies.

"Very well," he conceded. "Take what you need and depart before dawn. The rest of us will hurry to the ruins. I'd like to make it well ahead of the final moment."

"You'd do well to lose the wagon. It's only a few days. Carry your supplies on horseback and you'll move much quicker," Boen suggested. His feral grin inspired dread in Bahr's heart, making him almost feel sorry for the mercenaries.

"Agreed. I'm sure the farmer won't object to parting with a few horses."

"Can't see why he would. Cheer up, Bahr. This should be fun."

Fun? How can any of this be construed as fun? We're all going to die, but at least you get the opportunity to rush into Lord Death's arms the way you wish. "I'll take your word for it. This doesn't sit well with me, not in the least. Hurry back. We're going to need you, my friend."

Boen leaned over and slapped him roughly on the shoulder. "It wouldn't be a war without a Gaimosian involved. Get some sleep. You need it more than the others. I haven't seen you sleep in too long."

"I don't take much comfort in you watching me sleep," Bahr tried to joke.

Boen smiled. "I guess we've been in the field too long. Maybe I should stroll down to that village and find a nice wench for the evening."

"Do people still say wench?"

"Does it matter? Good night, Bahr."

SIX

Boen

The Vengeance Knight was gone long before the first rays of sunlight slit the veil of night. He'd packed his bags and oiled his sword before bedding down, making leaving all the easier. Everyone but Ironfoot was asleep as he saddled his horse. The two warriors clasped hands and said a terse good-bye before Boen slipped out into the snow. There was no room for emotion, nor were either inclined to show any. True warriors committed to the task, ever seeking to improve their martial prowess through the test of combat. Wars were won or lost on less.

Boen pulled his bearskin cloak tightly around his shoulders to prevent the wind from driving down between his armor and tunic. Winter had been excessively harsh in Delranan, leading to thoughts of finding a better job in the central plains. Averon was the greatest, richest kingdom in Malweir, surely there must be some odd quest Boen could accomplish down there. Not that it mattered now. He was trapped in a power struggle with no viable escape route. He long held a sneaking suspicion that any attempt to flee, to leave the group for safer climates, would result in being shuffled right back into the middle of it all.

Never a believer in fate or destiny, Boen carried his troubles on his back and faced each day like a true Gaimosian. Tomorrow was never promised, to anyone. He lived each day as if it might be the last and was content with it. Until now. The threat of an early demise clung to the quest like violent clouds raging in from the sea. Lord Death took interest in Bahr and the rest though for what purpose remained concealed. Boen couldn't help but feel matters were stacked against him. As if he was meant to fall. The notion proved particularly disturbing.

All his long life he'd done as his blood commanded. He defended the weak and innocent from the depredations of violent people. He'd fought in more wars than he remembered and bore hundreds of scars in memoriam. All the pain and suffering of being Gaimosian developed his life down roads most were too frightened to travel. This new war went far beyond the limitations of mere mortals. He was about to tangle with gods. The prospect was both frightening and exhilarating.

Gods! How does a mortal compete with a being as old as time? A being without shape or figure who controls the very core of power itself? The creators of the world! Boen couldn't wait to cross blades with one, whether it was light or dark. He didn't care much for either sect of gods. Living a good life and trying to do right was all that mattered to Gaimosians. Boen was no different. He long held the belief that if there were gods in the world they despised Gaimosians enough to let them fall into ruin. He had no need for gods if they were willing to do that.

He'd ridden nearly a league before the sun rose. Lack of camouflage or the need for concealment allowed him to move faster. He wanted to be found. Disappointment started to creep into his idle mind as dawn broke. He should have seen signs of the enemy by now. Could he be mistaken? Could Skaning and his force have ridden by the Gaimosian without ever crossing paths, even now readying to slaughter Bahr and the others? The prospect of abandoning his friends at their moment of need soured his great stomach. He briefly contemplated turning back before realizing even if he did the end would already have fallen.

Boen stifled a quick yawn, flexing his right hand. It took longer for him to limber up these days. Six decades of harsh living left him filled with aches and pains. He found he now spent more time stretching and preparing for a fight than fighting. Thankfully his skills with a blade weren't diminished, otherwise he'd be in the ground already. Clenching his fingers repeatedly, Boen looked down and was rewarded with the sight of numerous horse tracks. At last!

Nervous excitement fluttered in his chest. Sliding from the saddle, snow pillowing around his boots, Boen knelt to gingerly run his gloved fingertips over the tracks. *Fresh. No more than a half-day old. Seems old Skaning is in a hurry to have a sword shoved up his ass. Well, I'll be more than happy to oblige*. All he had to do was turn to follow the tracks and catch them unaware. More likely than not the young lord of Delranan bedded down for the night. Their camp couldn't be that far away, not and still allow them to remain within striking distance.

"Seems I'll get the chance to spill a little blood after all," Boen mused to his horse. The animal bucked its head in silent understanding. Having been bred for war, the horse was a willing extension of Boen's combat power. They'd ridden together for close to ten years. Finding him stable in Bahr's barns right before Harnin burned them to the ground encouraged Boen. The horse was perhaps his truest friend.

Climbing, slowly, back into the saddle, Boen snatched the reins and turned in the direction the tracks led. "Right back to where I came from. These boys are going to pay for wasting my time."

Boen took his time. A group as large as the mercenary band didn't move very fast, nor were they able to cover great distances. He'd catch them long before they knew what struck.

The trail ended outside of a large copse of firs. Boen remained mounted, trusting in a quick getaway and what he hoped would amount to a prolonged trek across half of Delranan. If his plan worked he'd be leading Skaning and his cronies to Arlevon Gale and the mounting conflict threatening to tear the world apart. Perhaps some of them would come to terms and abandon their wicked masters. Perhaps not. Boen doubted any of them were stern enough to survive the coming storm.

A guard was stationed on the eastern flank. Boen searched for a long while before arriving at the conclusion Skaning was a damned fool. He'd only focused on securing the portion of the perimeter where he believed the only threat to be. *How has this fool managed to gain a lordship? He should be dead already*. Ingrid and the rebels could be right behind, striking without warning. Boen concluded the mercenaries were no better than armed brigands. No real fighting force worthy of mention would find themselves so woefully underprepared in the face of imminent danger.

Fools with pointy sticks, he decided. Their previous engagements weren't as violent or climactic as the river men had been but there were more than enough mercenaries to cause trouble. Even Boen wasn't strong enough to defeat two hundred fighters. Satisfied the majority of the camp was still asleep and lacking any sort of vigilance, Boen drew his broadsword and charged.

The thunder of hooves awakened a handful but by then it was already too late. Boen was crashing through sleeping roles, trampling those unfortunate enough to be caught asleep. His sword hacked and slashed those precious defenders quick witted enough to get up. Ropes of blood flew across branch and snow. Men screamed. Boen roared as only a Vengeance Knight could. His pass through the camp lasted a handful of heartbeats. In that short period of time he'd struck down three and trampled another five to what he hoped was a painful death.

Boen raced off into the forests. Snow kicked up in his wake. Shouts and roars, oaths of vengeance trailed after him as the mercenary camp was struck. Skaning gave in to his fury and ordered them after the Gaimosian. All thoughts of Bahr, brother of the king, fled as the irrepressible desire for payback subsumed reason. Men strapped on their armor and weapons and climbed into saddles. The dead and wounded were forgotten, left in the care of a skeleton group consisting of the lone medic. Skaning led the charge, never realizing Boen had slowed enough to allow them to catch up.

The chase ranged across fields and small patches of woods. Boen took them due north, hoping to put enough distance between them and Bahr that they wouldn't be any hindrance in the next three days. Standing his ground wasn't an option. If the enemy was smart they would surround him at distance and gun him down with enough arrows to slay an army. Boen wasn't counting on them being intelligent, especially now that their ire was up.

Foresight would have given Boen time to plan a few surprises along his escape route, but time and necessity seldom cared for one's desires. Boen had no other option but to flee as fast and hard as he could. The rest would settle itself. Not even his great endurance was enough to outlast his foes forever. At some point his faithful mount would flounder, giving out long before they reached Arlevon Gale. His one hope, slender as it was, came from the need to reach safety by nightfall. Too bad the day had just begun.

Exhausted, horse covered in sweat, Boen dashed into the trees as the sun dropped. The snow was blessing and bane. No matter how hard he tried there was simply no way he was going to lose his pursuers. Not with several feet of snow covering the ground in most places. He'd tried running up streams and over rocks where the heat of the sun melted the snow and ice. None of it worked. Skaning's mercenaries continued, plodding their way closer and closer.

Boen tried, unsuccessfully, to get Skaning to split his forces but the young lord was wise enough to know that was akin to a death sentence. No good commander divided his strength, especially not when facing a lone warrior. Frustrated and hampered at every turn, Boen welcomed nightfall. Tired as he was, so too must be the others. The chase was long, arduous at times, and time consuming. He hadn't been involved in such a situation for as long as he could recall, leaving him certain neither had the mercenaries.

No doubt by now they'd been filled with complaints and argued to stop. Mercenary companies were seldom paid well during the campaign and, given the conditions afflicting Delranan, Boen wagered on this crew being no exception. He guessed he'd opened up at least an hour's lead, that time lengthening the longer the day went. It wasn't much but it was enough for him to leave something special.

Boen quickly dismounted and took the time to rub some feeling back into his aching legs. His body wasn't what it used to be. It took longer to recover from the simplest things. Frowning, he secured his horse under a small rock overhang deep in the trees. Boen cut a large branch from the nearest pine and hurriedly began erasing his tracks as he made his way back to the edge of trees. He didn't have long before Skaning's mercenaries arrived, if they chose to attempt an attack at all. Darkness falling certainly provided enough dissuasion, at least in his estimation.

Crouched down behind a large tree trunk, Boen produced his looking glass and scanned the surrounding area. He didn't like how easily his tracks led to the tree line but saw little else he could have done. Winter was his enemy. After a few seconds of searching, his efforts were rewarded. The lead scouts ranged into view. They were clearly in no rush to catch up to the man who'd singlehandedly removed nearly ten of their numbers in a matter of moments. No doubt rumors that they were chasing the Gaimosian had already spread. Skaning might be a fool, but he was more cautious than Boen hoped.

Dismayed, Boen saw his chances for a quick victory slip away. He was going to have to get results the hard way. More than half of the enemy force was already in view and there they stopped. Boen froze. Where were the others? Did Skaning suspect a trap and slip them up? Boen had no way of knowing, not without speaking to one of the mercenaries. A spark lit. He grinned. The Gaimosian watched as the mercenaries broke off and headed towards a suitable camp site. Settling down until true dark, Boen waited to make his move.

The armor was slightly too small and it chafed him awfully. The mercenaries didn't seem inclined to indulge in personal hygiene he presumed. Adjusting the gauntlets on his wrists, Boen resisted the urge to scratch. He needed to blend in if there was any chance of getting away with his scheme. Feigning confidence, Boen emerged from the dark and strode up to one of the four fires in the enemy camp. He'd never done anything so brash. The exhilaration quickened his heart. Made him feel young again. Young or incredibly foolish.

"Too damned cold for this sort of work."

"Quit griping. We're getting paid ain't we?"

"Not enough. That damned fool got us ranging across the middle of nowhere and for what? A single rider?"

"A big one too."

"You seen how quick he was when he hit our camp? Coulda killed the lot of us and that's a fact."

"You fool. If he wanted to kill us he'd a done so. I ain't never seen a fella fight like that. Like he was possessed."

"Some folk say demons haunt these parts."

"Demons. Pah! You've been at the bottle again? Skaning'll have yer head if he finds out."

"I ain't been drinking. Just repeating what some of the locals been saying."

"I've seen demons."

The speakers stopped and turned to the newcomer. Boen met their gazes unflinchingly. The only way his plan was going to work was by trying to blend in.

"What do you mean? You been drinking too?" the pock-faced mercenary asked and scowled. Half of his right ear was missing as well as a good patch of hair from his scalp.

Boen shrugged. "I ain't seen a drink in too long. Sitting my ass in the saddle for so long I almost forgot what it tastes like."

The other mercenary, younger and with a foul complexion, frowned. "See! He knows what I mean. Demons and monsters hiding in the forests."

"There ain't no demons!" Pock Face scolded.

Boen persisted, acting the part. "Maybe not around here, but I seen some."

"Where?" Pock Face insisted.

"Down in the jungles. Nasty bastards they were, too."

Scarface, the younger mercenary, barked a shrill laugh. "You ain't never been in the jungle."

Boen spun on the smaller man. His fists clenched, the Gaimosian rose a little higher on the balls of his feet and leaned forward. "You calling me a liar, *boy*?"

Realizing his mistake, Scarface immediately backed down. "No, uh…I was just sayin is all. Folks all have tales of monsters and such."

"I seen what I seen and don't need some snot-nosed kid claiming different. We're not going to have problems, are we?" Boen pressed.

Scarface threw his hands up and fervently shook his head. "Not from me."

Boen gave a curt nod. "Good. Now where was we?"

"Talking on heading into them woods to rout our prey," Pock Face answered smoothly, relishing the rebuke of his younger companion. "I heard tell Skaning wants us to go in tonight."

"I don't fancy tackling that bastard at night," Boen replied. "Did either of you get a good look at him this morning?"

Scarface shook his head again, much slower this time.

"I did. Bigger than an ox he was," Pock Face said. "Not the sort I'd want to run up against in the dark. You might be able to take him, or at least give him a good run."

Boen froze. He forced his hand away from his sword. There was no way he'd be able to fight his way clear of the entire camp if he was discovered. "I may be big but I ain't stupid. We got archers for that sort of work."

"Archers ain't no good at night."

"I don't reckon they are but neither is my courage. I don't want to die until after I get paid," Boen said quickly, hoping to distract them before idle minds began thinking.

Pock Face bit back a laugh. "Don't matter none. Skaning hisself is taking ten of the lads to try and get this bastard tonight. With a little luck we'll be done with this game and heading back to the real money. I'd like to be the one to take a swing at the king's brother. Think of the bonus I'd get!"

Scarface yawned and rubbed his lower back. "Been a long while since we was forced to ride like that. I need some sleep."

"Too bad you got next watch," Pock Face reminded him. "I'll be dreaming about your old lady though."

"Go on ahead. Make sure you get whatever new diseases she done picked up too," Scarface said and laughed.

"I'll take the watch," Boen offered. "I can't get no sleep no how and my turn ain't been called tonight."

"Thanks, friend, but you ain't getting a cut of my pay."

Boen shrugged. "Don't need it. Go and get before I change my mind."

Without needing additional encouragement, Scarface trudged off to his sleeping roll, leaving Boen and Pock Face standing in awkward silence. The two studied each other, sizing each other up. Boen could tell the mercenary was trying hard to figure out whether they knew each other or not. He reached up to scratch his jaw, careful to avoid the awful scarring on his lower cheeks.

"Got a problem?" Boen asked defensively.

"Maybe. I don't think I know you, *friend*."

Boen tensed, ready to attack and flee. "Don't see as to why you should. I joined up with that last batch of recruits when we was heading out of Chadra. Boss didn't want to take me on at first cause of my age but I convinced him otherwise."

"How?"

"By shoving this blade under his throat and telling him how much I needed the job," Boen growled, casually showing his broadsword to the mercenary.

Pock Face blanched slightly at the size of the weapon, knowing he'd have difficulties wielding it in battle. "Well…ah, sounds good. I'm gonna take a piss. Watch my post?"

Boen nodded. Nervously, the mercenary headed out into the darkness to relieve himself. Boen waited a handful of seconds before drawing the dagger tucked in his waistband and stalked after. He came upon Pock Face just as he was tying his trousers up. A whirl of movement disturbed the night. Boen's blade flashed once as it sliced neatly across the mercenary's throat. Blood bubbled and frothed as it ran down between fingers desperately trying to seal the wound. But Boen had cut deeply. Pock Face would be dead in a matter of moments, leaving the Gaimosian free to make his way back to his horse and figure out how to deal with the ten mercenaries heading his way.

He snatched the body by the neck and waist and dragged it off into a small clump of holly bushes. Boen didn't wait for Pock Face to die before wiping his hands clean on the snow and, after checking the camp a final time, sprinting off into the night. Sighing, he knew he was in for a long one. There was much to be done before he could appropriately welcome his coming guests.

SEVEN

A King Returned

Badron, deposed king of Delranan and tyrant of the north, stared at Harnin One Eye's corpse as it swung gently in the late morning breeze. Crows had already pecked out the eye and both cheeks. No greater fate was deserved for a usurper. Once friends, Badron and Harnin carved Delranan into their own vision. Badron still wasn't sure what went wrong. He'd gone off to war with the intent on bringing Rogscroft to heel and, potentially, forming the first northern empire. Harnin was supposed to keep Delranan running smoothly, pouring supplies and follow-on forces to the war effort. None of that happened.

Each person Badron questioned told the same tale. Plague and rebellion. What little remained of Badron's once mighty kingdom didn't deserve the title. Whole villages were gutted. The population, what was left of it, was downtrodden to the point they were ready to give up. Coupled with ferocity of this past winter, the kingdom of Delranan slowly faded away.

Badron was no fool. He knew that deep down at the core of the issue was the Dae'shan. Their eternal need to mess with mortals were already driving him mad. It didn't take much to think they would have done the same or worse to Harnin. Badron hadn't seen Amar Kit'han or the other Dae'shan since fleeing Rogscroft in shame. The betrayal of the Wolfsreik rocked his belief system. He lacked allies and, most of all, Kit'han's guidance.

Taking the first fort in the long string of defenses had been relatively easy. His return left him questioning his principles. This wasn't the same kingdom he'd left. Leaving for a different land where none recognized him wasn't possible. He was already committed to the course. One way or another he was going to stand at the end of the storm. Rumors of the Wolfsreik crossing the mountains already reached his ears. It didn't take much imagination to see their massive force crushing Harnin's meager defenses in short order.

He needed to find a way out. A way to change the course of the coming war.

"Isn't it amazing how unimpressive the mortal body is once the spark leaves?"

Badron screwed his eyes shut at the sound of the hissing voice whispering in his ear. His hopes that he'd lost the Dae'shan or fallen out of their favor were dashed like waves upon the rocks.

"Will I ever be freed from your curse?" he asked weakly.

Amar ignored him. "I've witnessed thousands of souls flee the mortal shell. Each is…unique despite the appalling similarities in life. More often than not the body clings to what little life remains, desperate to avoid becoming food for the worms. Would it pain you to learn how Harnin One Eye scraped and clung to his fading life, cursing your name with his last breath?"

"That is not the look he held in his eyes," Badron protested.

"Was it not? What else could a man have who held such hatred for his former mentor?"

Badron finally opened his eyes. "Relief. He was relieved his troubles were over. Does that surprise you, demon? That a lowly man was able to overcome your manipulations, even at the hour of his death, and find a measure of honor? You're not as all powerful as you wish to believe. There is strength left in this world. Enough to confront your mad quest for ultimate power and control."

The Dae'shan paused, finding Badron's change unexpected and disturbing. The northern kingdoms stood ready to fall. Rising amounts of carnage fed the Olagath Stone. Soon it would be filled with enough residual suffering to enact the ritual. Amar Kit'han spent generations cultivating Badron's bloodline to achieve his desired results. The weak were culled in the same manner as over aggression. Over and over he repeated the process until he was sure the bloodline that remained contained all the necessary requirements.

It was no accident Badron was the result. He was inherently weak, craven. Badron had no qualms with ordering others to go to war but was a far cry from the warrior kings of old. He'd grown lazy over the years, complacent to the point of lethargy. Amar found killing the king of Delranan's wife to be almost too simplistic. Surely another, more powerful catalyst was required to make the grieving king's mind susceptible to the Dae'shan's manipulations? Rather than fight, Badron willingly sank deeper into a darkening world.

Badron's sudden defiance proved most unsettling. Amar had come expecting him to be weak, ripe for the final push towards Arlevon Gale. Instead he found a man desperately trying to regain a measure of his former strength, his mind healing from decades of irrepressible damage. Badron had other blood relatives still alive. Options remained available to Amar and it was time to remind the king.

"It has never been my quest, king. I am a steward. I ward Malweir until the dark gods can reclaim what is rightfully theirs. Would you be the one to deny them? No. I think not. You've ever been a coward. Which is why I no longer need you."

Badron stiffened. His eyes narrowed. Veins popped on his neck and forehead. "What do you mean?"

Amar grinned savagely under his hood. "Your brother and…daughter are both returned to Delranan. Which would you prefer I use in your stead?"

Badron's voice turned dark, menacing. "I will deal with my brother. My daughter has no use to anyone, much less your lofty ideals."

"Ah, there is where you err. Your daughter is most powerful. More so than you ever have the hope of becoming," Amar taunted. "Does it disturb you to know Maleela, a creature you deemed pathetic and a waste of life, has the ability to conjure more terror than mighty Badron of Delranan ever could?"

Swift as a mountain cat, Badron was on his feet with sword drawn. He rounded on the Dae'shan, the point of his blade waving menacingly. "You seek to abandon me now, here? After all I've sacrificed to your whispered madness, I am not meant to be more than chattel? You claim immortality but I'm willing to put that to the test."

"Put away your sword, broken king. You cannot harm me. If I chose, you would already be a pile of ashes at my feet." Amar paused, hovering back slightly just in case. He hadn't anticipated Badron's great rage.

"No more lies. No more subterfuge. I've listened to you enough. I am the son of kings." He spread his free arm. "All you see stretching away belongs to me and no other. This is my kingdom, not yours or some damned dark god lacking the balls to claim it himself. Take your filth and leave me. I may die in the process, but I'm ready to test you finally."

"Perhaps you aren't as lost as we believed," Amar said through pursed lips.

"Leave me," Badron warned.

Amar Kit'han folded his arms across his chest. He noticed movement out of the corner of his eye. A squad of soldiers, fully armed and led by a young officer, was charging toward their beleaguered monarch. Amar decided it was past time to go. "Very well, but do not be so bold as to assume this is the last you will see of us. As we speak, the Wolfsreik have returned. They've laid siege to one of One Eye's fortresses and are preparing a campaign to reclaim the throne. Your brother and his merry band of misfits drives from the west. They come to kill you. Delranan is a pathetic shell of what it once was. Your petty rule is at an end. Enjoy what little time you have remaining, *king*."

Folding time and power, the Dae'shan evaporated as Badron's soldiers arrived. They abruptly halted, not believing their eyes. Unshaken, the young lieutenant marched up to Badron with a worried look.

"Sire, what was that?"

Badron kept his focus on the residual bits of power, dark colors of green and blue, gradually falling to the ground.

His mind struggled, and failed, to resolve what he'd just been told. When at last he shifted his gaze to the officer, his eyes were cloudy. "That, was a mistake."

"Well, is it true?"

Badron stood with meaty fists planted squarely on his hips. His face was twisted in concern. It had been a very long time since he'd last led soldiers in the field. The campaign into Rogscroft was never his. He begrudgingly admitted to be more of a bother than asset. Rolnir had warned him from the beginning. He chose not to listen. A king wasn't dictated by the whims of a field general.

Bergen, the same lieutenant who'd glimpsed Amar Kit'han, the only other person in Delranan to as far as Badron knew, nodded repeatedly. "The army has returned but it is far worse than you were led to believe, sire. We counted three standards planted near their field command. Ours, Rogscroft, and that of the Pell Darga."

Badron scowled. He had but a few hundred fighters. They were all that stood between the traitorous Wolfsreik and the heart of Delranan. They weren't enough, no matter how many fortresses One Eye managed to construct. He figured there were roughly between two hundred and fifty to five hundred soldiers strung out along the frontier in the seven fortresses guarding the eastern half of Delranan. Three thousand reservists against a force of nearly seven times that much, all seasoned, professional soldiers. Badron didn't stand a chance.

"It appears I have but one recourse," he said. "Send riders to every town, hamlet, and village from here to Chadra. Every able-bodied fighter is to report immediately for active duty."

"That will prove excessively difficult," Bergen answered amidst the open mouths and shocked looks of the assembled officers.

"I care why?"

Badron was tired of being countered with every order. Nothing had gone the way he'd planned since deploying the

Wolfsreik. He'd been fought every step of the way. It was time for the king of Delranan to put his foot down and remind his soldiers who wore the crown.

"Sire, what I meant to say is that the kingdom has already been picked over. Between Harnin's muster and the plague we are greatly reduced in manpower," Bergen quickly added, sensing the rising displeasure from Badron.

"Find people. These little wooden playhouses won't last long once Rolnir gets his entire force in the field. *Make* them come. I don't care if you need to clasp them in chains. Do not fail me, lieutenant."

Soldiers rampaged through the quiet village, rousing everyone in the middle of the night. Torches lit the central plaza as bleary-eyed citizens gradually filed in. Those who complained were lashed or kicked into action. A few desperate mothers attempted to hide their adolescent boys but it was already too late. Badron's soldiers, while clumsy, were wholly effective. Soon the entire village stood assembled.

A rough-looking sergeant with a long scar, pink and puckered, running down the left side of his face thumped up to the town square and the small flight of steps to the block where merchants hawked their wares on market day. He glared down at the villagers with open disdain. His uniform was soiled, torn in places, unbefitting of a professional soldier. For many, this was their first encounter with the new Delrananian army. The feeling of disgust left in their mouths drove many to spit.

"By order of the king, all military-aged males are ordered to march with us immediately. Any violators will be judged traitors and executed," the sergeant growled.

Murmurs rippled through the crowd. Angry fists waved from the middle. More than one voice rose above the others in protest. The sergeant, to his credit, curled his fists and planted them on his hips while the fury ran through the villagers.

"This ain't our war!"

"What right do you have to come here and roust us out of our beds?"

"Don't care about one king or the next! Go back and leave us about our business!"

Having had enough, the sergeant nodded gruffly to a squad of soldiers standing at the rear of the assembly. They brandished clubs and waded into the villagers, knocking heads and limbs ruthlessly. Villagers reeled back, eager to avoid the terrible swath being cut through their ranks. Bodies tumbled. Cries rang out. The soldiers didn't stop until they had beaten their way to the main aggressor and pummeled him to his knees. A loud crack brought their savage attack to an end. Hands snatched his prone form, dragging him up onto the market platform. He rolled once and stopped at the sergeant's boots.

"This is what happens when you openly rebel against the crown," he snarled through clenched teeth. "You now have five minutes before I lose my temper. Fifteen to fifty, kiss your loved ones good-bye, grab what gear you think you need, and assemble back here. Move!"

Reluctantly the crowd parted. Mothers wept. Old ladies hugged their husbands, knowing the odds of seeing them again were slim. Young boys feigned bravery. The same scene was played out across eastern Delranan throughout the night. Badron didn't stand a chance of raising enough conscripts to beat back the combined army. They were all going to die.

EIGHT

Invasion

"How much further?"

Maleela ground her teeth at the Goblin's impatience. She'd agreed to lead the fifty-thousand-strong force into her home kingdom in the hopes of punishing all those who had done her wrong in her short life. Goblins had already razed three villages to the ground without mercy. Bodies were hacked and cut to pieces. Feeding an army so large demanded sacrifices. Maleela wasn't prepared to reduce herself to cannibalism, finding the act revolting. Her Goblin minions lacked any hesitation. Meat was meat.

She glared over her shoulder at the battle-scarred Goblin general at her side. Thrask was as impatient as any human soldier she'd ever met. If he wasn't instrumental in controlling the ravaging horde behind them she would have had the impudent Goblin executed already. The notion of leading such an army never occurred to her before her internment--or rather, enlightenment--with the Dae'shan. They'd opened her eyes to a brand new world of despair and hatred. All those lonely nights spent dreaming of vengeance were finally being realized.

"Until there is no more to go," she replied through clenched teeth. "How many more times do you plan on asking that question, General?"

Thrask swallowed heavily, wanting nothing more than to rip the throat from the Human girl. "We came here to fight, not walk. This is war."

"Yes, war. War that we must walk to if we are to fight. My father and what remains of his army will be in the east. Our task, in case you have forgotten, is to march to the ruins of Arlevon Gale and await orders from our master." She cut off her statement abruptly. Memories of her eager submission to Amar Kit'han sickened her stomach. No amount of self-rationalization could ever reduce the fact that she'd willingly bent her knee.

Thrask bristled suddenly. "Your master, not mine. Demons want to destroy the world, not rule it."

"Why then are you here?" she demanded.

"To fight," Thrask said with unabated pride. "We kill because we were made to. I think we should have stayed to fight Dwarves. They die much better than man."

"I shouldn't think either death displeases you," Maleela said. "Your lot seems destined to die by the sword. Fighting the Dwarves wouldn't have accomplished anything but delay us from reaching our goals. Amar Kit'han wants us to be at the ruins within the next two days."

Thrask shook his head. Ropes of saliva flew away. His tusks, greenish-brown on the tips, were chiseled, sharpened for tearing flesh. "We should have stayed in the Deadlands. March and march all day. Goblins need to fight."

"There is a war coming, General Thrask. One that promises to launch our world into an unprecedented, new age of warfare. There will be blood enough, even for the likes of you," she told him. "What is the status of the stragglers?"

Thrask shrugged. "They either keep up or fall away. No other choice. I don't care about a few. The army will arrive in strength. You must give us bodies to kill."

"We have been assured my father and his soldiers are ahead of us," Maleela said. She considered telling the Goblin how the Wolfsreik was returning, along with a combined force of nearly twenty thousand. The Dae'shan's intelligence was often spotty but Amar Kit'han was convinced he was right. Urgency was the matter of the day. She needed to push her new army harder to get them entrenched around Arlevon Gale before her enemies beat them to it.

"Betrayer," Thrask spit out. "He will die. I promise."

Maleela didn't need his reassurances. She had a special torment in mind for her beloved father. Anyone who willingly abandoned his daughter to a lifetime of silence, cowering in the shadows while greater men strode the world around her, deserved a fate worse than death. Mental images of Badron's suffering sent shivers down her lithe form.

"Badron is not to be harmed. Am I clear?"

Thrask snarled. "Why?"

"I will deal with my father. Once all his soldiers are dead, once his great cities are reduced to ruins and his legacy ripped from the history books, only then will he be allowed to die. I intend to rip him to pieces, bleeding him just enough over time. Goblins aren't the only creatures with a penchant for violence."

"It appears not."

Alone in her tent of tanned deer hide, Maleela struggled to find sleep. Each time she closed her eyes a host of memories assailed her. She'd given up trying to figure out how her life had devolved to this point. Perhaps she'd never been intended for anything greater than the puppet of pure evil. Knowing wouldn't change her course. She was committed to seeing this war through to fruition.

A small mirror was one of the few possessions she allowed herself on the campaign. Reluctantly, she withdrew the small piece of glass each night and stared at her reflection. She'd changed since being abducted in the Jungles of Brodein. Her cheeks were sunken. Dark circles clung to her eyes. She felt tired, borderline fatigued. Red streaks riddled her once blue eyes. Her hair was a tangled mess. Worse, she felt dark. As if a great weight had settled on her soul and slowly gnawed away any resistance she once possessed.

"Am I evil?" she asked her reflection between sobs.

"Only as evil as you wish to be."

Maleela slowly put the mirror down and bowed her head as Amar Kit'han materialized before her. "Master."

"Doubt is a terrible thing, Maleela," he admonished. "It leads down many dark, twisted paths beyond our control. Madness might claim you should you pursue this train of thought."

"What else is there for me to consider?" she asked.

Amar cocked his head. He'd anticipated her question. Long nights had been spent watching her. Studying her thoughts and the absence of dreams. She proved the perfect specimen for his experiments. Maleela was broken, a tortured soul beyond salvation. Or so he hoped. She harbored great reserves of strength her father and uncle couldn't compete with. Turning her was no easy feat, but one he'd accomplished with relative quickness. The princess of Delranan had given herself to his cause freely.

"Tomorrow," he said.

Maleela raised her head, staring intently into the swirling shadows of his cloak. "What does tomorrow have to do with anything?"

"Careful, princess. You might not enjoy what you find by peering too closely at me. Many who have went blind from hysteria," he cautioned.

"I'm not afraid. The darkness comforts me," she said.

"Perhaps it does, but that doesn't prepare you for the nightmares I carry." He paused before returning to his earlier thought. Maleela wasn't a fool. The slightest chance she intended on playing him for one existed. He couldn't be foolish enough to trust her, not until her loyalty was proven. "Tomorrow is the promise of the future. A future where you are the last of your bloodline. A future where there will be no torment or mistreatment by lesser beings. If you continue to serve me, I will make you a goddess."

"A goddess? I doubt the dark gods will approve of my elevation in status," she snorted.

Amar bowed curtly. "I am assured certain.... privileges upon the completion of my task. The pantheon will be half empty, after all. The end of this struggle can only be decided with the eradication of the gods of light. Would you willingly ignore the promises tomorrow offers?"

Maleela reeled, shocked at his admission. She'd never expected to be more than the forgotten princess. Her life was one continuous string of disappointments. For the Dae'shan to openly admit to entertaining the thought of letting her rise above all her tormentors and peers and stand beside the very beings responsible for so much hardship and strife was astounding. She'd never been taken into confidence before, not even with Aurec as they planned their long, unending life together.

Those dreams seemed so foolish now. Heir to the throne, she intended on taking her army across the face of the world. No mortal obstacle could withstand the might of the Goblin force behind her. All she required was for Thrask to remain moderately loyal in order for her to achieve her goals. His worth expired once that was finished.

A sudden thought dawned, sparked by his demure comments. Maleela raised her eyes to peer harder at the Dae'shan. This mystical figure that shouldn't, by any means, exist, was apprehensive around her. Why? What untold powers welled within her that frightened a creature capable of toppling kingdoms to the point he made her a nervous ally? She wasn't sure she wanted to know. Some truths were best left undiscovered.

"You want to become a god," she whispered. "That's what this is all about. You're tired of your station in life and want something more. How has no one seen this before? Close you keep your secrets, demon."

"Perceptive, but it will not avail you," he seethed. "Yes, I wish to ascend. This world is trite, far beneath my talents. What better reward for millennia of servitude than to accept me into their ranks? Haven't I earned it? Countless souls have died by my manipulations, all in the name of what we are about to attempt. Malweir deserves new leadership. The kingdoms of Men and Elves must fall. It is the natural order of things."

Maleela turned her back on him. "I was a fool. To think you had my best interests in mind when you all but enslaved me."

"I serve but one master, the dark gods. I am the extension of their will. Should they deem my efforts here on Malweir worthy I will gladly accept their approval," he said and paused. Conflicting thoughts raged within his time-worn mind. "There are few certainties in life, even for one as old as the world itself. Your death is one of the very few promises you have to look forward to. Serve me well and I can change that. Fail me…and your suffering will become legendary."

Angered and slightly disturbed at the unveiled threat, the young princess meekly folded her arms across her chest and glared at him. She felt his pain radiating from the dark robes. The horror lurking in the shadows of his cowl. *What god could require such servants? To utterly destroy the soul and recreate the essence of his being without regard for personal feeling or compassion?* Maleela felt true fear for the first time in her life.

Amar Kit'han approved of her reluctance to further reduce her station. Perhaps she was the one after all. "Very good. Your tongue will land you in more trouble than you are worth. Continue pushing the army. I want them emplaced around Arlevon Gale by tomorrow night. Our enemies are gathering and these Goblins are all that stands between them and the ruins. The ritual must not be interrupted, even at the cost of all fifty thousand Goblins."

"They will obey their orders or Thrask will flay them alive." Maleela bowed her head meekly as the Dae'shan hovered closer. "The enemy will not penetrate our lines, but you owe me my revenge."

Amar laughed, a hissing sound reminding Maleela of a dying serpent. "You shall have your revenge. King Badron does not yet know it, but he marches to his impending demise."

"That's all I care about." Maleela scowled but held her tongue. She'd said her piece and was loath to push much further.

The Dae'shan collected power around him and dissolved away, leaving Maleela reeling in shock and sudden sickness. She dropped to a knee and retched her breakfast. She failed to see General Thrask peering cautiously at her from behind the command tent.

NINE

The Wolfsreik Returns

Smoke clouded the air over what remained of the enemy fortress. Vultures and crows flocked just out of arrow range, eager for the survivors to depart. Bodies littered the inner courtyard amidst a sea of broken spears and arrows. Soldiers searched the dead, ensuring there were no pretend victims capable of a surprise attack. The sickly sound of steel piercing flesh echoed occasionally throughout the fortress.

Piper clipped his helmet to his belt, removed a soiled leather glove, and wiped the sweat and grime from his face. He'd survived more battles than a professional soldier in his position should have. This was but another in a long, unending war. It pained him to look down on so many countrymen. The defenders weren't necessarily bad people. Just because they were forced to support Harnin One Eye on his foolish crusade didn't turn them evil. They were kinsmen, brothers in what had once been the strongest kingdom of the north. Greed and apathy changed all that.

"Commander Joach, we have a few prisoners. The rest of the garrison is dead," announced a grim-faced lieutenant. Blood ran from a small cut under his right eye.

Piper winced. He guessed there were over three hundred defenders. *Three out of three hundred. How many more need to shed their lives in this foolhardy crusade? Will the gods ever be satisfied with our sacrifices?* "Bring the survivors to me. General Rolnir will want to glean as much intelligence from them as possible before sending them away."

"Yes, sir." The lieutenant threw a crisp salute, impressive considering how long the army had been in the field and spun off barking orders.

Only three. Piper respected the defenders' willingness to fight until the last but failed to understand their passion. Most soldiers would have surrendered the moment they realized they were impossibly outnumbered. They knew they were fighting countrymen. Didn't they? What possible lies could Harnin have spun to drive them into such fervor? For the first time in many years Piper felt stymied with unanswerable problems.

There were no reasons he could imagine to make any soldier, especially part-time reservists, fight to the death against a battle-hardened, seasoned army. None. The Wolfsreik second in command assumed it was witchcraft or worse. Coldness prickled his skin at the very thought that the same dark powers ever lurking behind Badron might have worked their way deep into Delranan to corrupt all. Confronting armies was one matter, fighting full-fledged fanatics something far worse. He had no tools capable of fighting magic.

Seeing no point in pursuing such troubling thoughts, Piper looked back to the ruins of the outer wall. He'd hoped to be able to capture the fortress intact, using it as a base of operations once the army readied to make the push west. Such was impossible now, at least not without massive reconstruction efforts. Neither he nor General Rolnir had the time to dedicate to such a mundane task. The war needed to continue at as rapid of a pace as possible. King Aurec wanted the campaign ended and his army returned to Rogscroft before summer.

Stepping over a pair of corpses, Piper grimaced at the gruesome way both had been killed. Wide, red stripes ran diagonally down their chests, spilling out onto a grim combination of mud and partially melted snow. Their open eyes seemed to glare skyward, as if accusing the gods of failing them. Piper began to suspect drug use. It seemed the only viable assumption given how animalistic the defense had been.

None of the interior structures remained intact. Whoever had commanded ordered the buildings set on fire to prevent the Wolfsreik from claiming them. A prudent choice considering all the defenders intended on dying in the first place. Most of Piper's casualties were already removed from the battlefield. The dead were cataloged and carted off for burial while medics and surgeons filtered through the wounded. It was grim business, but one most of the soldiers had grown insensitive to. Limbs were hacked off. Buckets of blood slopped in corners when no one was looking. Piper always found the cries unsettling. It was no easy thing for a professional soldier to cry in fear of his life. Some wounds left little alternative.

Pushing thoughts of the triaged area away before he became sickened, Piper began slapping the odd soldier on the back or offering encouraging words to veterans who continued to prove themselves after nearly a year of unyielding warfare. His pride swelled at the pleasure in their faces. Not that they enjoyed killing or even fighting, it was his praise they sought. The knowledge that they had fulfilled their commander's orders and managed to live through the horrors of combat was all any soldier really needed. Of course, seeing their buddy still standing next to them at the end, in perhaps slightly worse shape than the beginning, didn't hurt either.

"When are we to the next one, Commander?"

"Showed them rebels, sir!"

Piper faked his grin. "Aye, that you did, lads. That you did. I was thinking of giving you louts a day off and letting the rest of the infantry take a crack at the next fort. They've been malingering in the mountains for a little too long if you ask me."

Rousing laughter circled the immediate area. The vanguard was never expected to become engaged in prolonged battles. Their job was to flood the front lines and either force the defense to flee or buy enough time for the heavy infantry battalions to get online and attack. Unfortunately plans didn't always go according to what was scribbled down on parchment. Piper's vanguard, now bolstered with soldiers from Rogscroft and the Pell Darga, had forced more decisive engagements over the course of the winter war than in the Wolfsreik's long history. A fact he was immeasurably proud of. Secretly he worried that Rolnir might have been correct when he guessed Piper would get killed long before his time was due.

"Sharpen your weapons, fix your armor, and I'll see about getting some hot chow," Piper continued. He looked around at the partially burned wood surrounding them. "Doesn't look like it's going to get too cold tonight. You've earned your rest, lads. Enjoy it. We're finally home."

They saluted as he stalked off. His mind was already wandering over the thousand tasks a battlefield commander was responsible for long before their arms dropped. The prisoners bothered him for reasons he still wasn't sure of. Worse, without any enemy commander, there was simply no way of knowing how strong the garrison had been. There was no telling how many, if any, people slipped away to warn the rest of Harnin's defensive line when the attack began. That old feeling of guilt and remorse started creeping back into Piper's conscience.

"This was a messy affair."

Piper immediately felt some of the tension leave. Vajna had started out a fervent enemy, but their alliance forged bonds of comradeship only soldiers understood. Piper had come to rely on the Rogscroft general's experience and opinions more as the campaign lengthened. He might even go so far as to say they were becoming friends. Men in their position seldom found the opportunity or desire to make friends. Friends die too easily over the course of a war.

"Tell me about it. I didn't expect the reservists to put up such resistance," Piper admitted. "It shouldn't have been this hard, Vajna."

"Makes you wonder just how bad taking all the other forts is going to be, eh?"

Piper wasn't ready to broach that subject just yet. He'd had his fill trying to sack the first one. Casualties were relatively light. He figured no more than twenty-five dead with another three times that wounded. Not that bad considering. Those numbers would be significantly smaller if he'd had artillery support. His memory danced back to the initial explosion though technically it was more of a collapse. The engineers had snuck in under cover of darkness and weakened a large portion of the wall while infantry and skirmishers crept as close to the fort as possible. The noise of so many logs and mortar collapsing in on itself was deafening. It was certainly loud enough to shake the garrison out of their slumber. Piper's respect for his engineer corps continued to strengthen.

"I don't suppose there's any coffee?" he asked.

Vajna snorted a brief laugh. "The battle's been over for almost two hours. The cooks had damned well better have coffee brewing. Breakfast as well. The boys work up a mighty hunger doing all this dirty work. I wouldn't mind a quick bite myself."

"I was under the impression generals ate last," Piper chided.

Frowning, Vajna agreed. "Aye, that we do. But the rules don't extend to coffee."

"As much as I'd love to indulge in your idea, I'm afraid it's going to have to wait for the moment," Piper said. "I have the prisoners being brought here."

"Prisoners? I wasn't aware we'd caught any."

"Barely. We nabbed three before they managed to kill themselves on our steel." He paused as he caught the three prisoners being escorted by a squad of Wolfsreik armed with crossbows and drawn swords. "It appears they've arrived."

Vajna scrutinized the trio. Killing had never been a problem, though he took no personal pleasure in any of it. Just part of the job, he told himself before falling asleep. "Let's hope their tongues are as loose are their swords. There had best be coffee waiting when we're done."

Piper smiled. The same lieutenant halted a few paces from Piper and saluted. "Commander, the prisoners as ordered."

"Very good, lieutenant," Piper said, returning the salute. "You're dismissed."

"Sir? he asked, momentarily forgetting proper military decorum.

Piper waved his caution off. "I think the general and I are more than capable of handling three bound prisoners. Just don't go too far."

"Yes sir."

"Oh and lieutenant, could you send someone over to the mess station and get General Vajna a mug of coffee?" Piper asked.

Trying, and failing, to conceal his sheepish grin, the lieutenant saluted again. "Yes sir. I'm sure the cooks will be more than willing to comply."

Piper turned to the prisoners. Two appeared to be in their late teens. Both had several bandaged cuts peppering their bodies. The one on the right had an eye filled with blood and was missing a handful of teeth. Their older companion looked to have been involved in more than a few scrapes over the years. His left arm was in a sling with three of the fingers on the same hand missing. Blood stained his chin-length beard. Piper knew where to begin.

"Gentlemen, I trust you've been taken care of, medically?" Piper asked. His eyes locked on the grizzled reservist.

Spitting a mouthful of blood, Blood Beard replied, "Ain't got nothing to say to the likes of you. Kill us or send us away."

"Haven't we been through enough? I don't think killing the three of you will satisfy any requirements," Piper said. "You've earned your lives, I think. Now, let us dispense with the posturing and foolishness. Why did Harnin order you to fight like that?"

"I ain't never seen the One Eye. We're fighting for our kingdom."

Piper exchanged a nervous glance with Vajna. "Your kingdom? The same kingdom Harnin One Eye has all but destroyed?"

"Like I said, don't know nothing about that," Blood Beard said. "We heard all about you murdering bastards coming back from the east. Don't none of us fancy dying without givin' our families a chance."

"I think your notion of what has transpired needs adjusting. What exactly have you heard about the Wolfsreik?" Vajna asked.

Blood Beard eyed him wearily. "You ain't no Delrananian. They got mercenaries to do their biddin' now?"

"This man is a general in the Rogscroft army," Piper growled. "You might not have heard we are allies now."

Blood Beard shrugged. "This was never my war. Old One Eye says we've been betrayed by you Wolf soldiers and the only way to survive is by fightin' to the last." He spat again. "Only regret I didn't go like the rest o' the boys."

"Pointless deaths are without honor," Piper said. "We haven't returned to kill you. Hells, we don't rightly care whether you fight or go back to your homes. King Badron betrayed the kingdom and we acted in Delranan's best interests."

"Says you."

Frustrated, Piper realized further questioning was pointless. "I'm having you sent back to the main army for holding. Your wounds will be treated and you'll be fed. Don't do anything stupid and nothing wrong will happen to you. Am I understood?"

The trio remained defiant, silent.

Scowling, Piper summoned the escorts to take the prisoners away. He didn't calm down until after they were out of sight and a steaming cup of coffee sat before both him and Vajna. The sun was slowly rising, pushing enough past dawn for them to make out the world around them. Smoke still clung to the area and more vultures were getting bolder.

"That went well," Vajna said and almost laughed.

Piper didn't know what to say. He'd expected demons and witchcraft but was met by pure ignorance. "How can simple persuasion be so powerful? Are we fighting on the right side of this war?"

"You're asking the wrong questions, Piper. My conscience is clear to this damned affair. We're not just fighting for ourselves but for the preservation of our way of life. These blind fools aren't much for great thinkers if you ask me."

"Perhaps, but the Wolfsreik has already switched sides once. There must be some conflict of interest in this mess,"

Piper persisted. "You would think those prisoners felt at least a measure of remorse for having watched so many of their kinsmen die."

"You can't change people's minds when they're convinced, no matter how hard you wish it," Vajna answered. "Those fellows knew what they were doing. Harnin had them all spun up to think we were coming to kill them all. If you think about it their defiance makes sense. I don't think I'd have the courage they displayed, though. Tough bastards, that's for sure. I only hope the other forts we run up against lack the same conviction."

Piper wanted to comment that the defenders were of the same blood as the Wolfsreik. Nothing was bound to be easy. His premonitions aside, he felt confident breaking the defensive line would be trying but a victorious endeavor before too long. He wasn't sure why, but he felt almost rushed. Time never meant too much to Piper, but now, finally back in his own kingdom, he felt the seconds slowly slipping away as they marched towards an uncertain end.

"Hey, you listening?"

Shaken from his premonitions, Piper turned back to Vajna. "Sorry, I was just thinking."

Vajna shrugged. "There's not much that needs thinking on. We've got a war to win, and I'll be damned if this isn't the worst cup of coffee I ever drank. The cooks need to be sent to the front lines."

"You presume they're better swordsmen than cooks. Ha." Piper laughed. "Of course, our enemies might not appreciate a bad meal."

"That makes two of us," the Rogscroft general agreed. "Looks like a rider's come in. I guess Rolnir is here."

"The army should have been moving down from the mountains the moment we launched our assault."

He didn't add that the operation's success depended on speed. The faster the combined army wiped out the defensive line of fortresses the faster they'd be able to push westward and reconquer their kingdom.

Instead Piper decided it was time to admit his orders to his friend. "Vajna, I'm afraid I already have my orders."

"Great, where are we heading next?"

Piper shook his head. "Not this time. Rolnir and Aurec agreed that I am to lead the assault on the second fortress while you maintain control of the vanguard. I'm heading out as soon as the lead infantry units arrive."

Vajna was instantly angered. He'd never wanted to be teamed up with one of his enemies in the first place but after several battles and days on campaign he and Piper had formed bonds that only soldiers can. They'd overcome kingdom differences to forge a near perfect union of military complements. Vajna was a born infantryman whereas Piper had a head for tactics and cavalry. Together they were responsible for winning seven battles for the fledgling combined army. No other pair of commanders matched their prowess or success.

"They're splitting us up? I should be going with you," he protested. "You'll need me in the next assault."

"I agree, but that's not my decision to make. Your king and my commanding officer believe you serve better purpose for the war by remaining here with the vanguard. I suspect, but can't prove, that they intend on driving the main body west while I slug it out with the rest of the defensive line." Piper paused, shifting his lower jaw slowly. "I'd rather be going with you. Taking another ten of these monsters isn't going to be fun, or easy."

"I expect you'll suffer fierce casualties given what we went through here," Vajna added. His voice darkened. Logically he should be the one to lead the assault on the forts. Delranan was Piper's kingdom, not his. The Wolfsreik needed to be seen leading the drive across their own lands in efforts to maintain a measure of security among the population. His people didn't take kindly to seeing a foreign army sweeping across Rogscroft. Vajna didn't imagine the Delrananians would differ much.

"Let us hope not," Piper concluded. He extended his arm for Vajna and the two shook as brothers. "Take care of yourself, old timer. I have a feeling our two kingdoms are going to need people like you when the dust finally settles."

Vajna laughed and gave his steadily expanding belly a soft pat. "Old my ass! You'll pay for those words when we meet in Chadra."

Nothing else needed saying. Both were seasoned professionals and had been through similar circumstances too many times before. It was just part of the job. Piper headed towards the front of their makeshift camp. Each had a specific purpose in this new phase of the war. Should the gods will it, they would meet again after the hostilities ended.

TEN

Homecomings

"My lord, we weren't expecting you."

Venten waved off the unnecessary concern from Elstep, the house chamberlain, as he swept into what remained of Rogscroft castle. The elder statesman begrudgingly admitted the renovations had come a long way since Badron's defilement. Men and women busied with sweeping, painting, cleaning, and removing broken furniture and debris. Few bothered to stop and acknowledge his passing. Nor did he expect them to. He wasn't a king or even a noble. In fact, Venten wanted nothing more than to fade back into obscurity, much the way he'd been transitioning before the war started.

Thoughts of being a retired general and politician had to wait as he was determined to uphold the charge Aurec had given him. He was the voice of the king, an extension of wills manifested in the form of one person with the unmitigated ability to choose how and where his kingdom began the healing process. Any self-assured whispers he spoke in the quiet hours of the night seemed insignificant in comparison to the enormity of the task before him. Venten was given a handful of ruins, the remnants of a broken people, a skeleton military force, and told to rebuild an entire kingdom. It was a daunting task, one he wasn't sure if he could accomplish or not.

The tenacity of his people already shined in the darkness before dawn. He viewed a ramshackle village housing more than five hundred refugees. Mounted patrols circled the city and castle proper, providing the necessary protection to assuage the general population's fears. The sounds of hammers and saws working throughout the night suggested all was not lost. That his people remained strong despite their losses. Venten took hope. Perhaps they had a chance of rebuilding it after all.

Venten glanced at the partially removed burn marks scoring the wall inside the castle entrance. “No need to fret, Elstep. I’m only an extension of the king, not the king himself.”

“Begging yer pardon, sir, but yer more than that,” Elstep protested. “Word’s already come from Grunmarrow that you are the acting regent.”

“Elstep, truly, I appreciate the deference but it’s only me. Now, where do we stand on reconstruction efforts?”

Elstep shrugged. “Eh, can’t speak for most of the city but the castle is almost habitable. Crews been working round the clock to remove the filth them Goblins left behind. Vile creatures they was. At any rate, the throne room is cleaned and ready for a new throne. Most of the royal chambers are getting there. The kitchen’s been running since before you left for the war so there’s food and drink aplenty for the work crews. All in all, I’d say the castle is progressing nicely.”

“Nicely isn’t good enough, my friend,” Venten said quietly. “We’ve got a very large charge set before us. Aurec expects the city to be taken care of first. Royalty has its privileges and our young king has decided the population comes first. I want all but a skeleton crew shifted over to the city. The sooner we get homes and shops rebuilt the sooner we can concentrate on renewing trade with our neighbors and try to get our economy moving again. Winter is nearly finished, despite the feet of snow still refusing to melt, and I expect our trials will lessen considerably once we have free range of the roads and mountain passes again. Who is in charge of the reconstruction?”

“Don’t reckon I heard his name but I’ll send a lad out to get him once the sun comes up. Why don’t you head down and get some food in yer belly before he arrives? I’ll send him up to the antechamber for you.”

“Antechamber?” Venten asked.

Elstep nodded. “Been using it as an administration center since the king left. The lads’ll be real glad to have you back. Not all them are as bright as me, my lord. They need some help over there.”

Venten smiled at the chamberlain's candor. "Thank you, Elstep."

Red streaks ran horizontally through his eyes. The ride back from the army encampment at the base of the Murdes Mountains had been long, though not particularly grueling. Venten found the only harrowing part was from not knowing whether all the Goblin threat in the lands between the castle and the mountains was cleared out. Fortune allowed him trouble-free passage and he was able to make the journey in three days. Limited food left him slightly famished, a condition he managed to remedy after meeting with Elstep. Stomach full, he only lacked sleep, but at his age he figured there'd be enough time for rest once he was put in the ground.

An unmerciful stack of unread reports and requisitions stared back at him from the corner of the small field desk. Normally he preferred something much bigger but all the real furniture had either been cut up and used for firewood or had been desecrated by the Goblins. Coming from the field, Venten found little room for complaint, though not even a full belly was enough to prompt him to dig into the paperwork.

Clerks and random administrative personnel busied about their work, just as eager to finish their day as he was to avoid it. Venten had hoped to be done with public life. He wasn't suited for menial tasks involved with the daily operation of a major city. Life demanded more than hiding behind reports or sitting in one meeting after the other. The open steppes often called to him during those brief moments of isolation when he was able focus on himself. Never one for love or material possessions, Venten tried his best to live a simple life. Devotion to Stelskor and the winter war prevented that from happening.

"Lord Venten, I have Major Brun here. He's the Wolfsreik officer placed in charge of the security forces."

Rubbing his tired eyes, Venten waved Elstep to continue. The chamberlain bowed and stepped aside so Brun could enter. The soldier of the Wolfsreik snapped a crisp salute, albeit an unnecessary one, and clasped his hands behind his back.

"Sir, welcome back to Rogscroft," Brun said with pleasant tones.

Venten took in the young officer. Slender with just enough muscle concealed beneath his leather-plate armor, Brun had thick black hair and almost piercing blue eyes. He stood a hand taller than six feet and wore a broadsword strapped to his right hip.

"Major, salutes won't be necessary. I am not royalty," Venten said.

"Understood, but for the sake of appearances I believe it wise to maintain proper decorum, especially in front of the rank and file. With the war so far to the west it is easy for them to forget there is still a very real threat."

"Of course. Very well, Major Brun, I agree," Venten conceded. "I trust you have something good to report this early morning. Elstep is a cruel taskmaster. I only arrived at dawn and he's yet to afford me the opportunity to sleep."

He grinned at hearing Elstep cough in the background.

Brun offered a curt nod. "Sir, to date we have yet to encounter any remnants of the Goblin army or loyalists to Badron. Bandits are our major concern. We've doubled patrols after discovering a few recently burned farmsteads in efforts to counter the threat."

No matter how dire times grew there were always others who preyed on those less fortunate, even amongst themselves. "Have there been any civilian-related casualties?"

"A handful, no more than fifteen," Brun confirmed. "Thus far they've been confined to a pair of families trying to endure the hardships on their own. We've also captured or killed over a score of bandits."

"I don't foresee these raids lessening until the king returns," Venten guessed. "Still, we must take a more active role in protecting the outlying properties, especially the farms. Too many fields will remain fallow come the spring."

Brun appeared uncomfortable with the order but was professional enough to follow it without question. "Yes sir, I'll order increased presence patrols. Might we also look into finding the source of these bandits and attempt to root them out?"

Venten gave the matter some consideration. He dreaded wasting resources on finding an elusive force more interested in self-preservation than occupation. Time, money, and manpower were in limited supply. His first priority was to ensure the city was able to support the current and projected population. That couldn't be accomplished without hunting down those who preyed on the weak. He felt trapped.

"Yes, but keep them at a minimum," he said. "This city must come first. Am I correct in assuming you are also in charge of reconstruction efforts?"

Brun flushed. "Unfortunately. I must confess to not being trained in nation rebuilding. I'm a warrior, Lord Venten, not a statesman."

"I can assist with that. I'd like to take a tour of the city after lunch. Once the people see there is a civilian at least partly responsible for helping rebuild, I believe they will calm down slightly," Venten said.

Brun was clearly relieved. Extreme stress had added years onto his face. The knowledge that Venten, a person the people of Rogscroft knew and respected, had finally arrived to assume control melted years of stress on the young major.

"Sir, I'll have a detail sent to escort you to my command post in the city."

As much as sleep hounded him, Venten couldn't allow himself to rest until after he'd made his rounds in the city. He returned Brun's salute and hesitantly reached for the first report.

Amazed was the best he could describe the efforts underway in Rogscroft's center. Hundreds of workers erected scaffoldings, hammered boards, raised trusses, or carried supplies back and forth. Venten was reminded of colony ants, ever busy and tireless. Dozens of houses had already been rebuilt along with a handful of shops. He spied two large warehouses further down the road. Progress was well beyond what he or Aurec envisioned at this stage.

Venten found Brun overseeing a series of outgoing work details. Reports indicated that reconstruction continued around the clock, suggesting strong feelings of hope among the general population. The elder statesman took heart. All was not lost after all. Waiting for Brun to finish issuing orders, Venten studied the crude map tacked onto the back wall the tent. It represented the city and immediate areas. All rebuilding efforts seemed to be working out from the castle. Work crews cleared one street at a time while others swept in behind to begin new construction. Checkpoints and way stations had been established at strategic points throughout the city to facilitate safe passage of personnel and supplies. Impressed, Venten helped himself to a clay mug of steaming coffee.

"I expect this street to be cleared by nightfall. Our pace has been slacking lately. It's time to pick it back up."

A silver-haired carpenter with thick webs of lines creasing his leathered skin frowned. "What's the rush? Winter's near done and we don't have any timeline to follow. Not like we're being paid for this, Major."

Brun's frown outdid his accuser's. "We've been through this before, Iocta. The war's not going to last forever and there'll be thousands of soldiers returning home when it's finished. This city needs to be as far along as possible to house so large a force."

"I'm not arguing that part, Major, but some of the folks are ready to head home and start seeing to their own lives again," Iocta pressed. "This ain't our war."

"But it is."

All heads turned toward the unassuming Venten. Most clearly didn't know who he was.

"Who're you to say? We done our part and now it's time to go home."

Brun spoke up first. "This is Lord Venten, regent of Rogscroft until the king returns."

Iocta's eyes widened. "My…my apologies, Lord Venten. We wasn't aware King Aurec had sent you back."

"I don't see as to how that matters any. We all have a duty to our kingdom. The war may no longer be active here but it is far from over. Our obligation, if ever there was one, is to restore our city and kingdom to as much of its former glory as possible before King Aurec returns. You are the blood of Rogscroft, Iocta. You and everyone else like you. The army fights for us, but the life of this kingdom flows through your blood."

"That's all well and fine but folks are tired of hiding in these stinking ruins. We got our own lives to look to."

"Indeed. Farmers need to be preparing for spring planting. Herds need to be replenished. Trade routes reestablished. Need I continue? Let the army worry about beating Badron and the Goblins. They aren't my concerns. I need you, all you, to help me try and restore order to this once great land. Are you willing to do that for me?"

Iocta rubbed his chin thoughtfully as he digested Venten's words. A lifelong carpenter, he'd never bothered sticking his neck out beyond the circumference of his business. Now he was one of the more prominent advisors to rebuilding an entire kingdom. The responsibility was enough to force him to the cups. He appreciated Venten's return, making his decision almost too easy. "I will keep the crews at work. Like you say, this is our kingdom too."

It was a minor victory but one Venten claimed vigorously.

"Commander Joach departed shortly before your arrival, sire," General Vajna said with a flare of disappointment.

King Aurec and General Rolnir exchanged deceptive glances. Clearly the decision to part their two most successful commanders hadn't been an easy one to arrive at, but both felt it was in the army's best interests. They hadn't expected such stiff resistance among Harnin's forces. Devoting time, effort, and personnel to the current problem distracted from the overall objectives both had set forth before departing

Rogscroft but was a necessary part of the reconquest campaign.

Aurec addressed Vajna's concerns. "General, I fully trust in your ability to defeat the enemy. If anything, our task is made more difficult with this line of fortresses."

"All the more reason to keep the vanguard together. We've already taken out one of these monstrosities. How much harder can the others be? The lads know what to expect now. Give us a week and the entire eastern sector will be broken wide open."

"Making Piper the correct one for this task. However, that doesn't mean I can afford to squander another general, especially not one of your experience and caliber, Vajna," Rolnir said. "You're more valuable to me, and the army, here."

Sense of importance suddenly inflated, Vajna felt humble. "This doesn't sit well with me, but I am honored in your opinion, General."

Problem solved, Aurec was able to continue, "Vajna, the army has occupied the foothills and immediate plains along the Murdes Mountains. As we speak, columns are forming for the push into the heart of Delranan. I'll lead one, Rolnir another, and you the last. Our objective the retaking of Chadra Keep. Do not stop. Do not wait. Attack with all possible aggression. Crush any who stand in your way."

"What of the other two columns? Surely we can't accurately coordinate our movements spread out across a third of the kingdom," Vajna protested.

"A calculated risk we must take," Rolnir said.

Vajna studied king and general while he contemplated what was about to happen. In theory it should all work. Harnin had a skeleton force at best, no more than seven thousand with a large portion dedicated to the defensive line. The rest would be spread out in vain efforts to engage the rebellion. He saw opportunity to win the war and be home before the spring.

"When do we attack?"

Aurec smiled. "All three columns are presently lining in order of march. They will push out under cover of darkness where we will each ride out to assume control."

"Our departure point will be here, at the ruins of Arlevon Gale. The army will splinter in two days' time. Once each column reaches Chadra they will encircle the city, thus pinning loyalist forces within," Rolnir explained. "Good luck, General."

"And to the both of you," Vajna replied. His heart was lighter than it had been for a long time. Confidence swelling, the old soldier felt invigorated enough to finish his portion of the crusade and finally head home for much-needed rest.

"How does it feel to be home?" Aurec asked Rolnir once the formality of tactics was finished.

"Not as good as it will be once I discover whether my house is still standing or not," the redhead general of the Wolfsreik replied. In truth he dreaded his homecoming, knowing he and the other officers in his command had been branded traitors. How many families had already been rounded up and put in slave labor gangs or, worse, murdered in their beds while the army was busy in another kingdom?

"I can't make any promises, though I sincerely hope your kingdom isn't in as much disarray as my own," Aurec answered. Barely twenty-one, the boy king was beginning to sound more like a seasoned professional. War and the hard cruelty of winter helped forge him into the king Rogscroft needed. Hard when necessary and compassionate when the situation called for it, Aurec was well on the path to becoming as great a king as his father had been.

Rolnir nodded. "Fair enough."

Nothing else needed to be said. All three looked inward as their thoughts gradually shifted back to what they hoped was the last stage of the campaign.

Horses snorted as they strode through calf-deep snows. Aurec's pathfinders, Mahn and Raste, had taken a platoon forward to scout out the nearest major roads to facilitate the army moving faster. They'd been in Delranan for less than a full day and were already thirty leagues into the kingdom's interior. Most of the roads were cleared, a dual-edged blade if Aurec had ever seen one. Clear roads meant enough columns of infantry or cavalry had already gone by, heading east, or the local villagers had gone stir-crazy from being trapped within their homes over the course of the unusually long winter. Either way it was a risk he needed to take. The drive west couldn't afford to be slowed down, not with the end goal almost in sight.

Aurec's real fear was that the discipline of the army would break down the longer the campaign lasted. Men would want to return to their homes as those repressed worries came to light. Each would be thinking of their own families at this point. Aurec sympathized with them, for he lamented Maleela's loss every night. A small part of his mind whispered that she was already dead, forgotten on some desolate stretch of Malweir he'd never heard of.

He'd ridden at the head of the five-thousand-strong column deep into the night and was borderline exhausted. Youthful exuberance was all but lost on the new king. He should still be sowing his wild tendencies, not burdened with the worries of the crown and a kingdom. Aurec missed his father, for that was the logical destination for all his worries. The pain of seeing Stelskor's beheaded corpse continued to war within Aurec's heart and mind. Yet the longer the war dragged on the more he felt less than the day prior. His nerves were numbed. His mind was hardened by brutal statistics and casualty reports.

He seldom saw faces, recalled names. Each soldier in uniform was a number. A statistic. The impersonal nature of his position left him hollow. He needed more than the war was willing to give back. Already he felt old, used up. Thoughts of a warm bed and belly full of properly cooked food, not the meager rations the army cooks prided themselves on producing once a night, mocked him through the chaos of battlefields. The war continued to change him on fundamental levels. Some were positive while most reduced his opinion of what a ruler should be. No one being should have the ability to decide who lived or died. No one. Yet he was co-commander of nearly twenty thousand soldiers, many of whom weren't going to go home alive.

It had taken many long nights before Aurec came to accept that casualties were an awful part of war. He despised losing troops in combat, but recognized they were almost necessary. War was the most brutal, twisted event any race could endure and it was entirely too common. His faith in the gods decreased daily, for what omnipotent beings responsible for the creation of the world would so casually allow their creations to wholesale slaughter one another?

Aurec turned inward. His thoughts centered on bringing as many of his soldiers home as possible. The war dominated his dreams. Thinking about anything else merely served to distract him from what needed his attention. Men were willing to die under his banner, proudly wearing his colors on their armor as they waded through the slaughter of others who might once have been friends. It was a grizzly task.

Mahn rode in a short time later, out of breath and red faced. His eyes harbored a nervous twitch that led Aurec to believe their easy march was about to end.

"Sire, we've come across tracks. A lot of tracks. We're not alone out here."

Aurec's frown was concealed, thankfully, by the night. He couldn't stop from looking left or right, though. "Are you sure they're not ours?"

The question was almost foolish, a desperate grab towards answers he hoped weren't what Mahn said next.

"They're Goblin prints," Mahn confirmed.

"Goblins? How? We destroyed them in Rogscroft," Aurec protested. "There's no way they could have gotten here before us."

"I don't know, sire, but after these last few months I'd recognize their prints blindfolded. All I can report is what I've seen."

"Pick riders to send word to each of the other columns. I can't have two-thirds of my army marching blindly into a trap," Aurec ordered.

Mahn nodded and rode on, leaving the king of Rogscroft and commander in chief of the combined army at yet another loss. The more he thought he was getting ahead, the more setbacks reared up to slap him back into place. *Goblins already in Delranan. What have we gotten ourselves into?*

ELEVEN

The Olagath Stone

The quest had been somber since Boen's departure. While they might have chided the Gaimosian for his singular mindset, he was the anchor that kept them moving. Bahr had grown increasingly silent as the days progressed. The loss of Maleela and his expected confrontation with his brother plagued him more than he was willing to admit. A man unused to answering for his deeds, the Sea Wolf harbored all the hurt and pain since being arrested in Chadra and kept it for his own. Not even Anienam correctly guessed the reasoning. Quiet, Bahr drove them ever eastward, towards the ruins of Arlevon Gale.

Everywhere they went were scenes of violence. Burned homes. Slaughtered animal carcasses. The occasional body partially buried in the snow. Whatever games the rebellion and loyalist soldiers were playing seemed confined to the far western stretches of Delranan. They feared that Skaning and his cutthroat band of mercenaries had already gotten ahead and were terrorizing their way across the kingdom in efforts to prevent the quest from finding safe harbor.

Sitting atop the horse they'd acquired in exchange for their broken down wagon, Anienam made a show of yawning and accidentally reaching over and slapping Skuld on the shoulder. Blind, he grinned at still being able to outsmart the former street thief. Their relationship was rocky at best, though nowhere near as turbulent as his and Bahr's. Anienam often found mixing with normal people mundane and difficult. He attributed that to growing up in the shadows of the last Mage. Magic was forbidden in many parts of the world and frowned upon in the rest. Only the Elves continued their practice in the arcane arts, though what really happened in their hidden forest cities remained the subject of much speculation.

"I swear you're not as blind as you claim," Skuld chided. His tone was playful.

Anienam laughed, a tormented cackling sound. "You doubt the handicapped? Not very polite of you, young one. Why, in my day I was taught to respect my elders. My father would turn in his grave if he heard you just now!"

"What happened to your father, Anienam?" Skuld asked. "We all know he was the last of the Mages but you never said what happened."

The wizard fell uncharacteristically silent. He'd never spoken about Dakeb, his father, to anyone before. Doing so was always so complicated in his mind. He seldom viewed the past with fondness. There was too much pain in Dakeb's life for Anienam to enjoy the memory of what his father had been. Who he was, however, was an entirely different matter. Anienam decided that he didn't need to shoulder the burden on his own any longer, not if he expected Skuld to step into his shoes when the time was right.

"Dakeb was…a different sort of man. He was the last of the old breed. A guardian of the collective hopes and dreams of the entire world. Not any easy task for anyone to take on, young Skuld. Malweir knew him as a true Mage, but he was so much more. Did you know he was the one responsible for taking the four shards of the crystal of Tol Shere and hiding them once the war ended? Few did. Sidian eventually discovered them and attempted to release the dark gods from their prison years later. The Silver Mage failed and the crystal was ultimately lost to the other dimension."

Eyebrows scrunched together as Skuld tried to piece important, or what he thought were important, elements of the grand tale together, and the young thief shook his head. "I don't understand it."

"Understand what?"

"The need for crystals and stones. You said something about an Olagath Stone to Bahr earlier. Now this talk of a crystal. Why would beings as powerful as gods fear something so simple as a stone?"

Anienam's sense of pride increased as Skuld tried to flesh out the center of the entire tale. "Gods aren't as powerful as you might assume."

"How do you mean?" he replied after a few minutes of thought.

"Gods need us to believe in them. Our faith gives them power and the ability to manifest in greater, different forms. Take away that belief and they are considerably weakened, but not dead. Long ago, or so the histories tell us, the gods were born from stone and rock, water and fire. They stored immeasurable power in Malweir, drawing on it as the ages sped by. Never underestimate the strength buried within the stone at your feet."

"Wouldn't doing that keep the gods from becoming more? From reaching their full potential?"

"Indeed. It was as damning as it was meant to be liberating. The greatest scholars theorize that's the source of the schism between light and dark. The dark gods wanted to pull their power from the ground while the gods of light sought to keep it buried, for all life on Malweir benefited from it. What started as debate quickly devolved into brutal warfare that continues to this day," Anienam explained.

"What is the Olagath Stone?" Skuld asked.

"A token of extreme power. There are several scattered across the world. Groge's Blud Hamr is one. Phaelor, the star silver sword, is another. The very wisest of our races learned the ancient secrets. Some say it was the gods of light who allowed it. I do not know either way, but the lore masters studied and developed their strengths around the power of the gods. Once the war became evident, a council was founded, in Averon. There the leaders of the free world met to decide what to do should the gods bring their war down from the heavens.

"It was decided that a series of stones would be created. Each stone would be capable of power undreamed of. They could confine the gods or release them. You see, the lore masters might have been highly skilled but they were not gods. Their knowledge of the power was rudimentary at best. The stones were flawed. Only one survived the creation process."

"The Olagath Stone," Skuld finished.

"Yes. It alone has the ability to free the dark gods from their prison or keep them confined for eternity," Anienam said with a smile.

"Through the Blud Hamr."

"Very perceptive. I grow more impressed with your development daily," Anienam complimented. "While each stone was intended on being all powerful, it was also realized that there was the potential for corruption. Even then there were subversive races at work in Malweir's shadows. Weapons were forged to counter the power of each stone. They too have all been destroyed over time. The Mages were partly responsible for hunting down and removing the weapons from the world."

"I don't understand why though. Wouldn't each weapon be a powerful item to withhold? It seems to me that there is more evil than good in the world. We need all the tools we can get if we're going to win this war, Anienam."

"Yes and no. The weapons were specifically tailored to their stones. Without the stone to draw power from, the weapons were all but useless. The orders of Mages couldn't take the risk of some dark sorcerer discovering long-forgotten secrets of the weapons and finding a way to turn them evil. The weapons needed to be destroyed. So it is that only the Olagath Stone and the Blud Hamr remain. Should we lose Groge or the Hamr, we are lost."

Silence fell over the wagon. Skuld tried, and failed, to digest what he'd heard. There was nothing natural about the direction his life had taken. Wizard. Magic. Gods. He was just a common thief until a few months ago when he overheard Dorl and Nothol talking about treasure in the Murdes Mountains. Skuld allowed his dreams of overcoming abject poverty to get the better of him and he stowed away on Bahr's ship. Nothing would ever be the same from that moment. Ever. Skuld was faced with many decisions to make regarding where he wanted to take his life. Few of them were good. All he knew was there was no going back to Delranan. That life was finished.

"Anienam, can we succeed?" he asked.

"I want to believe in my heart that victory belongs to us," Anienam replied. His voice turned soft. "It will not be easy, or pleasant. Some of us will not live to see the results of our efforts. A sad fact, but an inevitable one. The powers arrayed against us will be greater than even I can dream of. The Dae'shan will stop at nothing to achieve their goal. Even down to three they will not be easy to defeat. This is the final, great battle of age."

Skuld laughed suddenly, a gentle sound that was more awkward than mirthful. "And no one will ever know who stood there at the final battle. We are nameless heroes, Anienam."

"Sometimes those are the best kind."

Ironfoot tossed a small log on the fire. "Another two days. That's what Anienam says. Two days and this will be decided one way or the other."

"Doesn't seem so long now, does it?" Nothol asked as he stared deeply into the licking tongues of red and orange. "We could almost make a vacation out of it."

"Don't you dare look at me, Nothol Coll. One more rub and I'll blacken your eye," Dorl snapped from his spot beside Rekka.

Nothol grinned sheepishly and held up his hands. "Fair enough. I was just trying to lighten the mood. Besides, you're getting cranky in your old age."

Dorl made to stand but Rekka's lightning-quick reflexes clamped a hand on his shoulder and forced him back down. Despite her actions, the twinkle in her eye suggested she was beginning to appreciate the subtle barbs between the longtime friends.

Dorl wagged a finger at Nothol. "Just wait. You just wait."

"Your girlfriend seems to agree," Nothol laughed.

Ironfoot laughed so hard he spit a mouthful of water out. Even Groge enjoyed a laugh. Dorl could only fume harmlessly as the much-needed humor spread around the tiny camp. They'd been missing their greatest military asset, Boen, and struggling with a way to compensate for his loss. Many turned to Groge in the hopes the Giant youth would find his inner warrior and lead them into battle. Dorl was as frustrated as the others but had an outlet, even if it was the naturally taciturn Rekka Jel.

Bahr had grown increasingly reclusive the deeper into Delranan they drove, giving the sell swords cause for concern. He'd been their rock since departing to rescue the princess back in the fall. Whatever personal demons he combated when he thought no one was looking were starting to bleed over into the rest of the quest. Melancholy was as dangerous as enemy steel.

"That felt good. I haven't laughed like that since the feast after we crushed the dark Dwarves at Bode Hill," Ironfoot announced. "Dwarves often find humor in battle. It keeps us moving past the grief of loss."

Nothol said, "Makes sense to me. Let's hope we're all still around after this is finished so we can share a good laugh."

"Wizard, what do we do when we reach the ruins? I can't imagine our enemies will leave it unguarded," Ironfoot turned to ask. The Dwarf captain had had his laugh and wanted to get back to business.

Anienam paused as he noticed each of his companions slowly turning to look at him. The looks on their faces were heavier, more troubled, than any other he recalled seeing. Hope clung desperately against the harsh realities closing in around them. Deep inside, Anienam began to question whether he was the right person for this task. The fate of the entire world rested on the shoulders of the handful of collected souls staring back at him. Were they enough? What would Dakeb have done? His father had a knack for collecting assorted characters, forging them into a cohesive unit, and tackling intense evil. Anienam wasn't his father.

There was no way he'd ever be able to live up to Dakeb's reputation. The last descendant of the Mages felt his confidence slip, gradually chipping away with each new challenge or setback. He didn't know how much more he had left to give. Anienam lacked the resources necessary to feel inspired. His companions weren't hostile but remained cold to his advances. He recognized that he wasn't an easy person to get along with. Wizards seldom were. Magic continued to leave a sour taste in the world long after the Mage Wars.

Not that he could blame them. He often imagined he'd feel the same way if he hadn't been adopted by Dakeb when he was but a babe. Instead he'd grown up learning the nuances of magic and how to control his newly discovered abilities. Long decades spent in solitude all boiled down to this last task. One final quest to help right the wrongs committed by magic users since the dawn of time. Anienam Keiss wished it had fallen on anyone else but him. For all his bluster and bravado, he felt weak inside.

"No, the Dae'shan will have assembled as many dark agents as they deem necessary to protect the ruins."

"And keep us out," Nothol added.

Anienam nodded. "And keep us out. Exactly what they've collected won't be learned until we arrive, however."

"Isn't there some sort of spell you can cast to give us forewarning?" Ironfoot asked. He folded his burly arms across his chest as he glared at the wizard. Already his mind was racing through potential scenarios.

"That was never my area of focus. I can cast protection spells, the occasional attack spells, but long-distance scrying remains unknown to me," he replied. "Captain Bahr, what would you suggest? We are but two days' ride from our destination."

Bahr, a distant look in his eyes, casually glanced up from the fire. He hadn't been paying attention to the conversation. Thoughts of Maleela and Badron and the possible confrontations upcoming twisted his thoughts in unimaginable ways. That he was subconsciously abandoning his friends and allies to deal with their own futures was almost lost. Almost.

Reluctantly, he took a deep breath and answered, "Scouts would be best, but Boen isn't with us. I don't know if he will return in time."

"The Gaimosian will rejoin us, Bahr. That much I know," Anienam affirmed. "He's quite resourceful for an ogre-like sort. Vengeance Knights are crude, minimalist beings but their loyalty and devotion to duty goes well beyond any other tribe or race. He'll be at Arlevon Gale."

"That doesn't alleviate our need for quality scouts," Bahr pressed. "We can't just go into this situation blindly."

"I agree," Ironfoot added. "We need to scout the area first."

Rekka slowly stood. "I will go, if this task needs to be done."

"Absolutely not!" Dorl protested.

Rekka offered a thin smile. Her heart wanted to stay with Dorl, for if these were to be their last days alive she deserved to die happy, content for the first time in her two decades. The sad truth was the world didn't care whether one person was happy or not. Destiny and Fate marched to their own tunes, tormenting those caught up in the fervor. Some survived to great glory but eventually all wound up in the ground. Win or lose, Lord Death was stalking them all.

"I am the quickest and quietest of us all. The enemy will not spy me," she said. "You all know this to be true."

She forced the memory of her confrontation with one of the Dae'shan in the forests of Rogscroft away. Her guard had been down, despite the heightened caution of fleeing from armed soldiers. How one of the shadow agents of the dark gods managed to come upon her unawares remained a mystery. She'd always thought she'd been trained to deal with them. Her time with the dream masters of Teng and then in Trennaron deceptively allowed her to believe she had all the tools necessary to ensure the successful completion of this quest. Could she have been mistaken this entire time?

"She's right, Dorl. Rekka might be the best chance we have," Nothol told his friend. The words were difficult, even after all the gentle ribbing they gave each other.

The first arrow sliced across the camp, speeding over the fire to strike the nearest pine bole. Skuld cried out. A horse whinnied. Stunned faces had just enough time to look around before the first wave of mercenaries broke through the barrier of darkness.

"Attack!" Ironfoot roared. The Dwarf snatched his axe from the ground at his feet and charged without waiting for the others.

Shorter by far, Ironfoot ducked under an ill-timed swing and took one of the mercenaries just below the knee. The severed limb flopped to the ground an instant before the screaming man. Blood dripping from his axe, the Dwarf brought a heavy boot down on the wounded mercenary's throat, crushing his windpipe. Another sword aimed for Ironfoot's head. The Dwarf barely managed to bring his axe head up to block the blow. Locked in the dual blades, the sword was instantly rendered useless. Ironfoot twisted hard enough to jerk the weapon free and punch the mercenary in the chest with his axe head.

A third attacker ducked in, hoping to catch the Dwarf unawares. He came to an abrupt halt as a mighty hand clamped over his head and squeezed. The mercenary barely had time to comprehend what was happening before he died. Groge stormed into the light as he tossed the corpse off into the trees. The Giant was bewildered at the amount of enemies swarming into the tiny campsite. Any hope of Boen drawing them off the night they spent in the farmer's barn shattered. Groge guessed there must be more than a hundred enemy soldiers trying to kill his friends.

Unfelt rage suddenly welled to life. Groge grew angry, more so than he'd ever thought possible. He attacked with boot and fist. The war bar strapped to his back alongside the Blud Hamr smoothly pulled free and reaped a terrible cost among the enemy, but still they kept coming. Their tenacity was only matched by ignorance. Groge killed for the first time without compunction or hesitation.

Nothol, Dorl, and Rekka stood back to back as they desperately tried to fend off increasing, repeated assaults from the dozen attackers surrounding them. A handful of bodies, some wounded, others dead, already lay heaped around the trio. Arrows studded the trees and ground. More than one struck the packs on the ground. Cries of agony filled the night sky. Steel crashed against steel. The sickly sound of flesh being torn asunder hovered over the camp like Lord Death's very cape.

"Get down!"

Bahr perked up, pulling his gore-stained blade free from the mercenary he'd just impaled. The voice was oddly familiar. Enough to prompt him to obey. "Everyone down!"

A fresh hail of arrows, smaller and dark, flitted through the air where he'd just been standing. A moment later and the crossbow bolts would have riddled his body. Instead they slammed into the mercenaries, puncturing armor, helms, and flesh without prejudice. The unexpected assault was enough to drive the surviving mercenaries off. Poorly armored soldiers rushed in to fill the void but less than a handful remained in the camp. The others hurried off into the night to run down the enemy.

Bahr slowly picked himself up from the blood-smeared snow and took the offered hand. Surprising strength pulled him up. His gaze swept up from his rescuer's boots to the worn pants, dented body armor, and the haggard beard that only comes from not being able to shave for a few weeks.

"What are you doing here?" he asked, stunned.

Orlek snorted his amusement. "Nice to see you too, and don't mention it."

"Ah, sorry. We weren't expecting to see you. Thanks for bailing us out," Bahr said, suddenly embarrassed at not thanking the rugged-looking soldier. "But that wasn't your voice I heard."

"No, it was mine."

Bahr smiled. "Ingrid, what are you doing here?"

"We've been tracking this group since you left us. It appears our enemy is falling back to the east and we are hurrying to follow," Ingrid explained.

"We could have handled them. This wasn't your fight," he insisted.

Ingrid pursed her lips. "Perhaps not but there is more you need to know, Bahr. We've come across a massive force of Goblins driving up from the south. They are heading towards the ruins of Arlevon Gale."

Bahr's heart nearly burst. The great enemy Anienam had been warning them of. "How?"

"We haven't been able to figure that out. It appears they arrived a few days ago and have been slaughtering every village they find along their path. Their numbers are almost uncountable."

"You've seen them?" Bahr asked.

Ingrid fervently shook her head. "No but based on the debris trail they've left we can only assume they number in the tens of thousands."

"There is no force that large in Malweir," Ironfoot countered. The idea of running into a massive army turned his stomach. The long-standing animosity between Dwarf and Goblin fueled his sudden hatred.

"I don't know what more to say," Ingrid defended. "We're caught in an impossible situation. Harnin's forces are in full retreat and the Goblins are moving in the same direction."

"We figure this part of Delranan has already been destroyed. There's not much left of our kingdom to reclaim," Orlek added.

Bahr recoiled as if gut punched. He'd never wanted any part in ruling Delranan but to discover it was crumbling and without any hope of relief wounded him deeply. His strength of conviction renewed, Bahr knew what must be done. He had to confront his brother and end this cycle of violence before all hope was lost.

"Ingrid, we must find a way to get our people out of harm's way if there's to be any future for Delranan," he said in measured tones.

Ingrid smiled genuinely for the first time in days. Hope had been rekindled.

TWELVE

Fateful Decisions

The last body was tossed unceremoniously in the makeshift pit Nothol and Dorl dug shortly before midnight. Most of the rebels had returned. They'd managed to hunt down another score or so of the enemy before turning back. Smiles and exhaustion combined in the former civilians. Any semblance of their old life was gone. Warfare and loss transformed them from meager peasants and farmers to hardened killers with little room for compassion. Ingrid and Orlek ran them through constant drills, for each life was precious to the rebellion leadership.

The striking blond shivered under the warmth of her wolf-skin cloak. The furs would normally have been enough to ward away the cold. Winter was especially fierce this year, almost as if some fell power was enhancing it. Ingrid believed that there was no way the storms could continue into spring the way they had, not without evil influences. She had briefly conferred with Anienam when the two groups met earlier and was left with an unexplainable feeling of dread. The sudden arrival of the Goblins all but confirmed her feelings.

Her eyes were stern, watching silently as dirt was pushed over the mound of corpses. It was more mercy than they deserved. Foreign fighters had no place in Delranan and deserved the kiss of hard steel under the midnight sun. Orlek stood by her side, more for defending the image of her strength than for her well-being. She appreciated all he'd done for her and the love that had sprung from working so closely together during the toughest times. As much as it pained her to admit, her old life was gone. The loss of her late husband faded, replaced by her burgeoning love for Orlek. Never in her dreams had she expected to find another love. It was that fear that led her to the rebellion and into Orlek's mysterious arms.

"This is unnecessary," he told her without looking.

"We can't afford to leave the bodies lying around," she replied. "Skaning is still out there. If he discovers them we'll be hunted down for sure."

"I thought we wanted a stand-up fight? These mercenaries are filth. They don't belong in our kingdom." Orlek's voice darkened with undisguised contempt.

What secret are you keeping from me? Do you hate them because it reminds you of what you once were? Oh, Orlek, I wish you'd trust me. "I won't argue with that but we have to proceed with caution. Matters have changed. The Goblins threaten to undo everything we have worked for these long months."

"Do you think Harnin is behind this latest move? I can't imagine him willingly working with those filthy creatures."

Ingrid didn't know. At this point in the rebellion she wasn't willing to put anything past the One Eye. He was as shrewd as he was spiteful. Lives meant nothing to the current lord of Delranan. "We can't fight an army of Goblins. The best we can hope for is to destroy the loyalist forces and fall back until the Goblins retire."

"Goblins keep what they capture, Ingrid. Delranan will become a sordid pit used for their foul purpose," Orlek warned. "We must find a way."

She was about to break into tears when a thought came to her. "Do you suppose they're mixed up in this nonsense with Bahr? He's heading for the ruins as well. It might just be that whatever evil forces control Harnin and the Goblins is mixed up with Bahr's quest."

"To what end? He's already got the upper hand. None of this makes sense to me," Orlek said. "We need to get word to Harlan and combine our forces. Should any of the three elements be picked off by Goblins, our strength will be reduced, permanently."

"I'm going to find out," she said. Defiance twisted her once flawless face.

"Where are you going?" Orlek demanded.

"To make a deal. Send word to Harlan. I want all three columns to converge before we reach Arlevon Gale," she called back over her shoulder.

The leader of the rebellion stormed off to confront the Sea Wolf. Too many times she'd been behind on intelligence, leaving her struggling to improvise plans on the run. How many friends were left buried, much like these mercenaries, or shoved away in one of Harnin's dungeons? More than she cared to acknowledge. The pain of losing so many people she had counted on not only diminished her feeling of value but hampered the rebellion immeasurably. Ingrid needed to find that one key to change her lot. Otherwise….

"Captain Bahr, a word please," she snapped when he was within earshot.

Bahr winced at the sound of her voice and slowly turned from Anienam. The wizard, to his credit, stood with a barely concealed bemused look.

"What can I do for you, Ingrid?" Bahr reluctantly asked.

Ingrid continued until she stood a pace away. Folding her arms across her chest, she gave him her most defiant look. "You haven't been entirely honest with me. That needs to change, now. What do you know about this Goblin army? This can't be coincidence. Not with the rebellion already struggling for survival."

"I'm afraid the One Eye doesn't take me into his confidence the way he once did," Bahr snapped back. Traces of anger lingered in his dark eyes. He hoped his silent warning was enough to back Ingrid off, at least for the time being.

Her impatience got the better of her. Ingrid attacked. "Harnin knows he's losing the west. Each skirmish we fight depletes his forces. Badron's inevitable return keeps most of his troops in the east. Even with our diminished strength we are driving Harnin out of the wilder lands. Your coming changes everything. A return, which I might add, is highly suspicious. There is no magic in this part of Malweir. How then did you travel the hundreds of leagues from the Jungles of

Brodein to Delranan in the span of a heartbeat? Your blind wizard doesn't seem capable of such a feat."

She cut him off when he opened his mouth to speak. "Please let me finish. I don't care how you returned. That's your business. I am merely suggesting that whatever means you arrived by could easily have been duplicated by the Goblin army, meaning they are either hunting you or are entirely ignorant of your little band, heading towards the same conclusion. Either prospect is too unsettling for my tastes, Bahr. I can defeat the mercenaries and reservists. I can't fight an army of Goblins. Yet neither can you sprint the final stretch across Delranan unseen."

Bahr's eyes narrowed. The lines on his face whitened against his snow-burned face. "What are you saying?"

Good. Not as unreasonable as I imagined. "What I am proposing is an alliance. One of convenience to be sure, but an alliance. We will ensure you reach the ruins and you help us figure out a way to bring down this Goblin filth. Deal?"

Unaccustomed to dealing with rational people, Bahr hesitated. The immediate threat of being destroyed by dark powers fled behind the prospect of suddenly being responsible for the lives, and imminent deaths, of nearly two thousand loyal citizens of Delranan nearly dropped him to his knees. His options were gradually shrinking. This latest assault by Skaning's mercenaries left him rattled. More than anything he missed Boen.

"I won't be responsible for your lives, Ingrid. This quest is meant to be small, secretive. Our only hope of winning is by going unseen," he protested.

Anienam stepped forward. "Perhaps there is another way of thinking, Captain. We are very close to our goal but our strength is diminished. The sudden appearance of Goblins changes everything. Ingrid offers us increased strength and the potential of a diversion should we find the way barred."

"I have no intention of sacrificing my people," Ingrid said. "This is my kingdom as much as it is yours, Bahr. We will fight if we see fit, but I'm not going to fight a war for you."

"That's a fairly large contradiction," he snorted. "First you demand we work together and now you threaten to abandon my people when we would need you the most. Make up your mind, woman. I'm in no mood for games."

Ingrid glared hotly at the grizzled, old sea captain. The sound of her teeth grating could be heard. She admired Bahr's willingness to stick to his principles. Turning him to serve the kingdom wasn't likely going to happen, forcing her to take another route. Perhaps Bahr wasn't meant for the throne after all. She decided it was in her best interests to play along, for the time being.

"Very well," she drawled out. "We'll provide you with enough cover until you get close enough to do what you have to, but the moment it gets too much I'm taking my forces and heading back into the wild."

Realizing there was no way out of his predicament, Bahr nodded. It was a meek gesture at best. "Deal."

"So it's settled. We are coming with you," Ingrid said as she extended her hand to seal the accord.

Harlan slid his spyglass closed and returned it to the leather pouch around his shoulder. "Light infantry column. No more than a platoon. We attack the same as before. I want cavalry wings to sweep in from both flanks while pikes and swordsmen punch up the middle. Archers fire after all elements are on the move. We can't afford to let the enemy form a phalanx and defend properly. Questions?"

His officers and brevet noncommissioned officers shook their heads. This was a well-rehearsed drill they'd executed a score of times since taking the war to the wild. By nightfall Harnin would be down another fifty soldiers. These small-level engagements were tedious, but kept the rebels motivated enough to go on to the next one. Harlan used his natural guile to keep his forces in high spirits. The promise of plunder from the dead enemy went just as far. Smiling, Harlan wheeled his horse around to take his place on the right flank.

Horses lined up in the tree line, Harlan looked up and down his line. One hundred of his finest nodded their readiness. The field commander nodded back and slowly spurred his mount forward. Drawing his sword, he raised it above his head and slowly pointed towards the unsuspecting enemy infantry column marching into death's jaws. The line cleared the trees. He was rewarded by spying the second cavalry wing emerging from their cover. Trusting his infantry was already moving, Harlan ordered the charge.

The thunder of hooves echoed like the anger of the gods across the snow-covered field. Men roared. Horses snickered and whinnied. Shadows blurred overhead as the first two flights of arrows sped into the enemy ranks in rapid succession. Harlan grinned. Often considered foppish, he intended on furthering his reputation. One of the enemy soldiers was going to lose his head in an undignified manner. All for the legend of Harlan.

"Speed of horse! Attack!" he roared.

Seconds ticked slowly by. Hearts beat in slow motion. The world stopped turning long enough to watch as two hundred horses crashed into the lightly armored and confused infantry. Bodies fell in heaps. Caught unawares, the enemy infantry was quickly overwhelmed. Less than a few minutes later Harlan and his rebels were stripping the dead of everything useful.

"Bring up the infantry. We need to be moving in the event a relief force is en route," Harlan ordered. He knelt to wipe the blood from his blade. True to his word, he had singled out the enemy leader and took his head in one swoop. Men would sing his glory in bars and taverns across western Delranan.

Weapons, coin, supplies, and serviceable uniforms and equipment were pulled away from the dead, some of it exchanged for more worn items. The rebels were gradually turning the tide of battle but their personal belongings were being worn down. Each victory helped replenish their sorely depleted stores. Lost in their purpose, none of the rebels noticed their archers and infantry were already dead.

Snarls. Growls. The bitter hatred only made possible from thousands of years of animosity spread across the battlefield as thousands of Goblin warriors sprinted the final hundred meters to crash into Harlan's position. Men and women fell dead without being able to draw their weapons. Harlan's mouth dropped as he recognized the twisted irony of the moment. *Taken by my own ploys. But where did these beasts come from?* Harlan hefted his sword with weary arms and charged the Goblin mass. His only lament was that there'd be none left alive to capture his last chance at glory.

THIRTEEN

Chadra

Bahr took comfort in marching alongside so many fighters. He'd grown accustomed to sneaking across kingdoms with his brave handful, always doing their best to avoid confrontation, stealing when necessary. It wasn't a comfortable lifestyle but one he ultimately felt best given the dire situation he'd been roped into. Anienam's arrival on his front porch all those months ago was no accident. Bahr had been guided and played from the very beginning. He began to wonder if Badron wasn't part of this entire operation. Maleela admitted to not being kidnapped, but Bahr suspected his brother was behind staging the episode to facilitate his war.

He glanced to his right, noticing how close Ingrid and her swarthy-looking bodyguard were riding. She was a striking lady, leading him to question why she'd lower herself down to Orlek's level. Whatever he was now, Orlek was dangerous. No doubt if Bahr bothered to check he'd discover a checkered past filled with acts of murder or worse. Not that it mattered. Orlek was more than capable of taking care of both himself and Ingrid. Hooking up with him might have been her smartest move since abandoning Chadra. The rebellion needed hard people like Orlek. Delranan needed him.

Thoughts of his ancestral home disturbed the Sea Wolf. A very small part of his mind admitted missing his estate, and especially the *Dragon's Bane*. Rumors and accounts of what had befallen Chadra bothered him more than he was willing to accept. All his favorite childhood areas were more than likely destroyed. If Ingrid's reports were correct, all but the Keep was gone. Bahr suddenly understood what needed to be done to clear his conscience and liberate his dreams.

"Ingrid," he called softly. As good as it felt to be back in the saddle again, Bahr found himself almost missing their beat-up wagon.

She fixed him with her blue eyes, sparkling in the midday sun. “Yes, Captain?”

“How close do you figure we are to Chadra?”

“You can’t be serious,” she replied as her face visibly paled.

I wish I wasn’t. There’s too much pain and heartache waiting for me back home. Sadly, I can’t see any other way out and I owe it to my friends. “I need to see it. I need to know what Harnin and our enemies have done, if for no other reason than my peace of mind.”

“Peace of mind?” Orlek asked. His voice echoed traces of impatience and…something else Bahr couldn’t determine.

“Bahr, you don’t understand what happened there,” Ingrid replied with shaky voice. “The sheer horror of…Bahr, I’m begging you, don’t go back home again. You won’t like what you find. The old Chadra is gone.”

“I understand that, Ingrid, but it’s something I must do. I…I can’t explain why,” he stammered softly. An old hurt resurfaced, causing more pain than he was willing to handle. “I may have turned my back on my family and my rights as firstborn son, but, as you are fond of reminding me, I am still a part of this kingdom. The only way to clear my mind is to see my city.”

Orlek’s face darkened at the memory of his final look at what little remained of Chadra. The rings under his eyes from lack of sleep made him look decades older. “It’s a dead city, Bahr. You’ll be dead as well if you dare step foot there.”

“He’s right. Harnin is a monster. He’s lost all control and any sense of morality he once possessed. You’re wanted. I’m sure he has a special death in mind for you and your friends.” Ingrid shook her head, failing to understand what would possess a person as intelligent as Bahr to willingly stride into death’s grasp.

Bahr smiled weakly. “Death holds no promise for me. Lord Death will come at his own good choosing. Live or die, I need to ensure I’ve done all I can to help this quest succeed. I don’t expect you to….”

"To what? Understand? You old fool. I once thought you were the hope of our kingdom. Clearly I was mistaken. Whatever demons you've confronted on your quest, they have claimed the best parts of you and left a broken soul in your place. I understand more than you ever will. I was there during the plague. I was there during the Wolfsreik raids that killed scores of my friends. Where were you? Off pretending to save the world?" Ingrid was breathing so hard she found it difficult to speak. Her shoulders heaved from the exertion of her speech. That anger once gave her focus, but now left her feeling deflated. The sudden urge to break down and cry conflicted with her emotions. "I watched Chadra die even as I tried to salvage it. Bahr, whatever it is you think you need to prove, it is a lie. Focus on your quest. Perhaps then you will be able to deliver Delranan the salvation it needs."

Rebuked, the Sea Wolf stiffened his back and rode forward. Too many times over the course of the quest he'd been forced to abandon his own good instincts in the name of the greater good. While he found it nonsense, knowing there were a great many things he might have done differently, Bahr decided the greater good was what was important. Personal desires meant little if the world were about to fall. Trying to convince Ingrid or Orlek of that would be a monumental waste of his time. Time he didn't have.

"There is nothing you can say that will dissuade me, Ingrid. I need to see Chadra for myself. I'm not asking your permission or assistance. This is my personal quest. Anienam will keep the others in line and heading towards Arlevon Gale," he said with a measure of defiance. "Don't bother trying to change my mind. It's made up. This is something I must do."

"Bahr," Ingrid called out as he was already riding away. "Don't enter the city. You won't like what you find."

The ride to the capital city, rather, what remained of it, was relatively short. Bahr spent those few hours in silent thought, commiserating how far his life had spiraled out of control. The more he thought, the more he began to realize how dissatisfied he was. Dejection gradually transformed into raw anger. He'd been viewing the situation wrong from the beginning. There wasn't room for sorrow, not with so much on the line. Bahr had been manipulated from the beginning, forced to perform tasks to another's liking. That ended now.

The Sea Wolf took all his pent-up aggression and knew exactly where to funnel it: Badron. None of this would be happening if not for his brother's lust for power. Badron was the reason behind the ruination of Delranan. Behind Bahr's loss of home and love. Behind Maleela's disappearance. Behind the war. Behind everything. No other option remained but to remove his brother from this world. Only that would have to wait until after he dealt with the Dae'shan.

Vultures circled over the dying city in droves. Great flocks of the black-feathered carrion eaters hovered, making their roosts on abandoned rooftops, swooping in to tear strips of flesh from already desiccated corpses. Crows and lesser, smaller birds drifted in and out of the surrounding area. The city was quiet, reminding Bahr of a graveyard. Standing in a grove of trees to avoid being spotted by patrols, Bahr stared out on his birthplace. Tears welled in the corners of his eyes as long-forgotten memories rushed back.

He'd laughed here. Played and loved. Wasted his youth on dreams of fancy. Chadra was the one place he had felt comfortable enough to call home. The sadness of those memories tormented his already fragile ego. A time of reckoning was fast approaching. One in which he prayed he had the strength to outlast all else.

Sweeping his spy glass across the city, Bahr struggled to maintain composure. A large portion of the buildings had been burned to the ground. He spied stacks of bodies lining the main road like firewood for a cold winter's night. Wild dogs roved the streets in packs, fighting over the bodies to survive. The inhumanity of it revolted him.

"What has happened here?"

Bahr's question wasn't an easy one to answer, nor did he expect one. Nothing as foul as the scene played out before him was capable of being defined by any singular explanation.

Any thought he once entertained of entering the city in search of survivors or friends was dashed away. There was nothing left to the once grand city. To say that it was a skeleton of its former glory was being kind. Bahr tried but failed to find one redeeming quality of his home.

Eventually he shifted his focus to the massive, wooden fortress built atop the hill overlooking the city. Chadra Keep had stood for centuries, ever the watchful guardian of her people. Built by the first colonists of Delranan, the Keep was intended to house the entire population. Records said that nearly one hundred and fifty people had dwelled within the walls at one point. As time progressed, the inhabitants pushed out to build homes of their own. Soon the city of Chadra flourished under the Keep.

Bahr never understood how the wood didn't rot. He'd meant to ask Anienam during one of those rare down times during the quest but something else always seemed to pop up and steal the thought away. From what he could see, the Keep was largely untouched. Small fire marks scored the lower walls by the gate. Arrows studded the walls but the exterior of the Keep appeared as strong as it had always been.

He lifted his gaze to the tops of the walls where normally at least a score of guards would be visible. Instead he found nothing. No smoke drifted up from the dozen chimneys sprouting across the roof. The windows were shuttered. Doors all closed. A handful of bodies dressed in Wolfsreik armor swung lazily from the makeshift gallows emplaced on the eastern point. Bahr grew confused.

"Could Harnin have abandoned the Keep along with the city?"

Again, there was no answer. Bahr's only option was to either try and sneak into the Keep or ride back to link up with Ingrid and Anienam. He didn't relish either. The mystery of what had happened in Chadra Keep would have to wait, for his sole purpose now lay in stopping the Dae'shan from destroying the world. With heavy heart, Bahr closed his looking glass and turned back to his horse. He'd seen all he needed to. It was time to get back to the others.

He found them halted along a small stream several leagues east of their last position. Their spirits buoyed upon seeing Bahr again, so soon after his departure. Dorl secretly thought the Sea Wolf was gone forever and with good cause. No sane person would want to stick around to end of the quest. Only heartache and suffering awaited. The sell sword smiled and clasped Bahr's forearm.

"Welcome back."

"Dorl, did I miss anything?" Bahr asked. He carefully avoided any conversation that might lead to his discovery. Some pains were too near the surface to be exposed readily.

Dorl opened his mouth and shut it just as quickly. Whatever question he had on his tongue stayed there. "The wizard's grumbling again. Something about a proper meal. Ingrid doesn't seem inclined on stopping for the night, however. It appears dinner is going to have to wait until after this mess is ended."

"We're a day and a half away from the ruins," Bahr said. "Far enough away to risk campfires but close enough to begin worrying about scouts. Caution is prudent."

"Clearly you've failed to be around the wizard on an empty stomach."

"I'm old, not stupid," Bahr said and laughed.

The casual banter lightened the dread in his heart. The silence of his long ride back left him eerily disturbed, enough to have him constantly looking over his shoulder as if enemy eyes were upon him. Clearly Delranan was no longer his home. It was a strange, violent kingdom in which life and death were mere whim blown on the wind.

Dorl shrugged. "That remains to be seen. I think we all need to be a bit touched. What other explanation is there for sticking around this long?"

Bahr looked deep into Dorl's eyes. He'd neglected the sell sword's personal feelings this whole time, intent only on his own. *Yet another oversight I must correct*. "Dorl, I've been wrong to you. I know you want to leave and I don't blame you. This quest, I fear, will claim all our sanity before the end. Hard times demand hard people. There are is no finer group I'd rather have with me at this hour."

Dorl jerked back, a minute gesture but enough for Bahr to notice. Doubts sprang to life, prompting Bahr to wonder if his friend and loyal companion was already too far gone. "I…I don't know what to say. The gods know I am ready to hang up my sword and abandon this life. All we've done shows me that death is the only way out. How can we possibly succeed when so much hatred is allied against us?"

"It's been my experience that all are mired with petty hatreds. Overcoming them will be difficult and, as we've theorized, some of us might die, but we owe it to the rest of the world to stand up and fight for our beliefs. I can go to war but I can't win without your support. You and Nothol have been my two most valuable assets since I hired you in Stouds." Bahr shifted his weight to his opposite foot. Too many long hours in the saddle left his back sore and his legs restless. "Do you still have my back?"

Dorl didn't want to respond. He wanted to take Rekka and flee south. Avoid the terrible fate the gods had decreed for them. But as much as it soothed his fragile conscience to want to leave, Dorl knew he couldn't. Too much of his life was invested in those around him. He glanced over at Nothol, who pretended not to be eavesdropping. Rekka stood quietly beside the wizard, both staring in the opposite direction. Only Skuld dared look him in the eye, at least until the young thief noticed Dorl staring back and quickly dropped his gaze.

These are my friends. As much as I'd like to claim otherwise, I know I can't abandon them now. All our hardships and pain will have meant nothing if I choose to leave. Dorl scoffed at his cowardice. *What sort of hero left his friends in the middle of the night during their darkest hour?* He refused to be that person. Integrity still held meaning for the sell sword. Even if it was going to get him killed.

His mouth twisted in a funny way, as if the words refused to come out. "Fine. I'm in. I signed on to this fool quest in the beginning and I'll be damned if I leave all you now. Let's just hope the big Gaimosian returns. I don't relish the thought of tackling the dark gods without him."

"Nor do I," Bahr admitted, "but Anienam is quite certain he'll return in time."

"He'd better hurry up. Time is almost up."

Bahr nodded. Having said enough, he faked a smile. "I don't suppose there's any food ready? I'm famished."

Dorl's laughter was loud enough to get the others to look their way. "If there is I'm sure Anienam will have eaten it already."

"Best we hurry," Bahr slapped him playfully on the back and headed towards the camp center. All eyes were on the duo, most with that knowing look of satisfaction. Bahr felt better inside knowing that some questions could be answered after all.

FOURTEEN

Luck of the Draw

The fury of the Wolfsreik was unleashed for the first time upon Delranan soil mere hours after Piper Joach was given his new command. Warriors who'd been bottled up in the Murdes Mountains after weeks of inactivity attacked with ruthless abandon. The defenders were caught off guard and struggled to form ranks and recall their training. Piper knew it wasn't going to be enough. He had numbers and the element of surprise. All it took was scaling the wall and opening the gates.

Streaks of flame sped out from the fortress, trailing black, acrid smoke. Piper failed to understand the waste of ammunition. Surely whoever commanded inside recognized the need to retain as many shafts as possible for when the army broke through? He almost ordered a secondary assault, altering his plans to counter the fortress commander's sudden move. It was light enough that darkness wasn't a factor. Mind so wrapped around details and counter plans, Piper failed to notice the small moat ringing the fortress.

The first arrows struck the pitch filling the moat and exploded. Men screamed as they burned to death in their armor shells. Others, cut off by the wall flame stretching high into the sky, could only push towards the walls to be cut down by crossbowmen hidden behind the palisade. Piper Joach's carefully worked plan was about to be undone by the combination of guile and inexperience.

His initial instinct was to fall back and regroup but doing so would leave those soldiers cut off to their deaths. Wasted lives in a war that should have been avoided. Piper couldn't allow that to happen. "Push forward! Attack all sides at once."

Sergeants and junior officers gaped at his orders. They fully expected to die in the assault, but the Wolfsreik discipline was unmatched across the face of the world. Slowly they began moving. Some of Piper's tension left, replaced by the casual demeanor of a seasoned combat leader. He'd been a fool for not expecting tricks. Static defenses relied on misdirection and chicanery to survive. Most times they didn't work, leaving the garrison exposed to the predations of the attackers. Piper would be damned if he let a handful of reservists expose his momentary weakness.

"Commander, the flames!"

"Damn the flames! We must get under their fire and over the walls. Now!"

Piper shoved the startled sergeant forward. Hundreds of infantry massed just beyond arrow range, hesitant for the first time since encountering the Goblins. The task force commander frowned, knowing further exposure would limit his ability to succeed. Ignoring the incoming fire, Piper stormed over to his shocked troops. Heavy infantry had its uses but storming a fortress wasn't one of them.

"On your feet, lads! This is what you get paid for. Strike for the walls and don't stop until the enemy surrenders," he ordered. His voice strained into a bellow.

Soldiers reluctantly hefted shields and began to move forward towards the wall flames. Bravery and foolishness collided, as was its wont. Piper hoped it was enough. The other option was full-fledged retreat. He needed to give his assault force as much aid as possible to keep casualties down.

"Archers! I want your quivers emptied. Keep their heads down and don't stop firing until our lads are on the ropes!"

Longbows groaned as they were loaded and drawn. The first volley soared back towards the fortress, followed by ragged strings of successive shots. Order devolved into chaos as the battle intensified. Piper strapped his helmet on and joined his infantry in their charge. Smoke choked him. Coughing and sputtering, Piper forced his way through the advancing ranks to take his rightful place at the head of the column.

The smoke forced him to squint. Patches of tar and residue clung to his face and uniform. The heat from the flames nearly pushed him back. His nerves threatened to break. Piper Joach dug deeply, forcing aside his weakness and personal fears to inspire his soldiers. Or so he hoped. The thought of roasting alive shook him to the core. No one would label him a coward if he chose to retreat. But such lack of values wasn't in his character. He tucked his arms into his body, dipped his head, and closed his eyes the moment before running through the flames.

Intense heat seared his body. Steam rose from his plate armor, threatening to boil him like a coastal crab. What felt like a lifetime lasted but a few seconds. The smell of cooked hair and charred flesh sickened him, though he'd been around such too many times in the past. Piper kept charging, lifting his head as he closed the final few meters to the base of the wall. His enemy had established a poorly designed kill zone for their crossbows. Only a handful of Piper's disoriented soldiers fell under the deadly shafts before reaching the walls.

"Ropes!" Piper shouted above the roar of the fires.

Soldiers darted forward to throw their blackened grappling hooks over the top of the nine-foot walls. A fully armored Wolfsreik assault soldier could scale the distance in a matter of seconds, providing he remained in top physical shape. Piper counted on the harshness of winter and their trek across the mountains to fuel his assault. A dozen ropes went up. The first crashed back down before the soldier managed to grab hold. Soldiers scrambled up the others, barred steel in mouths. Short daggers were best for close fighting. Each soldier in the assault was specially trained for breaching defensive structures, having trained for months on designs exactly like the one they assaulted. Piper considered it payment for the lives he had lost in the initial attack.

One of infantrymen toppled over the wall. Blood ran in sheets down his armor. He was dead before hitting the ground. More soldiers climbed. The sounds of pitched battle atop the wall soon contended with the flames for dominance. Piper took his place in line and climbed. Muscles ached. He was more exhausted than he thought but couldn't stop. There'd be time enough for rest once the battle was won. His initial doubts of winning or losing were swept aside the moment he pulled his body over the wall.

His infantry was already surging towards the front gates, killing all in their path. Soldiers continued to swarm over the walls on all four sides of the beleaguered fortress. Bodies littered the area, reminding him of a slaughterhouse he'd visited as a child. This was war at its grimiest. Defenders fought with claws and teeth to stave off their imminent deaths. Desperation took hold on those few defenders still capable of acting. Many launched what amounted to a suicide charge into the armored ranks of the Wolfsreik heavy infantry. They died horribly, but at least with a small measure of honor.

Others were herded together and placed on their knees with hands over their heads. Abject failure lingered in their hollow eyes. Piper had seen it already and still failed to understand what could drive anyone to perform such against their own kinsmen. The Wolfsreik commander didn't have time to stay locked in deep thought, however. A pair of defenders charged him. Only one bore a sword. The other relied on fanaticism and paid for his arrogance.

Blood splashed across Piper's chest as his blade ripped a terrible score through his unarmed foe. The body collapsed even as the dying man struggled to register what had just happened. Piper took a half step back and brought his blade up diagonally to block a blow from the second attacker. The impact jarred his bones. Gritting his teeth, Piper pushed back and used the sudden separation to swing upward.

The blow was well placed but blocked immediately. Clearly this man was a skilled swordsman. Piper didn't have time to enjoy a bout. He needed to end the battle quickly and see to the rest of the fort. He was forced back another step as his attacker launched a series of blows. It had been a long time since Piper met his match with another swordsman. The challenge was appreciated at a fundamental level even as he snarled at having such difficulty.

Deciding quickly to let his opponent think he had the upper hand, Piper reeled backwards. Taking the bait, the other soldier charged foolishly. Piper ducked back from a blow aimed at his neck and drove the hilt guard into the man's throat. Blood fountained from the wound, telling Piper he'd struck the jugular. The enemy soldier dropped his sword and reached for Piper's throat. Hot fingers curled around his neck before he managed to punch a knee into the soldier's groin. Dazed and bleeding out, he fell back enough for Piper to deliver the merciful death blow.

Piper's breath was ragged. He looked around for another combatant but saw the battle had moved well beyond his tiny circle of influence. The main quarters were already on fire. More than a score of enemy had surrendered. Others were being forced to their knees and stripped of any weapons or personal possessions. He'd ordered his infantry not to take any chances until the final assault ended. Soldiers carried fallen comrades back through the gates, their bodies covered in cloaks. Medics treated those less severely wounded. Only a handful appeared to be seriously hurt. Piper winced as one soldier was carried past. The bandages swathed over the stump of his right leg were soaked through and dripping.

"Commander Joach, one of the prisoners talked," a grime-covered sergeant told him between half breaths. He bled from several small cuts across his right cheek.

Piper noticed the wounds and thought they could only have been made by fingernails. *Why in the world would these people do this to themselves? Is Harnin truly that powerful?* "Very well, bring him to me. I trust he's not as obstinate as the fool in the first capture."

The sergeant could only shrug as he'd still been en route with the main body when Piper and the vanguard made the first assault. He left and returned with the prisoner before Piper was able to finish drinking form his canteen. Disappointed, Piper put the cap on and replaced it in the holder strapped to his waist.

"I'm told you have information to give," he began with as much authority as he had left. He was much too tired to give a damn. The prisoner would talk or he'd find one who would. "Don't waste my time."

"No sir, I won't." The prisoner clearly recognized Piper, a fact he hoped to turn to his advantage. "Commander Joach, we didn't want to fight but the commander told us we was all going to be slaughtered by them heathens from the mountains. Been plenty of talk about them Pell Darga since you all marched to war back in the fall. None of us fancied being caught by them. It wasn't until we noticed there was nothing but Wolfsreik that some of the boys decided to throw down our arms."

"Admirable but unconvincing," Piper snapped. "What makes you different from the others we've encountered thus far?"

"Sir, I don't kill my own. I was once active duty. Served in the cavalry a few years back but mustered out due to my bad leg. Rider ain't no good if he can't ride. So I joined the reserves. A lot of the boys here done the same thing."

"Those would be the wise souls who surrendered I assume."

The prisoner nodded fervently. "Sure enough. We know a beating when one is due. Badron forced us here. Don't think many of us wanted this posting."

Piper exchanged surprised looks with his sergeant. Had he misheard? "Badron? That's impossible. The king hasn't been seen or heard since we ran him out of Rogscroft. You must be mistaken, trooper."

"No sir, I ain't. Was King Badron who gave us our marching orders. He come back one night not long ago and dueled old One Eye in front of the rest of us. Killed the bastard too. Bout time I says. He's been a wicked one since this all began."

Dead? Could it be? Piper wasn't one for gossip, despite it being a soldier's best friend. This sudden information was as unexpected as it was welcome. Badron was a minor threat without much backing or had been until now according to the prisoner. Yet another twist threatened to alter the course of the war. Normally Piper would take the time to investigate but time was the one element he lacked. Whatever time the combined army thought they had was slipping faster than sands in the hourglass.

"Sergeant, take this…what is your name, soldier?"

The prisoner stiffened. A measure of pride returned to his slightly broken form. "Fenn, sir. I be from Stouds."

"Very good, master Fenn. Sergeant, take Fenn to General Rolnir. He needs to know who it is we now face," Piper ordered.

Saluting crisply, the sergeant gestured for Fenn to head towards the gate. It was a long ride to catch up to the rest of the army.

Endless leagues of snow-covered fields and ice-covered streams rolled beneath the boots and hooves of the combined army. Rolnir pushed his force as hard as he dared. Man and beast were already close to their breaking points. As proud as he was of his army--though arguably it wasn't entirely his--he knew he couldn't keep them on the move forever. At some point they were going to have to rest longer than a few hours. Frowning in thought, Rolnir made his decision. The ruins of Arlevon Gale were still close to forty leagues away. The Wolfsreik general would lose half his combat effectiveness if he didn't halt now. He rationalized it by recalling an army needed an operational pause before advancing on the final objective.

Word passed through the column and the pace slowed to nothing. Soldiers busied setting up tents, establishing the perimeter, and foraging for any live game to bulk up their evening meal. Dried rations and hard tack only went so far. Rolnir made his rounds without complaint. His lower back screamed for relief and he had a headache deep within his skull. Partially dehydrated and stomach growling, the Wolfsreik general refused to take care of his personal needs until after all his troops were seen to. He was only as important as the lowliest soldier. They either made him successful or mired his legacy with failure.

The sun was already dipping below the horizon by the time he ambled back to his tent. A previous order kept his official command tent from being erected. Long marches in the field demanded efficiency, not decadence. He lived as a regular soldier would, but not without a few privileges of rank. Candles and the occasional bit of Rogscroft chocolate filled his saddlebags. He could do without the sweets but needed candles to finish correspondence late into the night.

The sudden commotion outside his tent forced him to slide back into sweaty boots and don his travel cloak. What he saw was the last thing he might have expected. The lone sergeant saluting him had a steady grip on a ragged-looking soldier beside him.

"What is this?" Rolnir asked, returning the salute.

"General, this prisoner informed us King Badron has returned. More, he also has information concerning the location of the enemy's main bivouac site."

Rolnir felt true hope for the first time since reentering Delranan.

FIFTEEN

A Dream Unrealized

Badron glared hotly at the roughly two thousand conscripted civilians assembled before him. Soldiers had worked to construct a platform for him to stand on for his address, reaffirming the king's dominance in Delranan. The rabble staring back didn't make him feel kingly. They were the bottom of the barrel, unfit to serve as retainers in the baggage trains. But they were all he had left. Delranan was picked clean of military-age males. Badron was going to have to fight with what he had, not what he needed.

"Whatever happened while I was gone is the past," he began slowly. "Harnin One Eye is dead and once again I am the rightful ruler of Delranan. Any who wish to deny my birthright may attempt to do so now."

None moved. Soldiers armed with wicked-looking spears hovered just behind them, ready to strike down any dissenter.

"We are at war. Not against enemies of state or neighboring kingdoms, but against our own kind. General Rolnir and the Wolfsreik have betrayed us. They have stormed back to destroy all you have struggled for. Rolnir is a ruthless foe, cunning and deceptive. He won't stop until the crown is placed upon his brow. Will you suffer his rule in chains? Your wives will be sold for whores. Your sons enslaved for his personal whim. Death will be your only release.

"I offer each of you the opportunity to save your families. To save your lives. I'm also not giving you a choice. I may be the rightful king of Delranan but you are my citizens. This is your kingdom. Stand and fight for your homes. Our enemies will most certainly kill you for theirs."

Badron fell silent. He wasn't an inspirational speaker, nor did he feel lenient. He needed bodies with weapons to slow the Wolfsreik advance. Most of the rabble staring blankly at him would be dead before the end of the week. Of that he had no doubt. They were the scraps of what had once been a strong society. *None of this would have happened if I hadn't allowed Harnin the option of assuming control in my absence. Killing him proved highly dissatisfying. Perhaps Rolnir's head will ease my troubles.*

"All officers will report for weapons-training instructions immediately. This camp will be ready for battle no later than nightfall. Our enemies are nearly upon us. The Wolfsreik will not spare a single soul. Fight to your last and defend Delranan's honor. Together we shall prevail!" Badron shoved a defiant fist into the air. Reluctant cheers rose from the crowd, gathering strength as they circled through the ranks all but doomed civilians.

Mildly pleased, the king of Delranan marched down from the platform and back to his command hut. He didn't expect a single one to survive the onslaught of Rolnir's assault. The wiser would break and run or throw down their weapons in surrender. Not that he blamed them. War was no place for farmers. Badron unclipped his cloak and draped it over a high-back chair beside his desk. Two oil lamps burned low on the desk. Black trails of smoke rising to a small cloud clung to the ceiling.

"Do you truly think your words are inspiring enough to snatch victory away from defeat?"

Badron winced. "My words are meant not for your foul ears but for what remains of my people. You may have broken Delranan, and perhaps me as well, but you will not hold your glory long. Even should I fall, Rolnir will reclaim Delranan and cast you out."

Amar Kit'han laughed. The wicked hiss seethed through the hut. "Ever so brave, eh king? There is no strength in the world of Men capable of halting my aggressions. The hour has grown too dark for any hope. And you, King Badron, have provided me with all the power I required. Your actions have brought about the end of the world. Soon the dark gods will return and Malweir will fall into a new age of darkness. For your loyal service I will ensure that you are slowly murdered over a thousand years."

Badron's hand reached for his sword.

"No mortal weapon can harm me, fool," Amar spat. "I am the instrument of the gods. What hope do you have of standing against me?"

"This will not go unpunished, monster," Badron ground out.

"It already has. Your kingdom is in ruins, that fool One Eye is dead by your own hands. Had you thought to work together you might have at least slowed my progress. Betraying Grugnak was a mistake. Little do you know an army of fifty thousand Goblins already rampages across Delranan and your very own Wolfsreik is but a few hours from this camp. You will not live to see the dawn. There is no power left in the north capable of contending with me."

Deflated, Badron resisted the urge to drop to his knees in defeat. *How did I let it come to this? The glory promised by my father squandered by my own greed.* Regret formed in the shadows of his heart. Attacking Rogscroft had proved to be a near fatal mistake. Jealousy destroyed the one kingdom that might have been able to come to his aid. None of that mattered now, not with Rolnir marching towards him. There would be no words. No offer of terms. The Wolfsreik would crush his meager force in hours, and rightfully so.

He suddenly felt unworthy of the crown. *I've failed. Failed at everything. Am I strong enough to earn my place beside my forefathers or will I be condemned to fate worse than death? I am truly cursed by the gods*.

"Cursed? An interesting notion. You know nothing of curses. For centuries I languished under the indifference of the gods of light. They allowed you foolish mortals to plod through life unmolested even as their dark brothers suffered torments unimaginable. My curse was born through servitude. Never again will I suffer."

"You didn't suffer enough," Badron retorted. His effort fell short, denoting how weak he was compared to the rising Dae'shan. That he managed to reply at all almost impressed Amar Kit'han. Almost.

He lashed out with bolts of vibrant yellow and orange power, striking the aged king in his chest. Badron crashed to the ground. Smoke rose from his armor. Burns scored his lower face and his hair had been scorched around the neck. He screwed his eyes shut as nausea washed over him. Strength fled his muscles. His bladder emptied. Badron groaned weakly.

"A shame he's not stronger. Perhaps the dark gods could have used him."

"Kodan Bak, you come unbidden. This is my problem," Amar snapped.

A third Dae'shan materialized beside the lesser Kodan. Pelthit Re glanced down at Badron's prone figure and then up to Amar Kit'han. Once responsible for twisting Harnin One Eye, Pelthit Re found his sudden lack of activity disheartening. He'd roamed the empty halls of Chadra Keep in search of inner solitude but repeatedly came up lacking, at least until Kodan Bak approached him with the seeds of rebellion. Pelthit Re followed his brothers to ascertain where he stood in the current Dae'shan hierarchy.

"This game is costing us, Amar," he chastised. "Our efforts need to be focused on the Olagath Stone, not meddling with a weak mortal."

"You should not be here, Pelthit Re. I gave you instructions to remain in Chadra."

Power rippled from his robes like heat waves from hot stone. "Instructions that made no sense with what time we have remaining. You would have me idle my time away only days before we open the path between dimensions? Armies are converging on the ruins, threatening our success and you squander valuable resources. This is not our way."

Amar's eyes flared brightly from beneath his hood. The pale yellow light turned vibrant, as if threatening to burn out. "Kodan Bak has been with loose tongue I see. Very well, come then. This will not be pleasant."

"No," Kodan interjected. "The time is fast approaching when our conflict will be settled but it is neither here nor now. The dark gods must come first. All other needs are secondary."

"Cowards," Amar hissed.

Kodan Bak laughed in his face. "I am not afraid of you, Amar Kit'han. We have languished under your flaccid rule. Our age draws nigh but it will not include you."

"I have waited for this moment. Whatever outcome the gods decree, your demise will surely be among it. Both of you will go to Arlevon Gale. Defend the Stone at all costs until Maleela and her army arrive. Bahr and the others must not reach the ruins alive or must be kept at bay until after the ritual. I will settle our affairs once that moment passes. You, Kodan Bak, I shall kill first."

The urge to attack surged through the lesser Dae'shan. Fists clenched. Teeth ground together. Kodan Bak held his ground for a moment longer before fading away. It was a tired game they played, one he aimed to finish for all times at his earliest convenience. As it stood, he'd accomplished his intentions. Pelthit Re now realized the full treachery of their leader, shifting his position in line with Kodan's. Together they had the strength to defeat Amar and select another to fill their ranks.

Amar Kit'han paused as Pelthit Re collected power around his willowy figure and dissolved back into the nether. Only when his companions were gone did he resume his attentions to Badron, but the returned king of Delranan was unconscious. Amar snorted his displeasure. Humans were pathetically weak.

Little did he realize Badron had heard every word of their confrontation and was already forming plans within plans. He must find a way to turn his daughter and brother against each other to stop the Dae'shan from assuming complete power over Delranan. The gods be damned. He only cared for his throne.

The great war machines of the Wolfsreik opened fire at dusk. Dozens of boulders and catapult rounds slammed into the bivouac site, throwing soldiers and equipment in every direction. Men screamed as they broke arms and legs. Others were crushed outright. Flames spread through the camp, sparked by a thousand burning arrows. All threatened to be lost in the initial moments of shock.

Gradually sergeants and company commanders started barking orders, lest the entire army be lost on a whim. Pickets and sentries were overrun in seconds, most of which were killed outright. A handful were captured and dragged back to the combined army's rear area for intelligence. No quarter was given when possible. The only way to guarantee success was through a lightning-quick assault.

Rolnir's gambit of using the Pell Darga to overwhelm the outer defenses paid off. Defenders were in shock from seeing the smaller, dark-skinned warriors emerge from the twilight. The bombardment began minutes after the Wolfsreik general was convinced his raiders were already reaping a terrible toll on the enemy. Cavalry formed ranks under the catapults, advancing at a slow walk. Rolnir wanted enough time to let the horror of what was happening sink in before committing his ground forces. Fear often drove wedges into the enemy's armor. The prisoners collected thus far from Piper's campaign told Rolnir one thing: fear was abundant in the people of Delranan. Exploiting it would bring an end to the civil war much quicker than he anticipated, providing all went according to plan. The redheaded general was experienced enough to know that most plans failed upon contact.

Archers from Delranan and Rogscroft continued firing at a measured pace. Each archer was intended to fire twenty arrows at a rate of five shafts a minute. Given the sustained rate of fire, that was more than enough to cover the cavalry's advance. Upon orders the archers would displace to the far side of the bivouac to screen deserters and retreating forces. Infantry support was already en route to cut off all escape routes. Rolnir had Badron right where he wanted him. The noose tightened with each passing second.

Horns bleated a dreadful wail, signaling the charge. The very ground trembled as hundreds of horsemen took off towards the poorly conceived defensive line. Badron may have been able to acquire bodies but they were raw, inexperienced peasants not made for war. Riders watched as some broke and ran. Others were cut down by their own sergeants. Fury burned within the chests of the cavalry as they watched the very people they'd sworn oaths to protect murdered for their will to live.

The wedge of horses crashed into the infantry line and tore a widening hole as it continued to pierce the depths of the bivouac. Rolnir watched through his spyglass. Men were running everywhere, many without weapons. Bodies littered the ground. He guessed there were between two and three thousand volunteers encamped before him. Less than a quarter appeared to have any military training. The slaughter quickened as his infantry plunged into the gaps created by the cavalry.

Orders were specific. Anyone wearing armor or armed with quality weapons was to be killed outright. Many conscripts were still in their civilian attire or given boiled-leather plates for armor, clearly distinguishing them from the reservists. That didn't prevent hundreds from being killed as the heat of battle overtook the Wolfsreik. Revenge for all the wrongs committed to their kingdom demanded justice. The Wolfsreik was the instrument of delivery for Rolnir's justice.

"Captain, strike the colors. We're riding to the fight," he ordered, adjusting his armor one final time.

"General, are…are you sure that is wise?"

Rolnir drew his sword and pointed the tip at his adjutant. "Question me in front of my command again and I'll strip you down before sending you in. Now, the colors."

Horns blared again, deep, resonating sounds that echoed over the din of battle as the command group surged to join the fight. *And hopefully prevent too many civilians from being slaughtered.*

Infantry formations cheered as their general blew past, sworn raised and pointed at the bivouac. They were the rearguard, designed to sweep in and mop up the battle. All were experienced veterans of multiple campaigns. Most were too old to stand the front lines or lock shields with their brothers. Rolnir didn't believe in disposable soldiers, however, and valued each and every life under his command including the Pell Darga and Rogscroft soldiers.

All flags of division were abandoned for the duration of the campaign, though he and his commanders agreed it was best to keep units together. Rolnir wanted them all to fight under one flag, to act as one army, not a band of several all vying for glory. He and Aurec both expressed concerns over too much carnage, for both wanted a strong Delranan as an ally once the madness of King Badron was ended. Their ploy worked and all three peoples attacked as one.

Swords clashed with axe and spear. The screams of pain from the dying lingered in his ears. Despite his orders, the increasing slaughter included a healthy portion of civilians who'd either been given no choice but to fight or were fanatics who bought into the lie. Those became dangerous quickly. Death became a tender mercy. He watched as smaller cavalry units peeled of the main thrust to form secondary wedges and head towards the supply trains and tent area.

The lightning-style offensive he and the council had painstakingly developed was being executed to near perfection. Already his artillery units were breaking down in preparation for movement. The army couldn't afford to be bogged down by any one engagement. Supplies, surgeons, medics, and rear echelon forces were already in column and advancing to conduct resupply and medical operations and the battle wasn't nearly finished. Rolnir recognized the need for speed if he was going to make the rendezvous at Arlevon Gale in two days. Aurec or Vajna wouldn't wait long to march on Chadra if he were late.

His sword was drawn though he never expected to get it bloodied. Frontline engagements were no place for the general of the army. The swarm of self-appointed bodyguards kept both friendly and enemy forces far away from their most valuable asset. Rolnir frowned at being protected so, but knew it was in Delranan's best interests. Aurec had already suggested Rolnir take the throne as regent until a suitable candidate was found. He scowled at his thoughtlessness. There was a battle to win first.

His advance pushed into the heart of the enemy bivouac. Hundreds of bodies, dead and dying, littered the immediate area. A few were from the combined army while the vast majority were Delrananian conscripts. Heartbreaking as the loss might be, Rolnir forced himself to view each corpse as an enemy of the kingdom. Anything less was paving the way for bad dreams. His vantage from horseback showed him Badron's command structure, which he immediately spurred towards. The only way to ensure total victory was by cutting of the enemy's head.

Flames already licked up the outer walls. Anything or anyone trapped inside would already be dead from smoke inhalation or the flames. Frustrated, Rolnir slid from his saddle. Sharp pain shot up his right leg, nearly dropping him to a knee. He leaned on his horse for support while the pain went away. More than one soldier jerked towards him before a foul-tempered look kept them at bay.

"Douse those flames!" he barked. "I want the inside searched. Bring any bodies directly to me. We can't let Badron escape."

Soldiers ran for buckets.

The attack came with such lightning quickness Badron had little time to recover. All his dreams and plans of rebuilding Delranan were swept aside as the full force of his former army crashed into the pitiful mass of conscripts. Compounding matters was his sudden dilemma of Bahr and Maleela, leaving his mind in a dark place. Badron was forced to abandon all his maps, plans, and personnel as he decided to flee. His life meant more than a few thousand peasants. Their deaths would be remembered with vain glory once he assumed the throne.

He shed his fine clothes and armor, snatching ragged clothes from a body as he hurried with an alarmingly growing number of deserters who decided their lives mattered too. The king of Delranan became a peasant. They ducked through tents and confused wagon masters trying to salvage their stores of supplies. *The fools. Can't they see they need to flee as well lest the enemy capture the much-needed supplies?* He bit down on his tongue to keep from giving himself away and kept running. Lord Death nipped ever at his heels.

The refugee column broke through the rear lines, attempting to reach the nearby forest. None could have expected the massed ranks of archers silently awaiting them. A lone voice cried halt just once. Peasants screamed in panic and ran faster. Badron growled at their mistake, knowing it would likely amount in his death as well. He wasn't disappointed. Arrows ripped into the unarmored conscripts, reducing their numbers by half in the first volley. It wasn't long before ranks of infantry popped up from the snow to encircle the few who remained standing. Badron threw down the nicked and rusted sword and placed his hands on his head along with the scores of fresh prisoners standing around him.

Wolfsreik soldiers swarmed in to begin roughly shoving the prisoners and binding their hands behind their backs. More than one was slammed down to the ground after snapping an unappreciated comment. While all were citizens of Delranan, the Wolfsreik harbored no loyalty towards those who had sided with Harnin One Eye or Badron thereafter. Chief rabble-rousers were gagged and blindfolded before being carted back to the command group. Wisely, Badron kept his eyes focused on the ground and his mouth shut. Anything else would arouse suspicion. Suspicion he could ill afford.

"Get them moving. The general wants us moving before the day's out," a scar-riddled sergeant barked. His ill-tempered look announced his displeasure with being placed in charge of prisoner escort duty.

Badron was secured and shoved in line. The weary column of deserters slowly began the march back towards the bivouac site. What they found went beyond expectations. Shovels were produced and given to as many prisoners as possible. Soldiers issued orders for the digging of a mass grave. Traitors, they snapped, didn't deserve individual graves while brave soldiers were lowered into the ground around them. Larger than many of his countrymen, Badron accepted his shovel and started to dig. Dark corners of his mind idly wondered if Rolnir was going to have them all killed and thrown in their hand-dug grave.

Briefly he considered turning himself in. Surely Rolnir would find mercy, or at least the political savvy to understand the importance of having the king alive. It was a decision he couldn't force, worried for his life. Amar Kit'han and the Dae'shan were ever lurking just beyond the corner of vision, leading Badron to believe that should he divulge his true identity it would be a violently swift demise. In the end the deposed king of Delranan slammed his shovel back into the frost-covered ground and dug a little deeper. He had nothing but time before making his move.

SIXTEEN

Refugees and Holdouts

Maleela narrowed her eyes as she stared at the bleak sun. Partially hidden behind a thin cloud bank, the normal brightness was faded, producing little warmth. She'd spent her young life dreaming of days when she'd be able to wander the world under the unforgiving glare of the sun. Badron's reign over her tightened up to the point when Aurec rescued her. Resentment forced her hands, pushing her into the arms of the Goblins and their Dae'shan keepers.

The day was half gone and Thrask's forces hadn't moved more than a league. At this rate they wouldn't arrive at Arlevon Gale until well after their deadline. She needed to get her army moving again. Revenge and destiny awaited her. Pulling her cloak tightly around her slender shoulders, the princess of Delranan turned her face from the sun, already forgetting the tender kiss of golden light as her mood darkened to deal with the Goblins. The sword at her right hip bounced gently off her thigh with each measured step.

She found Thrask standing alone. His short stature dominated the area. Thick arms were folded over his chest. A double-headed battle axe rested heads down in the snow. Saliva and blood painted his lower tusks. The hatred in his eyes threatened to burn the world down. Maleela snorted. She couldn't care less about the Goblin's aspirations for grandeur. He was a tool, nothing more. Malweir was a much better place without the Goblin hordes and she aimed to rid the world of the race the moment Amar Kit'han followed through with his promises. She need only bide her time until then.

"What is the meaning of this delay?" she demanded.

Thrask barely moved. His bull-shaped head turned ever so slightly to regard her with scorn. She was the means to an end. An end he'd already been given leave to execute once the dark gods were released. "We will move when we are ready."

Maleela stamped her food down and jabbed an accusatory finger. "I command this army and I say we move now. Your soldiers have done nothing but get fat of the corpses from those enemy soldiers. You've had your fun, now order the march. We must reach Arlevon Gale in enough time to perform our mission."

Thrask uncurled his clawed fingers. "You threaten me? Dae'shan or no, I will rip your heart out and eat it before you die. Mind your words, *woman*. Goblins do not take orders from Human scum."

"You will take orders from me," she persisted. She almost invoked Amar Kit'han's name but doing so would render her powerless in Thrask's eyes. The Goblin Lord respected power and strength. She needed as much of each if she hoped to maintain her already tenuous hold on such a large army.

"I could kill you," Thrask said, taking a menacing step closer.

She had her sword out and pointed at the Goblin's chest before he planted his forward foot. "You'll be dead before you can try."

The Goblin paused. He cocked his head, attempting to see how much resolve the small woman had. Slowly, Thrask began to laugh. "You are brave, perhaps. We will see just how much when the Wolf soldiers attack."

"The Wolfsreik is your concern, not mine. We have our orders. The ruins are less than a day's march if we move at full speed through the night. Our army needs to be in place and ready to defend shortly after arrival. Is that understood?"

Her sword waivered slightly, as if strained from the weight of holding it there for so long. Thrask knew he could easily shove the blade aside and tear her tiny figure apart without much effort despite her foolish notion of invincibility. "Goblins will do their jobs. No worry."

"Then I suggest you get my army moving. Time is against us," Maleela threatened. She sheathed her sword in a display of power meant to be witnessed by the growing throng of warriors around them.

Thrask backed down. The Goblin Lord was entrenched enough in his power he didn't fear losing it. All he needed to do was remain calm until Maleela's attention was diverted. Then he'd be able to reclaim leadership and bring havoc to the world of Men.

The refugee column stretched out for almost half a league. Hundreds of families had packed all their belongings, gathered as much supplies as possible, and joined the long wagon train south to escape the ravages of war. Dogs, cows, goat, and horses followed the winding column as it gradually made the long trek out of Delranan. Hope, what little remained, propelled them onward. Children sat quietly behind their parents. There was no sign of merriment. No laughing or playing. Each refugee focused solely on leaving the harsh reality of their homes behind. Nothing else mattered.

The column master, a self-appointed position claimed by the headmaster of one of the larger villages, drove them tirelessly down the snow-covered lane. Had he the necessary military training he would have sent out scouts and flankers. Instead he decided that pulling the refugees as close together as possible offered better protection in addition to peace of mind. A practical person, he tried to maintain order in the name of them all.

It wasn't enough. Lack of foresight left him vulnerable to attack. His world exploded slightly after dusk while the column was attempting to make camp. Short, grey-bodied Goblins swarmed from behind tree and rock with weapons flailing. Women, and more than one man, screamed, trying to break and run. It wasn't enough. The Goblin army marched straight into the long column without intending to halt. Nothing Maleela, or Thrask, said was strong enough to keep them from breaking ranks and slaughtering the refugees.

Every living soul was murdered as the Goblins rampaged through them. A handful of stragglers managed to gather their wits and hide before the horde ran over them. They watched in abject terror as their friends and neighbors were slaughtered for sport. Goblins laughed as they toyed with frightened children or bit into exposed throats. The smell of blood filled the air. A hush smothered the night, as if the gods were holding their breath in disbelief.

Sated from their earlier feast of butchered rebels, the Goblin army largely left their victims in the snow. Having no need for meat they wiped their cruel blades clean of blood and gore. Others set about desecrating the dead, turning their corpses into mockeries of what once had been. Arms were hacked off and shoved down throats. Women were stripped and carved upon. Depravity meant little to a race bent on the very destruction of the Human race.

Maleela watched it unfold with disgust. Her stomach rebelled, emptying twice on the blood-stained snow. As much as she wanted to command them to stop and resume the march she instinctively knew she couldn't without losing any gains she'd made from her confrontation with Thrask earlier. No fool, she recognized his acquiescence for what it was: simple posturing to allow her the pretense of being in charge. If she jumped in now and got involved she'd be sealing her fate. Goblins had no love for her, abiding her command only through the insistence of the Dae'shan. Given a choice they'd slaughter her for sport. Maleela stood on a very narrow edge. One wrong decision and she was dead.

"A good day," Thrask barked deeply as he strode up to her. Drying blood coated the front of his armor.

"Was this necessary?" she asked after wiping her mouth clean.

Thrask laughed. "Yes. We have killed many today. A glorious time for the Goblin kingdom. Your people were weak, Maleela. Killing them was a mercy."

"Mercy? They were mostly women and children. What mercy is there in murdering unarmed civilians?"

"Goblins have been at war with your race since the world cooled. How many thousands have you killed in kind?" Thrask asked. He surprised her with his depth of knowledge over the past, making him extremely dangerous.

Maleela gagged as the wind blew the raw smell of butchered meat and offal in her face. "No one living had anything to do with the past. This is our war. Our time. History is made through our deeds, not those of our fathers."

"Fathers, bah! I killed my father when I was seven. Malweir deserves to burn and I am going to be the one who does it," Thrask told her matter-of-factly. "The time of the Goblin is at hand. Mankind has had its time." He gestured back to the killing fields. "This is just the beginning."

What have I allied myself with? None of this is worth revenge against my father. Maleela struggled to find any words capable of countering Thrask's aggression. She fell short. Never in her short life had she encountered such raw hatred. Not even with all the hurt her father had inflicted did Maleela feel the sting or fervor like the murderous Goblins. A small voice in her mind whispered she might have made a mistake.

He took her silence for acceptance. "There is no such creature as innocence. Your world will burn just like these fools."

"Will you consume these children as well?" she asked.

"An army must feed. But no, princess. We have filled our bellies on Man flesh enough. These we leave to rot in the afternoon sun. They will serve their purpose."

She flinched. "What purpose?"

"Fear."

Thrask flashed his tusks and stormed away, leaving Maleela less sure than she'd ever been. Her world continued to crumble around her and there was nothing she could do to slow the progression. She feared it was going to be the end of not only her sanity but her immortal soul. Any semblance of honor she once possessed abandoned her. She was becoming her father. A twisted shell of a being incapable of knowing right from wrong. What was worse, part of her didn't mind.

Venom in her eyes, Maleela stared at Thrask's broad back. As much as she wanted to strike his head from his shoulders she recognized that doing so would alienate the rest of the army. She'd follow him in death. Whether Amar Kit'han succeeded or not wasn't her concern. She only wished to visit her personal vengeance on the wrongs committed by her father. All else was secondary by nature. The princess steeled her mind and stomach against the carnage and decided it was time to keep moving.

They marched throughout the night. More than once the princess of Delranan fell asleep in her saddle and would have fallen if not for the strap securing her tightly to the horse. Small, she wasn't meant to be a campaigner. Her life, while largely ignored by her family, was one of stark luxury compared to any other she had traveled with since leaving Chadra Keep in the fall. She was used to sleeping in beds with pillows and down blankets. Eating regular meals of fresh meat and breads. The Goblins lived by baser, harsher standards.

Several had already been killed over fruitless duels the rest reveled in. She'd watched whip masters flog their soldiers to the bone on whims. The madness of their race lacked inspiration despite being contagious. Insanity sparked like actions that revolted Maleela. Until now she'd never thought her life to be sheltered. The random brutality of war skewed all her previously held notions of sensibility. War was brutal, without purpose, and forever changing. One was fortunate if they managed to escape unscathed.

Through her daze she caught sight of a ghastly pale glow. Knowing little of this part of Delranan, Maleela stiffened immediately. The very air held the taint of witchcraft. The tiny hairs on her arms stood on end. She suddenly felt cold, as if the warmth were stolen from her blood. Never had she experienced such vile despair as in those initial moments when she first spied the glow.

Her unease spread through the Goblin ranks. They were naturally superstitious and took no luxury in being near such an unnatural place. The advance ground to a halt despite Thrask and his commanders' vapid urgings. Unused to having his army frightened to inactivity, Thrask snatched a whip and tore through the ranks.

Maleela watched him, hesitant to get involved. She wanted to turn and flee without knowing why. Evil permeated from the ground, seeping into her body. The fear almost subsumed her. Temptation nearly became too great and she almost broke and fled back into the night. Her tiny figure trembled under her riding cloak. Tears welled in her eyes.

"Despair often fuels our emotions, princess."

Maleela froze, instantly recognizing the rasping voice in her ear.

"You mind threatens to shatter under the reality of your situation. Death beckons but you are too afraid to accept his embrace. What tenuous hold remains on your army slips further from your grasp as you linger with indecision."

Clearing her throat, Maleela finally found her voice. "Demon, why do you torment me? Have I not brought your army to war? Give me my father and leave me in peace."

Amar Kit'han hissed laughter. "Peace? There will never be peace in this pathetic kingdom again. Already your people reduce their lives in squalor. They debase themselves on the shrines of forgotten gods who do not answer. Humanity is lost. What delicious atrocities you mortals exact against each other when you think no one is watching."

"What do you want?" she asked. Dark images of families locked in murderous embrace entered her mind. She couldn't fathom a parent willingly trying to kill their own children or vice versa. Head in a fog, Maleela shook violently to clear the images Amar Kit'han had placed in her mind.

The Dae'shan materialized in a shroud of shadows by her side. Only his violent red eyes were visible to the naked eye. "I come to congratulate you, princess. You have delivered the Goblins to Arlevon Gale in time."

Her eyes widened. "We have arrived?"

"Indeed. Begin your deployment immediately. Time is perilously short. Our enemies gather and converge as we speak. You have done well."

Any concept of success failed to translate in her limited scope of reality. Months of constant mental fatigue drove her down. She was a hollow representation of what she'd once aspired to become. Maleela wasn't quite broken but knew that seminal moment wasn't far off. She lacked the core of what she'd once been and needed to find a path of return.

Sensing her quandary, Amar Kit'han pressed his advantage. "You wish to find your father. To confront him for all the wrongs cast upon you over the course of your abused life."

"Yes," she all but whispered.

Amar nodded. "That moment in time approaches. I sense Badron is nearing. If the gods decide to grant your vengeance will you swear fealty?"

She hesitated, suddenly unsure of her true motivations. Her father was bitter, venomous at his core but still responsible for her life. His consuming hatreds were often taken for granted in her mind. But was there basis? Maleela had been largely ignored over the years, shunned at best but never mistreated. Badron kept her away but never went over the top. Had this all been a fabrication in her mind? Months of carefully rehearsed plans and speeches dissolved in her mind.

"He is coming here?" she asked.

"Indeed, though not by means of his choosing," Amar answered. "I will speak no more of this. Deploy your soldiers around the ruins and bring Thrask to me within the temple."

She opened her mouth to speak as he dissolved back into the night, leaving naught but the taint of his vile presence in the air. Maleela felt anger swell within her blackening heart. Her trepidations evaporated as she regained convictions. Her father could wait. Amar Kit'han and his band of demons were her immediate targets. Once vengeance was slaked, she could focus on her dispossessed father.

"General Thrask! Move your forces into position around Arlevon Gale."

SEVENTEEN

A Life Best Lived

Boen grunted as he ripped his massive sword out of his latest victim's chest. Blood and gore fountained, falling in puddles around his boots. The Gaimosian was covered in sweat. His muscles burned from excessive use without proper rest. He'd been on the run for so many hours time meant nothing. An endless stream of corpses traced his path across the wilds of Delranan. Bodies that never would have been this far north if not for the war. Not even a lifetime of combat and violence was enough to keep his great frame moving for much longer. Age and time had not been kind to him.

Vengeance Knights were rare. Their blood was slowly fading from the world's gene pool. Perhaps it was for the best. Theirs was a horrifically violent path only a few could manage without breaking. Boen was over sixty. His body a mass of scar tissues and memories best left forgotten. His beard had filled out since joining Bahr on his foolhardy quest. His wrinkles had deepened. He began to feel the weight of his long years.

A dog barked in the distance. His scent had been picked up. Boen grunted and wiped his sword clean on the body and headed quickly for his horse. He'd already reduced enemy strength by more than a score but it wasn't enough. Skaning had more resources at his disposal and Boen was running out of time. The mercenaries could feasibly keep him occupied for weeks, if not longer. He needed to find a way to force a decisive engagement to link back up with Bahr and the others.

"Damned dogs will track me down," he grumbled as he climbed into the saddle a little slower than usual.

Fresh aches and pains jolted the length of his body, prompting him to wonder if he gained too much weight in his old age. Frowning, the Vengeance Knight forced the thought from his head as it only made him hungry. He didn't recall the last time he'd had the opportunity to eat enough to fuel his massive frame. His horse buckled slightly as he settled into the saddle.

Boen leaned forward and pat him gently on the neck. “I know. I know. It will all be over soon. I figure two more days and nothing else matters. Let’s give these bastards a good show.”

As if bolstered, the horse snickered and stepped forward. Boen decided to follow the near empty streambed tracking east. The direction wouldn’t fool his trackers but it should give him enough time to confuse the dogs and get farther away. A thin layer of ice cracked and broke with each footstep. The sound was like thunder to his sensitive ears. Night was upon him and sound always carried louder on the cool winds of darkness.

Boen followed the stream for close to a half league before exiting the freezing waters on the south bank. Had he been forced to walk it he would have already been suffering with hypothermia or worse. The water barely came up past his mount’s hooves. He wished there were another way, a way to spare his trusted companion of many adventures from nature’s torments, but speed was his best, only hope for survival. There was only so much his sword could accomplish before strength left him vulnerable to enemy blows.

Darkness deepened the longer he rode. Delranan was largely open plains of gently rolling hills and light forests, making his trek easy despite the winter conditions. Heavy cloud cover helped keep what little heat from the sun close to the ground. Boen often reached out to wipe some of the lather from his horse, an act of miniscule kindness not returned. While his horse may be worked up and overheating, Boen didn’t suffer in kind.

He was freezing. Sitting in the saddle, while muscularly tiring, did little to prevent the freezing temperatures from seeping through his cloak and into his bones. Having to wear his armor didn’t help matters but it was a fact he was forced to live with. The boiled leather concealed by wrought iron from the Dwarven smiths in the Bairn Hills was a luxury in personal combat that did little to keep him warm.

Boen suffered in silence, knowing it wouldn't help his cause to complain. Such people often died from their ignorance as the solution to their problems passed them by. He was Gaimosian and in being so was meant to suffer. Whining didn't solve problems. Action and quick thinking did. His mind continually war gamed as he pushed east. Theoretically he held the advantages. Alone and unencumbered by logistics or orders, Boen moved at will and in which direction he needed to take. His only concern was diverting enough of Skaning's mercenaries to give Bahr time to reach Arlevon Gale in time to stop the dark gods.

Skaning didn't have that luxury. His forces were all mercenary from southern or eastern kingdoms. Not a one was a native of Delranan. Their lack of knowledge concerning the terrain matched Boen's, but whereas he was solo, they had to worry overstaying together or coordinating with splinter units ranging across the area of operations. They also had a master to report to. Additional pressure from Skaning left the mercenaries open to minor mistakes that were beginning to cost them lives. Boen took full advantage of their handicaps as he conducted a campaign of lightning-fast raids and executions.

Mercenaries were strong in numbers, but cut off from reinforcements and fresh supplies, they became vulnerable to his particular style of warfare. All he needed to do was stay ahead and continue his guerilla-style assaults. Boen worried that his strength would give out long before he managed to kill all his attackers or enough to force the others to retire. His enemies remained determined, forcing the Gaimosian to stay constantly on the move.

Thus far he'd been fortunate. None of his battles had resulted in any major wounds, though he suffered numerous small cuts and bruises. Boen struggled with the urge to stand his ground and fight. Doing so would only waste his life and delay the mercenaries for mere moments. If they were smart they'd have called for archers. Boen snorted, considering the concept almost cowardly. There was no honor in killing from distance. Gaimosians preferred the intimacy of close combat. There was satisfaction in watching stark realization enter the opponent's eyes the moment he realizes he is doomed.

"Only I'm the one feeling doomed," he grumbled under his breath.

Boen didn't enjoy running. He much preferred a stand-up fight. Skaning's mercenaries, keen to what they were facing, showed increased reluctance to engage him directly. As much as Boen enjoyed the reprieve, he couldn't fall back on it. Sooner or later the enemy was going to grow bold and gain the upper hand. It was only a matter of time. The only way he was going to escape his current situation, one of his own making, was by making the enemy pay so bad they lost hope. He just didn't know how.

Nothing he'd done thus far seemed to matter. He'd laid traps and ambushes for nearly twenty leagues. Bodies piled up in his wake yet still the mercenaries attacked. Boen couldn't figure out their motivation. Even an accomplished Gaimosian Knight with his reputation wasn't worth much of a bounty. What little he knew of Harnin failed to suggest much more than fanatic influence. Skaning and his goons must be operating alone in the hopes of crushing the rebellion. It was the only viable conclusion.

Boen frowned, unable to link a connection with Bahr's group and the rebellion. More so, he couldn't find a reason for Harnin knowing Bahr had returned. Logically it made no sense. There was no way Bahr could have made the return trip from Trennaron so quickly without the assistance of magic. Magic was rare in Malweir. Harnin had little or no reason to believe Bahr had access to magic, not even his failed torture of Anienam Keiss at the beginning of winter provided the One Eye with sufficient information.

Boen secretly began to suspect the Dae'shan had their fingers in more than just Badron's mind. It was the only thought that seemed to click into place. Their foul influence corrupted Badron. It was no great stretch of the imagination to think the same would have happened to Harnin. If that was the case, Bahr and the others were in for a world of hurt. Boen needed to return to the Sea Wolf as quickly as possible with his suspicions. He suddenly feared Bahr was marching into a trap.

"Come on, lad. We've got a long march ahead of us," he whispered to his horse.

Boen awoke with a start. Cursing himself for falling asleep, he dragged his sword from the scabbard and hurried behind a group of iron-grey boulders. Torchlight flickered nearby through the pines. The sound of boots crunching through the snow drifted closer. Boen clutched the leather grips of his sword tighter. His carelessness placed him in direct harm. His body ached worse now than it had before he stopped moving, but sleep wasn't going to be denied. Nearly falling from the saddle, the Gaimosian reluctantly took to ground for much-needed rest. Rest that left him in the middle of an attack.

His enemy wasn't sure of his exact location, else they would have killed him in his sleep and claimed his head for a trophy. Boen was awakened by the scrape of steel on stone. An accident to be sure, but enough of one to alert his keen senses from an unfit slumber. He slowed his breathing, drawing on the inner peace all Gaimosians took into battle. His mind centered. He became focused.

"Horse tracks are everywhere. So where is he?"

"Fool that big can't have disappeared."

"Already killed too many of us for thinking the same. Shut your mouths and keep on your toes. He's crafty, aye, but we got numbers."

Boen's eyes flew open. He marked the voice. The leader always stood out. All Boen had to do was link a face to the voice and remove the mercenary's command structure. The others should buckle under his assault. Torchlight broke through the trees, bathing his hiding space with red-orange light. Six figures followed, weapons drawn and ready. Boen burst from cover without waiting for them to get situated.

The mercenaries jerked back with a start. Boen roared an angry sound like a wounded beast. For the mercenaries, it was a warrior bent on murder. His sword plunged a foot deep into the first mercenary's belly. Blood fountained out of his back as he fell screaming. Ripping the blade free, Boen spun in a full circle while lowering his center of gravity. His backhanded sweep took a second man above the knee. The severed limb flopped away before the rest of the body dropped beside it.

Boen moved quickly and stomped his heavy boot down on his victim's exposed throat. The mercenary died with a loud crunch and soft gurgle. His last move gave the others enough time to recover and they fanned out in a rough semicircle. Their swords were lowered and pointed at him menacingly. Boen found it amusing and hardly the threatening gesture it was meant to be. They almost seemed to be toying with him.

"Got you cornered this time, you bastard," the leader sneered.

Boen offered his most ferocious grin. "Have you?"

"Kill him already. Bastard's already done too many of us."

"Best listen to him. I aim to kill you too," Boen taunted, hoping to force a rash decision.

Four against one wasn't bad odds, but Boen wasn't at his top condition. Tired, hungry, and ready to go south, he needed to find any advantage possible. Mercenaries weren't known for their valor or intelligence. Every so often a rare one took up arms and led his peers. Boen wasn't counting on the slender, foul-looking one calling the shots to be among the best. He pressed harder.

"Come on, scum. That steel's doing nothing but getting cold." He spat at the leader.

It worked. The mercenary captain lunged without thinking. Boen ducked back, raising his sword to block a savage swing. Steel clashed, sending sparks down to the ground. Boen grit his teeth as he absorbed the force of impact. Stronger than the Gaimosian anticipated, the mercenary tried to shove him back. Boen dug in his heels and shoved back.

They stood locked like that for tense seconds. Sweat beaded on their brows. Muscles strained. Boen gradually won. He outweighed the mercenary by a good thirty pounds and was several inches taller. It took longer than he figured but the mercenary was cast back. Boen charged in to finish him off. He slashed with a pair of jabs, taking the enemy off guard. Once he spotted his opening, Boen ripped his sword up diagonally. The tip of his sword caught the mercenary at the base of his throat, tearing out much of his neck and partially decapitating him. Hot blood melted snow. One of the mercenaries doubled over and retched.

Boen continued with a series of well-rehearsed attack moves on the nearest mercenary. Striking from high, the Gaimosian drove down with powerful blows. The strength of his assault forced the surviving enemy back. One tripped over a half-buried root and tried to roll away before he got trampled. Boen leapt over the fallen man and plunged his sword into the soft belly below the mercenary's armor.

Hands reached up to grab his ankle before he could jerk his sword free from the dying mercenary. Boen became off balance and fell. Weaponless, he kicked back and was rewarded with a muffled cry. He felt bone crunch under his boot heel. Both legs freed, Boen pulled himself up and fell on the prone mercenary. He rained down blow after blow on the already ruined face the mercenary was so desperately trying to protect. His defense was nothing compared to the inherent savagery of a Vengeance Knight. Boen didn't stop striking until the mercenary was long dead.

Chest heaving as he struggled to catch his breath, Boen slowly climbed of the corpse. He couldn't feel his hands but knew enough that several knuckles had been split open. He judged at least one finger was broken as well. As much as he would have liked to stop and inspect the damages, Boen lacked time. The mercenaries had alluded to having him painted into a corner, meaning they weren't the only squad in the immediate area.

Boen jerked his sword free, but not before having to put his foot on the corpse's chest and twisting hard. Again, the horrid braying of dogs sang over the night landscape. Prompted to move faster, the Gaimosian hurried back to collect his meager belongings. Using his hands proved overly difficult, making him regret not wearing his riding gloves. He rolled up his sleeping mat as fast as possible and secured it to his saddle bags. Untying his mount from the large-bole pine, Boen climbed aboard and continued the trek east, or so he hoped. With no moonlight to gauge his progress he could only use his internal compass and sense of direction to keep moving in what he hoped was the right direction.

He'd ridden through the remainder of the night and well into the dawn before daring to stop again. The stream had petered out, turning in a direction away from the ruins. Boen kept moving, stopping only long enough to take care of his horse. Both were exhausted and ready for the ordeal to end. Only Boen recognized the importance of the moment. He was supposed to link up with Bahr and the others by tomorrow at the latest. Time was quickly becoming his greatest enemy.

The Delrananian dawn proved uneventful, which suited his liking. He managed a fast meal of dried meat, a wedge of yellow cheese, and old bread before washing it down with stream water. His stomach grumbled for something warm, betraying all that his mind had so delicately established. The water cooled his inner core. Already trying to shiver away the cold from the night, Boen wished he had time for a fire. Instead of worrying over what might have been, he led his horse to the last bend in the stream and let it drink.

The first sign something was wrong came a short while later. He'd grown used to being alone despite numerous engagements with the enemy. Vultures circled ahead, enough to give him cause to worry. The smell came next: an overpowering stench of rotting flesh and spilled blood. Boen knew he needed to investigate, timeline or not. Climbing back into the saddle, horse and rider edged towards the vultures.

Boen crossed a large road littered with thousands of tracks, both horse and boot. His nerves tingled suddenly. Even his horse felt it. He slowed, eyes scanning his surroundings for any signs of mischief. The raw stench became almost overpowering. He kept moving, determined to learn the source of his unease. Boen emerged from behind a screen of boulders and witnessed one of the most horrific scenes in his long life. Nothing he had done came close to comparing to the vast amount of skeletons and partially digested corpses littering the ground for as far as his eyes could see. Boen leaned over and vomited.

EIGHTEEN

Despair

"We should arrive before too long. Another day at the most."

Bahr looked to Ingrid with a combination of doubt and worry.

As much as she tried to cling to hope, Ingrid slowly came to realize that their situation was growing increasingly dire. Bahr failed to get an accurate read on her despite multiple conversations and strategy sessions. Frustrated, he gradually accepted that she was his only chance for reaching his goal.

"I don't like it," he replied. "We've been hounded since returning to Delranan. Why has the enemy abandoned their hunt now?"

"You question being left alone?"

"I question the sudden change of tactics with us so close to Arlevon Gale," he answered.

Ingrid's blue eyes narrowed ever so slightly. "I've come to accept these moments as tender mercies best left unquestioned, Sea Wolf. Be thankful Harnin's killers aren't on our heels. I fear we'll all have need of strength before this ends."

Bahr held his tongue. Flashbacks of the ruins of Chadra continued to haunt him. It was a moment he didn't speak of, fearing it would invoke animosity among the two groups. She'd been there, but not after the fall. For him to recite what he witnessed would not only show incredible insensitivity but also demonstrate an ill-perceived weakness built into the rebellion. Bahr was no stranger to creating waves but not without proper cause. Reluctant as he was to admit it, the Sea Wolf needed Ingrid's fighters if he ever hoped to break through enemy lines and destroy the Olagath Stone.

"We must be ready to abandon Delranan if there is any chance of victory," he told her without pause. "I don't believe we can win if we hold on to the cities and villages."

Ingrid fumed. Her cheeks flushed. “That is all we have left. These people cling to the promise our rebellion offers. We can fight, but won’t win without their support, Bahr. Most are displaced, disenfranchised to the point they seek to flee south in the vain hopes of escaping this conflict. Even if they succeed our cause will suffer.”

“Hasn’t there been enough suffering? Delranan isn’t destroyed yet. We can rebuild the cities and grow new crops. It’s the people that matter most,” he defended.

“The old kingdom is dead, Bahr. It falls upon us to rebuild what little remains,” she told him. Her blunt tone left no doubt of her intentions.

His eyes widened. “You seek to reestablish the throne?”

“Would that not be the prudent course? Delranan needs leadership. Strong leadership capable of seeing her through these dark times. While I have no aspirations of claiming the crown I am desperately seeking qualified people. No, I’m not about to begin courting you. You’ve made it clear you want no part in the politics of the day.”

Her mood soured. She knew Bahr was the legitimate answer to all their problems but he was too stubborn, too stuck in an old train of thought to push aside his misgivings and do what was right for all. That left her with few choices. Orlek and Harlan would push for her to take the throne, but she wasn’t a ruler. Leading the rebellion hadn’t been her objective when the war started. She only assumed the position when Inaella and the previous council failed utterly.

“Bahr, I don’t mean to force you into a decision you have no desire in making. This isn’t your war, nor do I expect you to commit. We each have different paths to walk. You claim the very gods themselves have anointed your band to stop a war far surpassing the scope of our humanity. Who am I to disagree after all I’ve seen? If you must take the fight to the enemy in the old ruins we will accompany you to the forest edge as agreed.

“There our partnership ends. You fight your battles and I will take the rebellion to fight ours. Harnin One Eye needs to answer for his sins," she said with resolve Bahr admired.

"What happens when this ends? Will any of us be able to return to our old lives?" he asked without expecting an answer.

Ingrid surprised him. "Does it matter? There is no going back into the past. What's done is done. All we have is to look forward to the next dawn."

Bahr appreciated her words but heard them laced with futility. "I wonder if that will be enough. Maybe Dorl is right. Maybe it's best if we all just disappeared back into obscurity." He snorted. "The wizard wouldn't agree. The old fool is convinced we are here to serve some higher purpose that's been building for thousands of years."

"Anienam is a sage man. I wish I had a dozen like him."

Bahr laughed; a warm, tender sound as genuine as it was mirthful. "He's crazy enough to make anyone take to the cups. The old coot is half mad but a decent enough sort when you get past his mannerisms. I'm still trying to figure out if he's insane or just playing at it."

"He does seem a bit eccentric," she agreed. "But a valuable asset nonetheless."

"No arguments there. We would have been killed a long time ago if not for him," Bahr added. He and Anienam continued to think on separate paths but their wounds were slowly healing.

"Yet you torment him to no ends," Ingrid added, choosing her words carefully so as not to provoke another fit.

Bahr didn't have a reply. They were opposing personalities thrust into a rigid situation not of their choosing. He wondered what life would have been like had he not been born royalty and perhaps Anienam was passed over by Dakeb the Mage all those years ago. Would destiny still have found a way to involve them in this sordid tale? He supposed wondering didn't do anything productive. Their lot was cast and it would all be over in the next day or so. Live or die, he was at the end of the journey. At last.

There was no anticipation of what was to come. He wasn't the sort prone to worrying over life or death. Everyone ended up in the same place. Whether by fire or earth, darkness returned to claim them all. Bahr felt the irresistible pull of Lord Death growing as his days waned. The autumn of his life was quickly changing to winter and there was nothing he could do to prevent it. His time was nearly up, forcing him to stark conclusions a younger person wouldn't associate with. Bahr knew he was going to die. Perhaps not in the coming battle, but in the immediate years ahead. Already sixty, he was tired and ready to move on. After all, there was only so much one could accomplish in six decades.

"I do, but not without reason. He is enigmatic, making it difficult to relate to. We've all had our doubts about him over the course of the quest. He speaks in riddles and often holds back pertinent information, though for what purpose we don't know. I don't trust him, but I've come to respect him. Anienam may not be like other men, but he is most useful in tight situations."

Ingrid glanced over to him. The soft curve of her face reminded him of simpler times. "You have the oddest assortment of traveling companions I have ever heard of. These must truly be foul times for a company of misfits to hold a Dwarf, Giant, wizard, and Gaimosian." She paused. "I must admit I find that woman, Rekka Jel, intriguing."

Bahr nodded. "She is at that. I don't know what made me take her aboard when we left port, but she's got the fighting spirit of a berserker. I wouldn't cross swords with her if my life depended on it."

They rode on in silence for a while, each enjoying the illusion of solitude while in the company of several hundred others. The column of rebels stretched out behind them like a lazy snake crawling across the face of the world. Old legends spoke of a giant wyrm that would come at the end of the world to devour all unsuspecting souls. Only the bravest would band together and defeat the great wyrm but at terrible cost. Bahr wondered if the wyrm had been loosed upon the world and was slowly heading for him.

Far from superstitious, Bahr dismissed the ancient folklore for what it was. Myths were often forgotten over time while legends tended to live on. Bahr was living in an age of rising legends but the future was no place for the living. He turned his thoughts inward. It had been too many years since he had time, or the effort, to think of himself.

The rebellion finished what he never had the courage to start. He harbored no love for the rest of Delranan but struggled with the pain of so much heartbreak and devastation visited upon his people. Ingrid presented him with another side he'd seldom considered. The people were strong. Even after so much, they remained a force to be reckoned with. Bahr felt pride knowing he came from such stock but wasn't comfortable with the idea of belonging. Delranan wasn't his home anymore.

He'd lost everything but had gained a brand new world, a new life, to explore. The son of a king had gone on to visit Venheim and Trennaron. He'd drunk mead with a Dwarf king and battled impossible demon figures halfway across Malweir. How many others could claim such without falsifying their deeds? Yet of all the places he'd seen during his travels he could think of none suitable to call home. Perhaps he was becoming more like Boen than he wished to admit. Or perhaps, just perhaps, he already was exactly like the wandering Gaimosian.

Sudden commotion ahead of the column broke his train of thought. Bahr squinted into the midday sun. A handful of riders approached. Most were Ingrid's outriders. Two weren't. Bahr frowned the closer they came. The two strangers were haggard looking. Their clothes were torn and covered with old blood. He could see their eyes now and the sight chilled his blood. They were scared to death. Both shook uncontrollably, threatening to topple from the saddle.

Ingrid spurred her horse forward to meet them, forcing Bahr to catch up. She glanced at the newcomers over once and tried to keep the dismay from her face. "Gentlemen, welcome."

"Ma'am, we spotted these two riding like demons down from the north," one of her outriders explained. "Neither been able to speak yet. We figure they run into some pretty nasty action with Commander Harlan's troops."

"How do you figure they're with Harlan?" she asked, stiffening.

"Well ma'am, you can't really see it but they got the proper insignia sewn into their tunics," the second outrider told her.

Ingrid's blood went cold. Horrible images of what might have happened to Harlan and his column played havoc with her nerves. He was responsible for nearly nine hundred fighters. If the others were in the same condition as the pair sitting before her, she worried greatly. Fully a third of her field force might easily have been destroyed.

Ingrid felt pity for the pair but as a commander she lacked the luxury of expressing such. She licked her lips. "Trooper, what happened to you? Where is Commander Harlan?"

One of Harlan's people slowly raised his gaze, the thousand-yard stare looking far beyond Ingrid and Bahr. When he spoke, his words were broken, horrified. "He…they…all dead. We just mana…."

The onslaught of tears sent his haggard body into convulsions, effectively cutting off what little conversation remained. His mind hovered over the faintest definition of snapping, leaving him lost in the void until Lord Death came to claim him. Ingrid almost hoped it would be soon. No one deserved to live like this.

"All dead? How is this possible? He had one of the largest forces in western Delranan." She fumed, failing to admit the only possible conclusion. Harlan must have run across the Goblin army and been obliterated.

"Can we verify this?" Bahr said, speaking quickly to maintain Ingrid's grasp of power. Any lack of decisiveness would instantly erode her already tenuous hold on the fragments of the rebellion. "We need to have proof before we act."

"Lord Bahr, I've already ordered a pair of scouts to check the area these two came from," the lead outrider said with rigid formality.

Bahr waved his protocol off. "I'm no lord. Bahr is enough. Let us know the moment they return. If Harlan ran into what I think he did we all might be in trouble."

The Sea Wolf cast a worried glance to Ingrid, who merely sat atop her horse with trembling lips and fresh doubts darkening her eyes. Keeping her on course was going to prove problematic. From what he knew, she was the sort who was governed by her emotions.

Ingrid stared deeply into the fire without blinking. Her hands shook, ever so slightly, but enough for Bahr to take notice. She'd barely uttered a word since the bloodied survivors of Harlan's column arrived. The inconceivable had just happened and her power was greatly reduced. She lost the end of the war from her vision, knowing that Harnin One Eye would take his murderous forces west and crush her without effort. She had nothing left with which to stop him. Months of constant struggle and overriding sorrow crashed down around her carefully constructed world. She had failed.

Unused to giving in to tragedy, Bahr resisted the urge to reach out and slap Ingrid back to reality. She needed a firm yet cautious hand. Too much force would push her deeper into the misery of her mind's construction. The rebellion, and his cause as well, would be lost in mere moments.

"Ingrid, you still have almost two thousand people to see to," he said. His tone was gentle, quiet. "You can't be seen like this."

"And offer them false hope?" she replied. Venom dripped from her words. "It's over, Bahr. I failed. All this time I thought I was leading our people to victory but have only succeeded in getting them slaughtered. I wish I had never taken control."

"Talking like that will only make you more miserable. You can't change the past, Ingrid. Believe me. I've spent countless nights staring at the ceiling thinking about what I could have done differently. None of that matters. The only thing you need to do is look to tomorrow."

"To what point? I'm a fraud. This rebellion was doomed from the onset."

Frowning, Bahr decided to scold her like a small child. "Enough of this. Wars are fluid. Some days there is victory. Others defeat. You're a leader, whether you can handle it or not doesn't matter. These people look to you for guidance. What good will it do them to find you wallowing in your self-pity while the same despair creeps through their hearts? They need you. They need to see you sitting atop your horse with a rigid back and clear eye. These people are willing to fight and die for you. Don't abandon them now just because you've had a setback."

"Setback?" Her eyes flared hotly as she looked him in the eye. "Nine hundred of my fighters were killed by an impossible army. You and I both know it was the Goblins that did this. Even if Harlan had escaped what good would his paltry-sized force do to aid us against tens of thousands?"

"That's not your concern," Bahr told her. "All you have to do is see these people through the dark times. Find a way to win at all costs or fold back into the night. You've already fought a guerilla campaign. Your people know what to do. Have confidence in them and I doubt you'll be disappointed."

"I won't order them to their deaths. Our original agreement was to see your party to the ruins. My rebels were supposed to liberate Chadra."

Bahr paused, debating what to tell her. In the end, there was little real choice. She needed to know what he had seen in the capital city. The pain and distress of rampant destruction never dreamed of in Delranan. "There is no Chadra left to liberate, Ingrid. The city is completely destroyed."

"I warned you not to go back," she scolded.

He shrugged. Her wants didn't matter much. They seldom did. Bahr was used to dealing in needs, not wants, though he contradictorily forced his wants on them all. "I had to. This is still my kingdom, whether I want to be in control or not. Chadra's not the question. You need to come to a conclusion real quick about which way you're going to turn."

"How can it be that easy? When have you ever lost so much?"

Her scathing retort invoked unpleasant memories of watching his estate burn to the ground even as his beloved *Dragon's Bane* drifted to ashes across the harbor. How could he accurately explain he'd lost everything over the course of the winter without provoking further indignation? Unaccustomed to explaining his deeds, Bahr became infuriated.

"I have lost everything I ever loved and knew. What you see before you is all I have left. Don't you dare cry to me about loss. You said yourself I should be on the throne. I have no family. No home. No ship. I have only these hands and the quest Anienam Keiss has deemed me responsible enough to perform. When you have lost as much as I you can come and debate the morality of my decisions, but not a moment before."

Rebuked, Ingrid sank deeper into her blanket. Her shoulders sagged. The wrinkles around the corners of her eyes deepened. She felt the weight of another thirty years heaped upon her. Nine hundred souls reached out from the grave to condemn her for her sins. Ingrid hadn't known very many of them. She hadn't needed to. They were each valuable contributions to the kingdom and her efforts to return Delranan to normalcy. They were the future. And she had failed them all. The grief threatened to become too much.

Tears flowed freely. She didn't want them to stop. Her body racked with sobs but it felt good. Bahr leaned over and wrapped a fatherly arm around her. He enjoyed her company. She had sharp wit and was more than capable of handling her own on the battlefield, at least from what he'd seen. The rebellion still needed her. She was the backbone of their force. Their singular point of focus for hope and the future.

"Ingrid, I know you don't want to hear this. Especially now, but I need you to come back to me. Yes, nine hundred are dead but you still have nearly two thousand more looking to you. How do you want to be remembered? As the one who led her people to victory or the one who tucked her tail and ran the moment things got tough?"

Ingrid continued to cry.

Bahr continued, "Listen to me. This isn't the time for weakness. You need to take this sorrow, harness it and use it. Feed your anger with it and focus on tomorrow. The rebellion isn't dead. You're still the leader. Get out there. Tell them what they need to hear. Say anything. Just keep them moving forward. The rest will work itself out but it has to happen now."

She choked back her tears. Bahr's words slowly broke through her mental barrier. She found the slightest measure of courage deep within the reservoir of her heart and clung to it with all her might. Ingrid was a generally strong woman. After all she'd endured, from her husband's death to Harlan's massacre, she was the only one who had the ability to find a way to win. Bahr had given her the words necessary to carry on. The rest was up to her.

"Very well, what do I need to do?" she asked after wiping her tears away.

Bahr grinned. "That's a girl. We might have a chance to win after all."

NINETEEN

Honor Due

The rebels gathered nervously as they waited on Ingrid. Word had shuffled through the makeshift camp to assemble almost as quickly as what had happened to Harlan's column. Threats of desertion were rampant. Her officers struggled to maintain control despite their own misgivings. Everyone knew about the Goblin threat and it stretched the edges of their courage just to keep going day to day. The suddenness of their slaughter left many wondering just how much longer they could stomach a never-ending war.

Ingrid walked up onto the small platform a pair of former carpenters had made and surveyed her crowds. This wasn't how she wanted to speak with her people. They deserved better than a figurehead separated from them. Ingrid shocked Orlek and Bahr by climbing down from the platform and walking into the center of the camp. She spied Groge, the young Giant, at the back of the crowd. The innocence on his face was refreshing.

She raised her hands to quiet the chorus of murmurs, speaking only after silence settled over them. "My friends, it grieves me to confirm what most of you have already known. Harlan and his company have been killed. We suspect the Goblins did it but haven't been able to confirm so yet. I know many of you had friends, even family, in his units. Nothing I say can bring them back so I won't try. I won't insult you by saying they died for the kingdom or for you. They were ruthlessly murdered by our enemies."

Several broke out in cries. Others wailed their grief. Ingrid felt her heart burn with each raised voice. She wanted to join them but couldn't. Bahr had called it right. The rebellion needed her to be strong for them all.

"I know the urge to run away is in many of your hearts, for I once felt it too. My heart can only handle so much, but as easy as it would have been for me to abandon you under the cover of darkness I couldn't. You deserve better. We all deserve better. I won't make promises of vengeance. What I do offer is the opportunity to avenge your loved ones. To preserve their memories through your deeds. Your valor. The old kingdom is dead. It falls upon us to recreate the world as we see fit. The question is not who wants to go into battle beside me, but who will?"

Slowly, almost imperceptibly at first, the rebels broke out in ragged applause. Ingrid felt a great weight pulled from her. They were battered, beaten, and pushed to the breaking point, but the rebels of Delranan carried an unquenchable spark. Their kingdom was in flames. Their backs threatening to break. As easy as it would have been to turn and run, not a single person listening to Ingrid moved.

They realized that they were all that was left to defend and protect the people. Should they abandon sword and spear, the people of Delranan would methodically be wiped from existence. Not a soul among them was willing to let that happen, not without fighting to the last beforehand. Ingrid's heart swelled with pride. The sting of losing so many, and such a close confidant as Harlan, lessened ever so slightly. She felt pride again at the fighting spirit of her people. Bahr was right. They didn't look to him, for they never had. All eyes were fixed on her, eager to see how she handled the situation and took them to the next level.

"Sleep well this night, for it will be our last for some time. Tomorrow I intend on taking a small force to bury the remains of our friends. We will pause to give memory to their lives and deeds. After that we march with Bahr to the ruins of Arlevon Gale and meet our enemies head-on! We fight for the future of our very race."

She paused as cheers ringed the crowd again. "I will not order you to follow blindly. Those of you who wish to leave may do so with my blessing and good will. This will be no easy task and I fear many of us will not survive. Win or lose we will make such a name for ourselves that all history will tremble from awe!"

Ingrid walked off amidst undying cheers. Her voice carried conviction she hadn't felt since the beginning of the war. Proud of herself beyond measure, the blond warrior-queen of Delranan hurried to make plans. Much remained to be done if she was going to get her army to Arlevon Gale in time.

Two hundred volunteers marched behind her. They walked with dour faces and steeled resolve. Sword and shovel were sheathed and slung over their shoulders. The ground was much too frozen to dig in, so Ingrid and a handful of engineers devised a strategy to cover the remains with stone and pine boughs until the spring thaw. Some would be burned so that their trapped spirits would return to the gods. The rest would have to wait for months, if any rebels managed to return at all.

Ingrid marched at their head, her shoulders back and erect. She neglected taking her horse, knowing it would go further among her rebels to present herself as one of them rather than in charge. Bahr and Anienam accompanied them, the spindly wizard sitting aside a swayback horse. He cackled with bad jokes in an attempt at livening the mood. He failed. The rebels were too entrenched in their moods to think positively.

"How much further?" Bahr asked Ingrid.

She gestured ahead. "Not much. We should be there before too long. The scouts have already come back with reports the area is clear of enemy activity."

"That doesn't mean they aren't hiding somewhere. Goblins are known for their dislike of sunlight. They might easily be holed up for the day," he countered.

"With fifty thousand warriors? Where in Delranan could a force that large hide undetected? No, Bahr, I believe my scouts."

Ingrid fell silent, her thoughts already racing ahead to the scene she was about to witness. Her stomach felt ill and it was going to take all her inner strength to maintain control in front of the others when the killing grounds came into view. She'd grown accustomed, reluctantly, to the horrors of warfare but worried it might not be enough. Some atrocities just shouldn't be glossed over, especially when it concerned a full third of her fighting strength.

"Been lost like a pickle in a tree!" Anienam exploded suddenly and burst out in laughter.

Bahr's mouth fell open as he turned back to stare at the wizard. "Have you gone daft?"

Anienam broke his laughter. "Eh? What's your problem now? I haven't done anything wrong. Just minding myself and passing the time."

"With dreams of pickles?" Ingrid asked.

The wizard shrugged. "I like pickles. Crunchy or soft they both taste good. It's been a long time since I last enjoyed a good pickle."

"But what would one be doing in a tree?" she asked.

"Ha! Exactly my point!" Anienam fell back into a fit. Tears leaked from the corners of his eyes and down past his blindfold. He mumbled under his breath. "Pickles in a tree. As if!"

Ingrid looked back at Bahr. "Perhaps I was mistaken. He definitely seems to have cracked his skull."

"More times than I can remember, but I'm far from done. Don't you fret any. Just because I'm blind doesn't make me feeble. You'll see. You all will, I'm afraid. There's a terrible storm coming that none of us can escape."

"Thank you, Master Keiss, but I will keep to my own consort for the time being," Ingrid replied, her voice terse, strained.

"Still think so highly of him?" Bahr whispered.

Ingrid shot him an angry glare.

Work was slow, many pausing long enough to vomit. Rags were wrapped around mouths and noses to prevent the stench from overpowering them. Most of the corpses had been all but devoured, whether by Goblins or carrion eaters remained unknown. The rebels were slow at first. More than one made warding signs against evil while others closed their eyes to pray. Ingrid offered her prayers to the gods with less conviction than a season before. Bahr's explanation of his quest left the foundations of her faith shaken.

She personally counted more than seven hundred remains. Bodies wasn't a fair term considering so many had been devoured. Blood trails dragged off eastward into the snow. No doubt the Goblin army took the other bodies to consume along their march. It sickened her to think that Harlan was reduced to a meal without consideration of his rank or stature. All these bodies deserved better. They were the best Delranan had to offer, now nothing more than passing indigestion for the filth of a horrid race. Ingrid vowed to avenge them all.

"There's more at work here than a mere ambush," Bahr offered after exploring the immediate area around the slaughter. "Bits of armor and scraps of uniform. Your rebels aren't equipped like that."

"What are you saying?"

He pointed towards the road leading north. "I'd guess that Harlan ambushed a company of Harnin's forces before the Goblins struck. There are broken spears and spent arrows littering both sides of the road for a few hundred meters. One thing is for certain, there was a lot of fighting going on here yesterday."

"That makes sense. With his force engaging the enemy it would be easy for the Goblins to sneak up on them," Ingrid said thoughtfully. "He was no fool but becoming engrossed in a battle would take his eyes of the road, especially if he was certain the way was clear."

"Making the rebels easy targets," Bahr concluded. "This is more dangerous than I feared. Not only do we need to contend with a fanatical Skaning but now the Goblin horde. We'll get pinched between the two if we're not careful."

Ingrid grasped the gravity of their situation and felt her heart freeze. Logic suggested Skaning and Harnin's loyalists would abandon their attack on the rebels with the new, and far greater, threat the Goblins presented. No one could accurately say how such an army had arrived in Delranan but that didn't matter. The enemy had increased tenfold and possibly more in a short period of time. She couldn't realistically fight both sides but offering a ceasefire with Harnin wasn't possible. Skaning would stop at nothing to murder every last rebel and more than likely viewed the slaughter as a movement in his favor. The war would go on until no one in Delranan remained.

"What are we going to do?" She lowered her voice so only Bahr could hear. Ingrid had already avoided one panic. Driving them into another served no purpose.

Bahr placed his feet shoulder-width apart and his gnarled hands on his hips. He honestly didn't have an answer. "So much of my life has been driving forward, always moving towards a fixed location in the future. None of this makes any sense. Nothing Anienam or Artiss Gran said mentioned anything like this. My gut tells me to keep moving. Our mission is to destroy the Olagath Stone and thus save the rest of the world."

"Lofty aspirations but all this changes matters," Ingrid said.

"Indeed, but we can't turn back now. Too much is at stake."

He thought about telling her more, about how each one of his group had been handpicked by destiny to stop the dark gods. How could he possibly expect her to believe such mystic nonsense when he was still having issues with the concept?

"Do you truly believe you can alter the course of the world?"

Bahr offered a sly grin. "I certainly hope so."

The last remains were buried shortly before dusk. All told, there were more than eight hundred distinguishable remains. Most were undeniably human while a small portion were denser, shorter. At least Harlan had taken a toll on the enemy. Perhaps not as much as Bahr would have liked, but there was only so much a paltry force could do against fifty thousand. Smoke from the funeral pyres rose high into the fading daylight.

Bahr stared up at the smoke for a moment before turning away. He'd already secured permission to take a handful of Ingrid's best and scout the northern road in the hopes of ascertaining the truth of their predicament. Every minor bit of intelligence helped him form his final plans for the assault of Arlevon Gale. He feared he was going to need more than he was about to receive.

Anienam argued otherwise. The wizard's faith in his own capabilities clearly outweighed Bahr's. With talk of pickles subsided, the wizard agreed to wait behind with Ingrid. He quietly urged that time was nearly upon them. Only one more day and the Dae'shan would attempt to open the gateway between dimensions. Bahr had little time to dally with personal quests.

The Sea Wolf made it less than a third of a league before his senses began acting up. He drew his sword and tensed. Experienced eyes scanned the perimeter, catching every broken branch or disturbed patch of snow. The others crouched behind him, nerves getting the better of them. Bahr cursed silently at their skittishness. He wished for Ironfoot or Nothol and Dorl. They wouldn't shirk away from enemy contact.

"You can put the sword away."

Bahr froze before recognizing the voice. His grip on the sword loosened, slightly. Frowning, Bahr rose to full height. "You're not supposed to be here."

Boen stepped out from his cover with his hands empty just in case one of the rebels was armed with a crossbow and too thickheaded to recognize him. "I got lost and you showed up."

They embraced as brothers, Bahr perhaps the gladder of the two. "You look terrible."

"Ha, I feel worse. Skaning's mercenaries have had me on the run since I broke with you guys. There were a few moments I didn't think I was going to make it," the Gaimosian admitted. "Glad to see you."

"You too, but I don't think you understand the gravity of the situation we've landed in. There's more at work than just Skaning or Harnin."

Boen nodded, his face turned grim. "I know. The Goblins have struck. I stumbled on the scene earlier in the day. Damned nasty sight if you ask me. I don't think I've seen one worse. Any sign of them now?"

"No but we have to assume they're heading for the same place we are," Bahr answered.

"Doesn't look like any of us are meant to survive."

"Sure doesn't."

Boen scratched the stubble on his chin. "So what's our next move?"

"We don't really have a choice. Ingrid and her crew have finished taking care of the remains. We need to get back to the main body and drive on to Arlevon Gale. One way or another the war is going to end in the next two days," Bahr said.

"Guess there's no point in wasting time." He left the obvious unspoken. Should the Goblins reach the ruins first and have time to emplace, there was every likelihood of Bahr not breaking through to stop the ritual.

"What's he doing here?" Ingrid asked. The surprise in her voice bordered on suspicion. Gaimosians were a level up from mercenaries in her opinion. It wasn't inconceivable that he might have switched sides for personal gain.

"I got tired of wandering through the wilderness. Skaning's people aren't half as tough as they pretended," Boen answered with a deep rumble.

Bahr shifted his gaze between the two, picking up on the almost miniscule tension springing to life between them. *Just what I need, yet another power struggle in the group. What did I do to deserve this?*

"We're losing time here, Ingrid," he intervened before anything damaging was said. Bahr made a mental note to confront her once they were alone.

Her eyes flashed a hint of anger before her mask settled back into place. "Of course. The others must be growing concerned by now. Form up!"

Bahr fell into line beside her and began the short march back to the rebels. His mind was locked in a spiral of conflicting policies. At some point he was going to have to decide on which one was best to follow.

Orlek paced nervously around the supply wagon. His face was twisted in concern. Hands clasped tightly behind his back, the rebel leader walked faster the more he became worried. Ironfoot emptied his pipe on a boot heel and frowned. Still a stranger to Men and their unnecessarily intricate ways, the Dwarf resisted the urge to reach out and slap Orlek.

"Would you relax already?" he growled.

Orlek paused in midstride. "How am I supposed to do that? She never should have gone out there in the first place!"

"She doesn't seem the sort to take orders easily," Ironfoot replied. "That's the kind you want with you when things get dark."

"Ingrid is almost as stubborn as I am, making it harder to accept her place in this mess. We can't afford to lose her."

Ironfoot's thick, bushy eyebrow rose sharply. "We or you?"

Orlek gaped in shock. Until now he'd believed their love was secret. If it was that transparent to the Dwarf, how much worse was it to the rest of the rebellion? The consequences might become disastrous if word got out and it was received wrong.

Ironfoot chuckled. "Love is love. Doesn't matter what the race is. You have it in your eyes, Orlek. I'd be willing to bet there's plenty of folks here that picked up on it long before I did."

"Damned if that don't confuse all," Orlek muttered after regaining his wits. "Here I was worried over keeping the matter private and it's been written on my face the whole time. What would you do in my place?"

"Dwarf women are slightly fiercer than Humans. They tend to leave lumps on the skull. More than one warrior was forced to take a day of rest for being pigheaded."

Orlek grinned. "Yourself included?"

The Dwarf captain shrugged and barked a laugh. "Never said I was perfect."

"Excuse me, Commander, but Lady Ingrid has returned."

Orlek returned the makeshift salute of the courier. "Thank you. Inform group leaders to ready the march. We should be leaving shortly. I want scouts and flankers assembled in ten minutes. We're not stopping until we reach the ruins."

Another salute and the courier was away, leaving Orlek and Ironfoot alone again. The Dwarf chewed idly on a green stem, giving Orlek time to get his mind right. Some things needed to be overcome internally. Hefting his axe, Ironfoot gave a chuckle and ambled back to his group. No doubt Bahr would have plenty to discuss upon his return. Fond memories of his wife waiting back in Drimmen Delf kept him warm while he walked.

He found Bahr, along with Boen, already talking with the others. Ironfoot was just as surprised as the rest had been upon seeing the Gaimosian back among them. He had quietly figured never to see the big man again. Few were capable of fighting off a few hundred determined enemies. Still, it did much for morale to have Boen back. Ironfoot doubted even the stalwart Vengeance Knight would be enough to help turn the tide.

"…way I figure it we need to come in slow under the cover of night. There are no maps of the ruins and I haven't been there since I was child," Bahr said and paused. "Ironfoot, is all well?"

"Aye, was just conversing with Orlek. When are we leaving?" the Dwarf answered.

"Now. We're out of time."

Drums began to beat, sounding the call to march. Bahr rolled up his parchment and stuffed it back into his shoulder pack. Rebels formed ranks for accountability before joining the long column of march. Bahr and his group stood off to the side at the head. Their task was the main focus with the rebels being secondary players. The Sea Wolf looked back over the hundreds of Delrananians waiting to make the fateful walk to what would amount to slaughter on a scale none could comprehend. He didn't know why, but pride swelled in heart. He may not be the king, but these were his people nonetheless. Bahr found the task ahead slightly more manageable than a moment before.

TWENTY

Decision Point

Skaning folded his looking glass. Confusion twisted his features. He'd lost countless lives and valuable time in Harnin's court attempting to hunt down first Ingrid and now Boen. Weeks lost on the vain pursuit of glory. His dreams of catching and killing the king's brother while ending the rebellion would force Harnin to elevate him to a major leadership position, possibly next in line for the throne. That dream shattered like fresh ice striking stone.

He watched what had to be the full might of the rebel army assemble and strike east. There was no mistaking the Giant at the head of the column, meaning Bahr was with them. What dark alliance had they made and where were they going? Skaning wished he knew. His enemies had formed an alliance of convenience. His strength diminished to the point of combat ineffectiveness, Skaning could do little more than watch his dreams march under the boots of two thousand rebels.

His mercenaries presented another problem. Their last encounter with the Gaimosian turned many squeamish, forcing their dissent and the call for abandoning their job. Skaning had nothing to offer when they'd paid with nearly thirty lives. Many wanted to turn on Skaning and collect payment, thinking the rebels would be eager to have such a worthy prize presented. They spoke when they thought he wasn't listening, but word spread quickly in small camps. Skaning decided there was but one move he could make before the mercenaries came for his head.

"Captain Arle, summon the command. We have new orders."

The mercenaries, clearly unhappy with their lot, swore to conduct their task with their all. Never had they been this close to their ultimate goal, and payment. Skaning had sent the word for all splinter cells to return to the main body. They raced ahead of the rebels, hoping to get into ambush position in time to kill both Ingrid and Bahr before the rebels managed to gather their wits.

Dressed only in dark colors and without cumbersome armor, they stalked across the snow like arctic predators. Any metal objects were secured to their bodies to prevent excess noise. Their faces and hands were painted with charcoal. Weapons were blackened to prevent moonlight from giving them away. Secrecy was their only advantage. Secrecy and the rebels not suspecting such a bold move this far from their camps.

Skaning ran with them. He had little choice. The mercenaries would have killed him if he tried to back away. Men seldom risked their lives for others without proper cause. Mostly honorless, the mercenaries' foul-tempered glares were enough to force Skaning's actions. It had been a long time since he'd raised a sword in battle. What was supposed to be a punitive mission against Jarrik and Inaella left his honor dissatisfied. Jarrik had committed suicide and the pock-faced woman was nowhere to be seen. This raid was his only chance at redemption.

The mercenaries moved with surprising speed. Well-fed and hydrated, they practically sprinted across the windswept plains separating them from their prey. Skaning felt exhilarated. The thrill of the hunt caught in his veins and he quickly lost himself to the chase. There was untold promise with each movement. Lord Death followed in his chariot, gleefully riding their trail of disaster to the inevitable conclusion.

They were well beyond the point of turning back. Skaning committed the entirety of his force on one fatal move. More than likely he would only succeed in getting his command killed, but there was always that miniscule chance that they would kill their targets in the process. Ending the rebellion was his only official task but that had devolved into a quest for revenge. Ingrid and Bahr had conspired to murder a fourth of his crack forces, no doubt willing to continue until all were dead. This was more than personal now.

Talking quickly turned to hand signals. Skaning halted as his mercenaries dropped to their knees and drew their weapons. Footsteps and the jangle of armor and wagons could be heard coming down the abandoned lane. Skaning grinned savagely as he spied the first hints of torchlight dancing of the surrounding trees. They'd done it. They'd gotten ahead of the rebellion and taken them unawares. The lord of Delranan drew his sword and waited.

Cold breath came out in plumes of mist. His chest heaved from exertion. Young and relatively in shape, he hadn't expected to cover such long distances. The mercenary nearest cast an angered glance back to Skaning at the sound of his breathing, fearing it would give them away. The drawn dagger cupped at his waist told Skaning he was dead if he didn't get his breathing under control.

A pair of crossbowmen rose slightly, just enough for Skaning to catch their actions. No doubt others on both sides of the road were doing the same. He gripped his sword tighter. The first rebel scout came into view and was murdered from behind. Throat cut, the rebel died with a muffled cry as his body was dragged into the woods. The whiz of arrows cutting through the night air followed by high-pitched cries suddenly erupted around him. Skaning got caught up in the fervor, adding his roar to the others as he burst from cover and attacked.

Groge yawned, his great mouth a seemingly endless vacuum capable of swallowing the world. Tired, the young Giant was still capable of going several more days before needing to rest. His strength reserves far outlasted the others but he was part of a team and acquiesced to their needs and desires in the name of friendship and camaraderie. He had come to enjoy their banter, though far from professing to understand it. Most of all he appreciated the taciturn Dwarf. They were closest in kin despite their obvious size difference.

Ironfoot marched opposite of the Giant. They had the best night vision of the entire column and Bahr had no qualms about throwing them to the head of the column. The Dwarf relished the chance to show his tactical prowess this deep into what he considered enemy territory. Anienam reassured him the ruins were still too far away to worry about the Goblin army. All they needed to do was keep a clear eye out for roving patrols. No one in the command structure believed they were going to run into anything substantial. All thought was focused on the coming struggle against the Dae'shan and their army.

The unlikely pair was less than fifty meters behind Ingrid's scouts. With thoughts turned inward, the rebel army marching behind them, Groge and Ironfoot failed to spy the hidden enemy lurking ahead before they managed to kill the first of Ingrid's forces. Ironfoot reacted first, drawing his axe and ducking behind an ash tree. He bellowed warning back to the column moments before dark-clothed mercenaries burst from the shadows.

Groge stared down at the smaller figures in shock. A month ago he wouldn't have known how to react, but the series of running engagements with various enemies and the subtle urgings of power coursing through the Blud Hamr transformed him on fundamental levels. He no longer gawked wide-eyed as armed combatants came at him. The Hamr infused him with anger. Groge pulled his war bar clear and attacked.

The mercenaries recoiled upon seeing the Giant youth attacking. Their intelligence failed to mention the full extent of the menagerie Bahr had collected on his travels. Had they known a Giant was among them many wouldn't have stayed with Skaning. Not that it mattered now. Groge dove into the enemy with recklessness only youth possessed. He caught the lead attacker across the side of the head. A sickening crunch echoed through the trees as the mercenary was driven to the ground, dead before he hit. Two others died before they realized what was happening. Groge hurried after the others, oblivious to the dark crossbow shafts bouncing from his iron-thick hide.

Ironfoot watched the Giant attack and felt sudden shame at being outdone by a race who claimed to despise violence. Snarling savagely, the Dwarf used Groge's diversion to plow into the milling enemy ranks. His axe reaped a terrible toll in those first moments. An arm lopped off. A head rolled away. Slow to react, the mercenaries soon decided fighting the Dwarf was vastly preferable than trying to battle a Giant.

Figures dashed past him. Ironfoot knew there was nothing to be done about that. He now had his hands full with a half dozen mercenaries trying to stab him. No matter how many got past him they wouldn't amount to much trouble. Bahr and Ingrid had more than two thousand armed combatants with them, not to mention a Vengeance Knight. The enemy was as good as dead already. The Dwarf captain pushed those thoughts aside and hacked down to take a hand off at the wrist.

"What's going on up there?" Ingrid demanded to no one in particular as sounds of fighting drifted back to the main body. She, and the others around her, drew their weapons and fell into defensive positions.

Bahr and Orlek pushed her behind them instinctively, despite her protests. There were times when leaders were expected to be at the front of an advance but other times when they were needed away from the fighting. Both men felt this was one of the latter. Bahr had a sense of dread without knowing why. The first crossbow bolt took one of the guards to his right. Pierced through the chest, he died without a sound. Bahr drew his sword, wishing for a shield. Neither his experience or his skills were enough to stop a guided missile.

"Cover! Prepare for attack!" Orlek bellowed. Instincts dropped him into battle mode. Long sword in one hand and hooked dagger in the other, Orlek crouched as more than a score of the enemy came into sight. He offered a toothy grin and attacked.

Bahr tried to understand what was happening before launching into anything foolish. The Blud Hamr was already exposed. Should Groge fall, all their plans would be dashed against the rocks. The world would fail. Boen had no such reservations. The Gaimosian launched into a furious counterattack the instant he spotted their attackers. Cold recognition blazed hotly in his eyes, telling Bahr what he needed to know. They were being assaulted by Skaning's mercenaries. This knowledge led him to one inescapable conclusion: Skaning aimed to end his war tonight in an all-or-nothing gambit.

It was foolish at best. A maneuver that would likely result in the death of the entire mercenary company. Skaning either knew something the others didn't or had grown mad with despair over successive failures. Bahr quickly, and rightly, guessed the rebels held the advantage and followed Boen. He'd just gotten the Gaimosian back and wasn't about to risk losing him now. The Sea Wolf fell in a few steps behind Boen, intercepting a wild swing from a careless mercenary.

Bahr wheeled in a full circle, dangerously exposing his back. His opponent hadn't expected a second combatant and was off guard. Arm ringing from the shock of the blow, Bahr planted his feet and fended off a series of swings aimed at getting past his guard. The mercenary was skilled but not very experienced. Bahr all but disarmed him in three moves and swiped the tip of his sword across the enemy's exposed throat. Blood sprayed. Sword dropped. The mercenary raised both hands to his throat, desperately trying to keep from bleeding to death. Bahr kicked him over backwards and hurried to find another target.

Back to back, he and Boen fought against several dark-clad attackers. Sparks showered of angry swords. Bodies piled around them. The smell of blood and sweat tainted the air until nothing pure remained. All around the battle raged. Bahr guessed there must be hundreds of mercenaries all trying to kill as many rebels as possible. But why? Suicide made no tactical sense. Skaning would find no benefit in wasting so many lives. Bahr raised his sword to block and defect a forceful blow. His thoughts broken, the Sea Wolf was dragged back into the fight. Skaning's plan would have to wait.

"You need to fall back, now!" Orlek shouted at Ingrid over the roar of approaching mercenaries. His demeanor had reverted entirely back to his days in the line infantry. A seasoned veteran, he'd hidden that fact from her until now.

She gave him a queer look at his sudden boldness and opened her mouth to protest. The hard look on his face was enough to quell any rising argument she might have. Ingrid reluctantly did as she was instructed and not a moment too soon. Dozens of mercenaries broke through the front lines and converged on her previous position. Orlek, having sensed their strategy, summoned those rebels nearest him and formed a solid defensive line. The mercenaries threw themselves upon the massed ranks of rebel fighters, all trying to win through and murder the rebel leader. Her blond hair made her stand out, even in the night.

The tactic was bold but doomed to fail. Orlek snatched a man by his throat and drove his dagger deeply into the exposed belly. Shoving the dying mercenary backwards, Orlek left his dagger in the belly and brought his sword up. The enemy attacked with fury and passion he begrudgingly respected. Each had to know death was the only way out. That made them dangerous. Several rebels went down suddenly, exposing a small hole in the lines. Mercenaries poured through before Orlek rallied his forces to seal the gap.

He snatched the nearest rebel by the collar and roared, "Hold the line! No one else gets through or I'll kill you myself!"

The stunned rebel nodded determinedly and turned his attention back to the battle. Orlek sprinted after the mercenaries, knowing who their target was. Heart pounding with dread, the rebel leader slashed diagonally downward and ripped open an unprotected back. The mercenary screamed in raw agony as his nerves were severed. Orlek ran past his falling form and shoved the next mercenary off balance.

"Ingrid!"

Heads turned his way. Ingrid lunged forward to stab her attacker through the right eye. The squishy pop as her steel drove into his eye immediately sickened her. Orlek's blade could be seen dancing through his enemy. Other rebels responded and closed in on their hated foe. Fueled by memories of Harnin's harsh rule and campaign of oppression, the rebels killed with reckless abandon.

Boen ripped his sword from his latest victim and stared hard at the lone attacker still facing him. Defeated, the mercenary lowered his sword enough to stay Boen's aggression. He reached up and removed the hood covering his hair and half of his face. Both Boen and Bahr stared back hard.

Skaning spat a mouthful of blood on the ground as he dropped his mask. "Bahr. I've hated you for so long, building up your image in my mind to rival that of your brother. How disappointing it is to look upon you now."

Grinding his teeth, Bahr offered a wry grin. "Sorry but I don't seem to recall ever seeing you before."

"That's Skaning, one of Harnin's boy puppets," Boen supplied.

Skaning's eyes flared. His face tightened. "Ah, Gaimosian. I'll enjoy it when your kind no longer contaminates the rest of the world. Killing you will be a pleasure."

Boen responded with deep, booming laughter. "Be my guest. Better men than you have tried. They're all food for worms now. Come, join them."

The Delranan lord failed to respond to Boen's goading. Instead he held his ground and turned back to Bahr. "It doesn't need to be like this, old timer. I didn't come to kill you, well not specifically. Harnin doesn't care about you. He doesn't even know you've returned. Give me the blond bitch and I'll leave."

"There's only one thing wrong with that, little lordling," Bahr answered. "You're part of what's wrong with my kingdom. Getting rid of you all is the only way Delranan is going to recover. You need to die."

"Besides, we've already killed all your hired swords," Boen taunted.

Skaning tensed. "Perhaps killing a Gaimosian will seal my place in history."

He attacked with what little strength remained. Boen spied the move before it began and blocked it without effort. He backhanded Skaning across the mouth. Blood and teeth flew as Skaning stumbled. Boen didn't wait for him to recover. Kicking hard, he caught Skaning in the stomach and dropped him to his knees. Groaning in pain, the lord of Delranan didn't have time to look up before Boen's great sword drove down through his back and into the ground. Skaning died without a sound.

Boen jerked his sword free and turned to Bahr. "That…felt good."

Bahr had nothing to say.

The raid ended in abject failure. Only a handful of mercenaries were taken alive. Ingrid stayed their execution, instead offering them payment and the chance to live by joining her personal retinue. Orlek exploded in opposition but the offer had been made. All but one accepted. Snarling, Orlek stalked up behind the holdout and slit his throat. When Ingrid shot him a questioning look he merely scowled and returned to his place.

Several rebels were killed and twice that wounded. Those that could be moved were patched up by medics while the rest were given a small security detail and told to find the nearest village. This time Ingrid ordered the bodies left where they lay. Time was up. Efforts to resume the march began quickly. Bahr made his rounds with people, pausing only upon noticing the wild, almost untamable look malingering in Groge's eyes. He didn't know why, but the look left him feeling less than what he had been before the battle.

Orlek's harsh voice disturbed his thoughts. "All right, let's move. We've still got a long way to go."

The tired rebel column resumed their long march to destiny.

TWENTY-ONE

The Last Castle

Piper looked out over his force with admiration. They'd captured all but one of Harnin One Eye's defensive fortifications in less than two days. Casualties were acceptable given the almost unnatural conditions they'd been forced to fight under. His one regret was that hardly a prisoner was taken. Whatever Harnin and Badron had told them drove the defenders to near suicidal fervor. It was all Delranan blood in the end. The notion of killing his own people sickened Piper.

Fires burned around him. The warmth felt good on his face and hands, helping to remove some of the sting of battle. Nerves had already calmed. Piper hovered around that level of shock he experienced after every battle. He was beyond exhausted. It had been a continual battle ever since returning to Delranan. The mental strain threatened to wear him down to a fatigue level he hadn't experienced since the beginning of the campaign in Rogscroft. His eyes constantly burned. Decisions came slower. Sooner or later he was going to make a critical mistake that would cost lives. There were no breaks in combat. He didn't get to stop until the war was over.

Already his mind swarmed over details pertaining to the coming battle. Given the enemy's current tactics and their inability to understand surrender was the better part of valor, Piper didn't believe there would be much of an issue in capturing the last redoubt. Thus far he'd managed to attack almost unannounced, completely enveloping the fortification before the defenders were able to react.

Piper wasn't one to trust to luck. His mind raced over new tactics that would result in saving lives. As much as he wanted to avoid any casualties there was simply no way to break through to any of Badron's soldiers. They were pure fanatics wholly devoted to the deposed monarch. Piper didn't expect any in the coming battle to surrender either, forcing him to kill them all.

The idea sat ill with him. He'd always been a loyal son of Delranan and killing his own people, no matter how foul or corrupted they became, was a matter of intense sorrow. Reluctantly he forced aside the bonds of brotherhood and viewed the defenders solely as enemy combatants. It was the only way for him to retain what minor fragments of sanity he had remaining.

He took solace in this being the final battle before his task force could link back up with Rolnir and the main body. Piper figured they must be nearing the rendezvous at Arlevon Gale and preparing for the push into Chadra and, hopefully, ending the long war. Thoughts of any blissful future had to wait, however, as Piper Joach was once again called back into the combat frame of mind. He stretched, yawned deeply, and strode purposefully back to his command group.

"Commander."

Piper returned the salute. "Consolidate equipment and get ready to move. It's a three-league march to the final redoubt. I want ranks formed in ten minutes. Are there any prisoners?" He already knew the answer but had to ask.

"None. This lot was tougher than the others. Gave us a good bit of trouble but we finally rooted them all out," his senior sergeant explained. "I'll have squad leaders take accountability and send the medics through the ranks, sir."

Piper nodded grimly as his thoughts returned to the coming fight.

The march went swiftly. His field force arrived at the last redoubt in less time than he took account for and immediately set about preparing for the attack. There was an undeniable air of excitement rippling through them. At last their struggle was about to end. Many, if not most, wanted to return to the main body and carry out the war properly. While they viewed this task as important to the overall war effort, the redoubts were isolated and away from the front lines. Their friends and comrades were busy liberating the rest of the kingdom, risking their lives while the soldiers in Piper's task force wasted their time in dealing with fanatics.

That the end of this portion of the campaign was finally in sight fueled the soldiers. Axe and sword were sharpened. Minds were focused. All Piper needed to do was give the order. They'd all been through the drill enough times there was little need for much talk. Soon enough squad leaders and junior officers filtered through the column to lead their elements into assault positions. Hearts beat a little faster as the moment of attack quickly approached. Despite having done so nearly ten times already, the soldiers in Piper's command continued to exhibit nervous energy in the long moments leading up to their short charge across open ground.

The thrill of being peppered with arrows made them move faster. The scare of murderous swords and axes awaiting them once they gained the top of the wall sent fear coursing through many. It was all part of the great game of war. Few worried about death. Their time would come or not depending on the vagaries of fate. There was no rhyme or reason as to who died or why. War was as simplistic as it was complicated. Those who tried to over think were often the first to crack under pressure. Piper knew most of them had been weeded out long ago. What remained was the core of his fighting force.

Piper closed his eyes briefly to offer prayers to the old gods, hoping against hope they listened. He'd purposefully ignored the advice of his senior leaders and took his rightful place at the head of the main assault column. There wasn't much of an argument. He was a leader and, contrary to some belief, felt it necessary to lead from the front. A true leader could only sit behind the lines and direct for so long before the respect of his subordinates waned. As it stood, Piper had already been forced to worry over every other assault since returning to Delranan. If for no other reason than sanity's sake, Piper needed to be in the assault.

It took a bit of haggling, but Piper finally agreed to follow the orders of the senior captain. Piper quietly bit his tongue but knew it was for the best. This core group had been through numerous assaults already and was accustomed to working together. Realistically he was only going to be in the way and could easily get someone killed. He hesitated, thinking of changing his mind, but it was already too late. His only fear was that one of his soldiers would be injured worrying over their commander.

Arrows zipped overhead, signaling the assault. Piper broke out into a dead sprint along with one hundred of his best. Lightly armored, they moved much faster than normal heavy infantry. Piper hoped this ploy would play out again the way it had in the previous engagements. With a little luck his forces would be at the base of the walls before the defenders understood what was going on. Luck was very fickle.

Torches flared to life in measured intervals along the walls. The clang of armor and swords being drawn sang out into the night. Piper caught the telltale sounds over his own breathing and winced. This was not going to be pretty. He gripped his sword tighter and ran faster. Another salvo barraged the wooden walls, some arrows sailing over. Enemy casualties would be minimal but they'd be forced to keep their heads down long enough for the infantry to strike. Or so went the plan. Piper was veteran enough to know most plans survived first contact with the enemy. He briefly wished for one of the engineer's war machines. They'd make quick work of the outer perimeter. Wishing was a monumental waste of time. Piper had only his archers and infantry.

The lead soldiers reached the walls and began uncoiling ropes. Others hurried and slammed into the unforgiving wood. Breathing heavily, Piper did the same and pulled out the small, handheld shield from his back. Enough soldiers had arrived to follow suit and raise a protective barrier against incoming fire. A handful of archers stood on the flanks, waiting for any enemy foolish enough to peer down. More than one body fell from the walls, the price paid for trying to gain intelligence on the threat. Ropes went up and soldiers started scrambling up after.

On cue, another platoon of assault troops rushed the front gates. These soldiers were heavily armored and ready to bear the brunt of the enemy's wrath. Piper dared a glance as the massive iron wedge began hammering the gates with axes. Shouting sounded out from within the redoubt as forces were shifted to the gates. Whoever commanded was convinced the gates were the main assault. Piper didn't have time to dwell on it as it was his turn to grab the rope and climb.

Fighting was already breaking out atop the walls. A handful of bodies lay draped over the pointed wood. One was impaled. Most were defenders but a handful wore the Wolfsreik colors. Short sword in hand, Piper crested the top and dragged himself over. He was immediately confronted by a half-mad defender. Piper barely had time to raise his shield and block the blow. His enemy was quick, but he was more experienced. Piper dropped under the shield and stabbed into the defender's unprotected stomach. Blood frothed on his lips before he slid down.

The battle was in full swing now. Piper caught his breath and surveyed the scene. His group's primary objective was to swarm the walls and open the gates from the inside, thus allowing the rest of his force entry. The redoubt would fall in short order and the eastern campaign could finally draw to a close. The sheer number of enemy soldiers massed at the gates put all that in jeopardy. Piper opened his mouth to issue orders but was already behind. His captain was directing soldiers to strike the rear of the defense.

Their swords and axes hacked and slashed through the rear ranks, slaughtering dozens before the enemy managed to shift focus and defend. Even with the advantage of striking first, the Wolfsreik was heavily outnumbered and didn't stand much of a chance at breaking through. Piper sheathed his short sword and drew his preferred long sword. The time had come for him to attack. Collecting a squad-sized element, Piper hurried around the top of the wall, coming down directly besides the now furious fighting at the gate. His soldiers were given one task: open the gates no matter what.

Piper charged down the short flight of wooden steps, followed closely by his brave twenty. They fell upon those few defenders at the gates and rushed to remove the massive bar blocking the gates. Piper cut down one fanatic before being forced backwards by a dual axe-wielding opponent. It had been too long since he last confronted a worthy opponent and Piper was soon reeling in the vain attempt at gaining the advantage.

He smelled partially chewed meat caught between his attacker's teeth. Felt beads of sweat drip onto his hands and face. Piper stared into dark eyes filled with aggressive hatred and felt the strain of exhausted muscles as he tried to push back. All his focus lay in the struggle just to survive. He feared he might have made a catastrophic mistake by insisting to join the assault. Lord Death's chariot could be heard racing across the night sky.

Piper suddenly changed tactics. Giving in to his opponent's strength, the Wolfsreik commander jerked back and sidestepped. Momentum forced his enemy ahead and it was all he could do to stop in time and compensate for the lack of resistance. Piper had just enough time to recover and raise his shield. Two quick blows jarred his forearm. Sparks danced from his iron shield. Gritting his teeth, Piper launched into a furious counterattack.

Swords met. He attacked from a low guard, knowing it might prove his undoing, but this was close-quarter combat, not the open-field warfare he'd grown accustomed to since assuming command of the vanguard. It was intimate, far more personal, and Piper battled for his life. Every action was told in the eyes. Every move telegraphed without doubt. However much aggression his enemy bore, it was no match for the cold experience of a veteran. Piper eventually wore his enemy down and slipped past his guard.

His sword bit deeply, crunching bone in the right shoulder. Wounded, his enemy cried out and reeled back. Piper had the opening he needed. His sword moved like lightning. The tip caught at the base of the throat and plunged through the back of the neck. His enemy dropped in a pile of flesh, grasping his throat as blood pumped freely down his chest. No time to waste, Piper stepped over the dying man and cut down another from behind.

"Open the damned gates before we're all killed!" he shouted above the roar.

Instinctively he knew that several of his assault teams were dead. Soldiers fought harder, desperate to clear the way and let in reinforcements. Eventually the defenders were subsumed, dead to the last. Piper pitched a shoulder into raising the heavy bar. Ten soldiers added their strength while the handful of others still capable of fighting defended them from the melee going on in the courtyard.

The bar lifted with a groan. Men strained. Dust and wood chips fell to the muddied ground. Finally freed, Piper's group tossed the bar aside and hurried to pull the gates open. Scores of angry soldiers charged into the redoubt. Piper and the others barely had time to duck aside before they were trampled beneath heavy boots. With the gates open, the battle heated quickly and ended quicker. The defenders had no stomach for the level of violence the Wolfsreik brought. They fell by the dozen. Soon enough the enemy standard was ripped from the flagpole. The redoubt had fallen.

Piper sheathed his weapons and headed into the slaughter. His soldiers were well versed by now. Squads immediately set about collecting the bodies while medics and sergeants scoured their own ranks for accountability. A triage area was established near the gates. The cries and groans of the wounded were mercifully minor compared to what might have been. Memories of the hospitals in Rogscroft sickened Piper. Anything less severe was a blessing.

Blood-stained soldiers stormed through the redoubt. There would be no prisoners. Piper joined their ranks, eager to find any relevant intelligence in the offices. Thus far none of the defenses had given up any secrets. He quietly hoped to find Badron dead in one of them, but it was a dream only. The deposed king wouldn't be fool enough to get caught in one of these. Piper was left with pleasant thoughts but empty hands. He hoped Rolnir met with better success in the west.

"Commander, you have to see this," an ashen-faced sergeant said after coming out of the main headquarters building.

Piper's heart quickened. The look and tone of his trusted subordinate left him rattled without knowing why. The soldiers of the Wolfsreik were seasoned professionals. For one to be so visibly shaken whispered ill tidings. He hurried into the building. The stench of rotted flesh immediately struck him, making Piper gag. His eyes narrowed. *What evil has been done here?*

What he witnessed went beyond anything he might have imagined. Five decomposing bodies were laid out in a circle, heads all touching. Their hands were folded over their chests, feet placed together. The ground was stained dark with blood, enough to make Piper believe each corpse had been drained entirely. A closer look showed their throats and wrists had been slit. He took in their desiccated figures, immediately noticing how shallow their midsections appeared. The sergeant stopped him before he moved closer.

"They've been gutted, sir," he explained and gestured towards the far corner of the room.

Piper's gaze followed the pointing finger. He bent over to void his stomach. Intestines were nailed to the wall in intricate patterns lost on the world of men. Flies and gnats swarmed over the piles of organs on the floor. He regretted his decision and looked away. Piper stared back at the grinning corpses.

"They died with smiles on their faces," he breathed.

The sergeant nodded. "Be damned if I can figure out why."

"What dark arts have been at work here?" Piper asked a seemingly unanswerable question. Most of the army knew nothing of the fell powers lurking behind Badron. The scene played out in this room was one of nightmarish intent. Piper felt his knees weaken.

"Sir, I believe these fellows came here willingly," he said.

Piper's eyebrow rose. "Sacrificed? For what purpose? This was Badron's last defense. He had nothing to accomplish by holding it further."

The sergeant shrugged, answerless.

"I want the task force ready to march at once. General Rolnir and King Aurec must be notified of this…this ritual.

Burn this building to the ground. I want the entire redoubt razed from existence. Evil cannot be permitted to remain in Delranan unchecked."

Saluting, the sergeant wheeled about and began barking orders. Piper didn't know why, but he had a sinking suspicion that foul times were fast approaching. He was no practitioner of magic but knew it when he saw it. Whatever, whoever, had invoked this ritual had done so with purpose. Evil had been loosed in Delranan. He only hoped it wasn't too late.

TWENTY-TWO

With All Due Haste

"Six hundred and thirty-two."

"So many? How does this compare to the amount of dead on the field?"

Rolnir took a bite from a green apple. The juice trickled down his chin. "Insignificant but more than could be expected."

The battle was over almost as soon as it began. Less than an hour saw the demise of Badron's main army. An army of conscripts and has-beens. They were never more than an idle threat to the combined armies of Delranan and Rogscroft but presented a major hindrance in the march west. The true battle awaited them somewhere around Chadra. With the link-up fast approaching, both men agreed they had lost valuable time dealing with Badron's loyalists.

Their urgency was foreshadowed by an ominous threat lurking ever out of eyesight. Rolnir and Aurec both agreed that as long as Badron remained unaccounted for the threat was valid. There was no telling how many forces the former king had amassed in the capital or word of the defenses around the city. None of the scouts dispatched had returned--a minor but worrisome fact that didn't sit right with Rolnir.

"We don't have the capacity to deal with so many prisoners," Aurec told him.

"There's not much that can be done about that now. Executing them isn't an option."

"I wasn't suggesting that, General," Aurec said quickly to avoid raising unwarranted suspicion in his closest ally. "Nor can we leave them here."

"Making our position undesirable at best," the general concluded. "We're going to have to take them with us."

"A risk at best."

Their respective columns had converged after the battle. Rolnir immediately dispatched riders to summon the king. The battle proved significant in that it removed a massive fighting force in the central portion of the kingdom. It was an army they could ill afford to have roaming behind them. Rolnir hadn't required the additional strength in defeating the loyalists but was experienced enough to recognize the evolving threat. He didn't know what lay ahead but the ill feeling settling on the back of his neck was enough to change the plan.

Aurec wasn't that far away and their forces converged scant hours after the battle. Word was sent to General Vajna's column as well but with orders to carry on according to schedule. This way they'd at least be screened from any large forces moving down from the north. Aurec didn't suspect Badron had that many units to spare but without being able to discern where the battle against the rebellion was he wasn't willing to take the chance.

"Most of them were forced into service. They're not warriors, Aurec."

Rolnir took another bite, the tart fruit making him salivate. Fresh fruit was a luxury they hadn't counted on until raiding the first of Harnin's fortresses. The army scavenged all the supplies and food they could find, a rare sack of winter green apples going directly to Rolnir. Those closest knew the general greatly appreciated the fruit. That wasn't lost on him as he understood the desire of his soldiers to show appreciation for all that he'd done for them since the war began. Bringing any soldier home alive was cause for celebration.

"That doesn't make them any less dangerous," Aurec countered. "We're here on specific purpose, Rolnir. These people, kinsmen or not, are our enemies. Each is capable of plunging a blade into our backs the moment we turn away."

"I don't believe so. Look at them. We've killed the majority of their friends. There's no fight left in them."

Aurec disagreed. He'd seen the fight people had when all they knew was threatened. His own people hadn't given up even after their king lay dead and their city in ruins. Reminding one of those responsible for that calamity wasn't proper etiquette, especially now that they were fast allies and becoming friends.

"A cornered dog bites most," Aurec recited an old Rogscroft saying. He'd been that cornered dog but was able to find a way to turn defeat into victory, or what they hoped was about to become victory.

Rolnir nodded sagely. "Truth if I ever heard it, but that doesn't solve our dilemma. These prisoners are going to have to come with us. We can't afford to lose troop strength with taking them back to one of the redoubts and placing them under guard."

"Agreed, but what value is there in forcing them to march with us? We'll waste equal strength and time in making them march."

There was wisdom in that, but choices were limited. Rolnir wasn't going to allow his people to be senselessly slaughtered after they'd been taken prisoner, but neither was he willing to let them go about their merry way. The conundrum vexed him. He silently wished they'd have had the good graces to fight to the death instead of throwing down their weapons.

"Perhaps they can be turned?" Rolnir suggested.

Aurec paused. His brow knitted, he found the lack of thinking the matter through disturbing. His father never would have missed that. Then again, his father had the experience of over forty years on the throne and was expected to know such things. Aurec hadn't been king for more than a month. Mistakes were to be expected, but he'd never admit it. He was king, and kings were meant to make difficult decisions on a moment's notice.

"Turned how? You've seen the fanaticism they exhibit. Whatever Harnin and Badron did to them it is clear they are not the same innocent civilians you recall, my friend," he finally said. "They are poisoned by lies and ill intent."

"That may be so, but they are all we have to work with. If only a portion willingly join us I'll consider it a victory."

Aurec didn't see any other viable option. Time was running out. The urgency he felt resonated through the army for reasons none could explain. Something dark, sinister was drawing near and forcing the army to pick up their pace. He didn't know why, but the young king felt the inexplicable need to reach Arlevon Gale soon.

"Very well, General. Set your plan in motion. We need to be moving again," the king commanded.

Rolnir finished speaking and folded his arms across his chest. That patience was a façade, for he was most eager to get underway. The road to Arlevon Gale was short but would take doubly long now that his force had grown. Speed was an abandoned concept. Massive armies were only able to move at an insubstantial pace. He carried his gaze out across the sea of faces. Many were dazed, lost in the shock and despair of the battle's aftermath. Others harbored hateful feelings. More, he was satisfied to see, clung intently on his every word.

Having said his piece, the general of the Wolfsreik turned and went back to his tent to determine the order of march. Not more than a few minutes later, before he even had time to sit, a runner came in with news. Rolnir accepted the missive with joy and hurried to find Aurec. Yet another wonder had fallen upon the army.

"All the way to the ruins?" Mahn asked.

Even the brash Raste seemed to choke on the orders. Aurec resisted the urge to grin, knowing he was likely sending two of his closest friends and companions to their deaths. It was no easy task and one Aurec didn't take lightly. There was a time when he'd have gone himself, despite the urgings of Venten. Back when he was an irresponsible prince with more testosterone than wisdom and he cared nothing for duties. Aurec was often scolded for being reckless. Now he was asking others to do what he would have been chastised for.

Raste blurted out, "Those ruins are haunted!"

"Quiet, lad. He's king now," Mahn replied. "Sorry, sire. It won't happen again. He's nervous is all."

"I am not. I just don't want to go sticking my head out for no reason," Raste defended.

Aurec listened to them carry on for a while. Their camaraderie lightened his spirits, reminding him of why he wore the crown. Men like Mahn and Raste were the heart of his kingdom. So long as people like that were willing to follow, Aurec was committed to lead.

"If it's not too much trouble, I'd like you two to leave immediately," he said.

Mahn blushed while the younger, more impetuous Raste could only frown. "My apologies, sire, but you know how he gets from time to time."

"I do not. You're the stubborn one!" Raste countered.

Aurec held up his hands. "Gentlemen, please. Time is running out and I need to know what we're heading into. How soon can you get back?"

Mahn interlaced his fingers and thought. His knowledge of Delranan was more extensive than Aurec's but he was still a foreigner. "Less than half a day I suppose but I'd like one or two of Rolnir's scouts to come along just in case."

"Get them. Mahn, this is important. I can't commit our forces without intelligence," Aurec insisted.

"You'll get it, sire. We'll be back before you know it."

Aurec nodded his thanks. "Meet us on this road. The army will leave shortly after you. Don't stop for anything and return as fast as you can."

He watched the scouts depart. His mind raced ahead to the infinite number of possibilities waiting just out of view. The world had changed in the short span of the war. Kingdoms, once proud and glorious, were laid low by famine, strife, and rebellion. How many thousands lay dead were beyond his knowledge, but the king of Rogscroft feared it was beyond count. He knew, but would never admit, that neither kingdom would be the same again. That fear propelled him to move quicker than he liked.

"I bring good news!" Rolnir called excitedly as he walked up.

Aurec closed his eyes and exhaled deeply. It had been a long time since last someone delivered news that could be construed as good.

"Four hundred and fifty-one of the prisoners have agreed to fight with us."

Aurec broke into a wide smile. "That lessens our burden considerably. What of the others? Is there a chance they can be turned?"

Rolnir shook his head. "I'm afraid not. We've already separated them from the main body. They'll be under guard the rest of the way. I have to be honest and tell you I fully expect them to attempt to either escape or cause havoc among the ranks. Badron and Harnin were cunning. There's no telling what lies these people still believe."

"Malcontents are more trouble than they're worth, but they can't be that much of an issue," Aurec said. "Do you think it wise to keep the others together?"

"No. I've already got company commanders breaking down the numbers. Each battalion will take fifty or so but won't arm them unless we get into a serious fight," Rolnir explained. "Either way that's a sizeable addition to our main body that we hadn't counted on. I could use a mug of ale right now."

"We all could. I'll make you a deal, Rolnir. When all this is said and done I'll treat the entire army to a round."

"Done. That's one thing you'll never need to convince us on," Rolnir said and smiled. His red hair almost matched his wind-burned cheeks. His eyes sparkled brightly, knowing that their ordeal was at long last coming to a close. The war was almost over.

But it wasn't won yet. More would die before the end, and great many of the faces he'd looked at for years. Those were the losses that hurt the most. The empty seat at the table where a longtime friend once sat. Ghosts of old friends lingered in the haze of memory, prompting Rolnir to wonder just how many more were about to join the established crowd. No matter how many times he was forced to endure the personal loss, Rolnir doubted he'd ever get used to it. War might have been a natural state of affairs in the world but it left hollowed-out shells in the survivors.

Aurec caught that faraway look and immediately felt the attraction. He too knew what it meant to lose. Unlike Rolnir, the young king lacked years of experience. That fact didn't diminish his emotions. Aurec had lost count of how many graves he'd helped take a shovel to since the winter war began. How many more awaited them?

"That drink is going to have to wait. Best not to tell the soldiers yet. I need them focused on the war, not the aftermath," Rolnir finally said with a sigh. "How soon do you want to be on the march?"

"The scouts just left. We should give them a few hours' head start. If our suspicions are true it would be nice to have time to react accordingly."

Rolnir nodded agreement. "We're entering the tricky stage of the campaign. Caution and prudence should be our weapons of choice at this juncture."

"Indeed, but unfortunately time disagrees with you. Let's get them up and moving. Arlevon Gale awaits us," Aurec said.

"I pray that's all," Rolnir added.

The young king couldn't have agreed more.

They'd scouted half of the northern kingdoms over the past six months, often riding behind enemy lines in extremely dangerous situations. Mahn reckoned they should have been captured or killed no less than eight times, not counting the siege of Rogscroft. Blind luck and no small amount of skill saved them. At least it had until now. Mahn harbored no illusions that the task his king had given him was in any way minor or easy. He'd been around long enough to recognize danger without getting cast into it.

Aurec was hiding information that might be useful. Mahn was certain. There was something nefarious going on in the ruins, but what? The destruction of the enemy bivouac site reduced Badron's fighting strength considerably, prompting Mahn to wonder just how large of an army they were facing. The longer the war dragged on the more suspicious the veteran scout became. He'd give his life for Aurec or any of the others but wanted to know it was for the right reasons. Suicide was foolish.

The ruins of Arlevon Gale were said to be haunted by more than ghosts. Mahn knew next to nothing about them, though the pair of Delrananian scouts accompanying them spoke with extreme caution. Better had died for less and the sons of Delranan were no fools. They deflected Mahn's questions, mostly, and tried to focus on their mission. Mahn couldn't argue with them. After all, soldiers were expected to follow orders. They went to the ruins because their general told them to.

"How much further? It's so dark I can barely see in front of my horse," Mahn whispered.

The lead Delrananian scout squinted to try and get a better look at their surroundings. "Not much. We should be coming up on them once we clear the trees."

"Good. This place gives me a bad feeling." Raste's voice was low, anxious.

Mahn seconded the emotion. He felt a thousand pair of eyes watching. Each time he turned the feeling shifted. Always fluid, he couldn't pin down the location the feeling stemmed from. Without proof, he couldn't bring it before the others, not without sounding like a witless old timer. He bit his tongue, keeping those suspicions to himself while his hand crept closer to his sword.

The scouts felt a weight slip away as the darkness began to brighten. The trees spread out, growing thinner. Fresh sounds came to the four. Shovels and hammers. Torchlight broke the wall night. The scouts halted in place. Foul speech could be heard over the sounds of forced labor. The foul speech of Goblins. Whips cracked.

"Mahn, no," Raste cautioned as the older scout slid from his saddle.

Mahn waved off his concern and crept closer to get a better view. He danced between trees, edging ever closer to the tree line. His heart was wedged in his throat. No stranger to Goblins, Mahn thought those troubles were over after the ambush at the base of the Murdes Mountains where the Wolfsreik turned and helped destroy the Goblin occupation army. He never imagined encountering more in Delranan.

He used the trees and large bushes for cover until reaching the very edge of the forest. Close to one hundred meters had been cleared back, giving the Goblins a long killing field and removing the element of surprise from any attacking army. Thousands of soldiers busied with establishing defenses around the moss and ivy-covered ruins. Mahn tried counting, at least estimating, but the effort proved futile. No matter how many he saw even more lurked within the perimeter. They seemed endless. He knew the combined army would never be able to defeat such a large force, not without sustaining massive casualties.

"We need to get back, now. The army is marching into a trap," he said as he climbed back onto his horse.

"What is it? Mahn, what did you see?" Raste asked.

"Death."

TWENTY-THREE

The Old Alliances

Endless leagues passed by. Day and night blended into one unending, indistinguishable chain of events. The army grew tired. Muscles were sore. Feet hurt. Boots were cracked and replaced. Still the army trudged forward. The promise of war commanded them. Each soldier in the ranks was eager to join the cause and lend their axe to the cause of righteousness, though the senior leadership suspected many had come simply for the promise of violence. Not that it mattered. They'd all been assured unprecedented violence was about to be unleashed on Malweir should they choose to remain sidelined.

"We've passed into Delranan."

Thord looked up at Faeldrin. The Dwarf Lord took no comfort in the news. There were still many leagues to march before his army would come to their great battle. Excitement overpowered his sense of reason. The civil war with the dark Dwarf clans had been violent and bloody, but Thord viewed it as good experience for his army. They'd been assured that the enemy they prepared to encounter was unlike any they had ever faced. Thord took the challenge head-on, eager to prove the prowess of his people.

"That's great, but there's still a way to go if what you and the Dae'shan said is true," he countered.

Faeldrin grinned at his Dwarf companion. Elves and Dwarves had a long history of not getting along except in moments of extreme duress but the lord of the Aeldruin couldn't help but feel companionship with his shorter partner. War often forged strange bonds for which he was glad. He turned to the third member of their command group. Krek, the Minotaur king, marched with utter surety.

"What say you, my tall friend?" Faeldrin asked.

Krek snorted, clearing out his wide nostrils. "Goblins need to die. Krek will kill many!"

The Elf admired the Minotaur for his audacity, though often wondered why he hadn't been able to learn how to speak the common tongue fluently. Minotaur shamans had a long history of teaching their kings to fit in with the other races. Either Krek refused or he'd been too long in the ranks to seek change.

"Indeed, but we must arrive first. My scouts are already ranging into the kingdom," the Elf told them. "Artiss Gran spoke of dire occurrences happening across Delranan." Though he suspiciously avoided detailing those events. *Yet another round in the long game the Dae'shan seemed intent on playing with our lives.*

"I don't much care for the Dae'shan. What I want is another crack at these Goblins. They've killed too many of my kind over the years. Their time must come to an end and I'd have it come at the sharp edge of my axe."

Thord fell grimly silent. His hatred of the Goblins and their creators went deeper than anyone knew. Pure, unadulterated rage smoldered in his dark eyes each time he thought of the foul Goblins.

The Elf wasn't one to question old grudges. He too had had his share of enemies worthy of the term nemesis. The quest to slay the dragon, in what felt like a dozen lifetimes ago, helped him understand the Minotaurs and their crude ways. Scores of the mighty warriors fell when the Goblin army sent a punitive force to attack their underground home of Malg. Krek had been on a quest with the Elves and Dakeb the Mage, and unable to help defend his kingdom. Faeldrin understood the anger. He nearly let his thoughts take him back over a thousand years ago to a time when the world was raw. Many Elves were murdered by the dark powers. Powers he and his Aeldruin were assured to be marching towards.

"I think I like him," Thord said, gesturing up at Krek.

The Minotaur grinned; it was a menacing, spiteful glare.

"He does have his charms," Faeldrin agreed. "Thord, I believe we need to pick up the pace."

"Eh? Why?"

The Elf shook his head. Long, golden locks floated across his shoulders. "I cannot say why but my mind tells me much will go wrong if we do not arrive with all possible haste."

Thord grumbled. His face darkened. "I don't like it when you start sounding like a wizard. It was bad enough having to decipher what Anienam Keiss was saying."

"Anienam is our last link to the order of Mages. Without his guidance we might already be lost," the Elf Lord replied.

"And did he mention what fate awaits us?" Thord asked.

Faeldrin frowned, a minor gesture so small it went unnoticed. His crystalline eyes swept across the open fields before them. Faint rays of sunlight glittered over the pure, undisturbed white of fresh snow. Tufts of green struck through in places, bringing contrast to an otherwise serene world. Rock and stone jutted up at random intervals. Wisps of clouds danced across the blue sky. The Elf Lord closed his eyes and used an old method to calm his rising nerves.

"Not per se but trying to decipher a wizard's riddle is a feat best left to scholars, not warriors. I have my scouts out now but without having been in Delranan in a very long time I admit to being blind at the moment."

"We were told march west," Krek added.

"Right. We march west," Thord said. "My lads can pick up the pace, though we won't be able to maintain it for long, not with the long train for the cannons and ammunition wagons. I figure it will take at least two more days of hard marching to reach these ruins the wizard spoke of. That's a long time where anything can go wrong."

"Have we a choice?" Faeldrin asked. "I'm going to take my Aeldruin and ride out. Best not to be caught off guard."

Dwarf and Minotaur watched the Elves speed away. Powdery snow kicked up from their horses' hooves as thunder rumbled with each footstep. Thord glanced up at Krek, knowing it wouldn't be much longer before the seven-foot-tall bulls outpaced his much shorter Dwarves. For the first time in his life he cursed being short.

The Elves moved like ghosts. Far behind were the open fields of southeastern Delranan. Forested hills sprang up the further north the army ranged. Much of the deep snows of the untouched south were melting. Faeldrin found it discoursing, for the land was mired in countless tracks. There was no doubt in his mind that the Goblin army had come the same way.

"These tracks are but a few days old," Euorn said, his long fingers tracing one of the boot prints. "We've caught them."

"Not yet." Faeldrin wasn't certain catching the massive army was a good thing or not. They were clearly outnumbered even with the addition of the Minotaurs. The Elf Lord guessed the odds were better than seven to one. Even with Thord's cannons and black-powder weapons, their meager army would be hard-pressed to withstand any assault.

The scout rose to his full six-foot height. The crossed swords on his breast plate glimmered in the sun. "My lord, we've found them. The Goblins will be taken off guard."

"Euorn, there is no way we could have caught up to their army in less than a week. Look at the tracks around us. This was not created by fifty thousand soldiers."

"Meaning it's a raiding party," Aleor said grimly. Faeldrin's brother remained opposed to facing the Goblin army so outnumbered. "What are we doing?"

Faeldrin tensed. "What do you mean?"

Aleor gestured to the prints. "This. We are hopelessly outnumbered, Faeldrin. There is no chance of victory here. Our Dwarven allies are eager to do battle against a hated foe, but this is not our fight. We will not come away from this war."

"Have you so little faith in our abilities, brother?"

Aleor said, "I have little faith in our meager numbers. Fifty thousand, Faeldrin! When has Malweir ever seen such a force? These are the end days."

"Which makes our purpose all more important. Anienam Keiss warned us of the Dae'shan and their drive to release the dark gods. This is indeed the final battle, brother.

What other place would the Aeldruin be if not in the middle of it? Is this not the reason I created us? The world as we know it will fall or stand depending on our involvement."

"Faeldrin, we are all going to die," Aleor said, reaffirming his position.

"If such is to be our fate, who are we to avoid it?" his brother countered. Faeldrin reached out to place a reassuring hand on his brother's shoulder. "I need you at my side. While I cannot promise survival, I give my pledge that I will do everything in my power to preserve as many lives as possible."

Satisfied with the pledge, Aleor nodded. "Very well. Let us continue forward. If this is to be our fate I would see it done sooner rather than later."

The Elves mounted up and pushed ahead. Somewhere in the wild lands lay the ruins of Arlevon Gale and the fate of them all.

"We're in trouble," Faeldrin told his fellow lords.

Thord grimaced, unsure how to proceed. The look in Krek's eyes was plain enough. The Minotaur king wanted to attack.

"The Goblins are less than a half day ahead of us and already dug in around Arlevon Gale. They've cleared a fairly large field of fire in a full circle. We won't be able to sneak up from any direction."

Thord, staring down at the crudely drawn map, asked, "Where is the best place for my cannons? If we can get them in the right position I can break their lines."

"No, Thord. The enemy is dug in too well even for your cannons," Faeldrin said. "All is not dire. We've seen evidence of a large Human army camped to the northeast. They bear the colors of the Wolfsreik and Rogscroft. Krek, you'll be interested to know that the Pell Darga are among them as well."

The Minotaur grunted his approval. They'd fought together once before, long ago.

"How large?" Thord asked.

"Large enough to almost make a difference. I've sent my brother to form an alliance with them. Man and Elf haven't fought together in a very long time. It will be interesting to see if they are willing to do so now." Faeldrin pursed his lips. The tip of his tongue snaked out to gingerly lick across the top of his bottom lip.

"Has there been any sign of the wizard?" Thord asked. He folded his massive arms across his armor and glared north.

Elf and Dwarf both recalled their conversations with Bahr and Anienam during the battle of Bode Hill. It was no coincidence that all forces were converging on the ruins of Arlevon Gale. At the time, neither Thord nor Faeldrin paid much attention to the enigmatic wizard as he spun tales of gods and the end of the world. Their hands were full in dealing with the dark Dwarves. Little thought was given to Anienam once they were safely escorted to the Thorn River and sent south. Faeldrin guessed they had sorely misinterpreted the wizard's words. He only hoped it wasn't too late to correct his error.

"None, but that could mean anything. I believe the wizard was in good hands. Bahr led that group with unwavering fortitude. This was their destination and, unless my calculations are considerably off, this is the hour in which they need to be here."

"Scouts need to be looking out for them." Thord didn't particularly care much for the wizard's quest. His interests lay solely in his representative, Captain Ironfoot. The Dwarf commander was a valuable asset he dearly wanted back with the main army before they engaged the enemy.

"Agreed, but that would change our objective," Faeldrin told them.

Krek yawned, lacking interest in the conversation. His dark eyes, almost lost beneath the thick forehead and massive nostrils, were focused on fighting, not talking.

"In what way? There is a Goblin army in need of killing," Thord countered.

"If the wizard needs to get to the ruins to defeat the dark gods they're going to need help breaking through that army," the Elf replied. *Meaning we all stand a very high potential of dying in the process.*

Thord grumbled a deep sound that vibrated the ground. Krek snort a laugh just as deep.

"I'm beginning to not like you, Elfling," the Dwarf Lord snapped.

"What do you want from me? It can be no coincidence we are here. Perhaps our true purpose is to blast a hole through their lines to see the wizard through. Who are we to challenge the will of the gods?"

Thord wasn't convinced. "Dwarf gods are not involved in this war. It is the human gods who continue to destroy the world. I have half a mind to take my army home and let them deal with their own problems. Anything is better than spilling Dwarf blood for a pointless cause."

"My lords, pardon the interruption!" Mearlis all but shouted as he sprinted the last few dozen meters to their meeting.

Thord was silently thankful for the disruption. His fingers ached to grab his axe and settle his rising differences with the Elf.

"Mearlis, what is it?" Faeldrin asked.

"There's a large body of soldiers approaching from the west. They number several thousand at least. We were unable to determine who though."

Krek's flat ears perked. Rising to his full height, the Minotaur snatched his war bar in anticipation of crushing heads. "Good. We fight."

"Our Minotaur friend might be correct. Thord, I suggest deploying your army. It seems the Goblins must wait till the morrow."

Snarling, Thord spun away and bellowed, "Form ranks! Musketeers to the front. Prepare for battle!"

Horns sang out over the army.

TWENTY-FOUR

Destiny Awaits

Too familiar sounds echoed across the lightly forested plain. Men and women struggled to keep panic from taking over. Weapons were drawn. Battle lines drawn. Squad leaders snapped orders to their subordinates. Clearly at a disadvantage, the rebel army was stricken with the realization they were heading into a trap. Horses snorted excitement, their breath coming in crisp plumes of vapor that mingled with the rising mist.

The world turned dim. Light mist clung to the ground, growing thicker by the moment in unnatural ways. Trees appeared as demons, slender and wicked. Their branches turned to ripping claws threatening eternal pain. Sunlight filtered into the mist, turning their surroundings surreal. Every sound was amplified. The rebels could pick out the jangle of armor and…something else in the mist-shrouded distance. They looked to each other for comfort, finding none in the near terrified faces of friends and neighbors.

Orlek rode to the head of the column, sword drawn. His forest green cape billowed behind him as he flashed past the stunned rebels. Raising his sword high for all to see, Orlek shouted, "Calm yourselves! We are beset. The enemy is upon us. Ready weapons. Archers to the front!"

"I'm going to take a look," Boen said after watching Orlek's impulsive bravado.

Bahr frowned, unwilling to commit to jumping into the front lines of yet another battle. "I think we should get back and stay out of it. We're too close to the ruins for mistakes."

"He's right, Boen. This isn't our fight," Anienam added. Blinded, the wizard seemed more attune with their surroundings than any of the others.

The Gaimosian cast an empty hand towards Orlek. "What makes you think we'll be in the clear if they get into it? Like it or not we're stuck here. You say the ruins are close.

That means we can't just go around and avoid whatever's coming to us. Wizard, I am Gaimosian. War is what I do. Leave it to me."

"Do you not recall the prophecy?" Anienam barked, his voice high pitched, broken. "We are all needed at the final hour if the dark gods are to be stopped."

"Prophecy be damned! We'll never make it to the ruins if there's an army blocking the way! You can sit here and whine about it or run and hide in the night. I'm riding ahead."

"I'm going with him," Ironfoot seconded.

No one else moved. The long-awaited confrontation of wills had befallen them, leaving many wondering how to proceed. Bahr immediately noticed their group had divided, subconsciously, into two distinct groups. One wanted to be done with the quest and return to their lives while the other was ready to fight and become more than what they were meant to be. Both Dwarf and Gaimosian had been clamoring to fight since arriving in Delranan. Weeks of frustrations molded into aggression that could only be expressed through violence. Axe and sword, the duo headed off into the unknown confrontation.

Orlek crept alongside Boen, amazed at the way in which the bigger, heavier man moved. Never had he witnessed such a simple yet remarkable sight. Vengeance Knights were masters of their trade. Boen was in his element. An element where he excelled. Orlek was hard-pressed just to keep up.

To his right marched the Dwarf. Ironfoot might be shorter and stockier, but his footsteps had yet to make a sound. Orlek dreaded ever having to go to war against such foes. Blackened steel waivered in the dwindling daylight. Their faces were painted, lending each a menacing appearance. Snow-covered branches brushed off their armor, white flakes peppering beards and hands briefly before they melted. Orlek's heart beat faster. He'd never admit it, but he was tired of running, tired of fighting, and tired of forcing a life not meant to live. It was past time to put an end to this senseless war and try to find a way to rebuild.

That wasn't going to happen as long as fresh enemies continued to present themselves. Orlek flushed out those distracting thoughts and focused. Much of the snow had melted or had been trampled to the point it had become mud. There was no doubt the rebel force was on the trail of the Goblin army. What bothered him were the heavy sounds of an army preparing for battle. Goblins were bloodthirsty beasts as far as he was concerned, but they were hardly foolish. They had numbers and the advantage of being emplaced, forcing attackers to break on their defenses. From what he could tell, this new foe was moving their way.

Ironfoot's axe flattened against Orlek's chest, forcing him to stop abruptly. The Dwarf brought a finger up to his lips before Orlek could question the sudden move. Understanding, Orlek started to crouch behind the nearest tree. He brought his sword up and waited.

Ironfoot passed Boen a knowing glance and strode forward with his axe diagonal across his chest. The Gaimosian watched him go, confident in the Dwarf's ability in this type of situation. He and Orlek waited in silence as the Dwarf disappeared into the foliage. A shout of alarm quickly followed. Figures could be heard rushing through the brush. Murmured words of excitement flowed back and forth in a harsh, guttural language Orlek didn't understand.

They waited for so long Orlek felt his calf begin to cramp. The fervor died down, leaving him to believe Ironfoot had either been killed or taken prisoner. He was about to ask Boen why they were just standing doing nothing when Ironfoot returned, unharmed and unscathed. The grin on his face echoed immense relief.

"You can put your weapons up," Ironfoot said with unusual smugness. "Boen, you're not going to believe this."

"Believe what?" Orlek finally asked in frustration.

A squad of Dwarves emerged from the building gloom. Each was armed for war. A more frightening sight Orlek had never seen. "By the gods," he muttered.

"The gods have nothing to do with this," Ironfoot replied. "Boen, Orlek, the army of Drimmen Delf has arrived."

Reunions were conducted amidst the open-mouthed stares of several hundred rebels. Never before had the citizens of Delranan stood in the presence of so many different races. Elves, Dwarves, Minotaurs, a wizard, and a Giant. All allied with Delranan against the Goblin army. Many dropped to their knees in tears. Others warned that these were the end times at last. Dire warnings and predictions rippled throughout the small rebel army, now accompanied by over six thousand Dwarves and Minotaurs.

Nothol handed Dorl a mug of partially flat ale and gestured towards the meeting of leaders with his chin. "What do you make of this?"

"I don't know. It all makes me think Anienam's not the head case we've been playing him off to be. Why else would the Dwarves be here?"

Nothol agreed. Too much had gone wrong since arriving in Delranan for the sudden arrival of a massive combined army to be downplayed. He didn't think their quest had been fruitless or mired in failure. They'd gained the Blud Hamr and defeated countless foes along the way while only suffering one casualty and one missing. Maleela's loss stung Nothol most of all, but aside from that one incident in the Jungles of Brodein, their quest had been successful…thus far.

"Looks like we might stand a chance after all. Ironfoot's buddies should make quick work of those Goblins," Nothol told him. He'd hoped never to have to witness the awesome power of the army of Drimmen Delf unleashed again. There was nothing so terrible as watching cannons reap lives by the dozen from so far away.

Dorl shook his head. "It's not natural. Those gun-powder weapons will change Malweir if other kingdoms learn the secrets."

Nothol had nothing else to say. The Dwarves were likeable enough but contained savagery beyond imagination once provoked. Their prowess on the battlefield was rivaled only through technological innovation. Gunpowder might easily be the single most important discovery in the modern world. It didn't take much to let imagination get the best of him. Nothol saw vast armies sweeping across the face of the world, bringing death on unprecedented levels.

"Let's not worry about that. All we have to do is get the Hamr into the ruins in time to stop the Dae'shan," Nothol finally said.

"Right." Dorl drained his mug and handed it back. "What do you think they're talking about? How to get us killed no doubt."

"Probably, but what's it matter? We know our jobs. Live or die, it will all be finished tomorrow," Nothol told him.

"That's what I'm afraid of."

Rekka came over, the look on her face dour but pleasant. Dorl was immediately drawn to the way her clothes hugged her in all the right places. Her long, black hair hung down past her shoulders. The light brown of her skin blended with the dark blacks and blues of her fighting clothes. Her swords were tied to her hips in a nonthreatening way that could easily change in the blink of an eye. She was as dangerous as she was beautiful. Dorl counted himself fortunate to have the love of such a lady.

"We attack before dawn. Even now the Dwarves are rolling their cannon batteries into firing positions. King Thord is positive they can break the enemy lines enough to allow us passage into the ruins," she told them as she hopped onto the knee-high rock wall they watched the meeting from.

Nothol swirled his mug around, gently sloshing golden liquid over the lip. "I think I'll go see to my kit and leave you two for the night."

There was a time when Nothol and Dorl had been inseparable. Rekka's arrival convoluted their working relationship, leaving Nothol the odd one out. He didn't mind as long as she took care of him. Dorl Theed was a good person and a better friend. Nothol had been lucky to have worked alongside him for so long. They had enough stories to last a lifetime. Those lifetimes were about to be cut short come the dawn. He didn't suffer from the illusion of survival. Nothol, ever pragmatic, recognized death staring back at him. The

Goblin army was simply too strong to defeat, even with the unexpected addition of the Dwarves and Minotaurs. He briefly wondered if anyone would ever remember his name, his deeds.

The sell sword drifted towards the command meeting in the hopes of catching useful bits of information that might help him live longer. Smart enough to stay out of sight, Nothol leaned against a thick, white birch tree and listened.

"…enemy lines are too thick," Orlek complained. This was the rebellion's final hour. One he hoped they might escape. The longer the meeting dragged on the more he began to realize how futile that hope was.

"They won't be once my cannons get done," Thord assured. The Dwarf exuded confidence. "We'll rip them apart to the point the rest break and run."

Bahr added, "He may be right. We've seen these cannons in action. There is no other power on Malweir capable of causing such destruction."

"Enough to kill fifty thousand Goblins?" Orlek asked. Exasperation bled through his words. "How many of us have to die in the process? We never signed on to fight this kind of war."

"That doesn't matter," Ingrid replied. "We're here now and can't escape if we wanted to. The Goblins are entrenched in the middle of our kingdom. Even if we left they'd still be here. I don't think I need to remind you that they pose a far greater threat than King Badron ever did."

"So this is our fight now?"

"As much as I don't like to admit it, yes." Tears clung to the corners of her rich, blue eyes. She too saw the end of all they'd suffered for, only it wasn't the end they imagined. Ingrid rightly feared that Delranan as they knew it was coming to an end. Whatever happened tomorrow, their kingdom was going to be fundamentally changed forever.

Bahr said, "She's right. I didn't come here to fight Goblins either but they are in the way and too large of a force to ignore. King Thord and his cannons will do the trick, at least I hope so. We don't have much time left."

Frustrated, Orlek threw his hands up. "Time! Time for what? All you speak in riddles and half-truths. I don't believe your quest to save the world. Nor the reasons for these damned Goblins in my kingdom. Do any of you have an idea just how much blood we've shed fighting Harnin's army? How close we've come to breaking? Now you expect us to go into battle with a massive army who happen to be well rested and in defendable positions? You're going to get all our people killed."

"Individual life or death does not matter, Orlek," Anienam told him. His voice was even, measured so as not to provoke intense feelings. All eyes turned to the blind wizard. "What we face is a moment when the world might end. These times are not cast upon with consideration. Each generation has faced challenges and turmoil. That yours should be forced to endure such is no surprise."

"What are you saying? That we're just puppets in a never ending game?" Thord asked. He cast his gaze on the wizard, unable to accept Anienam was permanently blinded. The sudden change forced him to wonder if Anienam's ability to use magic was impacted enough to make a noticeable difference.

Anienam cocked his head as if in thought. "Perhaps, but we are still given free will to make our own decisions."

"I don't understand," Bahr said.

Clearly frustrated, the wizard continued. "The gods created all life on Malweir but they didn't intervene in how that life developed. Our individual races evolved on their own accord. We became good or evil based on our own decisions. Never once did the gods step in to alter the course of that development."

"What's the point of having gods if they're not going to do anything useful?" Boen asked. His eyes were narrowed with dislike.

Anienam flustered. "We don't have a choice in the matter. They created us, not the other way around, Gaimosian. You would do well to remember that in the coming hours."

Grumbling under his breath, Boen leaned back in the tiny field chair and let the conversation go on.

"Now, where was I? Ah, yes. The gods gave us all life, but they are not without the power to take it away. The gods of light understood that by allowing their dark brethren to continue to exist they were exposing Malweir to unyielding evil. They manipulated time and space to bring us various gifts. The Blud Hamr, for instance. These tools were designed with specific purpose. To use them would counter a specific dark power item."

"This grows tedious," Thord growled.

Even the slender Elf Lord agreed.

"It wouldn't if you would stopped interrupting me. In short, we are given free will to govern our lives but every so often there is divine influence that propels certain ones of us to act on behalf of the gods of light, or the dark."

"Anienam speaks wisely," Faeldrin said, coming to his rescue. "My people have witnessed many great and terrible events. Certain individuals spring forth in the hour of most duress and accept the mantle of leadership. I have seen it several times. The last was in the Deadlands when Anienam's father attempted to stop the Silver Mage. Now it appears that you are the chosen ones, though this task is greater than any in the history of the world, save perhaps the Mage Wars. The short answer to your question Orlek is yes. This is your war."

Rebuked, Orlek glanced angrily at Ingrid. His eyes pleaded with her to take the rebels and flee back to Chadra. They'd have more of a chance in the Keep or the city proper where they had defenses to hide behind. Charging into the massed ranks of Goblins was sheer suicide. Much to his dismay, Ingrid remained passive. He could tell by the way her brows furrowed that she was lost deep in thought. So much had changed since those first few days when Argis helped inspire the people to revolt against the tyrannical Harnin One Eye. The war continued to devolve into madness. Orlek reluctantly concluded that the only reason he remained with the rebellion was for his love of Ingrid. He'd lay down his life for her and it increasingly looked as if that were what was going to happen.

"Bringing us back to the initial point. What is our best course of action to break through enemy lines and get my people into the ruins?" Bahr asked.

Thord stroked his thick beard. "Cannons. Nothing else we have is strong enough to convince the Goblins to break away."

"We have made contact with the combined army coming in from the northeast. King Aurec is most willing to form an alliance," Faeldrin supplied.

Bahr and Boen exchanged a curious look. Neither could believe the same upstart prince responsible for all their woes was now a major player in the battle for Malweir. If Aurec hadn't kidnapped Maleela in the late summer, none of this might be happening, or at least not on the level it was now. Now Maleela was gone, lost, or perhaps dead.

"His army is large enough to give the Goblins concern and they have the advantage of cavalry," the Elf continued. "If we could coordinate simultaneous attacks, you and your group should be able to sneak into the ruins without much issue."

"There are too many shoulds and coulds in that statement, Faeldrin. I need something more concrete before risking our lives for nothing. Not to mention that if Groge falls, so to do our chances of success. He is the only one capable of wielding the Hamr."

"I didn't say it would be easy," Faeldrin smiled.

Bahr nodded understanding. "Anienam, just how long do we have left before the Dae'shan attempt to open the portal?"

Anienam made a public show of going through a series of calculations before saying, "The midnight hour. Just over a day from now the Dae'shan will attempt to bring their masters into our world."

"Faeldrin, is that enough time to get some of us over to Aurec and formulate a strong plan?" Bahr asked.

"I can have you there in a little over an hour provided our enemy hasn't expanded their lines. What do you have in mind?"

Bahr scratched a small cut on his cheek. "We need a diversion. The Wolfsreik and their allies are big enough to provide that for us. Once we get the Goblins to commit to shifting their main focus on the east, Thord can use his cannons and muskets to shred what remains of their lines on our front. Caught between two armies, the Goblins will have no idea which threat is the actual push. I take my group in under cover from the Dwarves…."

"And Minotaurs!" Krek snorted.

Bahr paused, trying not to grin. "Yes, and the Minotaurs, and cut through the ruins to find the Dae'shan. Wizard, will you be able to guide us to where we need to go?"

The question, while valid, irritated Anienam. "Of course I can, fool. My senses have grown tenfold since we arrived. Get me into the ruins and I'll guide you the rest of the way."

"Fair enough," Bahr said.

"What about us?" Ingrid asked. "Where do you want us?"

"Ingrid…no," Orlek pleaded.

The sadness in her eyes was felt by all except Krek. "I'm sorry, Orlek, but this is our fight. These Goblins are in the middle of Delranan. Whether we fight or flee doesn't matter anymore. I don't believe it ever did. We've been given the opportunity to free our people once and for all. Bahr, where do you need my rebels?"

"It would be an honor to have them fight alongside the Dwarves of Drimmen Delf," Thord told her.

Satisfied, and startled, with the answer, Ingrid graciously accepted. "It would be an honor, King Thord."

"Nonsense, woman. We Dwarves recognize strength when we see it. The honor is ours," he replied.

"It's settled. How soon would you like to leave, Sea Wolf?" Faeldrin asked.

Bahr answered, "Immediately. The sooner we get a solid plan in place the better. I don't like the idea of giving our Goblin friends additional time to prepare. If we know the hour is at hand they surely must as well. The Dae'shan are crafty beyond measure and will have numerous surprises in store for us."

Nothol finished the last of his ale as the command meeting dissolved. Bahr and the Elf walked away, followed closely by Ingrid, Thord, and Krek. They were a powerful group, capable of altering the course of the future. Nothol felt fortunate to have been born in such a time. Legends were born from moments like this.

No one in his old drinking haunts would ever believe him. Nothol Coll was too much of an ordinary person to be involved in such matters. The world went on with or without him. He scoffed at their assumed ignorance. Nothol made a living of being underestimated. He only hoped to take advantage of that fact in the coming fight. He thought about heading back to Dorl but his friend had already retired to his tent with Rekka in what promised to be their final night. Nothol reluctantly admitted he was jealous of Dorl but didn't relish the prospect of being separated before being able to marry. The sell sword decided to go and find a refill. He didn't plan on getting drunk but the need to dull his senses suddenly seemed like a very good idea.

TWENTY-FIVE

The Plan

The ride was mercifully quick. Bahr was tired of being in the saddle. Tired of roaming across the world and tired of not being able to lay his head on a pillow at night in his own home. Life didn't care for his wants or needs, however, so he kept going. The Sea Wolf took a small measure of comfort in knowing that all their troubles would soon be over. One way or the other his task ended tomorrow.

They arrived in the Wolfsreik camp without much fanfare. Pickets allowed them access after brief questioning. Aurec and Rolnir were awaiting them. Bahr marveled at the rigid structure of the camp. Tents were erected in orderly rows. Their dull, grey peaks extended further than he could see. The majority of soldiers were asleep, bedded down for what promised to be their final night of rest. Bahr got the sense that they were beyond weary, just as ready to see this through as he was.

Cook fires carried the aroma of roasting meat across the camp. Bahr began to salivate. He hadn't had fresh meat in a long time. Men stood in line for a late meal or huddled around the fire pits spread throughout the camp, exchanging stories or thoughts of what they might do once the war finally ended. It was a bond unlike any other in the world. Soldiers were a much tighter knit group than civilians gave them credit for. They laughed, cried, and bled together. Bahr reluctantly felt the attraction of being part of something so large. His own tiny group had fused together in ways his crew on the *Dragon's Bane* never had. His gaze swept over the rows of countless tents and his mind began to wander.

Having abandoned his claims on Delranan long ago, Bahr seldom spent time around the Wolfsreik. Their size and pride were beyond measure. His brother had been a fool to squander such a resource. Few bothered looking at him as his tiny group passed into the center of camp. Most were interested in Krek for they'd never seen a Minotaur. Elves and Dwarves were rare, but many had at least glimpsed one in the course of their service.

How many knew he was the king's brother? Probably less than he imagined. Knowing that didn't prevent Bahr from feeling eyes glaring at him. Their hatred of Badron must surely translate to him. His family had ground Delranan into the ground, breaking the kingdom to the point where it was almost beyond recovery. There was no atonement for such a crime.

The command group lacked the size he had imagined given the comparisons with the rest of the army. Rolnir and Aurec decided on smaller tents that were practically indiscernible from the others. If not for the double ring of armed and armored guards Bahr might easily have passed right by. He knew a little about the Wolfsreik general and virtually nothing of the boy king. This initial impression sparked a good feeling in him.

Rolnir was burly with red hair streaked through with silver. His hands were large and calloused from a lifetime of wielding a sword. His eyes were sharp yet tired. Red lines cracked the white. His wolf skin cloak draped over his shoulders gave him a wild and dangerous look. Lines began to accumulate around his face and hands. There was no give in his stance. He knew he was the master of this battlefield. Only in his thirties, Rolnir had been through more than a man twice his age.

Aurec, in comparison, represented youth. The boy was slender, almost untamed. An unconscionable weight was cast upon his thin shoulders. Bahr could only guess how traumatic it had been to have a crown placed upon his head at such a young age. He too had taken that test around the same age, only Bahr turned and fled. Though youthful, Aurec exuded weariness. He'd lost the most out of any of them and bore it in his eyes.

"Lord Bahr, welcome," Rolnir started off, offering his hand.

Bahr accepted the offer. "Please, just Bahr. I'm not lord."

Rolnir's lips twisted slightly before falling back into place. His secret hope that Bahr had returned to lay claim to the throne and lead Delranan evaporated. "Even so, you are brother to the late king. Allow me to introduce King Aurec of Rogscroft, Cuul Ol of the Pell Darga, and General Vajna."

Casting a glance to see if Faeldrin was going to step forward and take charge, Bahr said, "This is Lord Faeldrin of the Aeldruin, King Thord of Drimmen Delf, Ingrid of the rebellion, Anienam Keiss the wizard, and King Krek."

"Well met," Rolnir replied. "This is quite the collection of warriors. I'm told your army has…unique weapons."

"Very unique," Bahr said and went on to explain the gunpowder weapons to the combined army's leadership. When he finished, their looks were a strange combination of respect and abject horror.

Rolnir cleared his throat. "We should have no trouble breaking the Goblin lines with weapons like that, but they have a very large force. Close to fifty thousand or so we've guessed."

"A few less," Thord grumbled. "We've bloodied their noses back in my kingdom. They got a taste of what Dwarven might truly is."

"Have you any idea how they arrived in Delranan so fast?" Aurec asked.

Anienam answered, "Magic."

"Excuse me? There is no magic in this part of the world," Vajna said. His eyes narrowed in mistrust.

"Magic. There is great evil at work here. Surely you must have felt it lurking behind all Badron did? It is no coincidence that our armies have gathered near Arlevon Gale."

"These are just ruins, old one. Arlevon Gale may once have been important but their time has long fallen into decay," Rolnir said. "What could possibly be so special as to compel so many combatants here and now?"

"This is the final crossing point for the dark gods," Anienam said. His voice dropped to a conspiratorial level. "Tomorrow night the agents of evil will attempt to open the path between dimensions and release the dark gods into the world. This, my friends, is the final battle in a war that has stretched since the dawn of the world."

"How fortunate," Rolnir said. "Are there other surprises in store for us? I'm not willing to commit to the attack without knowing more. As it stands now we're going to lose too many soldiers just trying to break their lines, even with the Dwarf *cannons*."

The word felt awkward, almost unnatural. Rolnir wanted to see the machines in action but dreaded the effects based on Bahr's testimony. Until now war had been personal with sword or axe, made only slightly less so by the use of catapults and scorpions. He could almost envision there being no need for large-scale armies composed of infantry if the cannons were as effective as Bahr suggested.

"I assume plenty more we're not aware of. The least of which are the Dae'shan. Fortunately for us they are only three instead of four. Without a fourth their power is diminished, slightly. I can only assume that they've collected the remnants of creations of the dark to protect them during the ritual."

"You bear ill tidings, wizard," Aurec said. His voice was strained, for he secretly dealt with conflicting emotions. Rumor had come to him that Maleela was taken by Bahr and the wizard. Yet they came to his camp with open arms and in friendship. Their actions set his kingdom on a course for war, or so he believed. To have them standing before him now left him feeling raw, anguished.

"Magic seldom distinguishes between ill and joy. What matters is we have a chance, the slightest chance, of getting to the Dae'shan and destroying the Olagath Stone, thus sealing the dark gods away forever." Anienam paused to let his words sink in. "This will not be an easy task. The Dae'shan will be most determined to prevent our interference. They will stop at nothing to see us stopped."

"Are these the same demons who corrupted Badron?" Rolnir asked, folding his arms.

"They've often sought out soft targets with pliable minds."

"Makes sense. Badron was consumed with getting revenge on Rogscroft, though we've come to learn he merely needed an excuse to start a war," Rolnir said with respect to both Aurec and Bahr. He suddenly felt uncomfortable being caught between them. Any unspoken tension only added to the group dynamic. He wondered how well this newly forged alliance was going to hold together in the coming battle.

"The war was a cleverly crafted diversion from the truth. The Dae'shan have known for millennia this moment was coming and they knew where. We still have much going for us. We know what they intend to do and when. We also know that each time before has resulted in failure for them. This, my friends, is their final attempt."

"Making them all the more dangerous," Ingrid said.

"Indeed, but we have all endured much danger over the course of the winter," Aurec told her. "Rolnir is right, wizard, we stand to lose many lives."

Anienam shrugged. "Some losses are unavoidable. That is the nature of war, young king. Our Dwarven allies will lessen the odds, as will your siege engines."

"We've all fought Goblins before. The cannons and catapults will test their will, but they won't break and run," Thord added. "Not unless we manage to slaughter the majority of their strength. No, Anienam, this is going to be bloody for us all."

"How then do we proceed with the assault? If what you say is true, time is against us," Rolnir said, deciding to change the subject further. "How long will you need to complete your task?"

"Ha! The task itself is a simple smashing with the Blud Hamr," Anienam cackled. "Getting to the Olagath Stone is the trick. Some hours I suspect."

"Since Bahr and his people are already camped with us I suggest we begin the attack," Faeldrin said. "Once you hear the signal that the attack is underway you can commit your combined army in the support assault."

"What sign? How will we know?" Aurec asked.

Thord grinned, a savage look. "You'll know."

Aurec paced like a caged mountain lion. He wished he'd never sent Venten home. This was one of those moments where he needed his old friend's counsel. A moment he long dreaded was drawing ever closer. The battle on the morrow wasn't even a consideration. His sole concern lay on the brother of the king responsible for murdering his father. For destroying his kingdom and potentially ruining his way of life. Not only that, but Aurec desperately needed word of Maleela. If she was still with Bahr why hadn't he brought her?

Thorsson folded back the tent flap and coughed. "Sire, he's here."

His heart sped up. Sweat tickled his brow. Aurec's mouth went dry. His hands trembled. It took a concentrated effort to make his lips work. "Thank you, Thorsson. Please send him in."

The command sergeant major paused, as if determining whether his king was in the proper frame of mind for such a guest. Ultimately, it wasn't up to him. His job was to follow orders and offer suggestions. He knew, as did the others close to Aurec, that this meeting needed to happen in order for the king to go into battle with any doubts removed.

"You asked to speak with me?" Bahr said as he entered.

Aurec turned to face him. They stood for a moment, each staring back at the other. The king of Rogscroft struggled with the desire to strike the older Bahr. Until now he hadn't hoped to ever confront the one responsible for stealing his love. Aurec gradually got control of his emotions.

"Yes, Captain, thank you for coming," he said.

Bahr saw the turmoil etched on young Aurec's face. "I'm not my brother."

"Excuse me?" Aurec was taken off guard.

Bahr offered a thin smile. "You've been thinking it since we arrived. Badron and I are nothing alike. Nor am I the monster you think I am. Maleela is my niece. I was hired to return her from your…kidnapping effort. We didn't learn until much later that it was not all it was made out to be."

His words, while intended to assuage the anguish Aurec felt, had little impact. He saw Badron when he looked at Bahr. He saw the loss of the love of his life.

"Where is she?" he asked, the words coming out as a demand.

Bahr deflated. "She…she's gone."

Aurec felt his heart shatter. Months of repression finally broke free. The tears flowed. Reason and hope abandoned him. He'd kept the hope alive since the moment he'd awakened to find her missing. Death wasn't possible. She was merely secluded away in Delranan. Bahr's words shredded that illusion. With Maleela dead, Aurec feared he lacked the resolve to finish the war. He suddenly felt lost.

Racked with sobs, Aurec choked back his tears. "How did she die?"

Pain reflected off Bahr's dark eyes. His mind drifted back to finding Ionascu's murdered corpse. "I can't say for certain she did."

Aurec stiffened. "What do you mean? You're not making sense."

"We were attacked by a pair of Gnaals in the jungle. Nothol Coll took her to safety but was knocked out from behind. One of our own, who turned out to be a spy for Harnin, clubbed him and, we think, attempted to murder Maleela. Instead we found his body and no trace of her."

Frightful images played through Aurec's mind. He imagined her lying dead from starvation in the middle of a hostile land, dying slowly with no friends or comfort. The thought of being abandoned by those who claimed to love and protect her must have driven her into madness during those final few moments. Aurec's knees gave out and he collapsed onto his field chair, lowering his head into his hands.

Bahr shifted uncomfortably. He'd dreaded this confrontation from the moment Faeldrin led him into the Wolfsreik camp. The situation was beyond awkward. Heir to the throne, he was more of an outcast than anyone else in their steadily growing circle. Worse, the longer he stayed around them the more his perceived failures returned to haunt him.

He looked down on Aurec with immense compassion. Losing everything was no easy thing to endure. He knew. He'd lost his estate, his ship, and now his family. Bahr was alone in the world. No matter how tomorrow ended, his lot in life wasn't going to change. Accepting this fact was difficult but not impossible. He'd had countless hours on the road or river to ponder the course on which his life bizarrely twisted.

"How could you do that? You just left her to die," Aurec accused.

Bahr frowned, knowing he failed to properly explain the situation. "We have every reason to believe she was kidnapped after she killed Ionascu."

Aurec lifted his head slowly. His eyes were red and sore. Tears streaked his face, marring the dirt that had accumulated. "What do you mean? Maleela would never kill anyone. It's not in her nature."

"So I believed as well. My niece is a resilient young lady, however, and quite capable of defending herself. You've no idea how difficult it was keeping her from getting into battles. Which is why I fully believe she killed Ionascu and was abducted shortly thereafter. Nothing else makes sense. We found evidence of a struggle. Feathers and such." Bahr went on to explain their running engagement with the Harpies and Anienam's theory that the Hags were in league with the Dae'shan. Much of it sounded implausible to Bahr as he spoke it. Then again much of their journey since leaving Delranan seemed farfetched. He certainly wouldn't believe another if he were being told such tales.

Aurec reflected the sentiment. "You realize how impossible it all sounds? I've spent months locked in a war not of my choosing, all the while hoping against hope that she was alive and safe from harm. For you to stand before me and claim she's been captured by our enemy drives iron nails through my heart." He used the back of his sleeves to wipe his eyes. "I want to believe you, Bahr. I do. There has been much animosity between our families." He held up a hand for silence before

Bahr could counter the point. “I know you’ve been a minor player in this foul drama, but that doesn’t change things. I can look beyond your mission to Rogscroft, but not your negligence in keeping Maleela safe.”

“I accept that, but you need to keep in mind she is my blood. I may not have been there for her when she was growing up but my love for that little girl runs deep. If I could trade places with her I would, gladly,” he told Aurec.

The king nodded in total agreement. “As would I. Perhaps I was wrong. You are not your brother, Captain Bahr. I see that now. There is honor in you. It reminds me of my father.”

“Stelskor was a good man,” Bahr said. He’d met the old king twice before and came away impressed each time. Secretly he wished his brother would have aspired to be more like the king of Rogscroft. Delranan would have been a better kingdom.

“Thank you,” Aurec said.

They left the conversation at that. Each had said his part. Nothing further needed explaining. Bahr left in friendship. Heading back to Faeldrin and the others, he felt a great weight fall from his shoulders. His heart lightened. Making peace with the king of Rogscroft sealed a portion of the rift between their two families. Bahr didn’t know if it would be enough. Too much bad blood existed, but it was a definite beginning.

Despite the good feelings coming from his meeting, Bahr couldn’t avoid thinking about Maleela and what had become of his niece. Did she die in the jungle or was her fate much worse? He wasn’t sure why but felt the answer would soon be revealed.

TWENTY-SIX

Calm Before the Storm

Skuld watched the Dwarf army going through preparations for tomorrow's battle with awe. Once a common street thief, he never dreamed to have witnessed the sights and experiences of his long journey. Wars, monsters, and impossible races stretched his imagination to the limits. There were times when he regretted overhearing Nothol and Dorl talking about the riches in the Murdes Mountains. Times when he wanted nothing more than to retreat to his hiding spot in Chadra and forget the rest of the world existed. But he also found more times when he could do naught but stand in wonder at all Malweir had to offer.

His personal development took him through different courtships. Boen was his initial role model for he fancied himself becoming a great and powerful warrior. His own experience in battle left that desire deflated. No one should willingly want to go to war. Next came Anienam's subtle testing to see if he was right for assuming the mantle of Mage. Skuld didn't care for magic, though the strength and power of it was certainly alluring. He reluctantly accepted Anienam's promise that he held latent magical attributes that could be exploited into use but wasn't sure that was what he wanted from life. Skuld was more confused now than he had ever been in his brief life.

The rebels were his people. Many were from Chadra and he thought he recognized a few in passing. They were shopkeepers or smiths. Only a handful had ever been professional soldiers. They were nothing like the gruff professionals of Drimmen Delf. Skuld couldn't pull his gaze. He and a few others hadn't gotten to witness the Dwarves go to war during their stay in the grand halls. Bahr insisted that Skuld remain with Maleela while he and the others went to the battle of Bode Hill. At the time Skuld resented the decision. He wanted to help, to fight. Now that he saw how dedicated the Dwarves were to warfare his stomach felt unsettled.

"Isn't it a glorious sight?" Ironfoot asked as he came up beside Skuld.

Skuld didn't know what to say. He shifted his gaze to the normally taciturn Dwarf captain. "How can anyone be this good at destruction? I never imagined anything like this when I was living on the streets."

Ironfoot regarded the boy a moment longer before answering. "Dwarves aren't inherently violent, but we have great propensity to execute our will through the axe. You have seen this before. There are no surprises here."

"I wasn't allowed out of the mountains," Skuld protested. "Bahr thought it was best to keep me with the princess."

"Perhaps. I did not know either of you during those days," the Dwarf said thoughtfully. "Your race is full of surprises, young Skuld. I find myself constantly being taken off guard by your deeds. It is easy to see why Humans have become the dominant species on Malweir. The rest of us are too mired in the old ways, ways that don't exist any longer. Malweir was once wild, untamed. They were times for hard people. The weak perished quickly. Old hatreds were formed and continue to this day. What you see before us is a result of those hatreds. We will take our vengeance against the Goblins tomorrow."

Ironfoot fell silent. A battery of cannons was being pulled by. Four oxen were hooked up to each cannon. They strained under the several-thousand-pound weight of iron and gears as the animals dragged the weapons of mass destruction through partially trampled snow. Even packed for transport, the weapons presented an ominous scene. Skuld felt death as they rolled past. His argument with Ironfoot was justified, at least in his mind.

A sudden thought occurred to him. "Ironfoot, why are you not back with the Dwarves?"

"It seems my fate is not tied to theirs. Anienam told us that we were all required if the quest was to succeed. That means I am meant to fight alongside the rest of you." He paused as the last cannon went by. "Between the two of us, I think I would rather be with Bahr and that fool, old wizard. He makes life interesting."

Skuld was beginning to feel like he was the only sane one in their group. Confused, he said good night and went back to his bedroll. Dawn was coming fast.

Rekka rolled of a panting Dorl and pulled the blanket around her neck. She wasn't cold. Their lovemaking saw to that, but it wouldn't take long for the crisp night to turn their sweat into ice. Responding to her, Dorl helped by wrapping his free arm around her back and gently caressing her shoulder. Her eyes closed as she enjoyed the moment. Tomorrow could wait. It was much too late to worry about their destiny. All that mattered now was her time with Dorl.

The love they shared was undiscovered by either. She'd grown up in a rigidly structured world with no room for romance. Cashi Dam had tried to insist on his devotion, but it was misguided. The tribal leader of Teng let his desire turn to lust and eventually wound up with his death at the hands of a Gnaal. Dorl was unlike anyone she'd ever met. Rough on the outside, Dorl Theed bore the softest heart. He gave in wholly to her, willingly. The comfort she took from this was unmatched. It made her job easier and enhanced her life to the point where she could see abandoning the sword for children and a home.

Rekka propped up on an elbow and stared down into his soft eyes. Whatever fear she harbored melted as he stared back. Smiling, she traced a finger down between his chest muscles and sighed.

"What's wrong?" he asked.

She shook her head slightly. Her dark hair whisked against his exposed flesh. "Nothing. I'm trying to imagine what the day after tomorrow will be like."

Dorl was no fool. He couldn't imagine what tomorrow was going to bring, much less whatever fallout happened later. He didn't expect to live past the attack. A gnawing specter had been hounding him since their run-in with the Harpies in Fedro. He wanted nothing more than to close his eyes and get lost in the warmth of her embrace.

"Can't we just have tonight?" he asked.

Her smile faded, leaving only the slightest trace. "I want to give you so much more, Dorl Theed. Through you I have found a new sense of being."

"How do you mean? I'm nothing special," he protested.

"You are, though you don't realize it. I don't want to be the guardian of Trennaron any longer. I don't want to serve anyone other than myself. Dorl, I want to live. With you."

His heart skipped. Impossible futures raced through his mind. His young life had seemed aimless until Rekka entered it. She quickly became a fixed point for him to focus on as he trudged through misadventures and the endless string of daily hardships. To hear her words now, at this most terrible moment imaginable, meant more to Dorl than he'd ever be able to express.

"I never thought of settling down with anyone before," he admitted. "I've been travelling around with Nothol for so long I don't recall another life. Don't get me wrong, Rekka, I'm flattered you'd want to stick around with me."

"But?" Rekka's eyes narrowed. She withdrew her loving finger and tried not to glare down on him.

Dorl swallowed the lump rising through his throat. He hadn't intended on aggravating her but sometimes the tongue fails to express what the mind or heart feels. "Don't go jumping to conclusions. My only reservation to sticking with you is that I can't provide you the life you deserve. Nothing more."

Rekka tilted her head back and laughed. The sound was joyful, relieved. "Dorl Theed, you soft-hearted fool."

The corners of his mouth turned down in disappointment. "Like I said, I never thought about settling down with anyone before."

She brought her face close to his, their lips almost touching. "Will you think about it now?"

Dorl reached up and kissed her passionately.

Daylight faded; it was a gradual progression of colors from bright blue to dark purple. Birds chirped as they soared over the rebel camp. The mild brown bark from a dozen different types of trees looked like a carefully mended blanket. Groge was continually amazed with life in the lowlands. It was so unlike the harsh conditions of Venheim, high atop the jagged mountain peaks. So much life and variations kept him grounded. Young by Giant standards, Groge gained experience none of his peers could ever dream of.

Reluctantly he pulled his gaze away from the world. Groge never asked to become the one person capable of bringing about the end of the dark gods' threat and it wore on him heavily. All he wanted was to become a great forge master like Joden. That dream seemed further away daily. His disturbed gaze finally fell upon the Blud Hamr. The ancient weapon, though Anienam continued to contend it was a tool and not a weapon, stood head down in the snow. The handle stretched almost to his waist. Groge wasn't certain but he thought the very earth vibrated when the Hamr touched ground.

"I don't deserve this," he whispered to the Hamr. "You are too great of a responsibility for a simple apprentice. Am I even capable of doing the right thing when that moment arrives?"

Frustrated, he shook his head. He wasn't a great thinker or a trained warrior. Having never experienced the violence of combat before joining Bahr's quest, Groge was often left feeling stranded. In the months since he'd come down from the mountains he had not only taken lives, but was growing increasingly proficient at it. The notion horrified him. It became clear why his people abandoned the rest of Malweir all those centuries ago. No race should have the power to control and kill another.

Groge closed his eyes and tried to picture Joden's forge: the smell of charcoal and iron filling the air, the feeling of intense heat on the backs of his hands, the sounds of hammers clanging against anvils. It was the life he was cut out for, though perhaps not what he'd been created for. Clearly the gods of light had specific designs for Groge that the youth didn't share. Having almost no control over the direction of his life went beyond maddening.

'What makes me special?" he asked after long moments of reflection. "I haven't earned any rank or title. I'm not experienced. Would any other suffice in my place? I wish there were answers. Never have I felt so helpless, like a newborn. Will my actions keep my people alive?"

The Hamr began to glow bright blue as if in response. Groge took heart, knowing the Hamr was giving him a much-needed sign. Doubts began to erase as conviction rushed in to fill the void. Hope rekindled. The young Giant once again found purpose through the raw strength the Hamr exuded. Live or die, he instinctively knew he was going to perform well tomorrow. Should he live, Groge would never be the same after that. It was a small price he was willing to live with as long as he helped stopped the enemies of life and restore order to Malweir.

The eve of the greatest battle in generations did little to affect Boen's nerves. He was the definition of warfare. Gaimos had been vanquished millennia ago but her people continued to thrive under the worst conditions. They trained constantly, developing new skills in the art of killing. One popular theory was that the toppling of Gaimos by a coalition of nations was the single greatest tragedy in Malweir's rich history while simultaneously bringing about events that would alter the course of the future permanently.

Gaimosians were bestowed by the gods with latent magical attributes. A core group would go on to establish the library-fortress of Ipn Shal and the order of Mages. The ruin of Gaimos would be felt for generations. Many, Boen included, struggled through life in an attempt at championing the undefended. There was only one goal: the return of Gaimos as a nation and the finality of their life of exile. Boen wasn't sure what he'd do once he was able to settle down. At his advanced age it was beyond past time. His best years were long behind him. He had no heirs, no continuation of the bloodline. When Boen died so too would his family's history.

He shrugged off the feelings of dread lingering in the shadow-crusted corners of his mind and set his sword to the sharpening stone. Oils slickened the small slab of granite. It was an act he'd done over a million times. The repetitive nature soothed his nerves, distributing a sense of calm throughout his large body. His mind cleared. The prospect of hacking through enemy lines was all that mattered. Boen's purpose, his singular task, was to punch a hole in the Goblin ranks wide enough for Bahr and the others to get into the ruins. Nothing else mattered.

He'd given Bahr his word to protect his back for as long as necessary. Should that require giving his life in the process so be it. Boen was a warrior. This was his calling. All the pressure of politics and personal maneuvering went over his head as he prepared his mind for what must be done tomorrow. His only regret or fear, though he'd never use such a word, was that he had never even conceived such impossible odds. The war for the soul of Malweir was the largest in recorded history, or so he'd been led to believe. He considered it a great honor to be the only one of his people to be an active combatant. Once again a Gaimosian would be at the center of the world. His actions might very well be the spark that motivated the rest of the allies and tip the balance in the war.

Boen began to whistle softly as he repeatedly ran his sword over the stone. Tomorrow he would test his resolve. He would either be found wanting or deliver all those unspoken promises to his friends.

Dwarven work crews continued digging their cannons in throughout the night. Weapons were sighted in on lines of fire that would, theoretically, provide the most damage to the Goblin army. Aiming stakes were emplaced as far out as Dwarves were able to crawl without drawing attention. Cannon crews dug in their powder bags. They knew the Goblins had only one counter to the gunpowder: fire. Should any arrows drop into the ammunition pits, the entire battery could go up in flames. Piles of ammunition were rolled together beside each cannon. Gunners sighted in prefixed targets as work continued around them.

Individual firing lines were established for the musket-laden infantry. Over one thousand Dwarves went about cleaning their weapons, double checking their powder reserves, and ensuring they had enough ammunition to sustain a heavy attack. Barrels were brushed clean of dust and debris. Triggers were tested for reliability as the musketeers chatted quietly amongst themselves. They were already experienced, having stood toe to toe in the trenches at Bode Hill with their dark Dwarf cousins. Then it had been practically even. The Goblins had nothing comparable to their muskets. Tomorrow promised to be a glorious battle.

Back in the center of camp, the beleaguered rebels struggled with personal demons. Far from being real soldiers, the citizen army of Delranan individually had to come to terms with their mortality. The decision to stand and fight or flee wore heavily on them. Conducting the civil war campaign against Harnin's forces was a series of hit-or-miss ambushes and raids. Never had they stood the line against a proper field force. Imaginations threatened to run wild. The old timers recalled obscure battles where thousands were slain. These bits of history were kept silent from fear of routing their own army.

Several looked to the Dwarves and Minotaurs for motivation. They were true warriors. Many of the people of Delranan were inspired by the professionalism of their new allies. They set about readying their weapons and kit for the coming battle. Others floundered in self-doubt. They weren't heroes or even soldiers. Personal motivations ranged as greatly as the colors in nature. It was for each to decide how to handle their role. Some would break and run as the nightmare erupted around them. Others would drop to their knees and cry uncontrollably. Yet others would rise to the challenge and show the world the mettle of Delrananians.

Oblivious to the rest of the camp, the civilians went about their tasks with heavy hearts.

The Minotaur army watched them with amusement. Born and bred for battle, the bulls were ready to attack under the cover of darkness. Until recently the Minotaurs had remained in their forest home of Malg, far to the east. They seldom cared for the goings-on of other races and were intent on learning new secrets of warfare and savagery. Krek had come to power long after his experiences with Anienam's father in the Deadlands. He'd forged bonds with several from the kingdom of Thrae but his most important alliance was with the Pell Darga tribes in the Darkwall Mountains, the very ancestors of Cuul Ol and his tribes.

Both races were largely considered outcasts. Without the grand courts of the Mage orders to convene quarterly and bring order to Malweir, there was a growing discourse among those like the Minotaurs. Krek was determined to lead them back to an age of greatness where they were both feared and respected. It began in Delranan. The army was strictly punitive. Old rivalries remained between Minotaur and Goblin. Once subject to petty raids at the behest of the Silver Mage, the bulls of Malg finally found their opportunity to exact revenge.

They snorted and laughed. Sleep was long in coming. Seasoned warriors, the bulls spoke of grand schemes to kill everyone. They brandished weapons at each other and utter curses in their course language. Humans too close quickly shied away lest they get caught up in the melee growing in the center of the Minotaur camp. Young bulls charged into each other. The thunderous noise made many cringe throughout the camps. Blood spilled. Cheers raged. And the army of Malg continued its ritualistic endeavors.

Dwarves soon thronged to the edges, eager to witness the test of strength. True warriors appreciated strength. The Dwarves were no exception. While the bulls were all more than double the height, Dwarven soldiers looked on admiringly. They clashed axes in shields in a rhythmic song that made blood boil. Roars of approval went up when a bull fell. More than one injured warrior needed to be carried off to camp medics.

The ritual continued long into the night. Pre-battle jitters faded under the pretense of bravado. Blood mixed with snow and mud, painting the ground in shades of what tomorrow would bring. Gradually the crowds thinned. Warriors went to find much-needed rest. The Dwarves finished their pre-combat checks and bedded down. Cannon crews slept behind their pieces. Pickets were emplaced. Roving patrols circled the camps at intervals.

Incredible tension spread from person to person. Words went unsaid. Looks were exchanged. Those still awake skillfully avoided contact with their fellows. Even the trees seemed to feel it. Branches curled upward, their tips inching back towards the trunks. Birds and small animals fled lest they get caught in the middle. Clouds hung suspended in the sky as if afraid to move. The moon lacked its shine. Dull light barely reached the ground. A hush fell over the fields surrounding the ruins.

Night deepened. Armies bedded down. Nerves ran high and for good reason. The fate of all Malweir rested in the hands of all those assembled around the ruins of Arlevon Gale.

TWENTY-SEVEN

A Final Trick

Maleela, dark queen of the Goblins and heir to the hatred of the world, stood atop the hastily constructed watchtower centered on her command pavilion. Her slender hands were encased in black leather and clasped gently behind her back. Dressed in the colors of midnight, Maleela watched the plains of Delranan like a ghoul creeping through a cemetery. The sweep of her long dress had a thin line of sawdust clinging to it, marring the illusion of perfection. Her hair was tied back in a long tail that draped down between her shoulder blades.

Hard eyes stared down on the multiple armies camped nearby. She had no way of knowing for sure, but close to ninety thousand combatants were going through their final preparations before the battle was joined. So much death and hatred was going to happen Maleela could feel the electricity burning up from the ground. It stretched the height of the tower and tickled the soles of her feet. She suddenly felt stronger than ever before. Raw power flowed into her, imbuing her with the fortitude required to see tomorrow's events through. She closed her eyes briefly as power consumed her.

"Intoxicating isn't it?" Amar Kit'han asked. His raspy voice was the sound of rocks being crushed. "As if there is a direct connection with the heart of the world."

"What is it?" she asked.

Amar drifted closer, stopping as he drew even. Thousands of campfires burned to the edge of his vision. So impressed, the Dae'shan failed to find comment. "A link between Malweir's soul and the wielder of power. Very few have ever felt it and I suspect none will again once the ritual concludes."

"Has the end truly arrived?" she pressed. The desire to know her fate strengthened. "Will tomorrow be the end of the past and the beginning of your new, dark world?"

"Where I will ascend and you will be made a true queen," Amar replied. "Never before have I come so close. The dark gods strain against the mesh of their prison. They hunger for freedom. Time is nearly upon us. No longer will the Dae'shan cower in shadow. We shall take our rightful place as lords of the world. Malweir will be plunged into an eternity of darkness and nightmares. It is all so close now. So very close."

"There are many awaiting us that might claim to differ," Maleela countered. Power so strong it forced her fingers apart lest the currents burn them together.

Amar paused, his revelry disturbed. "There is more at work than you know, princess. Great armies have gathered. Many have come in the false quest for righteousness. Others simply because they had no reason not to. A handful, a very small minority are here for you."

She stiffened, bringing her hands from behind her. "Speak plainly. What do you mean?"

"Your uncle sits to our southwest. His quest will attempt to break my power while the armies ruin themselves around us."

Conflicting emotions raged within her. Deep inside, so deep she'd nearly abandoned it, the prospect of hope for the future stirred. Since devoting herself to Amar Kit'han and her fervent desire for revenge, Maleela had done nothing but hate. She'd lost faith in Humanity, her family, and most importantly, herself. Misery became her companion, comforting her in those long hours in the middle of the night when she thought no one was paying attention.

Amar Kit'han heard it all. His unique tortures were designed to break her mind under the false pretense of empowerment. Thus far it had worked perfectly. She was his willing tool. A tool he had every intention of discarding once the war was finished. Each night he continued to pour subtle traces of magic into her dreams, darkening them to the point where she was ready to take up a sword and spill blood. Her descent was nearly complete. All it needed was a final act.

"My uncle will be difficult to stop," she finally said as the war of emotions in her mind quieted. "He will be most formidable if he's managed to acquire the Blud Hamr. Killing them should be a priority."

Very ruthless, this one. Much better than her pathetic father ever proved. "Agreed. The Hamr must not be allowed to reach the ritual site. Are you capable of setting aside loyalties to accomplish this?"

Her face hardened in reply. "I am. Bahr has done nothing for me. Seeing him dead will serve as a brutal reminder for all who might one day cross me. You said a minority. My uncle does not constitute a minority. Who else must I face tomorrow?"

Amar grinned from beneath his hood. The glow emanating off his form was faint enough to go undetected by her mortal eyes. "Are you sure you can handle the knowledge I am about to bestow on you? You are only Human after all. An inherent weakness you are incapable of escaping."

"I grow weary of these verbal games, Amar. Tell me what I need to know so that I may win this battle. If you insist on speaking in riddles go find Thrask. Perhaps that foul-smelling beast would be better companionship for you." Maleela practically spat her words. Her disgust for the Dae'shan was rivaled only by the need to remain allied with him. For the time being.

"Very well. King Aurec co-commands the combined army to our east. They are the strongest, with thousands from your father's Wolfsreik. Aurec will stop at nothing to destroy the Goblins and end this war," Amar admitted.

Maleela turned slowly to face him. "Aurec lives?"

"Unless he just died, yes, and he is the crowned king of Rogscroft. Does this displease you? I can summon my…pets to dispatch him before dawn."

Her tiny hand raised. "No, if Aurec falls it will not be by your monsters' claws. He is…was a good man. He deserves to die with honor. I should like to see him one final time before the battle begins."

"Love still holds sway I see. Perhaps I was wrong about you," Amar hissed.

She fixed him with a deadly glare. "There is no love. You've managed to kill it. I am a creature of your making. I feel nothing but hate."

We shall see, puppet. We shall see. I wonder how deep your resolve runs the moment you are forced to confront your lover. Do you have the strength to take his life? "I am pleased to hear you say that. Aurec has grown to become a cunning foe. He will bring his army with all the might he possesses. Our Goblin allies are strong but they have seldom won great victories against man. We have numbers but I doubt they will be enough."

"I will make them enough. Do what you must to free your gods. Thrask and I will hold off our enemies long enough," she said with defiance. Already plans and counter plans warped in her mind. No strategist, she had grown up around the army and had absorbed enough to be confident about her chances tomorrow.

Amar appreciated her confidence but ultimately knew it wasn't enough. Thrask and his Goblins were weak. Otherwise their kingdom would have conquered half of the known world by now instead of wallowing in caverns in those places no one else wanted to go. Sadly, the Goblins served a singular purpose: kill as many of the allies as possible to make his mission easier. Nothing else really mattered.

"I think your proposal should be executed," Amar said without warning. "I suggest presenting a flag of truce to meet with our enemy leaders. It will be good to demoralize them moments before they order the assault."

"And you don't fear the same of me?" she asked.

"Should I?"

Maleela hesitated for the briefest moment, enough to cause quiet concern in the Dae'shan. "No. I will do my job as long as you fulfill your promise. I want my father's head."

Amar stared back at her hard. She would get her wish sooner than she could ever expect, for only he knew that Badron, the former king of Delranan, was cowering amongst the Wolfsreik just scant meters away. Oh yes, they would meet again. Remaining silent, Amar Kit'han decided to let Maleela learn the truth of this the hard way. Some secrets were too delicious to waste before their proper time.

The first tendrils of dawn crawled across the face of the world with lazy intent. Bright pinks and reds replaced the dark clouds, threatening an ominous future. Maleela viewed it as no better sign. Blood skies were proper for the amount of blood about to be shed. She watched from her tower as the small envoy of Goblins trudged beyond their trenches and partially erected palisades. The dingy white banner waving over their heads in the predawn breeze reminded her of a soiled nightgown. There was nothing dignified to it at all.

Frowning, Maleela stormed down the steps. Her mind raced through several possibilities. The growing desire to confront and murder her father filled her with rage, with purpose. She had never felt closer to her goals. Soon all the wrongs that had been thrust upon her during her short life would be avenged and the world would be open for her to ascend to her rightful place. Those desires proved almost too powerful, threatening to render her mind to fragments. Sanity and reality waivered back and forth as she slowly felt her core slipping away.

She didn't care. The dilemma within was paltry compared to the full force of her wrath. Nothing could deter her from claiming vengeance against a lifetime of mistreatment. Maleela was dressed in resplendent onyx armor. Intricately carved skulls poked out from beneath her full-length cape. Polished leather boots stretched up over her knees. Her sword belt was sprinkled with emeralds and sapphires. Hair tied back in a tail, the princess of Delranan wore a severe look. She had become the harbinger of doom for the northern kingdoms.

A pair of Goblins met her at the base of the tower. Maleela ignored their drooling glares as she marched past. They had become tedious to her. Foul beyond measure, the Goblin horde was merely a means to an end. Secretly she wished them all to die in the coming battle. There was no room in Malweir for such filth. Not in her visions. A handful of

Humans were secured among the ruins. Most, she guessed, were prisoners intended for sacrifice in Amar Kit'han's dark ritual to bring forth the dark gods.

The notion of Human sacrifice was sickening but concerned her little. Maleela tried to stay focused on her goals. Everything else was an unpleasant distraction from the truth. Mud sucked at her boots with each light step. She took the reins from a Goblin and climbed aboard her horse. Thrask was already waiting.

His tusks gleamed in the morning light, as if he'd purposefully polished them. "This will be a day long remembered."

Maleela grunted in reply. Her tolerance for the Goblin Lord was weakening the longer they shared company. "I want no quarter given. Their army is a nuisance at best. Can your forces handle them?"

Insulted, Thrask thumped a meaty fist to his chest. "We will kill every…last…one."

I certainly hope so, though not without suffering great losses on your part, my dear Thrask. It would be divine if you managed to get yourself killed as well. That would solve matters nicely for me. She nodded. "Good. Now, let us go meet with our enemies. I am most eager to hear what they have to say."

The lines parted enough for her column of twenty warriors to march through. Only she and Thrask were mounted. The others marched with grim determination. Their boots struck the ground with fury as if their anger was translated deep into the earth. Maleela cringed inwardly at the sound before steeling her nerve. This was war. It took several long minutes for them to reach the parley area secured between the lines--long minutes in which she dealt with questions and doubt. This was her first true test of leadership, though she knew neither Thrask nor Amar expected her to be much more than a figurehead. She vowed to prove them both wrong.

Maleela recognized Aurec immediately. Her heart threatened to get the better of her, overturning all she'd endured before she tightened up. There was no room in her life for love. Not any longer. There were others, but none she knew. Pennants and banners waved on the morning breeze, announcing the Wolfsreik in all its glory. She spied several other colors amidst the very large group. Rogscroft and the tattered remains of flags she failed to recognize. All told her enemies presented an opposing group.

Sliding to the ground, she walked side by side with Thrask until they stood under the hastily erected pavilion for the meeting. Maleela avoided looking at Aurec, though she clearly saw him start to move towards her. She could only imagine how much willpower it took to make himself stop and remain still, like a king should.

"So, at last all my enemies are gathered," she began without pause.

Aurec clicked his tongue on the roof of his mouth. "Enemies? I see several but only one I would not consider such. Why are you with this filth, Maleela?"

Thrask bristled at the insult, momentarily forgetting the banner of truce. "Mind your tongue, boy-king. I have killed many like you."

Maleela held up a hand to silence the Goblin. "This is not the world you once rescued me from, Aurec. I have made my choices and they lead me to an inevitable conclusion."

"That being?"

She turned to the redhead. "And you would be?"

"Rolnir. What is your conclusion?"

Madness twinkled in her eyes. "Ah yes, the mighty general of the Wolfsreik. I grew up listening to tales of your heroism. How paltry they seem to me now that I finally meet you. You're all going to die here. I trust you realize that."

"If that's what the gods decree, so be it, but I doubt that very much," he replied.

"Are you thinking of the second army massed on our western flank? We know of the Dwarves and their pathetic civilian force. Thrask and his Goblins are more than familiar enough with those stunted beasts. They will be dealt with efficiently."

Thrask passed a sidelong glance at her that lasted barely a second and expressed his doubts. Aurec was the only one who caught the move.

"Your *ally* doesn't seem to agree," he said quickly to seize advantage. "I see the doubt in his eyes. You are right to fear, naturally. Dwarves are formidable at their worst."

"We kill Dwarves!" Thrask snorted and said no more.

"Enough of this! I did not come here to bandy wit," Maleela snapped. "Lay down your arms and surrender. There doesn't need to be mindless death."

When Aurec spoke it was slow, almost casual in his argument. "When I agreed to accompany the Wolfsreik into Delranan I had thought it was to hunt down your father and restore order to both of our kingdoms. My experiences here have proven me wrong. There is a sickness in your kingdom, Maleela. No amount of talk or well wishes is capable of curing it. Only by excising this malady from the source will Delranan heal. Badron was a puppet of a great evil. I suspect you are now as well. The woman I knew, the woman I loved, would never have given in to such wicked temptation."

"I…am not the woman you loved," she said.

"I don't believe that," Aurec replied. Sadness filled his voice. "We don't have to go through with this, Maleela. Renounce your claim to the Goblins and help us drive them from Delranan forever."

She paused. The decent part of her mind wanted nothing less. Her hatred of the Goblin race was immeasurable, but so too was the lure of the Dae'shan. She wanted all the gifts Amar Kit'han promised. Power. Apotheosis. Maleela knew she was on the verge of becoming a god. All she had to do was win this battle and accept the power of the dark gods.

"The Goblins are not my problem," was her answer.

"They will be, princess," Rolnir said. "You can't possibly think they'll let you rule them, even should you prevail on the field?"

"They will do what they're told, general. This is not my war, but I will gladly trade all your lives to get what I want." Maleela pursed her lips as if debating to continue her thoughts.

Rolnir frowned, not getting the answer he was looking for. "This won't end well for you. You may have numbers but they are an undisciplined lot best left for murder."

Thrask roared. Hot saliva sizzled as it struck the already melting snow. "I will kill you myself! This is the time of Goblins!"

"Not if I have anything to say about it," Rolnir said as his hand dropped towards his sword.

"General, we came here under the flag of truce. Will you violate that because of petty grievance?" Maleela asked.

Aurec added, "She's right. There will be time enough for killing in a few moments, though I would gladly run this Goblin through and be done with it here and now."

Rolnir reluctantly withdrew his hand.

"This is the only chance you're going to get, Maleela. Turn away from here and take your Goblins back to the Deadlands. My army will provide safe conduct back across the Thorn River. We won't ask again."

Maleela broke out in a fit of laughter. It was a wicked sound, cruel and spiteful. "And here I thought to test your resolve. Do not think to cow me into submission, Aurec. I am my own person. A queen in my own regards. I don't want to kill you but I won't hesitate if you get in my way. All I want is my father's head."

"I would gladly give him to you if we knew his whereabouts," Aurec said darkly. "Your father is a coward. We've beaten his armies but he remains hidden. You ask what I cannot give."

Maleela's face darkened. Disappointment and anger clashed in her eyes. What she wanted. She wasn't even sure of that any longer. Briefly she considered ending it all, but dark purpose spurred her on. "Impossible. My father wouldn't abandon his kingdom like that. More than likely the snake is among your own ranks, skulking like a mountain asp. I would have been told if he were dead."

"Doesn't matter," Aurec said. "He's not facing you. I am. Is it truly your father that compels you into darkness? Maleela, abandon this foolish quest and return to the light. I beg you a final time. Please. If not for me than for what we once shared."

She paused. The power of words sank into the deepest recesses of her mind where she dared not look. Those special parts of herself where even the evil of the Dae'shan had yet to find purchase. Love. The power in such a word was beyond compare yet she couldn't avoid the strength of her promises. There was no room for love in her life now. She had become one with the dark.

"Enough has been said. It is time for battle," Thrask announced.

"Indeed," Maleela added.

Deflated, Aurec could merely nod. Without saying good-bye he and the others turned and left. The time for talk had ended. Thrask was right. There would be a battle the likes of which hadn't been seen in Malweir since the Mage Wars. Red light crawled across the sky. The blood-colored sun whispered ominous intent. Maleela couldn't have asked for a better omen: bloody skies to match the soon-to-be bloody ground. She hoped the world would drown in it. A single crow landed atop the pavilion and cawed. The call was muted but might have been a clarion call to war.

She watched Aurec and his commanders ride back to their lines. The subtlest hint of confusion echoed off her face. That tiny desire to slit Thrask's throat and race after her former lover mocked her. Maleela, too late, recognized that her commitment to evil had ruined any chance of a normal life. She doubted love would ever find her again, nor should it. The foulness contaminating her soul stretched deeply, confining her to self-induced torments and misery.

"Do not think to betray me, princess. Your blood will taste good," Thrask threatened once they were out of earshot.

"Is that supposed to frighten me, Goblin? You don't know the horrors I've seen. Nothing you could possibly do will ever compare to what the Dae'shan have in store for us all,"

Maleela told him. "Now, prepare your army for battle. I suspect the enemy won't give us long to retire."

Thrask grinned at the promise of bloodshed.

TWENTY-EIGHT

The Last Day

"Standby!"

The call was echoed by a score of voices ranged along the lines. Dwarves tensed with anticipation. Breaths were short, ragged. The moment had at last arrived.

"FIRE!"

Thunder erupted as the mighty Dwarven cannon batteries unleashed their fury. Flames belched from the cannon mouths. Projectiles screamed across the sky and struck with such vehemence the Goblin lines threatened to break. Bodies were obliterated. Earthworks were tossed into the air like rubble. The ground became drenched with blood. Cries of agony spread among the defenders.

There would be no respite for the Goblins, however, as Dwarves diligently reloaded and took aim again. Acting with drilled precision, the cannon crews were reloaded and ready to fire within less than a minute. Battery commanders again issued the command to fire. Death spit at the Goblins. Acrid smoke clung to the air, sealing the cannons within a miasmic cloud. A few Dwarves coughed but soldiered on. War drums beat a fearsome tune for the Dwarves reviled in killing their most hated foe.

The barrage continued for close to an hour. Elevation was adjusted to provide extra distance with each salvo once Dwarven spotters confirmed the front lines were all but devastated. Successive explosions had tossed debris and bodies well in front of the trenches. Hundreds of Goblins died in that first hour, less than hoped for but enough to bolster the spirits of the allied army.

Thord watched his cannon batteries execute his will with a grin. Killing Goblins was honorable and this day would see his legacy cemented for generations to come. His fingers flexed on his axe handle. Rage filled his veins. The Dwarf Lord was more than ready to lead the charge into glorious battle, but that was the old way. Gunpowder changed the way his clans went to war. So many of the enemy was dead, broken before his musketeers stepped off the line.

Despite their technological advances, Thord found the use of projectile weapons dishonorable. He was a Dwarf and expected to engage in hand-to-hand combat. Anything less was unworthy, until now. The vast number of enemy soldiers awaiting them demanded the vehemence of his cannons. Promise held Thord to task. He knew that no Goblin would ever again willingly face his people in battle.

"General Brug, sound the advance. The time has come to show our Goblin kin the full truth of our wrath," he ordered.

The black-bearded Brug snarled in reply. Fetishes decorated his plaited beard. War paint darkened his face. A hooked axe blade stuck up over his right shoulder. A pair of pistols were holstered around his waist and the long musket in his hands whispered danger.

"Today we will have vengeance for our brothers lost on the banks of the river," Brug announced for all those close enough to hear.

Dwarves cheered, the memory of the brutal yet short battle along the banks of the Thorn River when the army of Drimmen Delf first began to march west still close to their hearts. One hundred Dwarves and several Elves had given their lives to slow the Goblin advance. Today that sacrifice would be repaid in kind. Thord slapped Brug on the shoulder and nodded, adding his own bellowing voice to the thunder spreading across his army. Brug turned to take his place among the musket battalions.

According to the battle plan the Dwarf musketeers would advance and engage the enemy with a devastating wall fire. Krek's Minotaurs would follow. In theory the lines would break and Bahr's team would be able to enter Arlevon Gale. Thord and Brug both knew that no true battle plan survived first contact. He hadn't gotten an accurate count of enemy casualties since the bombardment began, a troubling fact but not one capable of halting the attack. Even as he watched his ranks form Thord knew that his Wolfsreik counterparts were already engaging the Goblins with catapult and scorpion fire. Confused by the dual assaults, the Goblins were ripe to fall.

The Dwarf Lord couldn't help but feel unnecessary, however. The days when kings were expected to lead their armies into battle were ending. This was the hour for generals and heroes to emerge. He could do no more than stand by and watch. Frustration boiled across his face as he watched Brug point towards the trumpeter. A single horn announced the charge.

Brug primed his musket and stepped off, marching in step with a thousand other Dwarves in four ranks. Standard firing procedures called for the first rank to kneel and both the first and second ranks to fire simultaneously. They would fold back behind the third and fourth ranks, reloading as their counterparts fired. Each salvo would see them advance another ten meters until their lines were so close it was time for axe work.

The haze began to lift, dissipating the further they marched into the killing grounds. It was then the full extent of how destructive the cannons had been was realized. Body parts littered the cleared area leading up to the Goblin trenches. Hands gripped weapons. Heads lay, faces twisted in agony from being ripped away. An occasional torso formed a fleshy lump in the Dwarves' path. The smell of viscera and blood was sickening. More than one Dwarf forgot himself and vomited.

Brug ignored the destruction. His gaze was locked on the milling heads poking over the battlements before him. Huge gouges were torn through the trenches. More bodies lay strewn over the tops. Fires burned in the tents and hastily constructed buildings behind the lines. Black smoke clung in thick clouds. The Goblins had paid dearly for being in Delranan but it wasn't enough. Whole companies were seen hurrying back and forth to reinforce the lines at their most vulnerable points. Brug spied ranks of crossbowmen waiting, their foul quarrels loaded and ready to slay Dwarves. Armor piercing, the arrows could kill even the best of Brug's forces.

However cunning the Goblins may be, they were no match for the raw power of the Drimmen Delf Dwarves. Brug gestured to the trumpeter again when the front ranks were within one hundred meters of the trenches. Overzealous Goblins leapt up, brandishing tulwars and swords. They shouted curses in their foul tongue, taunting the Dwarves. A lone flag waved proudly in the breeze. Dark blue, it bore a pair of crossed swords. The Dwarf line ground to a halt. Their boots stamped heavily.

Crossbowmen rose, taking aim despite being out of range. Brug snarled with delight as his enemies foolishly abandoned the cover of the trenches.

Turning to his adjutant, the general said, "You would think after the pounding our cannons just delivered they'd be wiser."

The adjutant grinned back. "Goblins ain't never been wise, sir."

"Indeed. You may fire at will."

Saluting, the adjutant turned to his musketeers. "Front rank kneel! Second rank aim!"

Muskets rose. Dwarves squinted down the barrels as they zeroed in on their targets. For a moment everything paused, as if the world had stopped moving. The order to fire changed that. Bodies fell as a cloud of pale grey smoke filled the space between lines. The thunder of so many muskets being fired was deafening, though nowhere near as loud as the cannons had been. What had begun as foolish pride turned to panic. Those Goblins who survived the first volley scrambled back for cover. It was already too late. The second firing order smoothly filed forward to take position and fired. More grey bodies dropped in splatters of blood and gore.

Brug continued his attack until his front rank was no more than ten meters from the Goblin trenches. Scores of wounded tried crawling to safety. Brug ignored them and continued firing on those still battle capable. The sheer amount of dead and wounded rendered the trench units ineffective but reinforcements poured in. Several were cut down well before reaching the safety of the trenches. Dangerously low on ammunition, Brug decided it was time to let their allies into the fight.

"Trumpeter! Now!" he bellowed.

A series of three long blasts washed across the battlefield. The Dwarves parted ranks, catching the Goblins off guard. Confused, they stared curiously as a dark brown cloud emerged from the acrid haze. The ground began to tremble. Dwarves reloaded and prepared to fire without their enemy realizing. All eyes were fixed on the mass of warriors barreling towards the trenches. Brug waited until he guessed the Minotaurs were almost directly behind his musketeers and ordered a final volley. Goblins were harvested like wheat.

Krek bellowed and dashed past the already reloading Dwarves. His army followed at his heels. They leapt into the trenches with savage fury, hacking and crushing all who stood in the way. Krek reveled in the task, knowing it was revenge for old wrongs. A pair of large Goblins rose up in front of him. Each brandished heavy war bars. Krek raised his own, a favorite weapon since his time as a young bull.

The Minotaur king attacked the Goblin on his right, almost ignoring the other as he brought his weapon down with both hands. The Goblin tried unsuccessfully to duck away but was caught on top of the head. A sickening crunch announced his shattered skull. Blood and bone flew apart. Krek came out of the swing and readied to wheel on the second. The war bar slammed into the back of his thigh first, dropping him to a knee. Waves of pain rippled through him. The Goblin reared back for a killing blow.

Krek was faster. He reached out and grabbed the Goblin by the throat, crushing the wind from him. Ragged claws tore at Krek's forearm. The king drew the dagger from the Goblin's own belt and plunged it into his enemy's groin. Screaming, the Goblin let go. Krek pushed his attack, stabbing the Goblin over and over until he hung dead in his grasp. He discarded the corpse and rose. Fresh pain lanced up his leg. Not feeling any broken bones, he turned his attention to the battle raging around him.

Similar battles were being played out. Goblin and Minotaur bodies littered the area. Krek frowned upon seeing several of his bulls down but took comfort in the kill ratio.

Already rattled, the Goblins offered naught but weak resistance to the onslaught of the Minotaur army. Hundreds died in the trenches. Horrid sounds filled the air. Bones breaking. Steel ripping through flesh. The wet sucking sound of fresh wounds. Cries of the dying. Groans from the mounds of wounded piling up. The world had gone mad and Krek was a willing participant. Limping, the Minotaur king lurched after a new set of foes.

Reinforced by another wave of shock troops, the Minotaurs drove deeper into the earthworks. Front ranks fanned out in a widening arc. Sword and axe rose and fell with killing blows. The ground ran slick with blood and offal. Several warriors slipped, their brethren leapt or climbed over to continue the attack. Suddenly the Minotaur army was in danger of being impossibly entangled. Snarls brought the front line grinding to a halt. Panting heavily, the bulls cut down the remaining Goblins and established a foothold for follow-on forces.

Having been brutalized, the Goblin ranks cracked and broke. Survivors fled back into the ruins to secondary defensive positions. The trench quickly became untenable as more Minotaurs swarmed into it. Soon the large warriors were forced to snatch bodies and toss them across the killing field just to continue unimpeded. Shock units surged through the gaps in the line, taking a new fight to the retreating Goblins. Scores fell, hacked down from behind as they fled for their lives.

Krek was at the center of it all. His dark bear hide draped across his shoulders flapped in the early morning wind. Sweat covered him in a thick sheen. His breath fumed from his nostrils. Naked from the waist down save for boiled-leather armor, the Minotaur king was drenched in blood. He paused at the inner lip of the trench and surveyed the battlefield. Most of the first trench was occupied by his army and the erected battlements were being systematically ripped apart. Reluctant as he was to admit it, the honor-less weapons of the Dwarves were highly effective. Krek brandished his war bar high above his head and roared.

A fresh battalion of bulls took the lead of the advance. Krek's personal guards, they drove past the captured trench and into the massed ranks just beyond. Word hadn't gotten through Goblin lines that the trench had fallen. Fresh troops were rushing to the battle while those already broken units fleeing the front hurried back into them. The result was a severe constriction that quickly devolved into a death mill.

Minotaurs fell upon the Goblins with unabated fury. Old grievances were expressed at the sharp ends of sword and axe. The Goblins struck back, hacking and slashing at their much taller foes. Deep cuts took Minotaurs at the knee and belly. Limbs flopped away, trailing ropes of blood. Grievously wounded Minotaurs fell to the blood-churned ground where they were set upon by Goblins and butchered.

Krek spied the danger and immediately moved to counter. He bellowed to his forces, who fell back, slightly, to allow for a rank of shield bearers with spears to advance. The body length of wood reinforced in iron successfully prevented Goblin swords from cutting low. Spears slashed forward, jabbing and plunging down into exposed shoulders and necks. Just like that the Goblin counterattack faded and died.

The Minotaur king wasn't content with simply holding ground. His army was designed for breaking the enemy and driving them from the field. The only way Bahr and his group were going to get into the ruins was by the Minotaurs and Dwarves forcing the Goblins far enough back to create a hole in the lines. Once accomplished, they would be able to make quick work of the rest of the perimeter, especially with the glorious distraction the Wolfsreik was providing on the opposite flank.

Hundreds of crossbow bolts flew from the second, more heavily defended trench twenty meters ahead. The force of impact drove several bulls back a step. A rare handful went down, the bolts slipping by the shield wall to embed deep in the flesh. Most hammered into the shields with a sound to rival thunder. Unlike the first line of defenders, these Goblins hadn't been caught in the cannon barrage. They were fresh and ready to fight. Krek enjoyed the challenge. This was where honor was met. A great and terrible reaping would be held this day and Krek aimed to get the majority of it.

His large, wide eyes surveyed the second trench. It appeared no Dwarf rounds managed to penetrate this far, leaving the defenses rather wholly intact. Sharpened logs were leveled at dangerous angles to prevent any normal army from making a head-on charge. The Minotaurs of Malg were anything but normal. Capable of leaping high, Krek intended on going over the defenses. Doing so would cause many casualties. He reckoned the first wave would be rendered ineffective.

Suicide wasn't in his tactical plans, however, and he was forced to consider a second option. Fires burned around him, the residue of the barrage. Ordering the follow-on ranks to collect as much burning material as possible, Krek intended on burning the enemy out. He just had to get there first. Enemy fire was picking up. Short spears and throwing axes joined the arrows. More bulls dropped. Clearly the ease with which the first trench fell was not about to be replayed a second time.

A series of small towers were erected every fifty meters. Filled with a score of Goblins each, they provided excellent overhead cover to continue raining projectiles into the Minotaur ranks. Sooner or later the range would decrease to the point they became effective. Krek needed more firepower to break the lines. Once accomplished, he saw a clear path to the center of the enemy camp.

Snatching the nearest warrior by his armored collar, Krek ordered, "Burn the towers! Bring up the shamans!"

The bull snorted and hurried through the massed ranks to follow his orders. Krek waited impatiently, adding his own shield to the wall for his wizards. Arrows, spears, and axes thundered into his shield. More than one had already cracked from continued strikes. It wouldn't be long before they all followed suit. He grunted under the force of multiple impacts before turning his head back to his army.

The wait seemed incredibly long but he was finally rewarded by several diminutive figures slipping through the ranks. His shaman corps, ten strong, marched with heads high.

Their long antlers reached up to an average bull's shoulders. Shirts of bones, alabaster white clung to their chests. Each bore a personally carved totem stick adorned with random fetishes of feathers and worse. Their skin was dull brown, almost green from practicing magic deep underground. Each was more dangerous than his entire army combined; they were a foe the Goblins hadn't reckoned on.

Krek nodded and passed his shield off to the bull directly behind him. He marched to the shamans, an imposing target several Goblins aimed for but failed to hit. As one, the shamans bowed to the waist. No time for formalities, Krek bade them rise. "Take out those towers."

He briefly considered trying to capture them intact, knowing they'd make the perfect vantage point for Brug's snipers once the Dwarves refit and got back into the fight, but the amount of losses he'd suffer trying to take them weren't worth it. Krek needed to break the second trench in a similar fashion to the first. Notoriously stubborn, the Goblins would die to the last before retreating from his bulls.

"As you command, sire," the eldest shaman replied. He grinned, wicked rows of pointed teeth showing beneath thick lips. He gestured with his hand and the shamans began to spread out through the lines.

Satisfied they would accomplish their task, Krek turned his attentions back to the stalled attack. Too many bulls were down, being dragged back to the hastily erected triage area at the first trench. Dwarf engineers were already turning the former defenses around to protect against the inevitable counterattack. Once the shock of the combined assault wore off, Krek and Brug alike had no disillusions about the Goblins bringing everything they had in reserve back on the trenches. This was their only chance to secure the foothold. The sound of shovels and pickaxes joined the clash of weapons.

The wait wasn't very long. Storm clouds rolled in, abrupt and adding further confusion to the Goblins. It had been too long since they last confronted the Minotaurs and had no working knowledge of their tactics. That ignorance was about to be exploited. Lighting crackled. Bolts of blue-red power lanced from the shaman staffs. Shockwaves rippled across the distance between lines. More than one bull was knocked to his knees as the shamans unleashed their full might. The smell of singed hair choked the air, adding to the necrotic aroma of death. Bulls howled in those first few seconds.

As one, the bolts of power struck the Goblin towers and exploded. Wood and charred corpses burst apart in the blink of an eye. Debris extended over both armies. Minotaurs roared in delight while Goblins wailed and began to understand true fear. Krek didn't hesitate. He bellowed and his army charged. The ground was covered in a span of heartbeats. Several large holes had been blasted in the Goblin defenses, forming natural ingress points for the bulls to swarm through.

The Minotaur king held back, knowing his warriors needed to secure the trench before he pushed forward. This was a dangerous moment for both armies. Momentum was fragile in the best situations. He knew it could easily swing back to the enemy should they recover their wits and reform their lines. Frustrated with having to stand idle and watch, Krek was pleased to see his army slip through the gaps in a trickle at first and then a steady stream. Others ripped the sharpened logs from the ground while others still wielded them like giant spears. The outcome was never truly in doubt. Stunned, broken, the Goblins were ripe to fall. All that remained to be seen was how many died in the process.

Krek felt a great weight slip away. He never bore any doubts to the veracity of his army. They were one of the strongest fighting forces in Malweir, but they hadn't been tested in battle since he was a young bull. Any apprehension slipped away. There would be numerous funeral pyres come the dawn, but his army had performed admirably and were cleansing the world of Goblin filth. He gestured to his flag bearer. It was time, now, before the Goblins regrouped. The Minotaur standard waved proudly over the captured battlefield.

Brug spied Krek's wave and quickly snatched his adjutant by the collar. "Now, go back and signal Bahr to advance. We've established a front."

He stayed to watch the Dwarf sprint back towards the headquarters. Hundreds of Delrananian rebels were slowly moving closer to the battle, ready to get their hands dirty for the future of their kingdom. Brug couldn't care less about the Humans, knowing they were more than likely only going to get in the way. His attention focused on the two carts bringing a resupply of ammunition for his musketeers. A seasoned veteran, Brug would have much preferred to engage the Goblins with his axe but there was no denying the killing power his new units possessed. As long as he had ammunition, he held the advantage. Satisfied, the Dwarf general turned back to the battle.

TWENTY-NINE

The Wolfsreik Strikes

Aurec couldn't stop fidgeting. A veteran of several battles, he knew this shouldn't be any different. Unlike his previous engagements, this was a battle of attrition. He'd been the guerilla force for so long his didn't know if his army could handle a direct assault on a fixed position. A well-defended position at that. The young king paced, cracking his knuckles much to the annoyance of Rolnir and Vajna.

Command Sergeant Major Thorsson watched his king with amusement. He kept his doubts private, having been on the opposite side of such a battle. A survivor of the siege of Rogscroft, Thorsson had been fortunate to survive but he knew full well just how terrible breaking a proper defense could be. Hundreds of his friends died within the city walls in a battle that ultimately proved unwinnable. Ghosts of his former comrades visited him during those long hours in the middle of the night when sleep refused to come. It was a sacrifice he'd never admit to Aurec or the others.

"How did you sleep?" Aurec asked of a sudden.

Thorsson almost choked on his laugh. "Well enough considering the shit we're about to get into, sire."

Aurec was secretly jealous. He'd tossed and turned all night, thoughts of the coming battle driving him mad. He'd thought the worst of it was over until they rode out to meet the enemy under the white flag. Now it was Maleela and what she'd become tormenting him endlessly. He failed to understand how a caring, compassionate woman willingly gave her soul to the dark powers. What had happened to make her so…foul? He feared the answer would never become known. Deep inside he believed that she was going to be one of the casualties in this sad affair. His only love, a beacon that had guided him since the loss of his father, Aurec would gladly trade his life for Maleela's.

"Relax, sire. This will work itself out. There'll be some empty seats around the table when it's done, but I don't see how any Goblin army, no matter how big, can survive against the power we've got assembled here," Thorsson admitted.

Aurec let his thoughts stray from Maleela back to his army. Nearly twenty thousand soldiers from three kingdoms stood ready to launch into attack once the Dwarves gave their sign. He remained confused as to what that sign might be. Thord was suspiciously reluctant to give his surprise away. Of the many attributes he attached to the stout warriors, entertainment wasn't one. Aurec and the others had been through so much since the war began, so many transformations, that he almost didn't recognize himself. It was no easy thing being at the sharp end of the sword for so long.

"Do you really think we can do it? Break them and…." He let the question drop, knowing it was his love of Maleela that set these events in motion. Aurec wasn't sure how the others would react to his desire to reunite with her in the middle of this nightmare.

Thorsson frowned. This wasn't a moment for any leader to show doubt, for doubt translated into weakness. A proper leader needed to be strong in the face of adversity, not mired in whether he'd done the right things leading up to the inevitable moment when steel clashed. Aurec was better than this, Thorsson mentally scolded. "Sire, this is one of the finest armies ever put to the field. The Goblins might have numbers but they're not true warriors. Our boys'll do it, don't you worry."

Aurec found comfort in the words, despite the harsh tone in which they were delivered. This was no time for selfish indulgence. He was a king and expected to act accordingly. Rebuked, Aurec said, "Thank you, Thorsson. It is easy to forget myself. I am still young and largely inexperienced after all."

"It's the young ones that keep the army fighting. Remember that," Thorsson added.

The generals arrived, engaged in deep conversation.

"...doesn't matter if we don't know what they're planning," Vajna argued.

Rolnir threw up his hands in exasperation. "For the hundredth time, Vajna, I don't think we'll be able to miss it. You heard the Dwarf king. He's a sly one and makes no mistake."

"I don't like entering an engagement, especially one this big, without knowing the proper moment." Exasperated, Vajna couldn't help but take out his frustrations on those around him.

Aurec wanted to grin but first ensured there were none of the rank and file lingering within earshot. "Generals. Are we prepared?"

"As much as we can be," Rolnir answered.

Vajna rolled his eyes.

Tension filled the space between them. It had only been a few moments since the end of the parley, but to each it might have been a week. Suddenly the ground shook and thunder filled the sky. Smoke and flame belched from the Dwarf lines followed closely by massive explosions. Aurec's mouth dropped open. Never in his wildest imagination could he have imagined such destructive power. Screams from the Goblin lines could be heard rising above the lingering aftershock in a grizzly chorus. The thunder boomed again with similar results.

Aurec turned quickly to his shell-shocked generals. "Gentlemen, I believe that's our sign. Proceed with the assault."

Each saluted, less crisp than it might have been, and went to their respective commands. Vajna hurried off to give the order for the catapult batteries to open fire. He couldn't help but look over his shoulder and jump with each new salvo from the Dwarven cannons. Flames and smoke billowed above the Goblin defenses. How much death and destruction being committed was beyond him, however, and he lacked the stomach to think long on it. He had his own task to perform and it was going to cost many lives. Nothing in the combined army arsenal was comparable to the new Dwarf weapons.

"What in the hells is that?" the catapult battery commander shouted as Vajna drew close.

Truthfully, the general didn't rightly know himself. All he knew was he was glad to have the Dwarves on their side. "It doesn't matter. Fire at will, commander. Let's strike some of that fear from our ranks. We can't let the Dwarves have all the fun."

"Yes sir!"

Satisfied, Vajna next headed for his cavalry. It had been too long since he had been given the ability to take his horse warriors into the field. Thousands of soldiers and horses milled nervously, riders desperately trying to calm their mounts as the artillery barrage continued. His company commanders were gathered, awaiting orders. One extended the reins for Vajna to snatch.

"My friends, this is it. Speed of horse is the key. We move fast and don't stop until after we're through their lines. I want three wedges for the attack. We go in directly behind Rolnir's heavy infantry assault forces. Don't stop. Aim for the center of the enemy camp. Drive them of the front line and we break them on our steel. Questions?"

There were none. Not that he expected any. He nodded his unspoken appreciation for all that they had endured over the past winter and what they were about to go through in mere moments. These were the defining moments of a generation. None of them knew what was at stake, Vajna included, but that changed nothing. They had a task to perform. The end of the war was in sight. Plans had changed. Enemies had changed. The unexpected arrival of the Goblin army threatened to throw the entire campaign out of whack but Aurec and his command staff adjusted admirably.

Vajna reached up and stroked his mount's dark neck. The horse snorted and rubbed its cheek against Vajna. Nerves ran high amongst them all. Not that he blamed anyone. The sheer madness involved in what they were about to attempt was staggering. The old general almost looked beyond the battle and to his well-deserved retirement. There was danger in that, looking beyond what needed to happen first. Fearful that his distractions might get his people killed, Vajna went over his instructions in his head.

Catapult rounds arced over the field and crashed hard into the Goblin defenses. Unlike the withering punishment doled out by the Dwarves, these were designed to crush and break. There would be no field of bodies to demoralize friend and foe alike. Vajna and the others accepted their place in the battle, secretly lamenting the amount of lives they feared were going to be lost. It was far too late to worry now.

He watched as scorpions were rolled into firing positions. The giant weapons were akin to crossbows but the similarities ended there. Each was capable of firing three six-foot-iron spears simultaneously. Cranked through a series of pulleys, the weapons could pierce stone as easily as armor. There was no safe place for the Goblins to hide.

Dust clouds rose from the trenches. The catapults increased their rate of fire. Unlike the cannons on the Dwarf flank, Rolnir's artillerymen had an infinite supply of ammunition. Heavy boulders went first, quickly followed by rolled balls of thatch covered in burning pitch. The fires had the potential of working against the infantry but it was a chance King Aurec decided to take.

The scorpions began firing. Spears whistled through the air before slamming into wood and flesh. Vajna flexed his hands. Massed ranks of archers marched to the front. They would cover the infantry approach and follow his cavalry into the breach. Normally cavalry wouldn't attempt to break through well-defended lines but Aurec and Rolnir agreed that the greatest threat was the amount of reinforcements the Goblins could bring to bear from the parts of the perimeter that weren't under siege. Despite having the luxury of open space, all three quickly decided that the enemy held the advantages.

Under the triple barrage of the combined army, the Goblins tried to dig deeper. They were an army made for rampaging across the world, not hunkering down in fixed positions while their enemies threw everything in their arsenal at them. Scores died in those first few moments, but nothing compared to the western flank. Morale remained high despite their losses, boding ill for the infantry grinding forward.

Wolfsreik infantry crashed into the Goblin trenches. Dozens were killed before reaching the wooden spikes. Goblin crossbows were murderous and highly effective against even the most heavily armored infantry. Infantrymen dropped as fast as the Goblins could reload. This was the danger moment, when the attackers needed to decide whether they had the resolve to see their task through. The defenders fought with everything they had. Wolfsreik continued to fall, leaving an armored landscape covered in red.

Swords reflected sunlight as they rose and fell. Vajna took hope as several squads appeared to have breached the outer defenses. They dropped into the trench, spreading quickly to enable follow-on forces in. The sound was sickening. The deeds being conducted in the trench were akin to cold-blooded murder.

Small fires sprouted up and down the line. Deadly quarrels slashed down from the Goblin towers. Without any magical attributes, Rolnir was solely reliant on the hopes of his catapults knocking the towers out. Thus far only one was in ruins. It wasn't enough. Frontline commanders ordered all fire directed on the towers. Though hastily constructed, the towers were well protected from rising fire. Rising fire, but not from the scorpions.

Iron spears slammed into the towers once it became clear they were the focal point of the assault. Battery commanders barked orders as their weapon systems shifted aim and reloaded. Several towers burst apart in showers of bodies and debris from lucky strikes. Most remained standing. Infantry continued to fall. Vajna felt the strain from his mounted position. Waiting for the orders to advance left his stomach crawling. His instincts demanded he join the battle. Perhaps his actions would save some of those infantrymen being shredded by Goblin fire. *More than likely I'll just get more people killed by getting in the way. Calm yourself, you old fool. We'll attack when the moment is right.*

Soon dust obscured his view. Vajna cursed. He needed to be able to see the battle to make the necessary adjustments. Snatching the reins, he quickly mounted. A veteran captain stepped in front of him with a firm glare etched on his face.

"Sir, that isn't going to happen," he said.

"Get out of the way, captain. I need to be able to see," Vajna warned.

Other soldiers came to help bar the way. "General, we need you here, ready to lead us. Getting yourself killed won't do us any good."

"Which is precisely what's going to happen if I can't see the gods' damned battlefield! Now, step aside."

"No sir," the captain replied with authority. He tilted his head to a young sergeant. "Take a squad forward and report back with actionable intelligence. Move."

"Yes sir!"

Satisfied, the captain turned back to his general. "Now sir, if you would please stand down. We've got this under control."

Fuming but knowing it was the right call, Vajna finally relented.

The wait felt long. He slid from his saddle and paced up and down the line. Whispered bits of conversation among his cavalrymen reached his ears but were blocked out by his worry. Catapults continued to fire but at a reduced pace. The scorpions were so far forward he hardly noticed the deadly whiz of projectiles being fired. Smoke and dust billowed in great clouds now, preventing any of his soldiers from seeing into the trenches. However infuriated Vajna was, he knew that Rolnir and Aurec were positively livid.

Soldiers eventually began returning, walking wounded and others being carried back on makeshift litters. It started as a slow trickle before the volume increased. Vajna was threatened with dismay. His only hope was that the amount of wounded far outweighed the dead. In just a few short minutes well over one hundred wounded returned to the marshalling area. Medics and surgeons rushed to meet them, desperately trying to save life and limb.

Clearly the assault on the trenches wasn't going well. Vajna finally spied the squad returning. Each of the young soldiers bore grim looks and had almost blanched skin. His worst fears were about to be confirmed. The squad sergeant offered a dull salute. His eyes bore horrors no one should ever be made to witness.

"General, the first wave is ineffective. Goblins still hold the outer trench. We've got a small breach established but are threatened with being pushed back. The enemy is moving massive amounts of reinforcements into their lines and are cutting our infantry down with those damned crossbows."

Vajna spat his frustration. His cavalry was next to useless as long as the enemy trenches remained intact. The worst part was he couldn't do anything about it. Colonel Udo and the heavy infantry were going to have to fight it out.

"Send word back to General Rolnir. We can't have the assault get bogged down at the very beginning. Move, quickly, before the day is lost!" he ordered and turned to his Wolfsreik counterpart. "Herger, how close do you think we can get to the lines without the Goblins catching wind of us?"

Colonel Herger, former enemy turned close friend, never took his eyes of the dust cloud concealing the battle. "Close, but we will lose the advantage of speed of horse."

Exactly what Vajna feared. The battle continued to rage but without the use of the thousand-strong cavalry force. As far as he was concerned they were a wasted asset. His frustrations gave way to curiosity as a lone rider barreled towards his position. The soldier was lightly armored and fresh from the fight. Blood stained his upper thighs and a broken arrow shaft plunged deeply into his leg.

Face pale from loss of blood, the soldier abruptly halted in front of Vajna. His look was one of pure terror, as if all the demons of the underworld had just been unleashed. "General, you need to ride now with everything you have or it's all lost!"

"Calm down, son, and explain what you mean. We can't even see what's going on," Vajna said, his voice terse.

Taking a deep breath, the soldier continued, "Sir, Colonel Udo has secured a small stretch of the trench but he can't hold it for long, not without your cavalry to break it open. The enemy is stronger than we thought. Our infantry is taking a mauling. Most of the first units to attack are down to fifty percent strength. It's a slaughter, sir."

Vajna and Herger exchanged looks, each processing the information in his own way. Hours of build-up were finally ended. It was time for the cavalry to draw spears and ride to war.

"Mount up! We ride now!"

THIRTY

Into the Breach

They ran as fast as the slowest among them. Separating now served no purpose. So close to Arlevon Gale and the dangerous energies swirling within, the time for unity had finally arrived. All arguments of disagreement and doubt were cast aside as they raced across char-blackened ground. Eyes were focused on the drab, grey stones that had once been grand buildings just ahead. There was no glory remaining here, only wanton death. Thousands of body parts littered the ground as they ran. Many more had simply been obliterated to dust.

No words needed speaking. Each knew what must be done. All were expendable save one. Groge carried his war hammer in one hand and the blind wizard in the other. There were no foes to stand in the way. No cheering armies as he plunged deeper into the chaos. Twice as tall as the others, Groge made an easy target for Goblin archers.

Bahr and Boen led the way, as they had since Thord called them forward. They were escorted by a squad of Aeldruin across the killing fields. Neither saw the need for the Elves but any assistance was welcomed at this point. Having witnessed the might of the cannons once before, Bahr's group was largely unaffected by what they now stalked through. Grim determination saw them through. Drawn swords displayed their readiness to fight, though Bahr secretly hoped there was little of it. He'd had his fill of fighting and wanted it all to end.

There was no time for words. Everything had already been said back in the marshaling area. Drive hard. Stay together and head straight for the center of the ruins. Anienam assured them the ritual chamber was located in the middle. Nothing mattered but gaining the objective and stopping the Dae'shan. Faeldrin offered his assistance and rode at the head of the group, preventing stray Goblins from rising out of the corpse field in ambush.

They'd covered most of the ground. The first trench was immediately ahead and with it the wanton death wrought by Dwarf cannons and Minotaur brawn. Dwarves and bulls now joined the body count. Their once majestic bodies were strewn at odd angles, draped over the trench or folded impossibly small around it. Bahr felt immense sorrow as the full effect of the assault came into view. War was never glorious, despite what Boen might preach, but this went far beyond anything that had ever occurred save perhaps the Mage Wars.

Faeldrin's Elves peeled away once Bahr was beyond the trench. They were lightly armored and posed more of a liability than asset in the middle of the fight. Besides, Thord suspected the enemy might try to circle down from the north and flank the army. The Elf mercenaries were needed to screen the far flank. Bahr didn't lament their loss. The Elves proved fine allies but would only get in the way.

Up ahead the battle raged on. Massed units of Minotaurs and Goblins traded blows. Dwarves armed with muskets desperately tried to swing around the Goblin lines and rake fire down from the side. Alas, the fall the first two trenches meant the Goblins had less to defend, constricting the defense and more than tripling the amount of strength they could dedicate to the battle. All the Minotaur might meant nothing if they couldn't find a way to pound into the guts of the Goblins.

Bahr couldn't allow himself to be distracted by the almost desperate plight of the battle. He knew Boen would argue to divert and join the attack regardless of their mission. Daylight was already fading and time was running out. It had taken nearly half a day for the allied armies to get as deep in the ruins as they had. Each moment spent in wait was one less they had in which to deal with the evil at the heart.

No, Boen's thirst for battle would have to wait. Only when they reached the spot of the ritual and finally faced the Dae'shan would he have an opponent worthy of a Vengeance Knight. If they made it that far. Several ranks of Goblins remained between Bahr and the ruins. Greatly depleted to fight the two-pronged allied assault, the stationary Goblins presented enough of a challenge to give Bahr pause. It didn't last long.

Boen roared and raced ahead. His massive thighs propelled him forward. Sword brandished menacingly, the sixty-year-old Gaimosian struck the Goblins with unexpected fury. A quick swipe took one in the throat. Blackish blood spurted on Boen's armor. His back swing caught another in the shoulder, gouging chunks of flesh and leather. A third Goblin tried getting inside his reach and tackling the bigger Gaimosian. Boen absorbed the blow and drove the pommel of his sword down on top of the Goblin's exposed skull. Bone gave way with a sickening crunch as the steel sank into brain matter.

Distracted, the Goblins failed to notice Ironfoot charge into them. His axe reaped a terrible toll. A spine was ripped open diagonally. The paralyzed Goblin dropped without a sound. Ironfoot stabbed his axe head into another Goblin's face and dropped into a half-body swing that clipped the knees out from a charging attacker. By then it didn't matter. Bahr and the others were among the bewildered Goblin host.

They fought with utter surety. Weeks and months of minor skirmishes and full-blown battles had honed them into a lethal group. Rekka's slightly curved sword claimed lives as quickly as she could swing. Nothol and Dorl hacked and slashed. What started as a lone duel devolved into a melee. Bodies dropped. Others slipped and fell in the mud and blood. Steel struck bone. Lopped off limbs and heads. This was war at its most brutal: a violent demonstration unparalleled in all existence.

Only Skuld and Groge hung back. Neither were particularly skilled combatants and more likely to get in the way than help. Skuld watched with sword clutched so tightly his hand hurt as his companions, those he'd come to call and think of as friends, mercilessly slaughtered every Goblin poor enough to get snagged. The battle was as brutal as it was quick. Nearly two score enemy bodies slumped around them in the span of moments.

Bahr looked back to the Giant. "Come on! Others will come."

Swallowing his apprehension, Skuld followed the Giant deeper into the ruins of Arlevon Gale. They slipped through the carnage and finally gained the first set of ruined buildings. Lengthening shadows cast eerie fingers across the area. They could have easily concealed Goblins but worked to Bahr's favor instead. He led the group into the deepest shadows where they collected themselves for the next stage. Now that they were in the ruins, beyond the madness of the battle raging around them, Bahr felt he could regroup and take a little more time.

"Is anyone wounded?" he asked, still trying to regain his breath.

The others were in similar shape. Goblins fought hard and his tiny group was hard-pressed to fight them off. Only Rekka seemed…normal. Bahr shrugged the feeling off and went back to scanning his group. Satisfied they were all in fighting condition, he looked to Anienam. The wizard appeared no more than a babe in Groge's massive hand. In another time it might have been amusing.

"Alright, wizard. You're up. Where do we go from here? Those Goblins won't be fooled long and they'll be looking for us," Bahr said.

A thick cloud of black smoke passed by, briefly obscuring them from each other's view.

Anienam cocked his head in thought. "We must find the direct center. More than likely the ritual chamber is underground."

"More than likely?" Boen asked with a low growl.

Nothol added, "You don't know?"

"Have either of you been here before?" Anienam snapped. He struggled to keep his voice at a whisper. "Find the center of this place and get me inside. I'll provide enough cover for Groge to do his job."

Scowling, Bahr knew there was no other choice and sticking around to debate the validity of Anienam's guess was pointless. "Fine, what do we look for? How will we know when we find it?"

"Look for? Why, a lot of guards. Expect the Dae'shan to have their most lethal agents protecting them," Anienam replied.

"Lovely," Bahr frowned. "Let's move."

One by one they filed after the Sea Wolf. Arlevon Gale was much larger than any of them had thought. Scores of what had once been grand buildings and halls littered the area. Most were reduced to a mere few feet in height while others retained nearly two stories. Not a one was wholly intact. The rubble was strewn across the former roads and walkways. Hundreds of square acres were filled with ruins, clearly marking Arlevon Gale as a once important city. Bahr had spent a lifetime roaming the world and never once bothered to inspect these ruins. Whispers of ghosts and fell powers stalking the ruins kept most sane people away.

The stomp of many boots forced Bahr to duck into what had once been a meeting hall. They filed against the largest wall, weapons gripped tightly as a column of infantry marched towards the battle. More than one in his group held their breath from fear of being discovered. They hadn't come to fight a war, just end the madness consuming the world. Bahr couldn't do that if they engaged every Goblin element that marched by.

He gently eased his head around the grey stone edge. The last rank of Goblins had rounded the corner and were well on their way to meeting the Minotaurs. Satisfied the path was clear, momentarily, he gestured the others to follow. He took them skulking deeper into the ruins.

The buildings grew taller, suggesting they were nearing the center. It became increasingly difficult to avoid further Goblin units. Whole battalions were massed in wait. Many were already mustered and heading to the front lines while even more were preparing defensive positions for the eventuality of the enemy breaking through. Clearly whoever commanded intended to make the allies pay for every step of ground.

Bahr began to feel frustrated. Any progress his group made was stymied by the continuous stream of Goblins moving about. Thankfully the squat warriors were seemingly oblivious to Bahr's task but he knew it wouldn't last. Sooner or later their luck would run out and the Goblins would discover them. That fear kept him driving forward, sometimes taking roundabout paths to avoid Goblins. Anienam hadn't mentioned it, but Bahr secretly began to suspect the wizard had placed an enchantment over them to prevent the Goblins from finding them. Regardless, he couldn't trust to luck. Only skill was going to see them through to the objective--skill and a river of blood.

The rumble of gears and wheels forced him down the nearest side alley. A battery of catapults was being dragged towards the front, narrowly avoiding running into Bahr's group. Groge barely managed to avoid detection as he ducked into a bank of shadows. None in the Goblin army expected the enemy to be so deep within their ranks and walked with the arrogance of supremacy.

Satisfied the way ahead was clear, Bahr continued to lead them deeper into the ruins. The deeper they went the calmer it became. The air took on an arcane atmosphere, confirming they moved in the right direction. Nerves stood on edge. Hairs danced on end, as if tiny jolts of electricity lingered in the air. Stomachs roiled, threatening to empty at the alkaline taste permeating tongues and nostrils.

The shadows had grown so deep it was near pitch-dark now. Bahr couldn't risk lighting a torch and was forced to rely on instinct. Fewer Goblins were noticeable. Most activity faded, ending altogether. Only the harsh whisper of winds kissing the sun-blasted stone accompanied the tiny group. The buildings were closer together, forming tight avenues nearly impassable for Groge. Frowning, Bahr had to find a way for the Giant to pass. They backtracked and swung to the right, immediately taking the first open lane before heading back in the same direction.

Bahr sprinted down a thin corridor and came to an abrupt halt upon hearing foul speech directly ahead. The sun was dropping over the horizon. Shadows deepened. Even with the rage of so many fires nearly a third of a league behind them, Arlevon Gale grew dark. He spied the reflection of many torches on the snow. Boen, catching his hesitance, nudged Bahr aside and crept forward. The Gaimosian returned a moment later, a look of sheer disgust on his face.

"We've found it," he told them.

Dorl pricked up. His nerves were beyond frayed. Nothing in his past adequately prepared him for what they were doing. "How can you be sure?"

Boen grinned in a way only a madman could. "Because there's a Troll standing in front of the door and close to one hundred Goblins."

Dorl Theed swallowed hard. *We're dead.*

Torches flickered in the supernatural gloom, revealing a chamber deep underground. The low hanging ceiling trapped the light, brightening the room more than any of the Dae'shan wished. The chamber was oval. A small hole was centered in the ceiling. Golden sunlight filtered in, widening when it struck the ground. Dust from several hundred years clogged the sandstone floor. Leaves and other detritus had been blown in and windswept to the corners. Had there been a point the chamber would have been cleansed. As it stood, there was no need.

A small pedestal sat directly in the sunlight. Knee high, it was made of pure obsidian. Five other stones, each as long as an adult, were spaced out in a star pattern connected to the obsidian. Stone runnels angled down from the curved stones to the centerpiece. Created for singular purpose, the chamber hadn't been used since Arlevon Gale fell into decay.

All three Dae'shan hovered scant inches off the ground. This was the chamber from which they would free the dark gods and ascend to the pantheon. A disturbance at the entrance forced them to part. A squad of Goblins marched in pairs with a bound prisoner between them. Humans all, the prisoners were hauled up and dropped on the stones. Their hands were bound as were their ankles. Each was blindfolded and gagged. They were the final sacrifices required to activate the latent power in the Olagath Stone. Squirming in the vain attempt at freedom, they'd each been told what was coming to them. Amar Kit'han enjoyed the theatricality of the moment.

"We stand a very real chance of losing this battle. Thrask's Goblins are of little real use," Kodan Bak said, his pale eyes never leaving the sacrifices.

Amar Kit'han frowned. Bringing the Goblins in had been a gamble from the beginning. His hopes of presenting a major military power to cow the other kingdoms into submission backfired twice. If they couldn't hold the lines long enough for him to complete the ritual it would all be over. A thousand years was a very long time to wait for the next opportunity to free the dark gods, even for an immortal.

"The Goblins are strong when need be. Give them the chance to hold," he replied.

Reaching into his robes, the Dae'shan produced an onyx athame. Fear brightened the eyes of the five victims strapped to the stones.

Pelthit Re, ever eager to prove his value, added, "They will not hold. Those new weapons of the Dwarves are an unforeseen complication."

Frustrated, sensing it was nearly time for one of them to make their play for leadership, Amar Kit'han drifted around to face his kin. "Send forth the Gnaals. We will make quick work of our enemies."

Ignoring the threat from his peers, Amar turned back to his victims. Their deaths would open the path between dimensions and usher forth a new age for all Malweir.

THIRTY-ONE

Counterattack

Maleela's stomach tightened as she watched the wholesale slaughter of Goblins on the western flank. She'd never dreamed of such violence from the Dwarves, having been sequestered deep inside Drimmen Delf when Bahr and the others had gone out to fight at Bode Hill. The cannons were impressive and world changing. She tried to calculate the implications of these new weapons and failed. Hundreds of Goblins were murdered in those first few moments. Close to a thousand by the time the Minotaur army attacked.

She watched her new army as it threatened to break under the onslaught of so many different foes. Her gaze reluctantly tore from the horrifying Dwarven weapons and centered on the Wolfsreik to her east. Aurec was there, standing in resplendent battle armor under a sea of waving banners. He'd grown to become a true king, despite her earlier protestations. She bore no doubts that he would soon take up the sword and join his army in the attack. Aurec often suffered from an excess of honor. Maleela didn't particularly want him dead, but she wouldn't hesitate to cut him down if he stood in her way. Badron was out there and she wanted him dead.

Her defense against the Wolfsreik was much stronger than against the Dwarves. Without those infernal weapons the Wolfsreik was forced to execute their attack the way it had always been done. She was prepared for that, or so Thrask assured her. The Goblin war machine had fought their way across the northern kingdoms for months, slaughtering and killing along the way. Maleela had no stomach for it. There was no glory to be had in killing. Her alliance with the Goblins was one of convenience. Amar Kit'han promised her the blood of her father before the end, leading her to the inevitable conclusion that Badron was on the field. *Most likely skulking in a soldier's uniform no doubt.* Her hand idly tapped the blade strapped to her right hip.

Too many thoughts swirled in conflict. Goblins. Aurec. Badron. She slowly felt her sanity being dragged away. Feelings of vengeance dominated her waking moments. Dreams had become nightmares threatening to consume what remained of her soul. She wondered how she had become evil. Had it always been there? Lurking in the hollow corners of mind and spirit? She only felt marginally different, as if these feelings were natural.

Far too late for her to care, Maleela watched the Wolfsreik smash into the Goblins. The press of bodies was massive. Despite the gnawing displeasure in her stomach, she couldn't take her gaze away. Bodies fell. Weapons rose and dropped, their crisp silver catching sunlight in menacing angles. Slowly, almost casually, the ground turned a dark shade of red. Blood. She shuddered. What made her cringe was seemingly commonplace amongst the combatants.

Frantic movement from the Wolfsreik lines drew her attention. Fresh units were being hurried towards the attack where those poor initial units were being torn asunder. If…if the Goblins could hold, there was the very real chance to win this battle. Surely the Dwarves would run out of whatever they used for ammunition soon. Once they did, she had numbers on her side. No amount of natural savagery could beat back the vast amount of Goblins waiting to get into the battle.

The east secured for the moment, Maleela turned back to the Dwarf front. Aurec would live or die without her interference. She noticed with dismay how much destruction had been wrought to her lines. Thousands of Goblins lay dead, twice that were wounded and trying to drag themselves away from the fighting. Plenty of Minotaurs were down as well, their near gigantic forms almost an aberration of nature. She marveled at the bull warriors. Until now she'd thought them to be myth, an extinct race having long since exited the world.

No matter how many enemy casualties littered the trenches it was paltry compared to the losses she was suffering. The battle had gotten close enough to render the Dwarf cannons obsolete but the constant report of smaller, centralized explosions continued to bother her. Puffs of grey-black smoke drifted away from ranks of Dwarves at measured intervals. Whatever fell sorcery the mountain dwellers employed went well beyond the cannons. She reluctantly deduced they had found a way to make smaller, handheld versions of the weapons. If Thord's army had enough of them….

Heavy boots thumped up the stairs of her observation tower. She didn't bother turning, knowing who it was. Maleela's only curiosity came from how long it had taken him to approach her.

"General Thrask, what is your report?" she asked, her voice smooth, polished.

Ignoring her, the Goblin Lord went to the edge of the tower and stared hard at the Dwarf line. He'd seen what a pair of their weapons was capable of and the cost was appalling. The battle along the Thorn River crossing was swift and exceptionally brutal. Nothing he had seen prepared him for the full fury lashing into his army.

"We must find a way to stop them."

Maleela clutched her sword, aching to plunge it into the Goblin's heart. "Can the army hold? Amar Kit'han will not tolerate failure."

"The demons are your concern, not mine. Kill Dwarves," Thrask snarled. "I must kill all the Dwarves."

She knew there were another ten thousand warriors waiting a short ride north. The ruins were a massive, sprawling complex but not large enough to house the entire fifty-thousand-strong force. With the northern flank secure and relatively quiet, Maleela figured it would be wise to funnel fresh troops in from the perimeter to counter the massive assault by the Wolfsreik on the east. Enemy forces were strongest there. The complications of the battle frustrated her. The Dwarf attack on the southwest was reaping massive casualties but their army was substantially smaller than Aurec's. There was no easy decision.

A flap of wings stole her attention. Rising from the center of Arlevon Gale were a dozen Gnaals. She'd only encountered the foul beasts, creations of dark magic, once in the moments before being captured by the Harpies. The very memory robbed her of strength. Gnaals were nothing short of the physical manifestation of hatred and evil. They appeared no more than bulbous, black masses flying through the sky but she knew the truth. Easily as tall as a Minotaur, the Gnaals had wide, leathery wings. Their bodies were the darkest shade of black, making individual characteristics almost indiscernible. Closing her eyes invoked vivid memories of puss-filled lesions, incredibly disproportioned muscles, whip-like tails, and eyes the color of pure malevolence.

She watched them soar into the sky, tucking their wings back and diving towards the Dwarf and Minotaur armies. Not even Boen or Groge had been strong enough to kill the Gnaals that had attacked her in the Jungles of Brodein. What could Dwarves do against a dozen of the killing machines? Maleela regretted the loss of life that was about to happen but felt relief at having one less problem. She could now direct her attention to the east, where she suspected her father cowered.

Thrask snapped his jaws together with appreciation. His warriors had strength in numbers but nothing comparable to the raw fury of the Gnaals. He quickly decided it was time to lead his troops into battle.

Maleela agreed. "Summon the reinforcements. Have them attack the Wolfsreik from the north. Between them and the Gnaals we can sweep our foe from the field and win this battle."

Thrask tapped a fingertip on one of his tusks as the notion of killing her entertained him. He didn't need her, despite what assurances the Dae'shan gave. She was weak, like the rest of her kind. The new world had no place for weakness. Thrask itched with the desire but knew it would only invoke the ire of Amar Kit'han. Instead he decided to wait until the battle was almost won before slicing her open and tearing out her heart.

"I go to fight the Dwarves. The army will attack your Wolf soldiers. This will be glorious day for the Goblin race. We will kill them all!" The Goblin Lord thumped a fleshy fist to his chest and stormed off. Killing Maleela could wait…for now.

With the foul Goblin gone, she resumed her mental quest for her father. Killing raged around her but her mind sequestered it away, lost behind the growing desire to see Badron broken and bleeding on the ground at her knees. The world dulled and faded until she saw but one figure. A solitary fighter lost amidst a sea of iron and armor. Badron. Oh how she wanted to slit his throat and bathe in his blood.

Gnaals dropped heavily into the massed Dwarf cannons. Weaponless, they attacked with tail and claw. No amount of Dwarf ferocity was enough to prevent bodies from being shredded. The battle raged as Gnaals cut their way through the Dwarves and reached the cannons. They bled from hundreds of cuts. Broken arrows and axe blades were embedded in their flesh yet not one had gone down. Close to a hundred Dwarves were already dead, torn apart without delay.

A few brave Dwarves managed to fire a final round into Arlevon Gale before their weapons were thoroughly destroyed. Gnaals crushed the barrels, snapping them like kindling. One blew up as the Dwarf valiantly lit the fuse in a last-ditch effort to launch another round. Both Dwarf and Gnaal disintegrated in a flash of smoke and flame. Temporarily dismayed, the remaining Gnaals recoiled and regrouped.

Fresh Dwarves drew ranks and prepared to fire. General Brug stood beside them, battle axe waving in the choked air. Having already withdrawn from the front lines, Brug's musketeers were busy rearming and preparing to head back into the fight when the Gnaals struck. Any terror he felt was deep-rooted but he barely managed to contain it. The Gnaals were evil on Malweir, a distant truth of vengeance and destruction stretching back generations. Few were strong enough to stand against them. The vast majority of races balked at the very sight as their nerves abandoned them. Dwarves, Brug reminded himself, were made of sterner material.

"Front rank kneel! Prepare to fire!" he barked.

Dwarves dropped into their well-rehearsed roles. Training took over.

"Fire!"

Muskets roared. Bullets struck the Gnaals in head and body. More than one screamed but they did not fall. As one, the Gnaals turned and advanced on the Dwarves. With no time to reload, Brug ordered axes drawn. He swiftly shifted to the center of the line and took his place among his warriors. Many cast sidelong glances to each other but none fled. If this was to be a battle to the death, so be it. Brug led the roar and charged. His musketeers followed step for step. Dwarf and Gnaal clashed in furious combat.

Using the Gnaals for cover, Thrask led fresh battalions of untested Goblins into the battle. They attacked the Minotaurs, still reeling from the force of the Gnaal assault, with belligerence. Krek kicked a Goblin knife thrower in the face. Bone and cartilage shattered as the Goblin dropped dead. Breathing heavily, the Minotaur king tried to withdraw and help the Dwarves but it wasn't possible. There were too many Goblins for the Minotaurs to pull away. His heart was torn, knowing the stout Dwarves were no match for the evil of the Gnaals.

Renewed cries announced the arrival of fresh Goblin troops. Thousands flooded towards the Minotaurs. Thousands that turned the tide of numbers. Krek was forced to forget his Dwarf allies and face the army threatening him. Chunks of flesh and hair coated his war bar with dried blood. His muscles were tight, heavy from exertion. His eyes burned from the smoke. Krek focused and calmed his breathing. There was fresh killing that needed to be done. It was only proper for the king to lead his warriors.

Morale remained high among his warriors. They'd suffered losses, several hundred as he figured, but were strong enough to repulse any attack the Goblins tried. Whatever pain the Minotaur army suffered was felt thrice over by their enemies. So many corpses littered the battlefield new units were forced to climb over mounds just to reach the Minotaurs. That made easy work for the taller, longer-reached bulls.

The line held for a while before so many Goblins arrived in force that Krek had no choice but to retreat. Combined with the loss of the Dwarf musketeers, Krek was heavily outnumbered and running out of vigor. Retreating would give him the time needed to recover and attack again. Bodies continued to pile up as the Minotaurs fought an organized withdrawal. Every inch of ground recaptured was paid for with many lives.

With the retreat came the sudden expansion of lines. Goblins were able to dash past the Minotaurs, suddenly eager to return the favor of carnage to the Dwarves. Nothing could be done to prevent that as Krek's bulls were faced with near overwhelming numbers. His bulls were hard-pressed to remain cohesive fighting units. Any breakup would mean death. Staying together was the only way his army was going to survive.

THIRTY-TWO

Brutal Survival

"What have we gotten ourselves into?"

The scene being played out before them was one the world hadn't seen in a thousand years. Very few living recalled an hour of such unmitigated darkness. Many of the one-hundred-strong company felt the old stirrings come back to life. Long had it been since the Giants of Venheim last went to war. Long since they were forced to give in to base instincts and take lives. Leaving their mountain forges was a difficult decision to make but one that couldn't be ignored.

So they came, with sword and axe, marching to a mournful dirge as vows of peace and non-interference were shattered upon the rocks. The long march from Venheim afforded each time for personal reflection, to decide if what they had volunteered to do was worth the cost of their soul. Belief in the old gods was gone, replaced by a lone deity who was both benevolent and demanding.

In the end there wasn't much of a choice. Whether the gods of light and dark were still around, lingering in the shadows just out of reach, didn't matter. All that mattered was the current war threatened to destroy the way of life of every single race on Malweir.

Blekling hefted his sword of his right shoulder. "It is as the Dae'shan said. This is a most grievous affair."

"Perhaps we should turn back? Return to Venheim and forget all this."

The Giant elder shook his head slowly. Long, black locks of hair dragged across his shoulders. "No. We gave our word. Groge is down there, lost in all this. He is our only hope of stopping the dark gods. Should he fall…well, at least there are more of us to pick up the Blud Hamr and stop this war. We continue to march. It is time for the Giants to return to war."

"Which front do we attack? South or east?"

Blekling studied the battlefield from atop the small rise the Giants had halted on. Tens of thousands of men and Goblins battled desperately on the right but they seemed almost evenly matched. His attention was drawn to the south, where Minotaur and Dwarf battled Goblin and…he froze as recognition dawned on him. He refused to believe what his eyes showed. Gnaals. Here, in Delranan. Until now he'd believed they were extinct, all killed during the Mage Wars when the dark Mages finally fell. Seeing so many at work now inspired dread.

"We go to the Dwarves," he said, his throat dry. *They need us the most. Once again our kind will engage those vile Gnaals. How many will die this time?*

Artiss Gran materialized at his side, gossamer robes simmering refracted rainbows from the sunlight. Face eternally obstructed behind the shadows of his cowl, the Dae'shan took in the scene being played out below and felt regret. Regret for not acting sooner. Regret for not standing up to his wayward brothers when they broke their pact with the gods. Regret for allowing the world to get to this point. He had much to make up for and, in his eyes, there could be but one possible outcome.

Blekling bowed curtly out of reverence. "Dae'shan. We have arrived, and it appears in the nick of time."

"That remains to be seen. Our allies are beleaguered. The Giants have not gone to war in a very long time. Are you sure you are prepared for this?" Artiss asked. He knew that by abandoning their principles the Giants would be fundamentally changed. There was latent danger in that. Vague memories of how terrible the Giants had become during the Mage Wars disturbed him. A great deal needed to change if hope and freedom were to survive the day.

Blekling, sensing the Dae'shan's doubt, grimaced. Fresh sounds of battle assaulted his ears. "This is not a matter of being prepared. Life is in the balance here. Great evil is at work down below. We have come to the aid of the free peoples of Malweir in the past when always the need was greatest. That pact continues to stand. Let no one say we do not honor our agreements. The Giants will go to war. Now."

Inwardly pleased, Artiss Gran nodded his consent. Perhaps there was hope for tomorrow after all. However pleased he might be, Artiss knew that the only way to defeat his brothers was through direct confrontation. The time of reckoning was at last upon him. Here, on this final day as the sun began to set, Artiss Gran was forced to find the destination to his long journey. It all ended tonight.

Blekling led his one hundred Giants down the slope and into the back of the Dwarf camp. Human and Dwarf stopped what they were doing and gaped as the force marched purposefully to the front lines without pause or comment. A cheer arose through the mire of desperation. Swords beat against shields. The army found new hope. Fresh life pumped into them as the Giants headed directly towards the Gnaal threat. What threatened to become a rout turned into defense. Hopefully, defense would lead to offense and the scouring of Delranan.

The Gnaals snapped to as they sensed their ancient enemies. Mindless with berserker rage, the Gnaals abandoned their slaughter of Dwarves to attack Blekling and his Giants. One hundred against eleven. The outcome was anything but certain.

Blekling led the charge. His blood ran hot. His heart pounded like the mighty forge hammers. His vision darkened. Nothing else existed except this battle. This moment. Picking up speed, he crashed into the nearest Gnaal. Limbs flailed as both bodies tumbled to the ground. Blekling gagged as an incredibly powerful tail curled around his neck and squeezed. Claws dug into his iron-like flesh. Intense pain washed over the Giant leader. He'd never been in a real fight before and it was threatening to be his death. Eyes burning, his vision swam.

Blekling reached deep into his heart and snatched hold of his inner strength. The Giant drove his right elbow into the Gnaal's exposed ribcage. It wasn't particularly strong, but enough to force the Gnaal to release its grip. Blekling slid from beneath the monster, continuing to slam elbows into exposed ribs. Enraged, the Gnaal whipped its tail about. Each blow broke the ground, kicking mud, snow, and dirt up.

Heavy, running, footsteps announced a trio of Giants rushing to help their leader. Axe and hammer struck the Gnaal repeatedly. Blood, so dark it appeared black, ruptured through broken flesh. Puss and ichor leaked from the monster as it was slowly, oh so slowly, beaten to death. Blekling managed to roll free, drawing his dagger in the process and plunging it deep into the Gnaal's heart. Exhausted and woefully underprepared, Blekling took the brief moment allotted to scan the battlefield.

While he might have killed a Gnaal, others were less fortunate. Several Giants lay dead or dying. The sight horrified him. A series of emotions erupted at once: hate, sorrow, despair, anger. Blekling snatched his weapons from the ground and led his host back into the fight. Eight of the dark Mage demons remained.

Inspired by the sudden appearance of Giants, Dwarves and Men launched back into the fight. Their weapons did little against the nightmarish hides of the Gnaals and more often than not they simply got in the way. Blekling didn't mind. The evil unleashed upon the world should have been eradicated centuries ago. That it had been allowed to endure was an affront to every sentient race on Malweir. Blekling intended on removing the stain for all time.

He watched, helpless, as Tobin's head rolled away from his already toppling corpse. Yarg grunted as a razor-sharp tail burst through his chest. His large hands desperately tried to keep his blood and organs from spilling out but it was of no use. He was dead before he struck the ground. A group of Giants systematically tore a Gnaal apart. Body parts littered the area at their feet. Blekling winced at the horrid screams coming from the dying creature. Madness had descended upon the world and he was but a small participant.

"Come brothers, let us end this brutality," he told those nearest him.

Each was panting and clearly struggling with committing acts of violence. He saw it in their eyes. Doubt lingered in the corners. They were hesitant to take that first step.

"This is not right. We should not be aiding in this slaughter."

Blekling fumed. His people were dying and these few suffered from lack of faith. "We did not begin this war but it ours to help finish. I did not wish to leave Venheim but the Dae'shan was correct. This war must end, here and now. We must do our part if life is to continue. Now, cast aside your doubt and fear. Follow me!"

Faith restored, at least somewhat, the Giants lunged forward to put an end to the remaining Gnaals. The Giant leader was immensely grateful for their cooperation. He asked them to do what he himself didn't feel right doing. Giants had once been mighty warriors, but those days ended and with good reason. Watching a Giant kill was a terrible sight to behold.

The battle had shifted away from him, forcing Blekling to run faster to reach his brothers. The Giant elder struggled for breath. Intense pain racked his sides. He knew some ribs were broken. The Gnaal nearly did him in and he knew it. Blekling decided to remain in the safety of numbers.

His first sign of trouble was the massive shadow suddenly drowning out the sun. Blekling looked up sharply in time to watch the largest Gnaal imaginable plant both feet on his shoulders and drive him into the ground. Bones snapped. Organs burst. Blekling withheld his scream though the pain was nearly unbearable. His weapons clattered away. Those flanking him were knocked aside as if mere children. Darkness swarmed his vision.

The Gnaal slithered off and wheeled quickly. Wicked rows of teeth, sharp and long, menaced from within the darkness of its mouth. Blekling looked upon the monster and knew death. Ignoring the crippling pain, he crawled and pulled towards his weapons. There would be only one chance. One chance only to salvage what remained of his name and legacy.

Overconfident, the Gnaal titled its head back and roared. Plants died at the sound. Rocks crumbled into dust. The

Gnaal took a ponderous step forward. Its tail snaked behind, whipping back and forth. It was then Blekling realized what he was facing. This was their leader. The toughest, meanest creation of dark magic alive in the world today. He snorted at the irony of it all. His head drooped. Eyes fluttered close. Tender relief flooded him as his fingers curled around the haft of his war bar. The Gnaal charged.

Blekling managed through great difficulty to prop himself up moments before the Gnaal struck. The stench of death hit first. The Giant vomited but held strong. Nearly two tons of genetic monstrosity slammed into him, driving both to the ground. Blekling grit his teeth at the moment of impact and was rewarded with his war bar impaling the Gnaal. Inch after inch of Giant-forged steel drove deeper into the Gnaal's vital organs. There was a terrible scream as the weapon burst through the heart and then spine. The Gnaal was dead.

Blekling lost consciousness as hands dragged the corpse away.

Three of the shamans were dead, slain by crossbows during the retreat. Krek ordered the remaining nine huddled in the center of his army where they'd be safe. For even one to have died showed great carelessness on all their parts. The shamans were not physically overpowering but they were the secret weapon in the ranks. Few of the other races had active magic users. With the shamans, Krek was able to maintain the balance of the battle until his numbers won out.

Fresh waves of Goblins poured towards them. The Minotaur king enjoyed fighting. It was the cornerstone of every good warrior, but he was tired. His muscles felt rubbery, overused for too long without a break. His mind, while sharp, was unfocused and almost lost in a haze. The battle continued to rage around him without pause or concern for those involved. It was an all-out slaughter. Any who survived would be scarred for life.

"Form ranks!" he barked and his bulls obeyed.

What was left of the Dwarf musketeers limped to their side. Less than a hundred remained and many were broken, ravaged shadows of what they'd been before the Gnaals struck. Krek looked for Brug but didn't find him. He hoped the Dwarf died a warrior's death. The ranking Dwarf saluted him and requested to join the lines. Krek was in no position to say no, despite how poor their condition was. Even a wounded Dwarf was deadly, he'd been told once. This was the hour in which to prove it.

Thord cursed and spit angrily. Too many of his kind were dying, slaughtered like sheep on a holy day. The Goblins possessed greater numbers. This had become a war of attrition and, if he didn't do something to change the trend, his army would be on the losing side. Hefting his axe, the Dwarf Lord collected his retinue and prepared to meet battle in the hopes of his presence inspiring the army.

Already the tide had shifted several times. The arrival of the Gnaals nearly broke the allied army before an unexpected force of Giants arrived. Thord wasn't one to question help when offered and used their arrival as a beacon to rally his beleaguered forces. The Dwarves and Minotaurs had already suffered greatly and there was still much more to come.

He'd watched as Bahr and his team slipped into Arlevon Gale and disappeared on their quest to stop the Dae'shan from completing their ritual. Normally that would have resulted in mission success and he would have pulled his army back to maintain a blocking force. The sheer size of the enemy army prevented any thoughts of that happening. Goblins continued to pour out of the ruins with murder in their eyes.

"You will only get in the way," Faeldrin said to him as the Dwarf stormed past.

Thord halted. "These are my warriors. What kind of king would I be to let them die without me by their side?"

He had a valid point. Faeldrin conceded he would be a poor king at best. Knowing the stubbornness of Dwarves, the Elf decided to change his method of approach. "They are strongest in the center. Whoever commands either has no concept of tactics or it overconfident. Use that to their weakness. Break the enemy in the center and the wings will collapse. I will take my Aeldruin and the rebels of Delranan to secure the western flank in the event our foe has hidden forces ready to strike."

Thord nodded his appreciation at the advice and marched on. Whether the flank was secure or not, this battle would be won in the center. His ranks swelled in passing. Wounded Dwarves filed out of the makeshift hospital and collected new weapons. Administrative and supply Dwarves followed suit. Those few cannon crewmembers still alive were the only ones who didn't. They desperately attempted to get the two remaining cannons back into firing configuration to add their thunder to the fight. Thord let them be. Enough had already died.

The march through the camp was mercifully brief. He could only take so much slaughter before growing restless. Now the time had come to produce his own. Brandishing his axe high above his helmeted head, the Dwarf Lord of Drimmen Delf marched his Dwarves into battle formation to the right of Krek's Minotaurs. The two kings passed knowing looks, each silently approving of the other's valor and readied to meet the heavy press of Goblins bearing down on them. The wait wasn't long.

Tides of Goblins crushed against the lines. Minotaur and Dwarf bowed back under the intense pressure but managed to hold. The musketeers fired off a volley that dropped scores of enemy soldiers. Having believed the Gnaals destroyed all the new weapons, the Goblins were taken off guard for a moment only. It was a moment enough for the allies to strike. Axe and sword fell and so too did hundreds of Goblins. Commanders barked orders and the line took a step forward before striking again. Hundred more died. The muskets fired again and the Goblins began to panic.

They'd come expecting an easier fight, not the hardened resolve of two races with a lot of fight left in them. Those in the back continued to press forward, unaware of what was about to happen in the front. Those closest to the enemy readied to throw down their weapons and turn to flee. Sheer weight of numbers prevented them from getting far. Dwarves and Minotaurs killed with glee. Their hated enemies of old continued to die in appalling numbers as they were gradually beaten back into the trenches.

Thord leapt over the outer trench, stepping on the fresh mound of bodies now filling it. He didn't pause to look down for there was no point. The vultures would pick the field clean regardless of friend or foe. Thord's focus was on doing as Faeldrin suggested. Break the center and their army will run.

Goblins were in wholesale retreat now, widening the gap between armies. Their confidence upon seeing the Gnaals unleashed had all but faded, leaving them with the harsh reality of their situation. Most were going to die. Neither particularly brave nor of strong will, the Goblin foot soldiers fled for their lives. Thord and Krek simultaneously charged.

They recaptured the second trench and held, for here the enemy defenses remained largely untouched. Thord spied a great beast of a Goblin whipping and hacking at his own ranks and immediately recognized their leader. He only hoped Krek hadn't spotted him as well. The Dwarf Lord cautiously stepped ahead of his army and slammed his axe against his leather-covered shield three times. Heads turned, pausing in what they had been doing to see what new spectacle had arrived, just as he hoped they would.

He could feel the gawking stares of his own soldiers behind him. Who in their right mind would expose themselves to enemy fire, especially given how lethal and accurate Goblin crossbows were, just to garner attention? The king of Drimmen Delf, for one. Unafraid, Thord waited until it was quiet enough to be heard. When he spoke, his voice was like waves crashing on the rocks. The raw intensity in his words made more than one set of knees quake.

"Goblin scum! Who dares claim authority to treat with me? I am Thord, son of Thorgrim, lord of Drimmen Delf, and cleaver of Goblins! Come scum, show me Goblin pride!"

He spat as far as he could towards enemy lines, satisfied to see their confusion blanking their wrinkled faces.

Trickles of saliva dribbled into his beard but he didn't care. This was war. One was expected to get…messy. Thord didn't need to wait long. Just as he suspected, it was the large, whip-lashing Goblin who forced his way through the ranks to confront the Dwarf king.

Krek watched the scene play out with great interest. His personal feeling that he should have the right to call out the enemy leader in single combat was substantiated by the sheer number of his dead and wounded. Thord had found him first, thus negating any claim Krek might have pressed. Angered at coming in second, the Minotaur king marched to stand behind Thord, offering silent support. Honor demanded a heavy price.

Thord pointed his axe at the Goblin and laughed. "You? This is the best you've got? A fat, broken beast who has to use a whip on his own soldiers? I should let my youngest nephew take his cuts at you, though you might not enjoy the whack of his wooden axe."

"Enough mocking, cave maggot," Thrask snarled at his hated foe. "I am Thrask, king of Goblins and lord of the Deadlands. Speak your terms."

So it is true. If your army is here who protects your lands? "Before I slaughter your army and leave the bones for the crows, I challenge you to single combat."

"There is no honor in it," Thrask shouted back. "I did not come to this miserable kingdom to barter with your runts. Go back to your army and meet death."

"Scared, eh? It's not every day a cave dweller like you gets to meet a real king," Thord taunted, hoping to lure Thrask into acting foolishly. "Perhaps I'll save killing you for last."

Thrask's rage boiled over. He took another step forward and threw down sword and helmet. "Weapons only. No armor to hide behind. I am going to enjoy watching *more* Dwarf blood spill onto the mud."

Satisfied, though finding it difficult to set aside the ignorance of Thrask's words, Thord did the same. He rolled his massive arms to loosen up the muscles. Cracking his thick neck brought cheers from his army. His dark beard was filthy with blood and gore, streaks of dried blood painted his face.

He looked every bit the berserker of legend. Killing Thrask wasn't going to end the battle but it would successfully demoralize the Goblins to the point it became a rout. Armed only with his axe and Dwarven tenacity, the lord of Drimmen Delf charged to meet his foe.

The Goblins were less vocal, though several cheered for Thrask as he hurried to meet death. They were close to the breaking point. More than a fifth of their force was already dead and nearly twice that wounded. What had begun as a simple defense was slowly downgrading into the kind of battles their armies had been hard-pressed to win in the past. Not even strength of numbers was enough to keep their spirits bolstered.

Thrask couldn't care less. He viewed this duel in the same manner as the Dwarf. Killing Thord would hamper his enemies, hopefully to the point they abandoned hope altogether. His hatred of Dwarves left him cocksure, arrogant. Lies whispered by the Dae'shan bolstered his ego and confidence. Once again Goblin and Dwarf met in single combat to decide the fate of the world. He halted when they were only a handful of steps apart.

They stared hard at the other, each trying to make the other flinch first. It was an old yet petty trick designed to inspire mental intimidation. Neither was weak enough to fall for such. Thord grunted and attacked. The time for action had come. Thrask stepped back rather than forward to meet the attack. The move, while simple, momentarily threw the Dwarf off guard. Momentum carried him past Thrask, who waited with his sword poised to cleave down the Dwarf's spine. Thord twisted at the last second and narrowly avoided being paralyzed. The sword slashed through air.

Spinning about, the Dwarf dropped into a guard. Thrask had already shown his hand. Rather than try to win through skill of blade, the Goblin was intent on trickery and foul tactics. Thord had seen it too many times before. Any hope he had of a quick, honorable victory was in tatters. Gritting his teeth, he prepared for a dirty fight.

Thrask took the offensive. "What's wrong, cave dweller? Haven't fought a true opponent lately, have you? My sword will slice you apart. Perhaps I'll have bacon made of your hide and feed it to my troops."

Silent, Thord shifted balance from his left to right foot. It took incredible discipline to keep from commenting, but he ultimately decided to let his axe speak for him. The time for taunts and petty chicanery was ended. Thrask became frustrated much too quickly and attacked, intending to punish the Dwarf's silence.

His sword moved fast but recklessly. There was no skill or precision. Thrask was an enraged beast fueled by bloodlust. Driving down from high, he used his minor height advantage to rain hacking blows down that Thord barely managed to parry. The Goblin sensed an end coming quickly. This Dwarf wasn't as strong or determined as many he'd already killed. No king worthy of the title would allow himself to fall so fast. Thrask renewed his efforts, seeking to humiliate Thord in front of both armies.

Thord let him come. The Dwarf skillfully fended off repeated blows, allowing Thrask to tire himself out. Once the force of the blows weakened, Thord shoved onto the offensive. He dipped his left shoulder beneath Thrask's swords and came up inside his reach. Shoulder struck chin and the bigger Goblin was driven back. In the same motion he dropped lower and swiped his axe across the tops of Thrask's thighs. Dark blood immediately spilled from the thin lines and Thrask screamed in agony.

Thord drove the head of his axe into Thrask's sternum, knocking the breath out of him before he leapt back into a proper defensive stance. Bleeding and angered, the Goblin attacked--exactly how Thord expected. Sword arced down in a wicked, two-handed slash meant to cleave Thord's skull. The Dwarf Lord sidestepped and swung his axe upwards. The steel bit deeply into Thrask's stomach with the sickening noise only steel and flesh meeting could make.

Eyes crossed. Blood frothed on his lips, bubbling over his tusks. Thrask dropped his sword. The weapon clanged uselessly on the ground. Thord wasn't done, knowing it takes more than one blow to kill a foe. He used his body weight to drag the axe through Thrask's abdomen, ripping organs away in a wash of blood. Ropes of intestines wrapped around the mighty axe as Thord jerked it free.

Thrask collapsed in a twitching mass of flesh. His clawed fingers flexed uncontrollably. His face twisted in that solitary question every fighter who'd ever lost a duel had in those final moments: how? Thord wasn't one to give in to procrastination. He'd spoken his piece before the duel began. This was all business. The Dwarf Lord gazed down on his defeated opponent one final time before chopping down. Thrask's head rolled away. Thord dropped his axe and retrieved the head. The Dwarf Lord raised it for all to see and heaved it towards the Goblin ranks.

Thord tilted his head back and bellowed at the top of his lungs.

Seeing their king victorious, the Dwarves of Drimmen Delf charged towards the Goblins. They were followed closely by Krek and his Minotaurs.

"My fighters have every right to march alongside them!" Ingrid fumed. She hadn't come looking for a war but the sight of what Arlevon Gale had become sickened her.

Faeldrin continued walking, eager to get back in the saddle and uphold his part of the battle. The Elf mercenaries weren't prepared to engage in full-scale combat but could harry any enemy pushing in from the flanks. Hopefully Thord and Krek had enough strength to do what needed to be done. He'd already lost a handful of Elves fighting the Goblins and didn't relish the prospect of losing more. Ingrid might be infuriated, but that was a personal issue she was going to have to overcome if there was any effectiveness to be found in her people.

"Damn it, stop and listen to me!" she all but shouted.

He paused, slowly turning. Amusement brightened his eyes upon seeing her standing there with hands defiantly thrust on her hips. She was every bit the leader whether she chose to accept it or not. Should they survive, Faeldrin had no doubts that the kingdom of Delranan would be in capable hands.

"Ingrid, this is not a game. Many of us will not be around in the morning. Don't be in such a rush to meet death. There is no glory to be found on this battlefield."

"Is that what you think of me? Glory? I've seen enough of war, Faeldrin. There is no honor to be had in this madness. All I ask is for my people to earn the right to redeem ourselves. This is our kingdom and I cannot help but feel partly responsible for what it has become." Ingrid paused as sour memories tormented her. "I…I need this."

"I do not doubt the strength of your convictions, but you must be warned that this is going to be brutal," the Elf told her. "There is a good chance you will be killed."

"Haven't I earned that right?" she asked. Her voice trembled, threatening to break down into tears. There'd be time for that when the smoke cleared and the final body counts were tallied. She couldn't cry now. Not yet.

"Perhaps you have. It would be an honor if your rebels would accompany my Elves. Though I did not speak it to Thord I believe the Goblins will attempt to flank us and strike from behind. The battle may be progressing deep into the ruins but our foes are cunning. This is not over by far."

"We're wasting time," Ingrid said.

Offering a genuine smile, Faeldrin nodded and headed out.

Ingrid mustered her forces, a mere fifteen hundred still in fighting condition, and marched in step behind the Elven mercenaries. Sounds from the fever-pitched battle in the ruins continued to mock them. Doubts and fears plagued each in their own way. None wanted to drive into the heart of the insanity but all felt it was their inherent responsibility. Live or die, they were all children of Delranan.

The Elves led them to the far edge of the tree line where sergeants directed the deployment of forces. Work went quickly and soon the army was emplaced and ready for the expected enemy counterattack. The wait wasn't long. Goblins advanced stealthily through the forest, hoping to take the rebels unawares. They failed.

Arrows plunged into the Goblin ranks. Cries arose from their ranks and they charged. Ingrid and Orlek exchanged nervous looks the moment before the Goblins attacked. The battle picked up quickly. Men and women died, hacked apart under the fury of Goblin blades. The line threatened to break.

"On me!" Orlek shouted and waded into the slaughter.

Ingrid's heart crawled into her throat. She couldn't bear to lose another love but was in no position to prevent Orlek from doing what he was meant to do. She steeled her mind against the inevitable and went back to directing the battle. Ingrid was no warrior and lacked the thirst for blood. That didn't stop her from using her knowledge of tactics to improve her army's odds.

Deep in the heart of the battle, Orlek plunged his blade into a Goblin's exposed throat. Blood squirted onto his chin and armor as he jerked the blade free to fend off a throwing axe. Another rebel hacked off the Goblin's hand at the wrist. The axe dropped away. Orlek stabbed, missing the first time but was rewarded with the sweet touch of steel driving into flesh.

Half deafened by the shouting, screaming, and clanging of swords, Orlek didn't spy the Goblin archer taking aim. The shaft thrummed away and struck Orlek in the left shoulder. The force of the blow knocked him from his feet, driving his breath away. Those not engaged in the front rank rushed to drag him to safety against his protests. Blood coated his sleeve and chest. The wound was deep. The pain near unbearable, but he refused to be taken from the field.

His last sights before passing out were of the Elves charging in from the side. Dominant on horseback, the Aeldruin killed without thought. Goblins crumbled under the pressure as nearly one hundred Elves rode deeper into their ranks. It took much effort to finally penetrate the entire length of the Goblin force. More than one Elf was dragged from the saddle and slaughtered.

Faeldrin wheeled his diminished force around once they were clear and prepared to wade back into the slaughter. Too many empty saddles converged on him. This was likely the final ride of the Aeldruin. The enemy was simply too large. It was a sad fact he'd known from the reports following the battle on the banks of the Thorn River. The willing sacrifice would place them on the pillars of heroes beside Elvendom's greatest. Faeldrin didn't want to be a hero. He merely wanted to live. Unless Bahr and his team managed to stop the Dae'shan, there seemed little chance of that.

Faeldrin pointed his sword at the Goblins and ordered the Aledruin back into the fray.

THIRTY-THREE

Glory Reclaimed

Catapults continued to drop rounds into the Goblin defenses. Rolnir ordered the batteries pulled forward to cover the infantry attack, hoping to relieve some of the pressure hammering into his army. With the attack all but stalled, he needed to find a way through the first trench line. All he needed was a foothold. The Wolfsreik general watched through his looking glass as the battle developed.

Anger and frustration clashed, their effects displayed by his bulging veins on his temples. His cheeks were red, flustered. His eyes were raw from lack of sleep and the natural irritation of so much smoke. He desperately wished for Piper Joach. The second in command was the voice of reason in the army and provided constant, sage advice. Advice Rolnir needed now. The attack was floundering, threatening to fail entirely. He needed to find a way to break through and turn the tide.

"Runner! Tell General Vajna to attack now," he ordered.

The young soldier dashed off without bothering to salute. Rolnir forgave the sudden lack of discipline and turned his focus on the Goblin towers. Each was packed with at least a score of crossbowmen who continued to slaughter his infantry. Rolnir had been in foul situations before but nothing quite so fierce. The siege of Rogscroft paled in comparison to trying to break through the Goblin defense. There the Goblins under Grugnak did most of the dirty work, leaving the Wolfsreik to mop up.

He cheered as one of the towers exploded. The catapult round continued to crash into the Goblin infantry. It was only one out of at least twenty. The Goblin held the advantage as long as those towers remained operational. Rolnir's joy turned to sorrow as what remained of the first unit to attack limped away from the battle. They were naught but tattered remnants of a once proud unit. Many dragged or carried wounded with them. It had been a very long time since any unit of the Wolfsreik was so thoroughly ravaged. Rendered combat ineffective in less than an hour, they wouldn't be able to return to the fight unless there was no other way.

"This is madness," Aurec said from his side.

Rolnir's scowl remained hidden by the looking glass. "The Goblins were much better prepared than we assumed."

"It's going to take more than what we've got to break those lines," the king said.

"Have patience. Our assault is in support of the main effort," Rolnir reminded. "The Dwarves will take the brunt of the fight."

He didn't bother stating the obvious: that only Bahr's mission was of importance. All else was mere secondary consideration. Rolnir held on to hope, that fragile string growing increasingly thinner as the battle continued. He wished he'd had the foresight to send runners over with the Dwarves but was forced to rely on a tenuous string of communication that meant delays in coordinating attack efforts.

The sign Thord assured he wouldn't miss nearly blew him off his feet. Never had he imagined such magnitude of power in weapons. Rising flames and smoke columns almost made him recant his position of being a warrior. No army on Malweir should be given this sort of power. The scope of warfare had changed forever. He hoped the Goblins were understanding that by the hundreds.

"Look, a breach!" Aurec nearly shouted.

It wasn't much but they clearly spotted soldiers funneling into first trench. Rolnir felt some of the tension weighing him down lift. His faith in his soldiers remained unchanged but doubts of their ability to break the Goblins arose. He had come into Delranan expecting to find Harnin and a band of reservists holding the line, not an impossible army of Goblins in numbers unheard of.

Rolnir silently urged his infantry on. They needed to smash the lines and secure an area wide enough to allow the rest of the army in. Once accomplished, the Wolfsreik would be able to crush the enemy from the inside. Silver and grey-armored soldiers began assaulting the nearest towers. Goblins and Men fell from the fortifications. First one, then another tower fell. Fresh infantry battalions, composed of Rogscroft and Wolfsreik soldiers, headed for the breach. Rolnir spied the diminutive brown-skinned Pell Darga ranging the lines in packs of hunters. They killed at random and were beyond ruthless.

Cuul Ol stood at their sides, watching his hunters go to war for the first time in generations. He chewed thoughtfully on a pine twig lovingly snapped from a tree in passing. The stress felt by Rolnir and Aurec failed to translate to the sage Pell leader. Living in the Murdes Mountains was a much harsher reality than either man could imagine. Where the lowlander armies struggled against impossibility, his Pell hunters reveled in it. There was little denying that the Pell Darga clans were the combined army's greatest assets.

Rolnir was infinitely grateful for their aid. They were artful warriors, if not properly trained. His respect grew with each engagement. The Pell continued to prove their worth since his first encounter with them in the mountain passes when they'd been enemies. Cuul Ol and his hunters all but brought the Wolfsreik offensive in Rogscroft to a halt by disrupting the supply lines and casting intense fear among the rank and file.

He hoped to use the natural animosity between Pell and Goblin to his advantage by disguising a large contingent of Pell hunters in Wolfsreik and Rogscroft uniforms. Once they infiltrated the first trench, they shed their false uniforms and attacked in the manner best suited to them. The effect had been brutal. Goblins in the immediate area faltered upon seeing so many of the almost-forgotten foes savaging them with short spears and daggers. Many Pell died in the attack, but the odds were always in their favor. They slew Goblins with every blow. Rolnir had no doubts it was the Pell who managed to secure the breach. Now it was up to the heavy infantry of the Wolfsreik to widen it.

This was yet another instance where he missed having Piper to confer with. His commander was in the wild lands somewhere to the northeast, hopefully destroying the last of Harnin's fortress line. Rolnir wished he had the additional five thousand soldiers for this campaign but their enemies were too many to fight one at a time. Still, the fifty-thousand-strong Goblin army occupying the center of his kingdom left the general with grave doubts. He needed his full army present if they were going to salvage the day.

"We Pell do our part well," Cuul said with pride gleaming in his eyes.

Shadows began to crawl across the face of the world as night readied to fall. The long train of wounded being dragged to safety grew. Hundreds, perhaps more, soldiers were carried, dragged, or limped back on their own. Rolnir found the scene disheartening. He'd expected massive casualties but none of their estimates prepared him for the dismal scene unfolding before him. Perhaps it was only an illusion brought on by the short distance separating the armies. Perhaps it was the ache in his heart upon watching his army fight a needless battle, one they weren't prepared for upon arriving. He didn't know, nor did he care. There could be only one outcome as far as he was concerned. The Wolfsreik was already home, now they needed to find a way to victory.

Rolnir cleared his throat, realizing for the first time it was parched. "Your warriors are fine indeed, Cuul. We are very thankful to have them."

"Many will not come home," Cuul added.

"Yet they will be remembered for generations, you have my word," Aurec told him.

Cuul Ol said nothing as he continued to watch the battle. Hundreds of soldiers had broken through to the second trench. Enemy towers were folding up and down the line. With each foot of gain hope was restored. Rolnir felt it ride the currents of the wind. They were closer to victory and ending the Goblin threat. The fact that it would all be for naught if Bahr failed didn't matter. He'd go to his grave knowing his army had done their utmost to defend Delranan.

As if waiting for Rolnir to make a fatal error, thousands of Goblins emerged from the north. If they managed to get into position they would trap Vajna and the cavalry between forces. He'd lose most of his army. The redheaded general collapsed his looking glass and decided to take matters into hand. He couldn't allow his greatest asset to get caught. The infantry was built for that sort of situation, horses weren't. He needed their range and speed to keep the battle fluid. The enemy understood that and aimed to remove the threat.

Any good feeling Rolnir had was dashed as this new force emerged. He'd grown overconfident with the taking of the trenches that he failed to prepare for what should have been blindingly obvious. Not even the Goblin commander could be foolish enough to marshal his entire army in the cramped confines of Arlevon Gale. The tide had turned in the blink of an eye. He had to act quickly.

"I need to get down there. Your Highness, I'm taking what's left of the army and hitting those new Goblins," he said with authority.

Aurec watched as fresh Goblins continued to flood the fields. All his carefully wrought dreams were undoing. His mind was made at the same time as Rolnir's. "I'm coming with you. This isn't just your fight, General."

Rolnir wanted to argue. Someone needed to stay behind and direct the battle. He was a professional soldier whereas Aurec was meant for loftier stations. But whatever the boy lacked in combat experience he equally lacked in tactics. Rolnir had no choice. "Very well. We move the command center over to Vajna's marshalling area and attack from there. Sergeant Major Thorsson, order the army to shift right and prepare to engage."

Thorsson shifted his gaze to Aurec quickly, as if to wish him good fortune, and stalked off barking orders. Time was running out if they were going to save the army.

The cavalry barreled towards the gap in the lines. Vajna and Herger rode at the head of the column. Nerves were on edge for never had either imagined an enemy so large.

Rogscroft's senior ranking officer focused his gaze on the melee just ahead. His cavalry would cover the space between lines in mere heartbeats, fortunately not giving many the time to think properly about what they aimed to do.

Lowering his short spear, Vajna broke away just enough to assume the point of the first wedge. Herger peeled off to do the same with the second. Those in Vajna's column followed suit, until the back rank was ten abreast. The crushing weight of so many would hopefully force the Goblins apart to the point the thousands of infantry would storm in and break the line for good. In theory it was a sound strategy. In fact, Vajna reserved his fear. There'd be time for that after his spear struck Goblin flesh.

The ground was rocky and filled with low stumps. The entire area had been lightly forested, making a series of natural defensive measures once Goblins cut down the trees. Snow made the situation worse. Vajna feared losing too many horses to broken ankles or worse during his charge. None of that could be helped. He would either arrive with his full force or get reduced along the way. It was up to the gods.

Infantry formations parted and filed in behind in his wake. Their confidence was bolstered by the thunderous charge of heavy horse. Goblins fought harder, desperate to keep their already slipping hold on the lines. Threatened with execution, they'd been ordered to hold at all costs. There would be no surrender or retreat. Fresh spears were brought in. The second trench was reinforced with new battalions of untested warriors. Horns bleated across the ruins in a weak attempt at inspiring fear in the horsemen.

Vajna's wedge was within meters of breaching the gap of the first trench when horns blew wildly from behind. He could just make out their beat from above the roar of battle and his horses. Fresh waves of panic gripped him. Thinking quickly, he thrust his spear wide left and wheeled in the same direction. Most of his wedge did the same. Vajna caught many confused looks on his riders' faces as they circled around. He was just as confused. But the signal was clear enough. Do not attack.

Once his wedge made the complete circle and headed back away from the battle, he paused to see if the others had followed. For the most part they had. Herger and his wedge were equally confused but the Wolfsreik officer was pointing towards the northeast where a roiling mass of squat, grey bodies were marching down on them. Vajna's blood chilled at the sight. Any thoughts of bringing a quick, decisive end to the battle at the trench dashed away like broken clouds. His cavalry was about to get bloody, but in the proper way.

Ignoring the groans and massed confusion of the infantry, Vajna didn't wait for new orders. Experience told him what to do. Thousands strong, this new Goblin offensive threatened to slash into the rear of the combined army's lines and reap a terrible toll. He pulled up alongside Herger and his other commanders.

"We're deceived!" Herger shouted.

Vajna nodded. What else needed saying? "Reform your wedges on line. We strike immediately before they have the opportunity to form ranks. Don't stop until we are through. Then we form up and do it again. Questions?"

There were none. These were seasoned professionals, veterans of two campaigns. Each knew what needed to be done. Wills resolved as the cavalry reformed their wedges, this time much tighter to make a greater impact on the enemy ranks. Vajna signaled his bugler with a nod and multiple horns blared out over the cavalry. Hundreds of horses lunged forward to the wild roars of their riders.

Fading sunlight caught the dull, silvered-spear tips as they lowered. Vajna welcomed the coming of night, knowing it would prevent him from seeing the full size of the force he was about to assault. Tantamount to suicide, it was his only play. The ground swept past. Meters disappeared as the lines converged. He braced, wincing once as his horse broke into the new Goblin army.

Bodies were trampled under the weight of hundreds of horses. Spears were cast, impaling their targets even as the riders drew swords and began hacking down at the shorter Goblins. Heads and reaching hands were lopped off. Blood painted the horses already lathering coats. Unsure which way to turn to avoid being crushed, those unfortunate Goblins nearest to the cavalry were mowed down without mercy.

Vajna figured they were halfway through the army by the time Goblins started to react. Crossbows took out several riders and their mounts. Angered Goblins fell upon them, hacking them all to pieces as the charge thundered past. Insanity gripped the field. There was no elegance to this fight. No honor. Vajna and Herger led their riders through impossible odds while killing as many of the enemy as possible along the way. Bodies carpeted the ground. Many were trampled underfoot while others were crushed. Finally, when he didn't think he'd be able to go any further, Vajna broke free of the last Goblin rank. Horses screamed approval as they thundered into open air.

Badron wasn't sure what possessed him to disguise as a soldier and join the second wave of the attack. Nor was he certain what made him think he could sneak past the Goblin defense and get away unscathed, but that was what happened. His old legs carried him across the killing fields, into the trenches where he exacted a small measure of revenge for the humiliation suffered in Rogscroft, and into the outer rows of ruins. Only when he was squirreled away in the shadows did he feel comfortable enough to shed some of his protection and breathe easier.

Comfortable. "I must be out of my mind."

If anything his position had worsened considerably. He'd gone from certain escape to almost certain capture. Even though the Goblins were distracted on two fronts he was most assuredly heading towards his ultimate demise. The promise haunted him as it had done since first agreeing to Amar Kit'han's lies. He took new umbrage against his enemies and readied to delve deeper into Arlevon Gale.

He wasn't sure what he hoped to accomplish. He never expected to make it this far. All he knew, and that not for certain, was his enemy was located in the center of the ruins. The Dae'shan had only hinted at this moment, never bothering to speak clearly enough for Badron to understand the severity of it. Killing Amar or the others seemed unlikely given their supposed immortality. *So why am I here? Vanity? Could the idea of trying to get revenge be more important than regaining my crown?* He didn't know. All he knew was that this ordeal was rapidly ending and his destiny was somewhere in these ruins.

He let his thoughts wander back to the devastating new weapons of the Dwarves. While none of the soldiers in his platoon had any idea what they were he instantly recognized the raw power of the weapons and decided he needed them for his vision of the new Delranan, whether the Dwarves chose to share their technology or not. Badron hoped Harnin hadn't destroyed too much of the infrastructure in his mad quest for fame. He needed his old spy network to enact his new strategies.

Badron crept through the ruins. Any surprise he felt at not finding Goblins impeding his progress went unnoticed as he spied the haunting glow just ahead. His heart raced. He'd found the Dae'shan. Weapon gripped tightly, Badron hurried to meet his destiny.

THIRTY-FOUR

Loss and Gain

Heart racing, Bahr was about to do the dumbest thing he had ever imagined in his long life. He gripped his sword tightly, as if afraid it would fail him when he needed it the most. Taking three quick breaths, he rounded the corner and prepared to charge into the mass of Goblins and the Troll. Boen's strong hand jerked him back at the last moment. Confused, Bahr turned on his friend with venom in his eyes. Boen's face remained impassive as he pointed.

Bahr squinted through the gathering darkness to where the Gaimosian pointed. There, amidst the angry rabble defending the entrance, stalked a slender figure no larger than a girl. Bahr squinted harder as he glimpsed her face. His heart fell. Mouth dropping open, he surged forward only to be held firmly in place.

"Not yet," Boen whispered in his ear.

"Let me go, you bastard. It's Maleela," Bahr snapped back.

"Think clearly you old fool. She's not here as a prisoner," Boen argued.

Bahr finally succeed in shrugging off Boen's grip but didn't move. Reason was blocked by emotional attachment. Days of worrying over her death finally wore him down, here when he needed all his strength. At the end of the quest Bahr found yet another obstacle preventing him from ending it all. Despair crawled into the shallow parts of his soul and he wept.

"Use the pain. It will make you stronger once we get inside," Boen urged.

Anienam whispered from a short distance away, "We are wasting time. The Dae'shan have already begun the ritual!"

"He's right, we need to move," Boen seconded.

Bahr risked another glance and was dismayed to see Maleela disappear within the ritual chamber. "There's too many. We'll never break through in time with that Troll standing guard."

Boen offered his most charming grin. "Leave the Troll to me. We can take care of the Goblins well enough."

"It has to be quick, before others come down on us from behind," Bahr said.

"Quick killing is the best. Are you ready?"

He wasn't, but that didn't matter. Boen used that momentary distraction to leap into an attack, stealing Bahr's place at the head of the group. The Gaimosian bellowed an almost monstrous roar as he raised his sword high above his head. Goblins turned, startled by the sudden appearance of enemies this deep within the ruins. The Troll roared back in challenge, knowing Boen for what he was. Shoving the smaller Goblins aside, the Troll rushed to meet Boen. They collided like mountains collapsing.

Boen struck swiftly. His sword ripped chunks of sickly green flesh away. In pain, the Troll tried to swat Boen's sword away and grasp his throat. Boen was quicker. His sword danced over the Troll's rough hide, scoring deep wounds designed to infuriate more than kill. His only chance was to get the Troll angered enough to where it didn't think clearly.

The beast was close to eight feet tall and five hundred pounds of muscle and anger. Boen had never fought an opponent so large, the Gnaal notwithstanding. This was a beast of the old world, a creature seldom seen outside of their mountain homes. Trolls weren't exceptionally bright but possessed the martial skills of a Gaimosian. Boen was in the fight of his life.

The Troll swung hard, clipping Boen's shoulder and sending him tumbling to the ground. Goblins backed away to give them room. None were in a hurry to die. Intense pain ran through Boen's right side but he struggled through it to rise again. Lip busted, a thin trickle of blood dribbled down his chin. Madness sparkled in Boen's eyes. This was the fight he'd been searching for. A fight where he'd either win or die. There was no alternative.

Boen lunged forward and ducked back as the Troll reached for him. He was rewarded by losing two fingers as Boen's sword sliced through. The Troll stumbled backwards, blood pulsing from the stubs.

"Now we're even, beastie," Boen barked.

The Troll attacked again, abandoning caution. He barreled towards Boen. Unaware of the surrounding area, the two battled with all their might. Sword hacked and cut. Fist pummeled and broke bone. Three of Boen's ribs snapped like kindling. The Troll buckled as steel ripped through his right hamstring. Blood peppered the ground. Both panted heavily. Exhaustion crept in for neither had gone against such a worthy foe.

Bahr and the others fired arrows into the distracted Goblins, felling several instantly. Battle erupted as Ironfoot and Rekka burst into the Goblin ranks. Sword and axe worked fast. Limbs and heads were hacked away before Bahr and the others managed to catch up. Though severely outnumbered, the group made quick work of their enemies. Not even the mighty Troll was enough to bolster Goblin confidence. Scores died within the first few moments.

Oblivious, Boen continued to fight. He felt the end of his strength fast approaching. He'd given his all, throwing everything he had at the Troll, but the beast was a monster of unchecked proportions. Bone from his shattered ribs pierced several organs. Boen felt death coming. He vowed not to die before killing the Troll. As if in agreement, the Troll attacked.

He wrapped Boen in a massive hug, crushing and squeezing the life away. Boen struggled but the grasp was too tight. His vision darkened. A series of pops burst up and down his spine. Tears flowed freely for the first time in his life. Boen raised his sword in both hands and plunged the tip down into the Troll's throat, driving the steel deep into the chest cavity where it burst the Troll's heart.

They collapsed in a heap of broken bones and cooling flesh. Boen slammed his head on a stone as five hundred pounds of lifeless flesh crushed him. Broken, battered, and bleeding from a dozen places, Boen lost feeling in his hands and feet. His vision began to fade. The Vengeance Knight, son of vanquished Gaimos, managed to turn his head and watch as his friends cleared the entranceway to the ritual chamber and rush inside. Satisfied he'd done his job, Boen died with a smile on his face.

The enemy held until Groge waded into the slaughter. Taller than the Troll, the young Giant kicked, smashed, and crushed any Goblin too slow to get away. Those survivors broke and ran. Bahr turned to go back and help Boen, for no single man was equal to killing a Troll. The gates to the ritual chamber were clear and, with time fleeing, Anienam urged the Sea Wolf to hurry. Bahr gave a final glance to his friend of many years and rushed into the passage.

Regret building, Bahr forced his legs to work, carrying him deeper into the unnatural darkness. Steps went by as he led his small group deeper into the unknown. The ground was smooth and steadily sloped downward. Humidity rose despite the winter chill. Bahr didn't know how far he marched before a haunting glow broke the curtain of dark in the distance.

All thoughts voided. His mind focused on what must be done. They had crossed half the known world in search of this moment. All Groge needed to do was smash the Olagath Stone and their ordeal would end. Bahr felt reinvigorated at the thought of finally being freed. He couldn't be concerned with who lived or died in the coming fight, for surely the enemies of light intended on fighting. Anienam promised this to be the final, desperate battle of their time and made no promises for success. Bahr didn't care.

Shadows detached from the tunnel walls and quickly formed to block the way. Bahr jerked to a stop and raised his sword. "Wizard! We are beset!"

Anienam, using Skuld as his crutch, hobbled to the front of the group and slammed his hands together. Violet light sprung to life, bathing the tunnel. Bahr felt his stomach lurch as the shadows came to life. They were a roiling mass of bruised flesh. Hundreds of different souls trapped by fell powers. Hands turned to claws stretched out for Bahr. He reeled back a step, knowing that should they touch him he would be lost forever.

The wall began to moan. It was a most horrid sound. Bahr felt lost. He couldn't fight what wasn't real. "Back, get back."

Anienam held his ground. "No. Do not show fear. It is an apparition, nothing more. Foul torments designed to induce fear." He took a step forward. "Go back to the nothingness of the afterlife and trouble us no more."

Laughter mocked him. The dead reached harder. The promise of living flesh spurred them on. Anienam clapped again, expanding the light between his hands. The dead wailed. The sound was so foul it made the wizard's nose bleed. Anienam felt strength leave his legs. He clapped again. This time the violet power surged forward to strike the wall. Shadows disintegrated upon contact, forcing the others to contract.

Anienam's lack of vision prevented him from experiencing the true horror the others suffered from. The Dae'shan had enacted a very old spell, dark magic from the time before Mages. He didn't know if his power was strong enough to stop it. Anienam attacked again. Violet light bathed the tunnel as he continued to attack. Shadows were blown apart. The wall shrunk but in doing so became stronger. He heard one of his companions retch. Noxious odors filled the tunnel. Anienam recognized them as poison. He had to end this or they'd all die.

Clenching his fists, Anienam whispered words that hadn't been spoken in thousands of years. The ground began to tremble. Sonic vibrations threatened to tear the already fragile tunnel apart. Anienam felt years bleed of his remaining life. He clenched Skuld tighter and was imbued with fresh energy. Revelations burst in his mind. He'd been right all along. With a mind-shattering scream, the wizard launched his collected magic at the wall.

Screams tore rocks from the walls. The shadows exploded into fine mist. Hundreds of years of pain and suffering were released with a final whisper of a groan.

Anienam slumped to his knees before Skuld could hold him up. Streaks of grey lined the young boy's hair. Wrinkles formed around his eyes. It took every measure of strength to lift the fragile wizard.

"It is done," Anienam told Bahr. "There will be no others."

Bahr resisted the urge to ask what he'd just witnessed. There was no real point to it. With the path cleared, they had a direct approach to the ritual chamber and whatever fate destiny had in store for them.

"Come on. Let's end this."

"The Goblins aren't strong enough to win this battle. Your Gnaals have failed as well. Our enemies encroach upon the ruins in waves. Do something," Maleela demanded without waiting to be acknowledged.

One by one the Dae'shan turned their heads to the impudent female. A useful tool but nothing more, Maleela quickly approached the point of uselessness.

"Princess, you should not be here," Amar Kit'han hissed. "Unless perhaps you wish to take the place of a willing sacrifice?"

He took pleasure at the way she swallowed harshly in response. He enjoyed her pale flesh and sudden nervous flicker in her eyes. The haughtiness she carried into the ritual chamber fled as she looked upon his face for the first true time. It was long past time for keeping secrets. Amar needed her to understand the despair of her actions. He wanted her to know how close to the underworld she had traveled by dealing with him.

"At last you begin to understand. There will be no dawn for you, Maleela," Amar taunted. "Your life ends tonight."

Amar Kit'han drew his athame and walked to the nearest sacrifice. The victim lay peacefully in anticipation of the liberation to come. He drove the athame into the chest of a middle-aged female. Blood fountained before spreading in a hot pool across her white robe. She died with a scream of pain.

The Dae'shan found the interruption more than troubling. The ritual had begun.

"You lied," she whispered.

"I merely told you what you wanted to hear. This is not a pleasant world and we are not pleasant creatures." He drifted around to the next sacrifice and repeated his killing stroke. "You are all but sheep for the slaughter. With these five souls, the Olagath Stone will be filled and I can finally release the dark gods."

He ripped the athame from the cooling flesh. Ropes of blood trailed away to splash on the cold, stone ground. Blood flowed from both bodies now, filling the runnel leading down to the dais where the Olagath Stone sat. The obsidian stone began to glow deep crimson. Amar Kit'han plunged the athame into the third heart, adding to the carnage.

The Stone continued to brighten. Unbridled power pulsed from the object. As the world continued to tear itself apart on the surface, Amar Kit'han enjoyed the relative quiet of the ritual chamber. He tasted the strength of thousands of souls trapped within the Stone and was rewarded with clarity of purpose. Never had he felt this impassioned for his task. Soon the dark gods would be released and his ascension promised.

"You can feel it, can't you?" he asked her. Blood dripped from the athame, sizzling as it struck the ground. "So much raw power just waiting to be claimed. I've spent generations awaiting this moment."

"This…this shouldn't be," she protested after finding her voice. "Life isn't meant to be lived like this."

"Perhaps you would care to claim the next victim? It is quite liberating, I assure you."

Amar floated around the ritual table to the fourth sacrifice. It was an elderly man with wrinkled hands tied across his lap. The twisted agony on his face was one of raw terror. Devoting his blood so that proper masters of the world could reclaim their throne was the fulfillment of purpose. To be one of only five was a high honor.

Maleela felt her stomach rumble at the thought of murdering a helpless victim. She looked down on the victim's face with regret. "You don't honestly expect me to believe these people are willing to die on purpose?"

"You don't honestly expect me to care what you think, do you?" Amar fumed. "I recruited you to perform a job, which is on the surface, not down here."

"I didn't think you were concerned with the battle," Maleela spat back.

"I don't but the Goblins must hold long enough for me to complete this task. You must return to the surface and oversee the battle. Where is Thrask?"

Maleela frowned. "He took a battalion of Goblins to confront the Dwarves and something else."

"Something else?"

"They are unlike anything I have ever seen. Great beasts that walk on two legs and have heads like bulls. They are slaughtering the Goblins at will," she admitted. Dire fascination laced her words.

Amar Kit'han found the news disturbing. He'd taken into account almost every angle from which their enemies could attack but failed to imagine the warriors of Malg would leave their forest homes. "Minotaurs. So Artiss Gran has managed to unite more races than we supposed. I believe our wayward brother is in need of cleansing."

"You should have never let him live," Kodan Bak snarled. His anger had boiled over. Sensing momentary weakness and distraction, the lesser Dae'shan decided it was time to make his play for control.

"Now is not the time, Kodan," Amar cautioned, his tone suggesting he knew what was about to happen.

"You will not be made a god. You've led us down wrong paths for too long, Amar Kit'han. The time has come to end your rule."

He and Pelthit Re spread out to either side. Raw power danced from their sleeves. Ripples of blue electricity coated their cloaks. The very air around them began to hum. Maleela stepped back and hugged the far wall lest the battle destroy her.

"Stand down, brother. It does not need to end this way," Pelthit Re ordered.

Hatred burned in Amar's empty eyes. "Oh but it does. Ever you have craved my standing. Tonight, after the dark gods elevate me, I promise I will torment you until the breaking of the world."

"No more talk." Kodan Bak launched his power at Amar. The other barely managed to deflect it in time, the magic exploding harmlessly across the ceiling. Rocks and debris fell heavily. Pelthit Re attacked from the opposite side, again testing Amar's defenses. Again the magic exploded across the chamber.

Maleela crouched and placed her hands over her ears to keep the deafening booms out of her head.

The sounds of fresh battle invigorated him. Badron picked up his pace as he delved deeper underground. The moment of retribution had arrived and once again he could claim the throne. All his trials had led to this one instant. He gathered his waning strength and raised his sword in anticipation of striking the Dae'shan down.

"Demon! I've come to claim what is rightfully mine!" Badron roared as he entered the chamber.

The battle halted immediately. Magic dissolved, leaving residual trails drifting in the air. The smell of blood, iron and foul, choked the air. Badron's eyes were drawn to the bodies slowly bleeding out on the stone slabs. Questions came to mind but this was no time for such idleness. He'd come to do murder and nothing would alter his course.

With but one sacrifice left and his brothers attempting to murder him, Amar suppressed the desire to purge the entire chamber in flames. Humans had always proved unreliable and taking a chance with this family had been a reluctant necessity. One he now regretted. Still, watching father and daughter try to murder each other should prove entertaining.

"Ah, the wayward king has returned," he chided. His voice was smooth, like water flowing over stone. "Alas there is nothing for you to claim."

Kodan and Pelthit paused their attack, suddenly fearful of a trick.

Maleela spun, drawing her sword in the same motion. “Father?”

“Maleela?” Badron said, confused. “This is your doing! You’ve sought to replace me from the beginning.”

“No, Father, I haven’t. But I am going to kill you now.”

Maleela leapt into an attack. Utilizing the momentary distraction, Amar Kit’han completed the ritual by plunging the athame into the final sacrifice. The world began to disintegrate around them.

THIRTY-FIVE

Even Gods Must Fall

The explosion threw Maleela and Badron to the ground. Dust and debris rained down from the ceiling. Amar Kit'han exchanged worried looks with his fellow Dae'shan.

"The wards have been breached. Our enemies are upon us," he hissed. "You let this happen!"

Kodan Bak, smoke rising from his tattered robes, clenched his fists and was instantly surrounded by a pale green glow. "You have caused this. So close to success you bring failure into our midst."

He unleashed the power. Amar reeled back, letting go of the athame. The magic burned holes in his robes. Weakened by the blast, he struggled to regain control as Pelthit Re swept in from behind. The Dae'shan clashed in a titan struggle. Skeletal hands clawed at each other. Robes were ripped to tatters. For a moment it appeared Amar Kit'han was on the losing side, but Pelthit was always the weakest of the trio. Amar managed to shove Pelthit away and attack with his full power. The lesser Dae'shan deflected the magic for a few moments before his hands began to crumble away. His robes flamed, turning him into a moving torch. Pelthit screamed once, a horrible sound from the darkest abyss, before his head exploded.

Power bristling on his hands in reds and oranges, Amar turned to Kodan. "Now for you, my traitorous friend. It is past time you learned your place."

Kodan Bak stared at the ashes of Pelthit Re floating in the air for a moment before reluctantly turning to face Amar. He'd made a grave miscalculation in Amar's abilities and was going to pay for it with his life. There was no backing away now. "Come then, let us end this now."

Amar raised his spindly arms in preparation to attack.

"What have you done, demon?" Badron demanded as he shakily picked himself up.

Amar and Kodan both paused, following Badron's pointing finger. The Olagath Stone was bleeding dark crimson light. The glow steadily grew larger until it bathed the entire ritual chamber. The last drops of blood flowed into the Stone and the ground began to rumble harder. A hole opened in the ceiling and grew larger.

Amar flashed Badron a wicked snarl. "I have liberated this pathetic world from the rule of you mortals. Soon the dark gods will be released and nightmares will come once again. You will bear witness to the end of all races in Malweir and my ascension to godhood."

"You're mad!" Maleela accused even as she readied her sword to murder to her father.

"Mad? I've spent lifetimes humbling myself before the world as I awaited this moment. You have had your chance to rule the world and been found wanting. This is the hour in which all hope fails. Welcome to despair, princess."

"Quickly! The ritual has begun," Anienam warned as they edged to the entrance of the ritual chamber. Desperation filled his heart. His worst fears were coming true. They were too late.

"Wizard, is this all for naught?" Bahr asked even as his mind raced through tactical possibilities. He spied the two Dae'shan in their tattered robes and immediately figured they had already fallen apart. What surprised him was finding his brother here. Worse, Badron was confronting Maleela. The five corpses on the stone slabs were inconsequential. It was the Olagath Stone that drew his attention. Bloody light drowned the chamber, emanating from the Stone.

Anienam wasn't sure. "Perhaps, but there is still a chance to destroy the Stone before the dimensional portal opens. We must hurry. Help me distract the Dae'shan so Groge can do his job."

"Arrows," he hissed and the wooden shafts sped towards the unsuspecting Dae'shan.

Without Boen, Bahr knew his chances of success were lessened but the Gaimosian had given his life so that they might succeed. He watched the arrows disintegrate on impact despite being imbued with magic. Trusting in Anienam's abilities, Bahr led the charge into the chamber. Ironfoot raced at his side, eager to drive his axe into one of the robed demons. Rekka, Dorl, and Nothol covered Groge as he slowly got to his feet after having to nearly crawl down the tunnel. The Giant was frightened but made a brave show. He drew the Blud Hamr which had been an inanimate object until now. This close to fulfilling its purpose, the Hamr throbbed in his hands and began to glow light yellow. Groge felt the power fill his veins, giving him strength unimagined. He might lack the strength to carry out his task, but the Hamr was not to be denied.

Amar Kit'han studied his enemies. Disappointment in finding Bahr alive after so many failed opportunities filled his heart with rage. "Kodan, stop the Giant! He must not succeed!"

The Dae'shan set aside their differences in the face of greater danger. They split to opposite sides of the chamber and attacked. Kodan Bak aimed directly for Rekka. She was easily the most dangerous of the group. Her slightly curved sword angled up to attack him. The Dae'shan was void of emotion as he deftly avoided her swing and knocked her to the ground. Dorl jerked to a halt and swung to confront Kodan, forgetting his charge to defend Groge. Having no other choice, Nothol did the same while screaming for the Giant to destroy the Stone and end this.

Kodan lifted a foot of the floor and spread his hands. Pure darkness radiated from his robes. He lashed out with both hands. Dorl Theed saw death approaching and was frozen in place. He dropped his sword as the bolts of power barreled towards his chest. His mouth dropped open in silent scream a moment before he was crudely slammed into the ground.

The blast caught Nothol in the stomach as he shoved his best friend out of the way. Intense pain gripped him but he couldn't cry out. Nothol Coll clutched at his stomach even as he began to shrink. Darkness spread across his lower body. His veins were aflame. One by one his nails popped off. His eyelids melted as his hair burned to cinder. He managed to look at his two friends one final time before he melted from the waist down and died.

"Nothol!" Dorl screamed.

"Dead. Your friend is dead as soon you will be,' Kodan hissed. He drifted closer to finish them off.

Bolts of magic struck his head and shoulder. The robes were shredded. Chunks of what little mortal remains he had ripped from his corpse. The Dae'shan turned to face his attacker, stunned to find the blind wizard continuing to unleash his power. Already under strength from dueling Amar, Kodan was blown back by repeated blows. Unable to defend himself, Kodan was pummeled to his knees.

Anienam stalked to his prey like a jungle predator. An unearthly glow poured from his eyes. He reached out with his left hand and plunged it into Kodan's hood. Anienam cried out in pain as he touched the necrotic flesh of the Dae'shan. Chanting spells that were all but forgotten since the Mage Wars, Anienam Keiss funneled his magic into what remained of Kodan Bak. The Dae'shan withered and died. His corpse collapsed in a pile of ashes. The last wizard leaned against the wall and hobbled after Groge. The Giant was his priority.

On the opposite side of the chamber the battle took a decidedly different path. Only moments after Amar realized his enemies had arrived, Maleela took the opportunity to attack her father. Her sword whistled through the air en route to slashing into Badron's right bicep. He roared in pain. Blood fountained from the wound. He narrowly avoided losing the arm completely by deflecting Maleela's second blow.

"Pathetic child," he sneered, regaining composure. "I should have left you in the woods to die after you killed your mother."

Years of pent-up anguish and suppressed rage flared to life. Maleela leveled her sword and shouted, "I didn't kill her!"

Badron laughed in her face. "It doesn't matter, for I am going to kill you."

"Not if I kill you first," she replied and lunged.

Badron parried her swing and sidestepped the next. Older, tiring quicker, the king decided to let Maleela exhaust herself before making his move. Youthful vigor was no substitute for age and experience. She continued to attack wildly. Her blows were poorly timed and often off center. She was a novice and showed it on every strike. Fresh pain numbed his arm. Badron knew that if he didn't finish this quickly there was the very real possibility he would bleed out.

He took a step back in preparation of driving his sword deep into her stomach but slipped on a piece of the ceiling. He crashed into the ground hard, breaking more than one rib in the process. Maleela glared down on him with unadulterated hatred. Two decades of confusion had boiled down to a final second before she killed him. Her sword fell.

And was blocked by Bahr's. Rage turned to shock. She started to speak but he swung a vicious right hook into her temple. Maleela collapsed in unconsciousness. "You'll forgive me for this later."

"You," Badron scowled from the ground. "I should have known you'd turn up here. The big brother too afraid to claim what was his. You'll die a coward's death now, dear brother."

Bahr looked at Badron's sleeve, now wholly covered with blood. "You'll be dead before you can try. That's a nasty wound she gave you."

"Come closer and see how much fight I have left in me."

Having gone too far to turn away, Bahr drove his sword deep into Badron's exposed chest and twisted until his brother died with a gurgle of blood frothing on his lips. Bahr collapsed. All his anger and tension faded. His strength fled. He was suddenly tired and felt every bit of his sixty years. Regrets filled his heart and mind. He'd never wanted harm to come to his brother despite their differences. Family wasn't replaceable. Bahr laid a hand on Badron's shoulder and let the weight of decades fall from his.

"You have rid the world of one tyrant only to fall to another!" Amar Kit'han rasped as he attacked.

Bahr began to laugh.

"You can't stop me. The ritual has begun and the dark gods will soon be freed. This is the moment of your demise, lesser son of kings."

"Stay your hand, brother."

Amar pulled up short as a blinding flash announced the arrival of Artiss Gran. The last of the true Dae'shan stood between Bahr and Amar as the hole in the ceiling continued to widen. Unimaginable power flowed into the chamber, heralding the return of Malweir's greatest foes. Sonic vibrations threatened to rip the chamber and all within apart. Artiss Gran clenched his spectral fists for he knew time was almost expired.

Amar Kit'han knew he shouldn't be surprised at his brother's return. All legends foretold the return of the Dae'shan in the final moments. With two others dead, it was down to them now. The fate of the world hung in the balance, a secondary outcome to their age-old battle.

"We should have killed you the moment you abandoned us, *brother*," he sneered.

"This doesn't need to continue. Stop the ritual and come back to the light," Artiss pleaded.

"There is no going back. Tonight this world ends. The ritual has begun. Our true masters are already returning. Can't you feel them? Forcing their way back into the world as all else fades into ash and memory," Amar taunted him to waste time. There was still the very real fear of the Giant crushing the Olagath Stone and ruining his dreams. Fear which prompted the Dae'shan to move slower.

"Nothing is eternal, Amar, not even you. The dark gods were banished for reasons above our rationale. Do not think to claim to know the will of the gods," Artiss chastised.

Amar Kit'han dropped to the ground, allowing his sandals to touch for the first time in years. The cold feel of stone was alien, unforgiving. "Enough talk. You can't change my mind and you're not powerful enough to defeat me."

"We shall see."

They attacked simultaneously. Magic, blinding and hot, flared through the chamber. The concussion knocked everyone to the ground. Wild, magic stretched forth and clipped Anienam not moments after killing Kodan Bak. The wizard gasped with unimaginable suffering as his bones were shattered and his organs began to melt. Using what little strength he had left, Anienam desperately tried to recover.

He watched helplessly as the battle between good and evil raged unchecked across the chamber. Bolts of magic struck the Dae'shan with unabated fury. Robes were torn apart. Desiccated flesh was blasted from bones. Each blow weakened the Dae'shan. Artiss was thrown back into the wall, shattering his spine and pelvis. Amar dropped to his knees with a gaping hole filling his chest cavity. Each ancient enemy crawled towards the other with the knowledge there was but one outcome to this affair. Amar gripped Artiss by the face and squeezed while Amar plunged his fist into the chest wound. Magic hummed, vibrating the very depths of the earth.

Parts of the ceiling collapsed around them. Heavy chunks of rock and stone broke the sacrificial slab, crushing bodies already drained of blood. Pitch-black surrounded the pedestal holding the Olagath Stone, steadily pushed back under the crimson light. Wails and moans from thousands of souls being funneled into the growing void made those survivors in the chamber cry freely.

The second explosion sent shockwaves up through the earth, ripping trees from the ground and flattening what remained of Arlevon Gale. Thousands of soldiers and Goblins were thrown to their backs. The weak of heart died instantly. Their bodies added to the lifelessness already gripping the world. At once the battle ground to a halt. Both armies struggled to pick themselves up and retreat in the face of this new threat. All were oblivious of what was happening below ground.

Artiss Gran and Amar Kit'han were locked in deathly grip. Neither was stronger than the other. Their magic slowly began to break down their molecular structure. Ancient bodies withered and crumbled to ash. Colliding colors washed between them in amplified rainbows. Amar opened his mouth to roar but flames and ash spewed forth. Artiss could barely blink before their combined power began to disintegrate them both. Soon only ash remained.

The Dae'shan were no more. Their evil was already washing away from the world as a far greater evil returned. Blood streamed from ears and noses as the dark gods forced their way back into Malweir. Millennia of endless torment drove them mad with impatience. They clawed their way back into the world before Groge could accomplish his task.

Foul power drove the Giant to his knees. He retched across the blood-stained stone. The Blud Hamr suddenly felt heavy. His heart beat fast, much too fast. His body threatened to rebel. Groge closed his eyes and began to pray to his god. The only god of his people. He opened his eyes with clarity of purpose, focusing on the wizard.

"Now Groge! Smash the stone!" Anienam cried out before he collapsed.

Groge tore his eyes from the prone wizard and hefted the Blud Hamr over his head. The Olagath Stone drew his attention, attempting to mesmerize him into succumbing to the irreversible power locked within. Spectral fingers reached down through the hole in the ceiling as the dark gods were desperate to stop Groge from fulfilling his role. Dark fire plunged down to strike his iron-thick hide. Terrible burn marks scored him as he brought the Blud Hamr down, fulfilling his destiny. The chamber was plunged into darkness.

Golden light suddenly flooded the ritual chamber. Anienam dared to gaze upon the light even as the sheer strength of it rendered his heart to stop. The last wizard felt darkness eclipse him and the world was lost.

THIRTY-SIX

Through the Hurt

The battle was ended but none of the survivors were fool enough to believe their world would ever be the same again. There was no explanation for what they had witnessed. The golden light showering Arlevon Gale wasn't natural. Some believed the gods of light had returned. Others figured Bahr and his group had succeeded in their quest but were destroyed in the process. Many just didn't have the stamina left to care. The battle was over. What was left of the Goblin army was in full retreat. It was a movement that would eventually fail. Already Dwarf and Minotaur commanders were planning to hunt down and exterminate them. Most of the people of Delranan and Rogscroft lacked the stomach for any more fighting, even the vaunted Wolfsreik.

General Rolnir stood looking down into what remained of the ruins. His burly arms were folded across his chest. Confusion stitched across his brow. Nothing in the last few moments had made any sense. An ill feeling clung to his nerves.

"Have the scouts reported anything yet?" Aurec asked from Rolnir's side.

"Nothing. I fear Bahr's group has met their doom."

Aurec wasn't so sure. There was no explanation of the gathered darkness nor the purity of light immediately following. Rather than waiting for his mind to conjure ghouls and stark images, he struggled to find conversation. "What do you suppose that was? All the light and dark?"

"Hard to say. I almost felt…a divine presence in the world," Rolnir admitted. The notion proved particularly disturbing. He'd never placed much faith in gods, light or dark, and to have come within the presence of so many at once threatened to tear the fragile constructs of his mind. "And now this," he gestured to the haunting glow in the sky. "It should be the middle of the night yet we stand in an ethereal landscape void of either light or dark. Are we dead?"

"I don't feel dead," Aurec said. "This is...something else. Maybe Bahr succeeded after all? The wizard seemed convinced this was the day of reckoning. They might have won."

"Perhaps. We'll find out soon enough. Dawn is approaching," Rolnir added. "I figure if the dark gods were freed we won't see the dawn."

They waited in silence for a time, apprehensive towards the dawn. Aurec's eyes stayed focused on the ruins. All friendly forces had been pulled back to form a perimeter once it was established what remained of the enemy was gone. Aurec wasn't willing to risk any further casualties without need. Sending Mahn and Raste in to find Bahr went against his better judgment but he needed to know.

Aurec spied movement amidst the rubble. It took a few moments before he was able to make out his scouts. Instant relief washed through him but was quickly replaced by excitement. Several others follow Mahn and Raste, the largest towering over them all. He tapped Rolnir's forearm and gestured. Without a word between them the duo headed towards the perimeter to greet the incoming.

Excitement instantly turned into panic the moment Aurec saw Groge carrying Maleela's limp body. He rushed to them with cold dread in his heart. The others continued to limp his way, oblivious to his silent concern. They were exhausted and near broken. All bore haunting stares that saw past what was before them. They struggled to accept what they'd just been through and, for some, it was a reckoning that would take years to accomplish.

Mahn cleared his throat. "Sire, it's finished. The enemy has been defeated. Delranan is safe again."

"Maleela? Is she...." He let the thought trail off, suddenly afraid of asking.

Bahr stepped forward, limping heavily on his right side. "She lives. I had to knock her out to keep her from getting hurt. She'll be fine soon enough."

Aurec was speechless. So many questions bothered him. What had happened beneath the ground? Where were the others? Was this war truly finished? As if sensing his confusion, Rolnir stepped in to shake Bahr's hand.

"You look terrible," the general offered. "I trust you did what needed to be done?"

He scanned the group, noting how a few of them were missing from the ranks.

Bahr nodded. "It is. The dark gods are gone. The Dae'shan dead. We lost a few friends along the way but the deed is finished. We can finally move on with our lives."

Even as he said it Bahr knew it was easier said than done. Personally he'd never be the same again. He was irrevocably changed. Bahr turned his gaze to the breaking dawn and said no more.

Rolnir sympathized with him. He'd lost thousands of soldiers in the past day, over a fifth of the Wolfsreik. While the army could be rebuilt, the sheer amount of quality veteran lost was irreplaceable. His kingdom was another matter. Kingless, Delranan would struggle for generations. No matter which way he looked at the problem, Rolnir found no easily obtainable solution. His life would be dedicated to rebuilding all that was lost.

"Where do we go from here?" he asked to no one in particular.

Only the wind replied.

Maleela awoke slowly. She winced as the pain in her head instantly assaulted her. Her eyes took a while to focus and when they did she found Aurec staring longingly back at her. Her first instinct was to recoil, thinking he'd come to do her harm. Vague memories of her deeds in the service of the dark mocked who she was. The Dae'shan influence dissolved the instant Amar Kit'han was destroyed, freeing her mind and soul.

"Aurec…I…." She fell into tears, ashamed of what she'd done.

He swept in to take her sobbing figure in his strong arms and pulled her close. Aurec whispered into her hair, "It's all right. You're back with me now and I swear I will never allow harm to befall you again. I love you, Maleela."

She gripped him tightly, as if afraid to let go. "I love you too."

Ingrid clutched Orlek's hand. The fighter had recovered from his wounds well enough to hobble about. He insisted on limping to an audience with King Aurec. She suspected he was withholding information but couldn't pry it out of him. The smug look he bore was proof enough as they entered Aurec's pavilion.

Aurec let them stand for a moment before speaking. He still claimed to not be ready to wear the crown but was growing accustomed to the idea of being in charge. "Ingrid, out of respect for your actions and your losses I think it only fitting that you are bestowed a proper gift. One worthy of a regent."

"Sire, I don't need any…excuse me?" she said, changing direction mid-sentence.

Both he and Maleela smiled warmly. "You heard me right. We are making you Regent of Delranan. I can think of no better person to lead this kingdom out of the dark hole it is now in. But there is more."

Ingrid struggled to maintain her composure. "Go on. I'm listening."

"Delranan will no longer be an independent kingdom, nor will Rogscroft. Maleela and I are combining our two kingdoms into one. Together it is our hope that we will maintain peace and order throughout northern Malweir for many long days to come. Rolnir has already been appointed General of the Army and plans are being fleshed out for permanent bases across the kingdoms. Never again will evil be allowed to thrive in the north. Are you comfortable with this decision?"

She pursed her lips. Ingrid was a natural leader, but a regent in what amounted to a small empire? She didn't know if she could handle that or not. Of course, with Orlek at her side, she felt as if she was ready to take on the world. “Yes sire, I believe I am. Thank you for this opportunity.”

“No, it is we who owe you the thanks. Without your guidance all that was good in Delranan might already have been lost,” Maleela told her.

The two embraced as sisters, leaving a smug Orlek grinning like a child.

Groge tilted his head back, enjoying the brisk spring breeze. The snows had melted and life was returning to Delranan. His hand was still wrapped in heavy bandages, though he doubted it needed the care. Burned to the bone, Groge accepted the wound and pain for services rendered. The Blud Hamr had flared with burning magic as it struck the Olagath Stone. Both Stone and Hamr exploded, their purpose in this world accomplished. Groge had been burned in the process but it was a small price.

The surviving Giants unanimously elected him their new leader. It was an unexpected role he wasn’t prepared to accept but they wouldn’t allow him to back away. He was a proven warrior now and it was his right to rule. The savior of the free world deserved no less.

“Feels strange, doesn’t it?”

Groge looked down with a fond smile as Ironfoot strode up to him. The Dwarf brandished a fresh set of rank epaulettes denoting his promotion. “It makes me wonder what the world is coming to. I never wanted to be a leader, just a forge master.”

“Huh, I guess I never wanted to be a general. There’s no way King Thord will let me scamper off on any quests or missions again,” the stalwart Dwarf replied with a hint of disdain.

“I shall miss you, my friend,” Groge told him. “It has been an honor to fight alongside you. Dwarves and Giants once shared their knowledge of the forge. I believe the time has come to do so once again.”

"What do you mean?" Ironfoot asked. He narrowed his eyes in suspicion.

Groge broke into a grin. His massive teeth, crooked and stained, reflected sunlight. "Thord has agreed to exchange smiths to regain what was lost. You are going to escort the Dwarves of Drimmen Delf to Venheim and remain until he calls you home."

Ironfoot opened and closed his mouth before barking a deep laugh. "It looks as if I'll have myself another adventure after all!"

Together, Dwarf and Giant returned to their camp. They had much to plan before leaving.

Thord was the last Dwarf to leave the battlefield. He watched, assisting when the mood struck, as the dead and wounded were removed to either be taken to the massive funeral pyres constructed on the edge of the camp site, or to the overflowing surgeon's tents. Great sorrow settled upon him, for he had lost much.

The army of Drimmen Delf accounted themselves as only Dwarves could. They reaped a terrible harvest of Goblin lives but at great cost. Close to half of the army was dead or wounded. It would take generations for the community to recover.

"What is to become of us?"

He turned to look up into Faeldrin's eyes. "Doesn't matter now, does it?"

"Of course it does. This war has changed everything. The world we knew is already fading. Tomorrow presents a brand new challenge for all peoples to accept. I do not enjoy the thought of returning to Elvenara with this news. The old ways are dead."

"Some old ways should have died long ago," Thord replied.

"Indeed. I shall have my Aeldruin attend the funeral services of your Dwarves. It was an honor to fight alongside you…friend."

"The honor was ours. Dwarf and Elf. We've never been stalwart friends."

He grinned through his beard, brownish teeth clashing with his hair.

Faeldrin's thin lips remained pressed for a moment. "Perhaps it is time to end that. Change is, after all, coming whether we wish it or not."

"I can live with that," Thord said, making a show of running fat fingers through his beard.

"My Elves depart after the wedding. If you'll have us, we will accompany you back to Drimmen Delf. I admit to having an affection for your ale."

"Ha! It takes you Elves far too long to get drunk," Thord replied, "But I accept the challenge."

Elf and Dwarf stood for a moment longer, their minds trying to forget the horrors conducted on the battlefield.

No one ever saw Inaella again. Some say she went mad and was lost to the last winter storm, her body devoured by wolves. Search parties scoured the kingdom, for she was yet a severe threat. Life would go on in Delranan, her memory slowly fading into obscurity. The fate of Inaella, once noble-born, devolved into mystery.

On cold winter nights, the coldest of course, travelers came to bear witness to a terrible wraith-like creature stalking the countryside. Emaciated, dressed in tattered robes, the creature strode across the snow covered fields moaning like a banshee. Future legends would name it a witch-woman and a warning to avoid the frozen wastes of western Delranan spread.

Dorl Theed knelt beside the freshly dug grave. He was speechless. Nothol Coll was his best friend and it had nearly broken his heart to return to Arlevon Gale to collect the remains. What little remained of Nothol had been hard to view. No one deserved to die in such a manner and it was all Dorl could do to keep his stomach. Rekka Jel had helped. Her impassive demeanor made the task easier.

They gathered Nothol's remains and brought them home to a sleepy village south of Chadra where Nothol had grown up. He was given a quiet funeral with but a handful of guests to bear witness. Bahr and the others were there, as were Aurec and Rolnir, Ingrid, Thord, and Krek. It seemed only fitting for the leaders to be present.

That was days ago and only Dorl and Rekka remained. Their bags were packed. Horses were saddled in preparation for the long trip southeast.

Rekka's slender hand offered just enough pressure to his shoulder to reassure him of her presence. "He was a good man. One of honor."

"He was my friend," Dorl replied. "I will miss him."

"That is good since you will have to explain to little Nothol how he got his name," Rekka said with a smile.

Dorl's head snapped up in confusion. "What are you…what do you mean?"

She laughed and hugged him fiercely. "I believe it is time for me to put down my sword and look to starting a family. A son would be a fitting tribute to Nothol Coll."

Dorl Theed spun her around three times before setting her back down. The ride south wasn't going to be half as bad as he imagined.

Trumpets blared out across the land. After nearly a year of continued hardship and warfare, peace had settled across the north. Thousands of citizens from Rogscroft, Delranan, and the Pell Darga clans converged on the growing city of Grunmarrow for the wedding of Aurec and Maleela. Their union would cement the bonds of fellowship between kingdoms and usher in a new age of prosperity. Envoys had already been sent south to Averon and the King was in attendance. Seldom were the times when such grand affairs kissed the world.

Pacing nervously in her chambers behind the wedding chapel, Maleela wrung her hands. She'd loved Aurec from the moment they'd met. This day never seemed like it would arrive. She was scared and excited. The combination of emotions threatened to make her go crazy before stepping out in front of so many people.

"Relax, you're already queen in all but name," Bahr told her.

He was the one person allowed in her chambers before the wedding once she'd succeeded in shooing away her attendants. Being the only family she had left, he was her rock during this storm. That didn't do much to ease her nerves.

"I'm trying to but it's not every day one gets married and crowned at the same time," she told him.

He chuckled softly, admiring the way this young lady had grown into a responsible individual. *Through no part of my own, nor her father's.*

"If anyone deserves this moment it is you," he said.

She stopped and looked him in the eyes. "You're leaving, aren't you?"

Letting out a deep breath, Bahr replied, "After the wedding. I've done all that was asked of me and it is time to move on. Don't think I won't return to check up on you from time to time, though. You may be a queen but you've not a quarter of the experience I do."

"I've only just now gotten you into my life, Uncle. I don't know what to say," Maleela said while trying to keep the tears from coming.

Bahr embraced his niece for the last time. Sadness clung to the corners of his eyes. "I love you, child. Your mother would have been proud of you. Now go, before you make this old man cry. You've a husband to accept."

"Thank you, Uncle," Maleela said and hugged him fiercely around the neck.

EPILOGUE

The roads wound across the face of the world, stretching endlessly in sheer amazement for Skuld. Born a street rat in Chadra, he was now a hero of the realm, whatever that meant, and a valuable friend to some of the most important people in Malweir. Never in his wildest imaginations did he think he'd live long enough to see the end of the war much less the dawn of a new chapter in his life.

Youthful eyes stared out across the landscape, absorbing all he could in passing. The world was wide and far and he'd live several lifetimes before seeing it all. Skuld wasn't too keen on spending so much time wandering the back roads and using his years collecting knowledge. His travelling companion felt otherwise.

Anienam Keiss, once last descendant of the order of Mages, had been granted life eternal by the gods of light and made custodian of Malweir until they deemed it necessary to return. His battle with the Dae'shan had left him near death, perhaps making it easier for him to pass into this new life. Now he was the only Dae'shan. His role was to replace Artiss Gran as the defender of Trennaron and to replenish the ranks to four. The quest would last long after his friends and companions were dust in the ground, but time no longer concerned him. Eternal, Anienam meant to right all the wrongs committed through the years out of his lack of vision.

"Anienam, what is Ipn Shal like?" Skuld asked when the tedium of endless roads grew too much.

"Naught more than well-preserved ruins these days I'm afraid. Time has not been kind to magic users," the wizard replied.

"Can it be made great again?"

Anienam smiled from within his gossamer hood. His flowing white robes were pristine in their innocence. "I've dreamed of the day when Ipn Shal returned to its former glory and became a place for the wealth of knowledge of all races.

Those days are returning. I can feel it in my soul. Others will soon come to join you, Skuld. It will not stand empty for long."

"But the magic failed before. What can prevent it from doing so again?" the boy asked.

Anienam was both pleased and impressed with his train of thought. "The gods are gone now, Skuld, both light and dark. Their influences are removed from the world and they have given us all free will to make what we will of the future. I cannot promise the road ahead will be easy, nor should it be. With great wisdom comes even greater responsibility. You are now charged with rebuilding all that was lost. I think your hardest task will be in convincing the leaders of the world to allow their subjects free practice of magic. The Mage Wars were long ago but many kingdoms continue to maintain…protective policies designed to prevent another war.

"This is an exciting time, young Skuld. No matter how difficult you find the road ahead, always remember that I shall never be far away. As the guardian of Trennaron it is my responsibility to ensure the world uses magic wisely. It would not do well to squander the gifts of the gods. Together I believe we can forge a better world."

Skuld beamed at the thought, though his mind couldn't escape the seemingly impossible task awaiting him. Frightened and excited, he couldn't wait for his chance to finally make something grand of his life. Dreams of treasure seeking and glory hunting faded as the burden of responsibility settled over his shoulders.

"Will it truly become a grand world, Anienam?" he asked.

The wizard nodded. "Anything is possible."

Sea spray washed his face as the *Regret* broke waves. Bahr named his new vessel for all that had happened over the last year, choosing to use it as a reminder that, while he had made mistakes, his life ahead was unwritten. Now that his niece was married to King Aurec and Delranan was in the capable hands of Rolnir and Ingrid, he no longer had any ties to his homeland.

Life wouldn't last much longer. He felt it in his bones. He was tired, mentally and physically. The war against the dark gods had removed certain parts of him he could never get back. Bahr didn't mind so much. A world traveler, he decided it was time to set sail and see those remote parts of the world he'd missed in his youth. Perhaps there was another adventure waiting over the horizon.

The Sea Wolf gave one final look back at the rocky coast of Delranan and smirked.

END

AFTERWORD

I hope you enjoyed reading this tale as much as I did writing it. To be fair, I never intended to write a series. Hammers in the Wind was originally meant to be stretch into two books. My first publisher saw potential and well, you know the result. Thank you all for seeing this campaign through with me and rest assured, there are plenty of other adventures to explore. The world of Malweir was born in the lowly village of Bagram, Afghanistan in 2002. I never imagined that the Armies of the Silver Mage would spawn so many novels, with plenty more envisioned. Hopefully you will stick around and take that journey with me. If you are up to the challenge, I humbly request you leave an honest review, be it good or bad. Every little bit helps.

OTHER BOOKS BY CHRISTIAN WARREN FREED

Malweir was once governed by the order of Mages, bringers of peace and light. Centuries past and the lands prospered. But all was not well. Unknown to most, one mage desired power above all else. He turned his will to the banished Dark Gods and brought war to the free lands. Only a handful of mages survived the betrayal and the Silver Mage was left free to twist the darker races to his bidding. The only thing he needs to complete his plan and rule the world forever are the four shards of the crystal of Tol Shere.

Having spent most of their lives dreaming about leaving their sleepy village and travelling the world, Delin Kerny and Fennic Attleford never thought that one day they would be forced to flee their town to save their lives. Everything changes when they discover the fabled Star Silver sword and learn that there are some who want the weapon for themselves. Hunted by a ruthless mercenary, the boys run from Fel Darrins and are forced into the adventure they only dreamed about.

Ever ashamed of the horrors his kind let loose on the world the last mage, Dakeb, lives his life in shadows. The only thing keeping him alive is his quest to stop the Silver Mage from reassembling the crystal. His chance finally comes through the hearts and wills of Delin and Fennic. Dakeb bestows upon them the crystal shard, entrusting them with the one thing capable of restoring peace to Malweir.

THE FRACTURED UNIVERSE I

DREAMS OF WINTER

CHRISTIAN WARREN FREED

The gods have been dead for 3000 years. Only a handful remain. Secret. Hidden.

Humanity has carved an empire across the stars in that time. It all stands on the brink of collapse as ancient evils resurface and the greed of men rises.

Senior Inquisitor Breed is dedicated to stamping out heresy wherever he finds it. When the Inquisitor General assigns him to investigate the escape of one of history's greatest threats he quickly finds himself at the center of a budding conspiracy with far reaching implications. He soon discovers the truths told to humanity are built upon lies.

Dark forces gather in the shadows. They ready to strike at the heart of all men hold dear. Should Inquisitor Breed fail to stop the spread of heresy there will be war without end. Unfortunately for Breed, it may already be too late

.

The wheels are in motion. The quiet threat grows.

Deity and humanity clash.

Perfect for fans of Erikson, Weber, Herbert, and Martin, Dreams of Winter marks the first must-read volume of the Forgotten Gods Saga.

THE
LAZARUS MEN
A LAZARUS MEN AGENDA

CHRISTIAN
WARREN FREED

It is the 23rd century. Humankind has reached the stars, building a tentative empire across a score of worlds. Earth's central government rules weakly as several worlds continue their efforts toward independence. Shadow organizations hide in the midst of the political infighting. Their manifestations of power and influence are beholden only to the highest bidder. The most powerful/insidious/secret of these, The Lazarus Men, has existed for decades, always working outside of morality's constraints. Led by the enigmatic Mr. Shine, their agents are hand selected from the worst humanity has to offer and available for the right price.

Gerald LaPlant lives an ordinary life on Old Earth. That life is thrown into turmoil on the night he stumbles upon the murder of what appears to be a street thief. Fleeing into the night, Gerald finds himself hunted by agents of Roland McMasters, an extremely powerful man dissatisfied with the current regime and with designs on ruling his own empire. To do so, McMasters needs the fabled Eye of Karakzaheim, a map leading to immeasurable wealth. Unknown to either man, Mr. Shine has deployed agents in search of the same artifact and will stop at nothing to obtain it.

Running for his life, Gerald quickly becomes embroiled in a conspiracy reaching deep into levels of government that he never imagined existed. His every move is hounded by McMasters' agents and the Lazarus Men. His adventures take him away from the relative safety of Old Earth across the stars and into the heart of McMasters' fledgling empire. The future of the Earth Alliance at stake. If Gerald has any hope of surviving and helping saving the alliance he must rely on his wits and awakened instincts while foregoing the one thing that could get him killed more quickly than the rest: trust.

BIO

Christian W. Freed was born in Buffalo, N.Y. more years ago than he would like to remember. After spending more than 20 years in the active-duty US Army he has turned his talents to writing. Since retiring, he has gone on to publish over 25 military fantasy and science fiction novels, as well as his memoirs from his time in Iraq and Afghanistan, a children's book, and a pair of how to books focused on indie authors and the decision making process for writing a book and what happens after it is published.

His first published book (Hammers in the Wind) has been the #1 free book on Kindle 4 times and he holds a fancy certificate from the L Ron Hubbard Writers of the Future Contest. Ok, so it was for 4th place in one quarter, but it's still recognition from the largest fiction writing contest in the world. And no, he's not a scientologist.

Passionate about history, he combines his knowledge of the past with modern military tactics to create an engaging, quasi-realistic world for the readers. He graduated from Campbell University with a degree in history and a Masters of Arts degree in Digital Communications from the University of North Carolina at Chapel Hill.

He currently lives outside of Raleigh, N.C. and devotes his time to writing, his family, and their two Bernese Mountain Dogs. If you drive by you might just find him on the porch with a cigar in one hand and a pen in the other. You can find out more about his work by following him on social media:

www.ingramcontent.com/pod-product-compliance
Lightning Source LLC
Chambersburg PA
CBHW010139030826
48979CB00023B/1038

* 9 7 8 1 9 5 7 3 2 6 2 4 5 *